SKY RAIDERS

MICHELLE DIENER

To Tab and Julia

Praise for Michelle Diener's award-winning science fiction novel
DARK HORSE:

(Winner of a Galaxy Award & the PRISM Award for Best Futuristic)

". . . truly exceptional . . ." *RT Book Reviews*

"Dark Horse had everything I would want from a sci-fi story." *Heroes & Heartbreakers*

"[Dark Horse] truly is a gem, highly polished and a wonderful read." *First to the Last Page Book Reviews*

"... this is one of my top reads of 2015. If you enjoy science fiction at all I encourage you to pick it up for yourself. I don't think you will be disappointed." *All About Romance*

OTHER TITLES BY MICHELLE DIENER

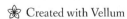

ABOUT SKY RAIDERS

When the people of Barit first saw the silver glint of sky craft, they felt awe. Then awe turned to fear. And they found a name for the mysterious newcomers. Sky raiders.

Garek's one year of duty as a guard walking the walls of Garamundo was extended to two when the sky raiders appeared. Two long years away from home and his lover, Taya. When he finally returns, the town is empty. While Garek was protecting Garamundo, the sky raiders were taking their victims from his hometown.

Taya can't bear looking into the night sky. All she can see is Barit, her home planet. Impossibly, the sky raiders have brought her and their other victims to Shadow, the planet that shadows her own, and looking up makes her aware of everything she's lost. Garek is out there somewhere. She knows he'll look, but he'll never find her.

She and the other captives have to find a way to escape. Without the food the sky raiders bring them from their raids on Barit, they'll starve on the almost barren wastes of Shadow. And when they've finished the job the sky raiders have brought them to Shadow to do, they'll be left behind to do just that.

What Taya doesn't realize is she'll have some help with her escape plan. Because Garek isn't giving up on finding her. And he's even more resourceful than she could ever have imagined.

Nothing is going to keep him from Taya. Not even space itself.

ONE

HE'D ASKED her to wait for him, and then he'd disappeared for two years.

As he reached the top of the pass and started down the steep path to the valley below, Garek wondered just how angry Taya would be.

That she would be angry enough to have taken someone else sat like week-old loaf in his stomach, heavy and sickening.

He'd had no choice, had come as soon as he could . . . He tried to shake off the chill that touched him, despite the bright day. He'd take her anger, her fury—he'd take it all if it meant he didn't find her with someone else.

He forced himself to pay attention as the path became steeper still, and frowned at how badly maintained the way had become, as if no one had repaired the damage a winter in the mountains could do to a narrow track. The spring thaw had come and gone, replaced by a golden summer, and the snow had retreated to the tops of the mountains.

Kas should have done something about the erosion by now, even though this path was a shortcut few besides the villagers knew of, cutting across the Crag and shaving hours off the journey through the foothills.

The familiar landscape tugged at something inside him. He hadn't thought himself sentimental, and though he'd missed Taya with an ache that hurt worse than a knife to flesh, he hadn't thought the sight of the rolling hills and high peaks would affect him. The crowds and enclosing stone walls of Garamundo had been something to bear stoically, but he was surprised how easy it was to breathe here, and it wasn't just because the air was sweet with the scent of summer grass.

When he'd left two years ago, the only thing he'd regretted was leaving Taya behind him, and he'd come back only to fetch her.

Fetch her and run, as fast as possible.

As far away from West Lathor as they could get.

The shadow cast by Garamundo had a long reach, certainly long enough to reach out and try to grab him again if he stayed here, and he'd sworn when they'd finally released him that he would never go back.

He wouldn't give them a chance to conscript him again.

He was halfway down the mountain when he noticed there were no leviks on the slopes.

He stopped a moment, shading his eyes against the bright midday light of the Star to search for any sign of their golden, curly coats.

He could find none.

A breeze rose up, swirling about him, and he was struck by the silence.

His hearing was exceptional, and there was no sound of life. No ring of a hammer on anvil, no murmur of voices from the street.

Impossible.

His home town was small, but not that small. Pan Nuk had at least a hundred inhabitants when he'd left. And it was directly below him. Hidden by the thick line of trees it would take him only ten minutes to reach, but there nonetheless.

He started to run.

At first he ran under his own steam, and then, as the silence seemed to deepen, become more sinister, he opened himself up to the Change and felt the curious, slow, honey-thick flow of the air around him, the inbetween, and he was suddenly at the village gates.

He drew back to himself, stumbled a little at the feeling of disorientation such a quick Change generated.

He stood still, looking around him carefully. Took it all in.

The ripped doors. The shutters hanging by a single hinge. The smashed pots and baskets lying in the street.

The emptiness.

While the city of Garamundo had held him, forced him to help them protect themselves from the sky raiders, the sky raiders had been helping themselves elsewhere.

Helping themselves to Taya.

TWO

THERE WOULD BE BLOOD.

Taya moved her gaze from Jerilia, weeping in soft, keening sobs, to the big Kardanx who gripped her arm, to the way Kas and the other men and women of the Illy began to gather to one side of the open area in front of the mine where they waited to be collected and returned to the camp.

The Kardanx shifted his grip and Taya could see there were already dark smudges ringing Jerilia's upper arm where he held her.

The spike of anger that ripped through her made her gasp, made her force in a breath of dusty, cold air.

If she couldn't keep a cool head, she couldn't expect Kas and the others to do the same.

Behind the Kardanx, some of his fellow countrymen began to gather as well, their expressions more muted, more severe.

They didn't want trouble with the Illy. It seemed the big man who had grabbed Jerilia wasn't so worried.

Kas had already told him to let Jerilia go. Jerilia herself had demanded it. Taya looked into his eyes and knew he would not do it.

Perhaps if Jerilia hadn't screamed so loudly, made such a fuss. Perhaps if Kas's bellow of outrage hadn't made every head turn.

Or perhaps not.

Whatever the reason, to let her go now would be a loss of face the Kardanx would not be prepared to accept.

Taya could see it in the way his eyes narrowed, the way his mouth tightened. She had always had the gift of reading people's intentions from the way they moved their bodies, and the Kardanx was screaming pent up rage and defiance with every pore.

A small movement caught her eye. Kas, drawing something from the back of his pants, gripping it tightly in his fisted hand.

Was that a *knife*?

No.

She wouldn't let another she loved be hurt. Not because of the lust of a stupid Kardanx. The Kardanx were supposed to worship the Mother, but either this one wasn't an adherent to the belief, or he was simply one of the majority who twisted the meanings of their oaths so they could treat women with less respect. She saw the evidence before her now, in the way the Kardanx thought he could have Jerilia, even against her will.

Taya had heard another, even uglier whisper. That the reason there were only six women amongst all the Kardanx the sky raiders had taken was because their men had killed them, rather than have them taken by the enemy.

Taya had heard Kardanx men swore an oath to protect the Mother, and her avatars, all women, with their lives. But if they had killed their women to protect them, they were not honoring the Mother as an equal. They had killed them like they would kill their livestock, so the invading army cannot use it. As they would burn their house, to give their enemy no shelter from the weather.

As one treats a possession, not a person, with their own will and choices.

The Kardanx took a step toward his own group, dragging Jerilia with him, and Kas and three others took a step forward.

The other Kardanx shouted something to their countryman, and he turned to look at them over his shoulder. He shouted back, and though Kardanx was close enough to Illian, it was said so fast Taya couldn't understand it. But the meaning was clear enough.

The Kardanx would not back down.

She wished, not for the first time, for Garek. Felt a need for him as strong as for her next breath. Then she shrugged off the paralysis of wanting something she could not have, and her gaze came to rest on their guard. When they'd first been brought here the metal skin of the two-legged, squat vehicle that enclosed him had been gleaming and new. Now she could see flakes of it falling off, and it was dull and corroded.

He was the only one on watch and his guns hung at his sides, mounted sleek and black on the stiff arms of his protective cover, above the pincers he could use as hands.

Kas took the first step out from the shouting group of the Illy, and without another moment's hesitation, Taya ran toward the sky raider.

He noticed her before she got to him, the head of the machine tipping down to look at her.

"Stop them." She looked straight up into the glass, and the dark tint faded to clear. For the first time, she found herself face to face with one of her captors.

Pale yellow eyes watched her with an interest that made her want to stumble back a step or two, turn tail and run.

She forced some saliva down her throat, worked her tongue off the roof of her mouth. "You need to stop it."

The robotic suit stayed still, but inside it, the sky raider tipped his head. "Why?"

The sibilant tones which made everything they said more frightening hissed over her. But now she'd been given a window into the helmet, she saw there was a disconnect between when the sky raider had spoken and when she'd heard the question.

It came to her in a flash that this wasn't how they sounded. They were using some device, some method of translating their language into Illian. It made her less afraid to know she wasn't dealing with something that sounded like she would expect a slither to sound like, if slithers could speak instead of hiss.

"We are different groups, we come from different parts of Barit. We are the Illy, they are the Kardanx. The Kardanx have different beliefs, different ways to us."

"We do not care." Again, his mouth moved and only after a beat did the hiss of his answer wash over her.

She shivered.

"Then you are stupid." She banged his leg with her fist in frustration, felt the gritty crunch of rusting metal. "If you want less work done in the mines, then you'll let that Kardanx take Jerilia. Because we're all mixed up in there. Kardanx and Illy together. And if he takes her, it will be against her will, and that will make us all feel like we have even less control than we already do. The Illy will fight the Kardanx. Fight them down in the shafts. Where you do not go."

She saw the pale yellow eyes blink in their narrow, sharp face that was otherwise not that different from her own, if you discounted the long, sharp incisors she caught the briefest glimpse of and the pale yellow fur that covered his face. He spoke again, although this time there was no hiss of reply to her.

She had the feeling he was talking to someone else. Getting advice. How he could do that, she didn't know. But then, most of what the sky raiders could do was new and magical to her.

He gave a sharp nod within his metallic cocoon, as if receiving an order, and then lifted both arms.

She heard something in the metallic suit whine. And the sky raider shifted, lifting up his arms. The barrel of one of his guns came level with her face.

But before she could think anything, feel any terror, the guard swung away from her and in two long steps was beside the Kardanx, gun leveled at his head.

"Let the woman go back to her kind." The hiss of the order fell into the silence that had descended, licking the air like a hungry tongue.

Without a word, the Kardanx released Jerilia, and she ran toward Kas and the others, stumbling in her haste.

They opened ranks for her, and then stepped back in to fill the gap, closing the line again.

"All who are the Illy, go this side. All who are Kardanx, go this side." He pointed with the guns, and Taya moved over to her group.

Some had been standing a little way away, watching without getting involved, and they began to move, pushing and weaving through each other to reach their people.

In the confusion, Taya saw one of the few Kardanx women in the camp slip amongst the Illy. The woman caught her eye and stumbled, and Taya realized her horror, and her anger, must have shown on her face.

If they sheltered one of the only Kardanx women left, if they took her to their side, that would be reason enough for another scene like the one today.

But hadn't she just seen how some of the Kardanx treated women? And hadn't she in these last few minutes come to the realization that the ugly whispers about men killing wives, sisters, mothers, and daughters was true?

Could she send a woman back to that against her will?

"Please." The woman was at her side faster than it seemed possible. Her hands came out to touch Taya's arm, and then drew back, fists clenched. "They don't want me anyway. They think me a witch. It's why I'm one of the few women in the group. I was living outside the village, and there was no man to kill me when the sky raiders came.

There was truth and desperation in her words. Her accent was thick, the vowels round and plump as a ripe plum, but she spoke Illian fluently.

Taya studied her, looking for some trick, some hidden motive.

She was a few years older than Taya and her eyes were a pale, almost glacial green. Her skin was honey-gold, close to Taya's own skin tone. Her dark hair hung down her back with a glint of auburn in it.

With a grimace, knowing only trouble could come of it, Taya gave a quick nod and pushed the woman deeper into the crowd. She felt a brief, light touch of thanks on her shoulder, and the woman was gone, burrowing deep into the mass.

Silence fell as the last of the prisoners sorted themselves into Illy and Kardanx.

The Illy, with their equal mix of men and women, were the bigger group, because most of the Kardanx volunteered for night shift.

If it were true that for nearly every man standing here, at least one woman had died, the sky raiders must have had to attack many towns and villages in Kardai to get this many of them. And the blood must stain the ground in Kardai dark red.

Looking at the Kardanx, thinking of that many bodies, Taya felt the burn of nausea in her throat.

She should be thankful to Garamundo. Thankful for the protection they offered. For keeping the sky raiders away so that only a few places in West Lathor were hit.

But giving even a drop of thanks to Garamundo was beyond her because of Garek.

She felt something on her cheek, and lifted a hand to brush it away. Her finger came away with a single tear, and she rubbed it into the filthy tunic she wore.

The guard swiveled the head of his suit to her, one gun held steady on each group, then walked slowly back, so that he could see them all without having to turn. The glass of the dome that covered his head was opaque again. "We understand now. Your ways are different. It is decided. You do not mix. You do not fight. You work together peacefully. There must be no break in production." The sinister voice that came from the sky raider's suit drifted on the fading light of the evening as the Star sank down in the west. The threat in the words, the very sound of them, made her shiver.

In the distance, the transporter skimmed over the open ground toward them, bringing the night shift.

There must be no break in production.

She shivered again.

There had been a few demonstrations of what would happen if production should slow or even stop, right at the start.

She watched the Star as it lit the sky a deep violet, low on the horizon. She liked to think of it slipping away from them here on Shadow to rise in the east on Barit. Taking a part of her with it.

Kas came up next to her and put a hand on her arm, and when she looked across at him, she couldn't tell what he was thinking. He looked tired. Tired and worn.

She'd run to the enemy. Made a decision without consulting him first.

"I don't regret it."

Kas gave a slow nod. "This was the culmination of two weeks of antagonism." He blew out a breath, looked across at the Kardanx. "It was only a matter of time."

"Tell me." Taya's voice came out on a croak. "Are the rumors true? What they did to their women, that there are so few here?"

Kas looked away. "So I hear."

"Then I'm doubly glad I did it. That some man who has no woman in his bed because he slit her throat like a goat tried to take a woman from the Illy, rape her . . ." She couldn't finish the sentence, her throat too tight. She took a breath. "I'll deal with the sky raiders before I deal with them."

Her gaze was drawn to the big Kardanx, to his hands. She imagined him holding a woman against his chest, running a knife across her throat.

She could hear a singing in her ears, like the sound the massive sky raider ship had made when it hovered over Pan Nuk, and taken them all. A singing, soaring sound of rage.

"Taya."

She turned to Kas, and he took a half-step back.

"What?" The word came out slowly, and she frowned at him. "*What?*"

"You were . . ." Kas wet his lips, set his feet apart. "Taya, you were starting to call the Change."

THREE

THE NEAREST TOWN to Pan Nuk was Haret, and Garek
mapped out the way in his head and called his Change before he'd
taken more than two steps.

There would be a price for that, using the inbetween to travel
always took the highest toll, and the further the distance, the bigger
the drain, but he would pay it to get there fast. To see if some had
escaped and sought refuge in a bigger, more secure settlement.

He'd been careful not to use the inbetween to shorten his journey
from Garamundo to Pan Nuk.

He'd decided to conserve his strength for when he dealt with
Taya. Had told himself the day or two he would save would not make
a difference, but arriving alert and strong, able to talk to her, win her
back, would.

If the sky raiders had come while he was walking the back roads
—while he'd been slipping past the towns along the road so there
would be no witnesses for Garamundo to question on which way he
had gone when they came for him again—he would never . . .

No.

He pulled himself up short even as the walls of Haret came into sight through the lazy, mirage-like view of the inbetween.

The state of the path. The weeds in the street. They spoke of months gone, not days.

Months.

He went through the town gate in an explosion of wood before he had a chance to pull back, diving into a roll and then coming up, light and ready on his feet.

He could feel the headache from traveling the inbetween twice in less than an hour putting its fingers out to gain a hold, but he could fight it off for another hour, maybe two. Long enough to find out if Taya was here.

He turned to look behind him, and the guards on watch duty were staring at him, mouths hanging open. There was nothing left of the gates but splinters good for kindling. He rubbed his hair to get some out, and shook out his tunic.

"Garek!" The shout had him spinning around, and down the main street a boy came at a dead run toward him.

It had been two years, and the boy was tall and lanky now. But he would know that blond hair anywhere.

"Luca." He waited for the boy to reach him, expecting him to stop, but he came on, leaping the last distance, so Garek caught him and swung him round.

"Garek. They took them. Took my father. Took Taya. Took your father. Took everyone who wasn't too young or too old." The words were whispered in his ear, the boy's head pressed tight under his chin.

The last thread of hope inside him snapped.

"Garek of Pan Nuk."

Garek lifted his head, and saw the guards had been joined by three more. The man who'd spoken wore a chain across his uniform, and Garek gave a nod. "Guard Master."

The guard master said nothing more, but looked over his shoulder at the non-existent gate. Looked back.

"My apologies for the loss of your gate." Garek rubbed at his hair again.

"You will replace it."

A blinding, white-hot rage flowed over him, and Garek let Luca slide to the ground. "Do you know where I've been, these last two years?"

The guard master shifted.

"I gave myself up willingly for one of those years, because that is the agreement between our people and the liege, but at the end of my time, I was told I could not leave, because in the last month of my year, the first sky raider was seen." He spoke quietly, noticing more and more people shuffling out of their houses into the street to watch.

"I was told, instead of taking someone from Haret, they were keeping me an extra year. Haret could not offer them someone who could call the Change as well as me, and the sky raiders were coming into our skies more and more often, with no acknowledgment, no friendly greeting. Garamundo needed the best in what they thought would be a war soon to come.

"When I objected, they told me I could take it up with the people of Haret. They showed me an agreement, signed by the Town Master, swearing that Haret, as the liege town to Pan Nuk, had made the necessary reparations to my village, and any reluctance from me would result in Pan Nuk being in forfeit." He rocked back on his heels. "What say you to that, Guard Master? What say you to a year of my life, stolen?"

There was a long, long silence.

"You can bring your questions to me, Garek. My guard master had nothing to do with it."

Garek turned. "Town Master. You are right. The guard master would have been responsible for not producing a good Change candidate for Garamundo, but you are the one who signed the deal."

Behind him, he heard the guard master draw in a breath at the insult he had offered, and with his back turned as well, as if there could be no threat to him from that quarter.

The town master crossed his arms over his chest. "I regret signing it. But I swear to you, it was done with the tip of a knife to my throat, and the promise that no matter what I did, whether I signed or not, they would still keep you one more year. At least by signing, I was able to keep one of our guards here, to help protect against the sky raiders, rather than losing him or her, and you as well.

"We would rather have had you here, Garek. Just over the hill in Pan Nuk and close at hand to help, rather than in Garamundo."

"But I wasn't. I wasn't here."

The town master looked away. "We took in everyone they left behind. No one has gone hungry, or without shelter. We are aware of our debt."

Garek recognized old Opik and one or two of the old women who had worked leather in their rocking chairs near the warmth of his father's furnace coming closer. He rubbed a hand over his forehead, trying to fight the headache off. "How many? How many left?"

"There are sixty, with the children." Opik spoke up. "The town master is right. They have been generous." But he looked at the town master with cooler eyes. "Though I don't recall any talk of reparation from Haret to Pan Nuk a year ago, for the use of our Guard for another year."

There were murmurs around him, more and more people he recognized, and children, at least twenty, hanging on to grandparents or carers. All that was left of Pan Nuk.

The town master rubbed a hand over his face. "I spoke to Kas. He told me that the reparation was owed to you, Garek. You had done all Pan Nuk could ask of you, and you should be the beneficiary, not Pan Nuk. He took the reparation in trust for your return."

"And where is that reparation now?" Opik asked. "You took all of Kas's things that were left." There was a shake to his voice.

"I have it safe. I have it here." The town master gestured to his house. "I knew you would be back, Garek."

"You sold Garek to Garamundo for money?" one of the old

women called out. "What good is that money now, with my daughter gone? With everyone gone?"

"Garek is the strongest guard I've ever seen." The guard master had come up beside him. "But even he could not have stopped the sky raiders. Not alone."

"We would have had a chance. Some of them would have had a chance." The old woman rocked, arms tight about her waist.

The headache was drilling into Garek's head now, hard and sharp as his father's chisel on the anvil.

The guard master was right. Garek had fought the sky raiders enough in these last eight months to know one guard, no matter how good, would not have stopped them. And passing blame now was nothing but a waste of time. "We can be thankful Garamundo gave the money at all. I'm going to need it." He looked directly at the town master.

"Why so?" Opik asked, frowning.

"Because back in Garamundo, there's a sky raiders' ship. I brought it down from the sky."

Everyone looked blankly at him.

"I'm going to steal it, and get them back."

FOUR

"ARE YOU ANGRY WITH MY FATHER?"

Garek opened his eyes and saw Luca sitting on the small stool next to the fire. He vaguely recalled being helped by Opik to this small room at the back of a house, of falling into bed to sleep off the headache. He'd been awake for five minutes, eyes still closed, listening to the sounds around him.

That Luca had realized he was awake was interesting. Taya could read people by the smallest movement of their bodies. Perhaps her nephew was born with the skill, too.

"Why would I be angry with your father?"

"Taya was. Taya shouted at him." Luca reached out and took a piece of kindling from the wood box and began stripping off the bark, throwing it piece by piece into the fire.

"Because of what the town master spoke of, the deal with Garamundo?"

Luca gave a miserable nod. "Taya said it was wrong. That she would go to Garamundo, fight them to get you back."

That would have been dangerous. And useless. Garek's heart

sped up, just at the thought of Utrel, his guard master, getting a look at Taya.

"What did your father say to that?"

"He said no. He said she would be making things worse for you, drawing attention to you. That Garamundo couldn't extend your conscription for a third year without some special dispensation from the West Lathor Council, and he didn't think they would risk that. Risk drawing the liege's attention to what they were doing, keeping strong guards longer than the agreed year. He told her not to tell anyone else in the village except your father why you weren't back. To keep quiet and let the year run out without any trouble."

"Your father was right."

Luca's head rose. He blinked, then relaxed. "You aren't angry?"

"No, your father did the right thing." Garek pillowed his head with his arms. "What did my father say?"

Luca gave a small smile. "I'm not supposed to know the words he said about Garamundo when it was just him, Taya, my father, and me. Taya had him over to dinner almost every night since you left."

Garek knew the old man would have loved that. About the only thing he and his father agreed on was that persuading Taya he was the only one for her was the best thing he'd ever done. And as an added bonus, seeing his father for dinner every night would have served to keep him in Taya's mind every day. If he saw his father again, he'd have to thank him.

"She . . ." Luca bit his lip, turned his head away. "She cried when you didn't reply to her letters."

Garek rose up, let the warm down cover slip to his waist. "Letters?"

"I thought you were cruel, in the beginning. Cruel to not write back." Luca threw the last piece of bark onto the fire. "But then I found them. All the letters Taya had written. My ball rolled under my father's bed, and I had to wiggle right under to get it. And there they were."

"Did you ask him about them?"

Luca nodded. "I'm telling you this because the letters were taken by the Haret town master when he cleared our house. They are with the money he has for you, and I want to explain before you see them."

"So explain." His voice was an octave lower.

Kas had not liked him for his sister, Garek had always known that, but to let Taya think he didn't care enough to return her letters .
. .

"He didn't want her to send you the letters. Letters are forbidden for the length of the conscription, yes?" Luca looked up, a quick dart of his eyes, and Garek was forced to nod.

"But she said one year was long enough. That if they wouldn't let you come home, not even for a week before making you stay another year, she would write. She had to hear from you."

Garek thought of the nights he had lain, thinking of her, of the sweet scent of her skin, the feel of her soft golden hair brushing his chest as they lay naked in the meadows high in the hills, and something hot and joyful burned in his chest.

"When I found the letters and confronted my father, he looked gray. Older. He had read her first letter. Not with her permission, but to protect her. He didn't want anyone in Garamundo to read it and find some way to use it against us. She was so angry, he feared she might have said something a guard would consider treason. He didn't know if they would read your letters before they gave them to you, but he thought they might, from things that had happened to him when he did his year. He didn't tell me what was in the letter, but from then on, he took them, and hid them, without reading them."

"How many letters?"

"One for every week you were gone," Luca whispered.

Garek closed his eyes. Slowly lowered himself back onto the bed.

It pained him to acknowledge it, but Kas was right again. They would have read anything that came for him before they gave it to him, if they deigned to give it to him at all. But for Kas to pretend he was sending them, to let her believe . . .

"He was wrong, wasn't he? To let her think the letters were being sent?"

"He was wrong." Garek rubbed his face.

"There is no one else for Taya." Luca said. "She told me that herself. Even when there was no word, even when Hap and Lynal and the others came calling, trying to court her, she said until she spoke with you, learned the truth from your own lips, she could not let you out of her heart."

"That is good." Garek cleared his throat. "That is very good."

Luca waited a beat. "Are you really going after them?" He fiddled with the stick. "What are the chances you'll be able to work the sky craft, if you can even steal it? And how will you know where to go?"

Garek swung up again, put his feet on the cold stone floor. "You're right, the chances aren't good. But they're better than doing nothing." He thought of Taya again, in the clutches of the sky raiders for weeks on end. "And doing nothing is not a choice for me."

THE CAMP WAS A GRIM, gray place, tucked up against a bend in the river, with water on three sides.

Black soil coated everything with a thin layer of grit. The trample of feet and the hot blast of the transporters as they came and went had killed all the grass, and it looked like a dead place, long abandoned.

The jousting tent, one of the many things the sky raiders had stolen from Barit on their raids to house their prisoners, looked bizarre, almost insultingly jolly with its colorful streamers and flags in the center of the makeshift settlement.

Taya hunched her shoulders and closed her eyes as the transporter took off behind them, lifting into the air with a scream of its engines, and churning up a whirlwind of dust.

When it was gone, there were only the prisoners standing in a bedraggled group in front of the camp, and the two guards on duty.

It was a prison with no walls or fences, no bars. There would have been none even if they'd had actual buildings rather than the makeshift shanty town of tents, pieces of wood and tin, and even a small boat, upended and suspended on poles with canvas draped down the sides.

Where would they run to?

She tried to shake the dust out of her hair, and then came up short. Something was wrong. The guards stood on either side of them, guns raised.

"No trouble here." The hiss fell into the sudden silence as the transporter winked out of the atmosphere above them. "No fighting." The guard in front of them lifted his gun and aimed it at the big Kardanx, held it there.

For the first time, the Kardanx looked truly afraid, and something nasty and satisfied sang in Taya's heart.

"Each go to your own side. No mixing."

When they had been dumped here, in this desolate place, the language issues and cultural differences had made it natural for the Illy and the Kardanx to set up their shelters at opposite sides of the jousting tent, which they used as a common meeting hall. But it was the behavior of the Kardanx men that had kept the divide as rigid as it was.

The night terrors, the walking around at all hours, the sudden explosions of temper; they'd become more and more noticeable. And more and more an indication that they had lived through something horrific. It was only as time had gone by that the Illy had learned it was something the Kardanx had done to themselves.

Taya wondered if they hadn't kept to their sides, if everyone was intermingled through the camp, what the sky raiders would have done.

They couldn't tell them apart by features; both had an equal mix of hair color, eye color and skin tone. Illy and Kardai shared a border and until one or the other opened their mouths to speak, it was impossible to say who was who.

The guard finally lowered his gun, and as if unable to let the loss of face go without challenge, the Kardanx pointed a finger.

"She doesn't belong on their side." His Kardanx was understandable to her, now he was speaking more slowly.

Taya followed the direction of his finger, but she knew who he was pointing to. The Kardanx woman with the green eyes stood alone, the Illy moving back from her, leaving her exposed.

Trouble.

Taya had known it.

"You say I don't belong on your side. Now you say I do?" The woman lifted her head, and glared across at the Kardanx.

There was a mutter among them, and someone reached out to lay a hand on the Kardanx's arm. He shrugged it off without looking around.

"They have taken one of our woman, but we can't take theirs?"

The guard looked between them. "No trouble," he said, and raised his gun again. Something in the way he held it was too eager, as if he'd had enough of petty squabbles. The other guard moved closer.

"Why do they say you don't belong on their side?" Taya forced her suddenly weak legs to move, forced herself into the open ground between the groups. She caught Kas's head shake, the flare of temper on his face, and ignored it.

"My father was Illian. They've said over and over I should return to the land of my father. They've said it since I was a child. They even call me Min of the Illy. When they aren't calling me witch."

The Kardanx bared his teeth at her.

"If she is of both places, and the Kardanx have said she should be on our side, not theirs, why are you making trouble?" Taya addressed the Kardanx, and he turned his bared teeth in her direction.

"Yes." The guard was watching her. Although she couldn't see through the tint of his window now, she remembered the intent, focused yellow gaze from the guard at the mine site, and forced a little more steel into her spine to keep her legs from trembling. The guard turned back to the Kardanx, and the hum of his gun engaging could be heard by all. "Why are you making trouble? Again?"

"He is not." An older man stepped forward, level with his big compatriot. "There is no trouble. The woman can go to the side of her choosing."

There was silence for a beat, then the guard disengaged the gun, and everyone let out a breath.

"Disperse."

As if the bell had been rung for a town meeting, everyone was suddenly in motion, moving to their shelters, or the open cooking areas.

The woman stood alone and uncertain.

"You can never stop. Never leave well enough alone." Kas stood beside Taya, his anger coming off him like sparks from a fire.

"Whatever happened here, it was far from well enough." Taya gritted her teeth.

"Well, she's your responsibility, then. You can ease her into the camp."

Taya lifted her shoulders. She hadn't expected anything else. She took a step towards the woman. Min, she'd called herself.

"And Taya? We have to talk. About before. At the mine."

Taya knew it. She looked over her shoulder, gave a reluctant nod.

Kas rubbed a tired hand over his face. "And be careful of that Kardanx. By the look on his face today . . ." He shook his head. "If he gets you alone, he'll kill you."

FIVE

"HERE IT IS." Lait Pollar, the town master, opened the door of the small storage room within his stables, and pointed to a wooden chest.

Garek opened the door a little wider, to let in more light, and saw the small space must hold the full contents of Kas's house. Some of the things were Taya's and he forced himself to turn away from them, pull the strongbox out, and close the door.

"I put the money, and all of Kas's letters in there." Lait handed him the key.

When it was open, Garek saw there was a fair sum inside. He was surprised Pollar had left it untouched, or if he had helped himself, he couldn't have taken much. There were parchments addressed to Kas scattered amongst the money bags, and then, in a substantial pile, the letters Taya had written to him.

He pulled the money out, put it in the sack he'd brought along, and then chose three letters. One from the bottom, one from the middle, and the one from the very top. He would read the rest when he had her safe again.

There was a small crowd around them, mostly from Pan Nuk,

but a few local Haret townspeople as well. When he rose from his crouch, Pollar put a hand on his arm.

"You aren't going to bring Garamundo down on us, are you?"

There was silence as everyone absorbed that. Realized the possibility.

"I'll try to do it without them knowing who has stolen the craft." Garek hefted the money bag over his shoulder. He reached down for a second bag at his feet, the bag he'd brought with him from Garamundo, with everything else he owned.

"And if they realize it's you?" Pollar's voice was panicked.

Garek smiled, and Pollar took a quick step back. "I'm from Pan Nuk not Haret. Send them there, if they come to give you trouble about this."

"You don't play games with Garamundo. They won't accept us sending them to Pan Nuk. They'll be looking to make an example." It was the guard master. He leaned against the door frame to the stable, and there was a tic in his cheek, as if he was having difficulty holding himself under control.

Garek shrugged. "I'll try to be discreet."

"Try very hard."

Garek cocked his head. "You seem to know a lot about how Garamundo will react."

"It's my job to know. My job to keep them informed. I can't inform them of what you're about to do, because they'll want to know why I didn't stop you. So make sure they don't find out."

"Did you tell Garamundo about what happened at Pan Nuk?" Garek heard the way his voice dipped lower.

Pollar and the guard master exchanged a look, and it was Pollar who replied. "We did."

"Exactly how long ago was everyone taken?" Something was building in him. Something dangerous and hot.

"Two months." Lait tripped over the words.

"So." He took a breath. Taya had been in their hands for two months. Two months wasted walking the guard walks of Garamundo, looking for sky raiders. Sky raiders who had already taken everything precious to him.

"You sent them a report. Did you ask them to tell me what had happened?" He knew he was drawing the Change. The room was fading in and out of clear detail.

"We did." The guard master's voice was low, almost guttural.

"Funny, they didn't pass the message on." He was drawing more and more air to him, until the room was thick with it. Almost too thick to breathe.

"They wouldn't pass it on, and you know it." It was Opik, his voice, fearless and calm, helped Garek find his own inner peace. Helped him bring it down a notch. "They were already keeping you longer than is allowed. If they told you, you would have come home, no matter what, and they would not have had much recourse to stop you."

"Yes. That's exactly what happened." Garek could picture Utrel, the guard master of Garamundo, reading the report and then flicking the parchment across his desk, his mouth in its familiar thin line. He'd have had no problem hiding what had happened in Pan Nuk from Garek. Especially with only two months left of his conscription.

Garek's cold fury at the thought was tempered by knowing the rage Utrel would feel when someone stole the sky raider craft from the city. The satisfaction of that helped to bring him fully back from the Change.

"I can help you." Opik held something in his hand, and Garek realized it was a travel sack, much like his own.

"How so?" He didn't have time to wait for old men. He planned to call one Change a day. Enough to get to Garamundo fast, but not be too tired when he got there.

"You aren't the only one here who calls the air Change, Garek." Opik pulled a little Change to himself, draping it around him for a single moment, and then releasing. "And I grew up in Garamundo, I can smooth your way there."

Garek considered. He couldn't approach the friends he had made amongst the guard, not without endangering them, and himself. He could use a helper. "If you can keep up." He gave a cool nod.

"I think I can." Opik tipped his head to look Garek in the eye. "You aren't looking forward to going back."

"I swore I'd never set foot in Garamundo again." He closed a tight fist around the necks of his sacks.

Opik rocked back. "Something tells me they'll wish you didn't have cause to return, either."

WHEN TAYA WASHED the grit and sand from the mine off her, she felt calmer. More her old self than before.

Even though it made sense that she would be happier when she was clean, she couldn't help but think the sand itself had something to do with it. When she touched it to brush it off her skin and clothes, it was as if something reared its head inside her. Like she was hungry but didn't know for what.

She scooped water from the bucket in front of her, and sluiced her arms, the water dripping onto the rough hessian sacks they had laid as a mat over the meager grass of the river bank.

No one would get into the river itself. The water was dark and cold, and they couldn't see the bottom. Instead they'd taken to scooping buckets of it up and washing on the bank and hauling what they needed for cooking and drinking back to the open kitchens to boil.

Beside her, Min, the Kardanx woman, shivered as she lifted her tunic over her head. They had the privacy of the dark of early evening, and a thick sheet strung between two poles to shield them from view.

"Thank you." Min splashed water on her body and rubbed, keeping her eyes down. "For earlier, at the mine, and here in the camp."

Taya pulled her own tunic off, hurrying to get the wash over with as fast as possible. Now the Star had set in the night sky the air was turning cooler by the minute. "I couldn't let you go back there against your will."

"The man in charge of your side. He was angry with you for doing it. Will you have trouble?" Min rubbed herself with a small square of cloth lathered with soap smelling of warm, sweet spices, and rinsed herself.

"I won't have trouble with Kas. He's my brother."

Min picked up a towel to dry herself and looked across, her dark hair clinging in wet tendrils to her neck and shoulders. "I'm sorry he's unhappy to have me here."

"He isn't unhappy you're here. He's angry I risked myself." Taya shrugged, and took the soap from Min. It smelled more lovely than anything she'd ever used before.

While she washed, she watched Min pull on a bright green silk gown. It had short sleeves, but swirled down to her feet, clinging to her body where it was still damp.

The clothes the sky raiders provided for them never failed to bemuse Taya. That went for the soaps and the towels, the sheets and the pillows, too. Whoever was in camp was made to unload the transporter when it arrived, carrying everything the sky raiders stole from Barit to a small tent just off the landing area. Everyone called it the Stolen Store.

She guessed some of the things must have been raided from a rich merchant train between Kardai and one of the far countries to the east. Some had definitely come from Garamundo or Juli, from the traders coming or going from the two big cities of West Lathor. She lifted up the pale blue robe she had chosen to sleep in tonight, with its silver embroidered edging and wide sash.

This one could well have come from the castle of the liege of West Lathor.

"Do you think they do this on purpose?" Min fingered the silk bodice of her gown, and then leaned forward to touch the silver thread edging Taya's robe. "Do they understand the strangeness of working all day down a mine, in the filth and dust, and then coming back to these clothes, this soap?" She shook her head. "The soap alone would be a month's wages where I come from. And the gown." She pulled the skirt out and let it go, let it twirl around her. "I would never have worn a gown like this in my old life. That I wear it here makes me nervous."

"I don't think they know. Or if they do, they don't care." Taya dipped her fingers into a jar of perfumed lotion and smoothed it into her hands, rough and callused from hauling rocks. "They don't care if they steal from the rich merchant trains or small, poor villages. And there are goods from both in the Stolen Store. They're stealing right now—" she pointed to the large crescent in the night sky that was Barit, "to get us food. Whatever they scoop up with the food they'll dump in camp as well. It's nothing to them but a way to keep us alive, warm, and able to work."

Min followed her finger. "Why do you point there?"

Taya frowned at her. "Because that's Barit. Right there." She took Min's hand and lifted her index finger to the correct place.

Min's hand shook beneath her own. "How do you know?"

"The position of the constellations. And there is Lanora." She moved her hand to Barit's moon. "We're on Shadow. Barit is just where it should be."

Min sat. Almost dropped straight down onto the ground. "This is Shadow?" She reached out a hand and patted the ground, as if to make sure it was still beneath her.

"Yes. You didn't know that?"

Min shook her head. "If some of the Kardanx know, they haven't shared it with the rest of us. Certainly not with the women."

"It's no secret." Taya wound a towel over her hair and squeezed out as much water as she could. "We can see Barit, and the Star warms us, just as it did on Barit, but that doesn't make escape any more likely."

"No. But it doesn't feel so terrible, somehow. So frightening. I know about Shadow."

Taya tipped her head up to look at the sky. "I think that's why we were taken. I was taught at school that Shadow was once part of Barit, back when the Star was young. That something happened and a big part of the planet was smashed off and became Shadow. Even if the plants and animals aren't exactly the same, you can see what their cousins on Barit would be. We can survive here."

"That's why the sky raiders hide inside those metal suits. They can't survive here." There was an edge to Min's voice, a certainty.

Taya snorted. "Even whatever their ships are made of can barely survive. Do you see how quickly it breaks down? That's why the transporters lift off into the sky every night. Not so we can't take one over and commandeer it, but because every moment it's down here, it's rusting that much faster."

"The guards' suits, too." Min lowered her voice. "They are getting worse and worse."

"Taya." Kas's voice came from a few feet away. "Are you finished?"

Taya stepped out from behind the sheet. "Yes. Sorry. Didn't mean to take so long. Where will Min sleep?"

Kas looked back at the camp, then to her again. "Pilar moved in with Noor a few days ago. He says Min can take his old tent.

Min stepped out from behind her. "Thank you."

Kas gave a shrug. "It's Taya you need to thank." He waited for them to join him, and Taya could see the strain around his eyes, and the worry.

She knew most of it was for Luca. An impossible journey away, and on his own.

They'd been taken so fast, so violently, they didn't even know what had happened to those who hadn't been taken with them. Thinking back to that cold, cruel interest in the eyes of the sky raider guard at the mine, she shivered.

But some of the worry tonight was because he was convinced she'd started to call the Change at the mine site. He hadn't said anything to her in the transporter, for fear of listening ears, and they hadn't had a chance since then, but she knew it was weighing on him.

It was certainly weighing on her.

No one from the Illy could call their Change properly since they'd come here.

Kas thought it was because, while Shadow had once been part of Barit, and was similar, the air wasn't exactly the same. It was a little harder to breathe here, everyone was out of breath more quickly.

The sand was different, too, not completely so, but enough for it to be noticeable.

Those who had tried to call the Change, out of sight of the watchful eyes of the guards, behind canvas and wooden walls, could only sustain it for a few minutes, before they were forced out.

Kas called the earth Change, and he could barely lift a thin line of sand from the ground, and even that was a struggle.

Of the six Changed amongst them here on Shadow, every one had a similar experience.

The problem was, Taya wasn't one of them. She had never been able to call the Change.

Until now.

SIX

THEY ATE their meal around the fire with Min, Pilar, Noor, Quardi and a few others; Harvi, one of the farmers who lived just outside Pan Nuk, and his wife, Pec, along with their two sons who helped them with the leviks. Jerilia sat with them, much quieter than usual, but composed and calm.

It had been Kas and Pilar's turn to make dinner for the Pan Nuk villagers tonight, and it was as eclectic a mix as the clothing.

The sky raiders had taken all the leviks with them when they'd raided Pan Nuk, with enough hay and grass to sustain them on the journey to Shadow. But once they were here, they'd died of starvation in two weeks, unable to get the sustenance they needed from the strange grasses and vegetation.

Harvi and Eli, another Pan Nuk farmer who worked the night shift, had watched at first with horror, and then cold anger, as both their flocks, built up over a lifetime, collapsed and died.

They'd eaten nothing but levik for over a week after that, until the left-over carcasses had spoiled and had to be buried.

There had been a growing fear of starvation in the camp, but they needn't have worried. The sky raiders weren't about to let production slow due to lack of food. Particularly when they could steal it from Barit.

When the last carcass was buried and everyone had gone over a day with nothing to eat at all, a big transporter had arrived. The guards had organized the unloading of crates, shimmering with condensation from their time in cold storage. Exotic foods Taya had never seen, as well as very familiar local Illian dishes. The whole of Barit was their marketplace, and if there was anything to enjoy about this experience, Taya didn't know whether the clothes or the food were better.

Tonight's dinner was fish, char-cooked over a hot fire, and tiny green peas, eaten raw, so sweet and plump they exploded in her mouth. The bread was buttery, with a crusty texture and a musky spice mixed through it, warmed over hot coals.

She ate sitting next to Quardi, as she always did; making sure he was comfortable, checking on his legs and how they were healing, bringing his food to him. He loved the fuss, and she loved him. Even if he hadn't been Garek's father, she would have loved him, but because he was, there was no filter on her heart when it came to him.

It was the memory of Quardi, lying crumpled on the ground outside the mine, that had forced her to approach the guard today. To make sure Kas didn't end up their victim, too.

She noticed Min had taken her food cautiously, but she soon relaxed and struck up a friendship with Noor and Pilar, and ate the bread with gusto, as if it were familiar to her.

It tasted like something that would come from Kardai.

Eventually everyone drifted off to bed, and she was alone with Kas in the small structure they'd built from planks of wood and thick gray canvas. She took off the strange open shoes she'd found with the clothes, with their gossamer thin straps that wove over her feet in a complex pattern, and sank down onto her mattress.

It was thick and soft, and so wide, there was only room for it and Kas's mattress in the room, with a thin space between the beds for walking. The thick down stuffing cocooned her, and she groaned with relief at lying down after another day hacking at rock with a pick. She brushed her hand over the sheets, so soft and smooth, she didn't know if they were very fine dar fibers or thick silk. When she'd first unfolded them, they'd carried the scent of sweet perfume and far away places.

"These remind me of that scarf you bought me last year." Taya ran her hand over the sheets again, and turned to look at Kas. He was sitting on his low mattress, elbows on knees, watching her. His fair hair was still damp from his own wash and it stuck up slightly over his forehead in an endearing way. "The fine blue one that matches my eyes."

He sighed and leaned back, propping himself up on his elbows. "I didn't buy you that."

She frowned at him. "Yes, you did, you met a trader coming over the pass—"

"I lied."

That stopped her.

"Garek sent you that scarf."

Her heart stopped beating for one terrible, painful moment, and then started up again, hammering in her chest. She couldn't speak.

"I think Garek is dangerous." He bunched his hands into fists, and his arms bulged with muscle honed into even more definition after over a month working down the mines. "I don't know anyone who can draw the Change as strongly as he can, and he will always attract the attention of the powerful. He will either be a tool of destruction for the liege of West Lathor, or he'll be too big a threat to be allowed to live. I've known that since his first Change."

He was watching her, and when she said nothing, he sat up properly. "Taya, I don't want you caught in the middle, damn it. You never have any sense of self-preservation. You made a deal with the sky raiders today, for Star's sake. And you manipulated everyone, including the sky raiders, during that scene the Kardanx made when we all got out the transporter. And for what? So a Kardanx woman could live on our side? What more will you do for Garek? You'd take on the liege himself if you thought you had to. And you wouldn't win."

"Why are you telling me this now?" She didn't know what to feel.

Anger. Rage. A terrible, terrible sadness. And an understanding. An empathy with her brother.

He loved her.

But he was such an *idiot*.

"Because today taught me something. Nothing I did to ease you away from Garek had any effect, did it? You set a course, and even if it means hitting a sky raider on the metal leg of his suit with a bare fist, you see it through."

She shrugged. Looked up at the ceiling, such as it was. Decided to change the subject. "The sky raiders look like us, more or less, but bigger, and with thin faces. Their skin is covered with short, smooth fur, which is a pale yellow. And they have too many teeth. I didn't see his hands, but his shoulders and neck were like ours, the head was about the same shape. The eyes, though." She shuddered. "They were golden yellow. And . . . cruel." She felt foolish saying that, but she thought it accurate.

"You saw him through the visor?" Kas leaned forward.

She turned to look at him. "He did something to the visor, cleared it so it wasn't so darkly tinted any more, and let me see right in."

"Why?"

"Because we were having a conversation, and I think he wanted me to look him in the eyes."

"How did you get them to intervene?"

"I told him if they allowed the Kardanx to take Jerilia, production would slow because the Illy and Kardanx would take the fight underground into the mine."

Kas blew out a breath, and gave a reluctant laugh. He opened his mouth to speak, then closed it again, shaking his head.

"Where did you get the knife, Kas?" She hadn't forgotten the reason she'd forced herself across the clearing to take on the sky raider guard. The quick flash of Kas taking a knife from the back of his pants.

He went still. And then understanding slowly crept over his face. "You didn't act today for Jerilia so much as me, did you? You didn't want me to fight."

She held his gaze, said nothing.

He rubbed his forehead. "It was in the crate of star fruit that came a couple of days ago. It's just a fruit knife. Must have been left inside by mistake, and they didn't check it like they do the clothes and the furniture they bring us. They don't expect anything but food in the food crates." He paused. "Quardi sharpened it for me in his forge."

"Try not to use it." She closed her eyes.

"Don't put me in a situation where I'll have to."

Her eyes flew open in outrage. "I had nothing to do with Jerilia being taken by that thug. I'm just the one who fixed it without resorting to violence."

"True. But later, you needled that big Kardanx—Ketl, I hear he's called. He lost face today. He'll go after either you or Min. He won't let that insult slide."

"I'll keep Min close. And stay close to you." She stretched, heard a bone click into place in her back.

"And now that we've danced around it, and talked about everything else, let's talk about you calling the Change." His voice was so low, she was forced to turn on her side to face him again.

"Are you sure I did?"

He tapped the long, blunt fingers of his hand on his knee. "I'm sure. What did it feel like?"

"I was angry. So, so angry that the Kardanx had killed their women. Just looking at them, realizing for every man standing there, at least one woman was dead. It was like I was in a tunnel, and there was a high-pitched roar in my head."

Kas lay down on his bed at last. "There is something here on Shadow that's calling the Change in you, Taya. It's the only explanation. Something down that mine, perhaps, that's buried too deep on Barit for it to affect you back home. Strong emotion is what calls the first Change. The strong emotion of adolescence is usually the trigger, but you're past that. So you used the anger you felt. Every time you let a strong emotion take you, you'll be a step closer to calling a full Change."

"You think it's an earth Change. Like you?"

Kas looked across at her. Then blew out the lantern between them and plunged them into darkness. "I don't know. If there is a chance you can call a Change here, you should try it. Out of sight of the guards. No matter what Change you call, it could be useful if we have a chance to escape. My Change is useless here, so are the others, and the Kardanx killed their Changed off over two hundred years ago."

"Do you think that's why they call Min a witch? Because she can call the Change? Her father was Illian."

Kas made a hum of interest. "Perhaps. Ask her. Ask her what she can do, and if it's been affected by Shadow."

They lay quietly for a few minutes. "We should tell as many people as we can about my calling a Change here."

"Why is that?" Kas sounded reluctant.

"Because if I can suddenly do it, maybe others will be able to, as well."

SEVEN

ONLY WHEN THE city gates disappeared behind them, and the cart he and Opik were sitting in had rumbled its way deep into the twisting cobbled streets of Garamundo, did Garek start to relax. Even then, he kept a surreptitious watch from under the deep hood of his cloak, searching the crowds around them for signs of a spy or a watcher the guards at the gate may have sent after them.

"This is as far as I go." The merchant turned into a yard that lay next to a large warehouse, and jumped down.

Opik and Garek swung down as well.

"Our thanks."

Opik had done the talking on this journey, and Garek didn't see a reason to change that now. He let the old man hand over the coins they'd negotiated with the grain seller and then followed him out onto the street.

"You're scaring the natives." Opik flicked a glance at him as they shouldered their way through the crowds.

He tried to relax his body, move less like he was about to charge into battle, grudgingly conceding that people were making an extra effort to get out of his path. The grain merchant had looked a little nervous, too, come to think of it.

Tension had ratcheted tighter within him with every mile they'd journeyed closer to Garamundo. He'd wanted to smash his way through the gates the same way he'd done back in Haret, had had to force himself still and calm at the back of the cart as they'd waited for the noon day opening of the gate.

Garamundo only opened its main gates three times a day. Morning, noon and sunset. If you got there early, you had to wait.

It was a sensible precaution against attack, but Garek struggled not to resent the arrogance of it. They had to control everything in Garamundo. Even the flow of traffic through their enclosing, imprisoning walls.

"Did you see the guard party stopped at that tavern back in Pan Itan?" Opik led them into a quieter lane running at an angle to the main street, but even though the crowds were thinner here, he kept his voice low.

"Yes." Garek gripped his sacks a little tighter. "I'm surprised it took them that long."

"You think they're after you?" Opik made the question light, but Garek wasn't fooled.

"They could only have left Garamundo after sunrise this morning to be in Pan Itan at ten. They gave me six whole days."

"But if they wanted you, why didn't they simply stop you leaving in the first place?"

"They offered me a full commission in the guard before I left. Well, the town master did. My guard master didn't want me to stay. He knows I'd take his job in a few years if I did. When they made the offer, I said I'd think about it, but I hadn't seen my family in two years and I wanted to go home." Garek rubbed his cheek. "But I knew they'd get twitchy. Start thinking about the other city states that would take me. And how they hadn't exactly made a friend of me when they'd forced the extra year of conscription. I knew they'd be coming with . . . let's say an offer I couldn't refuse." He let the dry sarcasm he was feeling come through.

They'd have approached him with a combination of a carrot and stick, he'd known that long before they'd even made the first offer. Known he'd need to get to Taya as fast as possible and then run.

Even if running was against his natural inclination.

He was much, much better at standing his ground.

But sometimes a smart fighter knew when the odds were against him.

"Were you tempted?" Opik asked. "A man with your talents could do well for himself in Gara."

Garek gave a thin smile. "No."

"You'd think they would have left sooner, if they already knew what had happened in Pan Nuk. That everyone was gone."

Garek stopped. That wasn't something he'd thought about. Why had they waited so long? It would have been a good opportunity to persuade him back, fresh from finding his village decimated, while vengeance sang loud and strong in his heart.

"The guard master may not have told anyone. Either he did it deliberately, because he doesn't want me back, even though the town master does, or he forgot about it." Garek started walking again. "Both make sense, knowing him."

"Well, the good news is that the guard party after you will take two days to get to Pan Nuk, even at a hard ride—" A high-pitched whine cut Opik off. A sound Garek knew all to well, and hated now more than ever.

He looked up, saw the liquid silver of the sky raider craft as it hurtled low over the city, dipping left, then right as it screamed overhead.

It would be targeting the merchant trains leaving the Far Gate, from the direction and the height of it.

When he'd been part of Garamundo's Guard, the reports they'd had in for the last two months were that the sky raiders had switched from stealing people to stealing food and trade goods. Of course, they could be taking people from outside of West Lathor, but the little intelligence they received from Kardai and some of the far eastern countries was that the same pattern was being repeated there, as well.

Pan Nuk must have been one of the last villages they'd hit.

He stared after the craft until it disappeared beyond the high roofs of the palace and the Hall, and wished he could call the Change without giving himself away and ruining his plans. He'd have to let this one go.

"Get down!" Opik was crouched on the street, and grabbed at the hem of his cloak, gave it a tug.

Garek was about to tell him there was no danger, not in the narrow streets where the sky raiders couldn't reach with their craft, when he noticed he was the only one standing. Everyone else was crouched with arms over their heads, pressed up against walls or in doorways.

"They're gone," he said, and pulled the old man to his feet.

Opik hunched his shoulders and drew his lips back in a snarl, his teeth white against his dark skin. "You stand out too much. Let's go."

THE RIDE to the mine in the pale dawn was smooth and uneventful, and when Taya stepped out, she kept her eyes on Barit, a fat crescent of pale blue and white in a gold-tinted sky.

It looked close enough to reach out and touch.

She thought of Luca down there, alone, and Garek. He would be coming to the end of his second year in Garamundo. He might even be on his way home.

She shivered at the thought of him, coming to Pan Nuk. Coming to that empty, ruined place that was once his home.

What would he do?

She rubbed her arms, suddenly agitated. Afraid for Garek in a way that confounded her. The hairs on her neck rose, and nausea burned her throat.

Let him not do anything crazy.

It took her a moment to realize the night shift were already waiting to one side, filthy and far quieter than usual.

"Eli?" Kas called to the Pan Nuk levik farmer who worked the night shift.

"We finally found what they were looking for." Eli shuffled forward with the rest of the crew. They looked more exhausted than usual, as if they'd been pushed harder.

The way it usually worked, they'd hack at the rock, bring it up, and the guards would look it over.

But the sky raiders were never happy with what was presented to them. Everyone had worked out they were looking for something their prisoners had yet to find.

She would have to ask Eli later what had happened when they had finally found what the sky raiders were after. Had they danced around? Whooped for joy? Or just hissed?

The sky raiders didn't go down the mine's long, meandering tunnels—couldn't, she guessed—not without making themselves vulnerable to attack in the narrow, circular burrows that stretched in all directions from the mine entrance. But more than that, their machines didn't work well in the shafts.

She'd found no pattern to the tunnels, no logic. She'd seen the robotic diggers they'd originally used to dig the tunnels abandoned and rusting down some of the dead-ends, as if they'd broken down and simply been left, sometimes with a sharp digging claw still embedded in the rock. It looked to her as if all sense of direction, all control had been ceded the moment the diggers got underground. Like a compass point too close to a magnet.

They didn't use the diggers any more. Hadn't since they'd brought their first transporter full of prisoners to Shadow.

Now they used the Illy and the Kardanx.

If the diggers didn't work well below ground, Taya guessed the machines the guards sat in wouldn't either.

To compensate, the sky raiders made sure they didn't need to go down the tunnels. They used a strange screen set up near the mine entrance that showed each person down the mine as a red and yellow blur, and they could measure how much work had been done.

Neither the Illy nor the Kardanx had understood what the screen was at first.

Quardi went down the mine the first day they were put to work, after the camp had been built, and then sat up against the wall of the tunnel. He swore he would not lift a finger to help their abductors. A few of the Kardanx had joined him, and one or two other Illians.

The sky raiders had waited until the shift was over, and then shot everyone who had sat instead of worked in both legs.

Clever, Kas had said. Wounding served as a more constant reminder than a few dead bodies, which would have to be buried. The injured were a burden for them all to carry, to care for, in the camp.

But Quardi joked their captors had lived to regret it, probably more than he did.

On the third day of work, the sky raiders' picks had crumpled in a heap of rust and fatigued metal on the first strike to rock, and they'd had to come to Quardi with a pile of metal taken from Barit, had to set up a forge and put him to work making picks that could withstand Shadow's atmosphere.

A guard watched him constantly, making sure he didn't craft other, more dangerous things that could be used against them, but he had to work sitting down while his legs healed, and the sky raiders had had to give him Pilar as an assistant to help him.

But whether they regretted injuring their only blacksmith or not, no one had spent the day leaning against a tunnel wall after that.

"Take your equipment." The hiss of the guard jerked her out of her thoughts, and she moved with the others to the picks the night shift had piled to one side. The transporter took off behind them, and she closed her eyes against the swirling dust.

But they weren't handing the picks out to everyone, today.

The men were given tools, and the women were herded to one

side. "Go to where the seam was uncovered. The stronger ones break the rock, the others carry it out."

It was one of the longest sentences she'd ever heard a guard speak. She saw the pile of ore was to one side of the mine entrance, away from where the transporter landed. Away from where the guards stood.

It was the rock they had been hacking at since they'd arrived on Shadow, but as she got closer she saw thick veins of a dark purple, almost black, ore glinting through each hunk.

It was beautiful, but Taya didn't think they were going to be making jewelry with it.

Something about the placement of the pile, so far from the sky raiders' equipment and the guards themselves, fired a thought in her head, and she picked up a chunk.

A feeling of nausea spiked inside her. It was the same sensation she often had down the mine, but more intense. She breathed through it as she turned and walked back to the guards.

"Do you want us to move the pile closer to the transporters? To make it easier to load?" She was holding the rock, thick with veins of ore, in front of her, and the guard began to raise his weapon, paused, and lowered it again.

"No." The command was forceful. "Take it back. We will let you know when we're ready to load."

She nodded and turned, keeping her face blank until her back was to them.

Then she smiled, even though her skin felt too tight for her body, and she had to breathe to keep her breakfast down. It wasn't definitive proof but it was close enough.

They were afraid to get close to the ore. If she were to guess, the shadow ore was what sent the diggers off course, and why the guards couldn't go into the tunnels in their protective robotic suits. It must affect their ability to function.

This is what would bring them down, if she could think of how to use it against them. The very thing the sky raiders wanted so badly would be their undoing.

She wondered how they planned to load it into their transporters if they didn't even want it near where the big ships landed and took off for fear of what it would do to their systems.

"Get to work."

The hiss of the guard galvanized them all.

The men started for the mine entrance. Taya moved after them with the other women.

She would have to plan their escape later.

EIGHT

THE BOLTHOLE OPIK had arranged for them was perfect.

Straddling the line between the just-respectable Seventh Wedge and the dodgier Eighth, the gaming house had a constant stream of traffic through its doors. To the one side of it were neat row houses, marching towards the eastern wall, and on the other, stretching further south toward the Hot Gate, the crowded, crumbling buildings of the Eighth sat sullen and dark.

The room Opik's friend, Haak, had given them above the gaming rooms even came with a large chest to keep his money safe.

Opik rolled his eyes when Garek ignored it, and carefully and quietly levered up a floorboard under his bed, and stuffed his sack into the narrow hole.

Garek didn't trust Haak not to steal from him, but he thought Opik was right to trust him not to squeal to the Guard.

Haak wouldn't want them sniffing around any more than Garek did.

As soon as their things were stored away, Garek left again, leading Opik out through the back.

"Must we do this now?" Opik panted, struggling to keep pace

with him as Garek wound his way through the twisting streets toward the palace.

He looked down on the old man. "As opposed to what? Having a shot of Haak's firebrand? Having a rest?" He didn't bother to hide his contempt.

Opik drew in a deep breath. "You're right. I'm older than I thought. Older and not half as tough as I once was."

He said nothing for a whole block. "I'm doing this for Taya, too, you know. I've got no living family left. But she was good to me. Always was. Doted on that father of yours, but never left me out."

Garek slowed his pace a little, so the old man could catch his breath.

"That Kas. He tried everything to get her to forget you. Not that I blame him." Opik gave him a sidelong look. "You're a big, dangerous bastard, Garek. You're trouble on two legs. Can't blame a man for wanting to keep his sister away. Had his work cut out for him the first year, of course. Bad form for the other lads to try it on with a conscriptee's girl. And she was your girl, clear as day." He cleared his throat. "But the second year, they didn't know Gara had held onto you. And Kas certainly didn't tell them. They thought you'd forgotten her."

Garek couldn't answer. Was there an answer to that, anyway? He could no more forget Taya than forget to breathe.

"But it didn't do them a blind bit of good. That little Taya—she may look like a fairy, with that pale blonde hair and those big blue eyes, but soon enough, you work out if she *is* a fairy, she's the fairy queen. And a very focused, very fierce queen, at that." Opik chuckled. "I feel sorry for Kas, really. All that effort. Wasted."

Garek fought to keep his face impassive.

The palace loomed ahead, and he used the sight of it to rein in his thoughts.

"Last I knew, the sky ship was in the courtyard near the western tower." He pointed to the tower he meant. The western wedges of the roughly round pie that was Garamundo were the affluent ones, and the houses were large, but not as high as the communal buildings of the north and the east. No house would overlook the western tower's courtyard, and he was sure that was why the town master's scholar, Falk, had chosen it.

"How do you want to get in?" Opik leaned against the side of a building while he studied the tower, and Garek realized he'd probably pushed the old man too far for one day. He should have left him back at the gaming house.

"The scientist working for the town master is a man called Falk. He may have worked out how to fly the ship by now. I'll need to speak to him, and I'll get in through him, too."

Opik had his breath back, and he pushed off the wall. "He a friend of yours, that he'll do all that?"

Garek studied the tower. "No. I've only met him once, when he came to get the craft from where I'd brought it down."

"Then how—?"

Garek looked back at him and Opik snapped his mouth shut.

He shook his head, but Garek saw a glint of eagerness in his eyes. "Poor, unlucky Falk."

TAYA STUMBLED as she and Min carried a large chunk of ore between them, the third time she'd tripped over nothing since they'd picked the piece up from the growing pile the men had hacked from the rock face.

"What is it?" Min peered at her in the dim light of the fireless lanterns the sky raiders had given them to fix at intervals through the tunnels.

"I don't know."

She felt sick. Her skin still felt too tight and she was shivering and hot all at once.

"Could the air be bad?" Min lifted her head and sniffed. "You might be more sensitive to it." She peered closer at Taya. "You don't look well."

Taya hefted the rock that was pulling on her shoulders and back. Unlike the first one they'd carried out, the surface of this one was mottled with thick veins of ore. Shadow ore, they were calling it. She ran her thumb over the wide stripe of iridescent purple, and a frisson ran through her.

She dropped her side of it in surprise, and with a startled cry, Min let go her side and jumped back before it landed on her foot.

The rock smashed to the ground and sheered down the middle, and the thick, rich center of it glinted back at them in the weak light.

"At least it split almost evenly. Can you carry your piece?" Min bent and lifted her bit up, and Taya forced herself to do the same. It was easier to carry her own ore than to carry with Min, but cradling the rock in her arms made her feel worse than she had before.

"Let's get you out into the open. I'm scared it's the air." Min started walking ahead of her, and Taya followed, feeling a strange disconnect with her body.

She didn't notice Min had stopped until she almost ran into the back of her. She lifted her head, and over Min's shoulder she saw the big Kardanx, Ketl, arms crossed in front of him, blocking the way.

"Let us by." She was frightened, and her voice came out on a croak.

Ketl leaned against the tunnel wall. "You owe me for the trouble you've caused me."

"You've caused your own problems." Min's voice was cool. "My friend isn't well, let us pass so I can get her to the surface."

There were sounds behind them and ahead, others coming down the passage. They were in the main thoroughfare, and Ketl could not have expected anything else. He cocked his head, listening, and she thought he would stand down. Try again another time.

Instead, he shoved Min against the wall, and as she was flung back, Min threw the rock she carried at him. It hit his side before smashing to pieces on the ground, and he jerked with pain.

No matter who was coming, Taya could tell he would hit her for that.

Fury ripped through her and she could almost hear the sound of tearing as her control slipped.

The world went a little gray.

"Step away." She hardly recognized her voice.

Ketl must have heard something in it, too, because he looked over his shoulder, one hand clamped over Min's throat, the other in her hair, pulling her head back.

He let both hands drop, and turned to face her. "Witch." He breathed it out, not accusing, not contemptuous, more surprised. Utterly surprised.

She looked down at the rock in her hands. And let it go. Watched it hit the ground and shards of rock explode outward. A splinter of shadow ore, shaped like a strange battle spike, was freed from its surrounding rock, bounced, and as it flew up, Taya was able to grab hold of it with her thoughts, and hold it in the air in front of her.

She looked up from it and saw Ketl and Min both watching her with wide eyes. She locked gazes with Min, and tipped her head left.

Before Ketl could react, Min dived left, out of harm's way.

Taya noticed the rock Min had thrown at Ketl had also smashed and left pieces of shadow ore free of the rock, and she reached for them, too. They all rose a little way, then dropped back down, so she concentrated on the thick spike in front of her.

"It will be a pleasure to kill you." Ketl bent and pulled a knife from his boot, and at the sight of it, Taya thought back to the Kardanx women, slaughtered by their own men.

A burst of voices came around the corner, and then stopped on a shout of surprise, but she couldn't look away from the danger in front of her.

Ketl lunged, and fear and rage crackled through her, fast and hot as a lightning strike.

She flung the shadow ore at him as he jumped, and like the spike thrower Garamundo boasted of as one of their best weapons, the sharp vein of metal tore into his shoulder and slammed him back against the wall, driving deep into the rock of the tunnel to pin him there.

"Taya!" Kas's shout came at her as if from a great distance, and she turned to him.

It was a relief to turn away from what she had done. Blood leaked from Ketl's shoulder.

Kas reached her, cupped her cheek, and then looked over her head. "You're lucky she aimed for his shoulder, not his heart." He wasn't talking to her, but Taya was glad, too. She didn't need Ketl's death on her hands.

Taya looked around to find both sides of the tunnel were packed, and every eye was on her.

She lifted a trembling hand to wipe away the perspiration stinging her eyes, and turned back to Ketl. He had gone white and still, looking down at where the spike was sticking out of the meaty part of his shoulder.

She tried to grab hold of it with her mind again, but only felt nausea and the shivery cold of a fever when she tried.

She leaned forward and grabbed it with her hand, careful not to touch Ketl, and tried to pull it out. It wouldn't budge.

Kas stepped up, gave it a yank, and got it out, threw it down at Ketl's feet. The Kardanx slid down to the floor, eyes flashing with pain and fury.

"Keep the chain on your dog," Kas spoke to the older Kardanx man in the crowd, the one who'd promised the sky raiders yesterday there'd be no more trouble. "My sister may decide to pin more vital pieces of him next time."

NINE

GAREK LET the night wash over him; the smells and sounds of Garamundo, the cool flow of air as autumn ran its fingers through the last muggy strands of summer. He thought he'd never experience this again, and was surprised by the comfort he took in its familiarity.

Opik sat close by, leaning against a wall, his eyes closed.

They'd had four hours of sleep through the afternoon—Garek knew they couldn't operate without some rest—but now they watched the western tower.

There was someone inside. Lights shone from the narrow windows and Garek could see a figure moving about, but unless he was willing to call the Change, he wouldn't be able to get in without confronting the four guards that stood watch.

He considered the implications of calling a Change.

He would get in to the tower, but the guards would send reinforcements. Yes, he could hold them back, but he would have to convince Falk to talk and learn how to fly the sky raiders' ship at the same time. And both the town master and the guard master would know he was back in Garamundo.

And yet, every second he stood here, Taya was in the sky raiders' hands. He hadn't allowed himself to think about what happened to the people they took. But he thought about it now. And it was ripping him to pieces.

He was about to tell Opik his patience had run out when first one light, then another, was extinguished inside the building.

Garek prodded Opik with his foot, and kept his eyes on the tower door.

A man stepped out, and Garek recognized the tall, lean figure of the town master's scientist. Falk Pallica called good night to the guards and then walked through the gates.

He wore only a thin tunic over his trousers, and, caught unawares by the sudden cool of the evening, he hunched his shoulders and rubbed his arms as he walked.

"Go ahead," Garek told Opik. "Walk fast and try to overtake him, if you can. I'll trail him from behind."

Opik stumbled to his feet, but by the time he'd reached the street, he was walking briskly enough, and Garek kept to the shadows as he walked behind both men.

Falk slowed his step as he approached a bakery, then swung in as if giving in to temptation. He came out less than five minutes later with a large paper bag and a small pie in one hand. He ate it in quick, clean bites as he walked.

Up ahead, Opik lurked outside a fruit seller's shop, lifting the fruit in the barrows and sniffing it. Falk slowed again and took out a key, opened up a door in a building just down from where Opik stood.

The scientist disappeared inside, and Garek called a tiny bit of Change to keep the door open with the thinnest of air wedges.

He waited until he could hear Falk on the stairs and then he opened the door and waited for Opik to join him.

They went in together, closing the door silently behind them.

Falk's steps rang above them in the four story building, and Garek began to run, completely silently, up after him.

Opik trailed behind.

The sound of footsteps stopped as Garek reached the third floor, and Garek was just in time to see the dark brown door of Falk's rooms swing shut. Again, he called on the smallest Change, on invisible fingers of air to hold the door open just enough.

He waited for Opik, and when the old man pulled himself up using the handrail, panting, he let him take a moment to catch his breath before he opened the door.

He left Opik to close it, moving fast and silently down the short hall and then left into the kitchen area.

Falk was standing beside a table, a jug in one hand and a glass in the other.

He looked up, startled at Garek's appearance. He lowered the jug, but kept the cup, and took a sip. "What have I done to deserve a visit from the Guard?" He spoke slowly, and far too calmly.

Garek kept his face still, but he sensed something. A tension in Falk that was not the reaction of an innocent man being visited by the Guard in a highly unorthodox way.

That Falk recognized him at all was surprising enough. Garek thought he'd had eyes only for the sky raider craft Garek had brought down when they'd met, barely acknowledging the guard who had managed what no one else had managed before.

He obviously didn't know Garek had left the Guard, and Garek weighed up the pros and cons of telling him, or not.

They both heard the door snick closed, and Garek hid his surprise when Falk seemed to relax, and tried to pretend he hadn't heard the sound.

So there was someone else either living here, or who Falk had as an ally. He thought his friend had just arrived.

"That would be my colleague, not yours."

Shock flashed across Falk's face and Garek smiled.

Falk lowered the cup. "That's disappointing."

Garek would bet it was. "So who were you hoping would come rushing to your rescue?"

Falk narrowed his eyes. "Something's off here. You aren't representing the town master, are you?"

"Why do you say that?"

"If this was official business, if the town master suspected me of treachery, I'd be halfway to the east tower by now."

"You're right. He doesn't know you're not loyal to him." Garek was fishing in the dark, but Falk's lips thinned, and he felt the satisfaction of a true strike.

"So what is this, a blackmail attempt?" Falk splayed his fingers on the table, leaning forward, his eyes searching Garek's face. "What do you actually know?"

Garek watched him back. Cocked his head. "I'll lay it out for you honestly. I don't know anything, and I don't much care. In fact, your . . . lack of loyalty to the town master is most definitely to my benefit. But whether you want to cooperate with me or not, you will."

Falk sized him up, and Garek had to admit that for a man who spent most of his time in a laboratory or bent over books, Falk had the long, lean build and muscles of a man who exercised regularly. He wouldn't be easy to take in a fight. But Garek was a trained guard, bulkier, every muscle honed, and even taller than Falk. And he could call the Change, which rendered any resistance Falk offered up useless.

It would never be a fair fight.

Falk suddenly straightened. "I recognized you right away, but now I remember where from. You're the guard who brought down my ship."

"Your ship?" Garek lifted his eyebrows.

Falk waved his hand dismissively. "I've done nothing but eat, sleep, and breathe that ship for the last three months. It's mine." He rubbed his hand over his face, and his shoulders slumped. "I don't have a chance against you, do I? You single-handedly brought down a sky raider craft. I actually wondered at the time if the town master would try to have you assassinated after that, because that kind of power . . ."

"He tried to woo me to his side, instead." Garek hadn't thought of the possibility of an assassination attempt, but Falk would know more of the political double-dealings of the Council than he would. He was lucky the town master was more greedy for power than afraid.

"It obviously didn't work." Falk gave a snort.

Garek folded his arms. "I need access to the ship. And I need to know everything you can tell me on how to fly it."

Falk went still. "The ship?"

Garek held his gaze.

"It sounds like you want to fly it." Falk rubbed the side of his head.

Opik, obviously tired of hanging around in the hallway, stuck his head into the kitchen. "That's exactly what the mad bastard is going to do."

TEN

"YOU'RE SAYING the ore went through skin and muscle and into the rock?" Quardi leaned in closer, and Taya nodded.

"Straight in."

"What kind of ore is that hard, straight out of the ground? No tempering, no folding. The raw ore?"

"This might help." Min appeared from the river, hair still damp, and fiddled with her sleeve. She pulled out a thin vein of ore, slightly thicker than a rug hook and the length of a finger joint.

The dizziness Taya felt before came back with a rush, and she lifted a hand to her head as the world flickered.

"Easy." Kas put a cool hand on her forehead. "It takes a while. It won't always be this intense."

"And you say you could manipulate the shards?" Quardi took the shadow ore from Min and turned it over in his hands.

Taya nodded. "Just the one properly. The others reacted, but then fell back down again. I didn't really know what I was doing. Was there something I did wrong?" She looked over at her brother, and he shrugged.

"I don't know. Garek calls the Change in the air. I call it in the earth. By their very nature, there is a lot to call of both those things. When the thing that calls the Change in you is in a much smaller quantity, perhaps what you see is a more precise, clearer view of what Garek and I do on a larger scale."

"The way you can only call a thin line of soil since we arrived. Because there is only a tiny amount of the type of soil you call on Shadow compared to Barit." Quardi glanced at Kas. He held the shadow ore to the light. "I wonder what you could do with this if I smelted it, Taya, while it was liquid . . ."

He stared at the piece, and there was a change in his face, a sudden dawning of enlightenment. "The Star-cursed bastards! Those mangy, flea-bitten, blood-thirsty Star-cursed bastards!"

"Keep it down," Kas hissed as Pilar, Noor and a few others from Pan Nuk moved closer, and then found places for themselves around the fire.

"The Nordren." Quardi waved the slender baton of ore as if conducting a band, and Taya could feel the tug as it waved in front of her. "I always *knew* they couldn't work metal like that with their hands. Superior skill my big hairy buttocks. I *knew* there was something else involved."

"Quardi, what are you talking about?" Pilar leaned forward and tugged the ore from his grasp, and Taya felt an uncomfortable lurch.

"The Nordren and their very intricate, very highly-prized metal-work, would be my guess." Kas spoke quietly. "You think they call the Change on iron?"

"I know it. I'll know for sure when I smelt this, and Taya sees what she can do with it. But yes. Those bastards have kept the secret well, I'll give them that."

"But how?" Min's silk skirts rustled as she leaned forward to scoop a ladle of hot stew into her bowl. "Surely they can't have the only Changed who call iron? The Illy or the Kardanx would have it too." She paused. "Well, not the Kardanx anymore. But I've never heard of calling the Change with iron. Only water, air and earth."

That reminded Taya that she hadn't yet asked Min what Change she could call, but now was not the time.

"Simple. We *can* call it." Quardi looked around at them. "When I was a lad, I was good in the forge. Helped my Da, and had the touch, even then. The Nordren came through, just a few of them, selling their wares, always with that snooty 'our metalwork is far superior' air about them, and I remember . . ." His eyes lost their focus, and he stared into the distance. "I remember them asking me to do a test, to see how good I was. I was determined to show them the Illy could work metal just as well as they could, and they were . . . relieved when I was finished. Like they didn't have to do something they didn't want to do."

"They'd have killed you? If your skill was more than just skill, if you were calling the Change?" Taya's gaze snapped to his.

"Or kidnapped me." Quardi nodded his head slowly. "The story that the Nordren steal babies in the dead of night might not be such a story, after all."

"And how many of us come into continuous contact with metal, after all? The miners at the iron mines, perhaps, but that's it." Pilar was nodding his head, too. "It must be a rare Change, or we'd know about it, but those few who might be able to draw the iron Change may never know it, just like Taya with the shadow ore. Unless they're exposed, like when they join the guards, of course, with the swords, and armor. But most of the guard are already Changed, calling something else."

"The Iron Guard." Kas lifted his head, and everyone stared at him.

"What?" Min put her bowl down with a thump. "What's the Iron Guard?"

"The scariest, deadliest guard in West Lathor," Taya murmured. "I thought they called it the Iron Guard because of all the iron they wear. Not that I've ever seen them, just seen paintings and heard about them."

"But wearing iron isn't the reason for their name at all." Quardi leaned back, shocked. "Somehow, the liege of West Lathor knows about the iron Change. Has found enough Changed to create a guard. And all that iron covering them is simply . . ."

"Part of their arsenal." Taya thought of what she could do covered in a suit of shadow ore, or with pieces of it, nicely sharpened, attached to her clothes and body. And shivered.

"Well, we're certainly uncovering a lot of Barit's secrets up here on Shadow." Noor's low laugh brought them all back.

"It's finally being able to see the bigger picture." Taya looked up to where Barit hung, low on the horizon, and couldn't help but grin. You could only be sad, angry and heartbroken so much of the time.

"The wood from the trees," Pilar agreed.

"The fire from the sparks," Quardi chimed in.

"The mountain from the rocks," Kas said, deadpan.

"You are all very strange," Min told them, her accent rich and thick, but she was laughing, too.

Taya didn't know how she knew, perhaps the inclusion of the water Change in the list Min had given earlier, but she guessed if Min had added her saying, it would have had something to do with water droplets and the ocean.

───────

"I NEVER BRING strangers in with me. Certainly never at night." Falk Pallica sat in the small area off his kitchen on one of the two creaky armchairs Garek would guess he'd saved from the tinker's cart. "They'll be immediately suspicious."

"Do you ever need contractors? Carpenters or something like that?" Opik sat on the other chair, chewing on one of Falk's pies.

"I've been asking for a wooden frame that will allow me to lower myself on top of the craft, and view it from above, to see if I'm missing something only visible from that angle." Falk tapped his foot. "I can probably get you in if you have the right equipment, and look like you're there to actually build something like that."

Garek spoke from his place at the window, looking down on the street. He hadn't forgotten that Falk had a friend somewhere about. "That won't be a problem. What time do you get in, usually?"

"I go in at nine because I work so late at night."

"Well, you'll come with us now, and you can arrive at nine with us in tow."

"Why must I come with you?" Falk threaded his fingers together and rested his hands on his stomach. "You don't want me trailing around after you, surely? I could meet you at the tower."

Garek almost smiled. Falk was certainly optimistic, he'd give him that.

There was someone coming down the street, whistling as he strolled along. Garek recognized something about the man, but he was wrapped against the cool night with a cloak and Garek couldn't see his face, even when he looked up at the window where Garek lurked in the shadows.

Without a doubt, this was Falk's backup.

Garek turned and looked at Falk, and Falk sat straighter in his chair. "Let's go." He was talking to Opik, but his eyes never left Falk. He saw the moment when the scientist decided to make a run for it, and let him take the first two flying steps from the chair. He called the Change, and slammed two columns of air into Falk from either side. It was the same as slapping someone on both ears, but a lot nastier, and Falk went down with a strange half-cry.

"I hope you haven't made him deaf." Opik swallowed the last of the pie, and stood up.

"Me, too. It'll make it harder for him to hear my orders when I ask about the craft." He toed Falk's limp form. "But I think he'll be all right. I've gotten better at judging these things."

Opik grunted. "Good."

Garek bent and took the strain as he lifted Falk over his shoulder. "We've got company. Falk's got a guard dog, and he's on his way up."

Opik opened the front door and held it for him, a strange look on his face as Garek shifted Falk to a more comfortable position. "What do you want to do?"

"Go down a level, hide, and then leave when he goes into Falk's place."

Opik nodded and Garek followed him down to the second story. There was a nice blind spot down the passage, and no lighting, so they could stand in perfect darkness.

He heard the light, quick tread of a man who was fit and agile, and waited for the sound to reach Falk's floor before moving out and down.

They slipped out the door, as much as you could slip, with a grown man over your shoulder, and started toward the Seventh Wedge at a jog. Falk's head bumped his back with every step.

"Hey! Stop!"

The shout came from the same window Garek had been leaning against less than five minutes before.

Garek couldn't help himself, he turned to look, and then swung back and sped up, following Opik into the darkness.

He knew who that had been. What he couldn't understand was how Aidan Hansard, from his Garamundo barracks, was involved with Falk Pallica. And why.

ELEVEN

TAYA WATCHED the transporter take off with the usual day shift, reluctant to turn back into the camp.

Kas and Quardi had managed to convince the guard that Pilar needed to spend the day at the mine, to see what machinery would be needed to separate the ore from the stone.

The sky raiders had some of the men and women working the mined ore, but picking at it with axes or slamming it with hammers was yielding a very slow return.

They put her forward as Quardi's helper in the forge while Pilar was away.

They would be watched, but Quardi seemed to think they could smelt the shadow ore, and she could try to manipulate it in its liquid form, without being noticed.

Quardi always had been mad.

It was why he and Garek fought so much.

Garek was quiet; a solid, strong presence who thought things through and considered his options before he made a move.

Quardi leapt into things without thinking, said things without censoring himself, and generally lived larger than life.

She sighed and turned back to face the camp. The night shift were eating a quick breakfast around the fire and washing themselves on the banks of the river.

She raised her hand in greeting to Liah, a friend from Pan Nuk, and began to weave her way through the tents to the forge.

Quardi had set it up close to the river so there was an easy supply of water.

The area around the forge looked like a slum tenement in Gara's Eighth Wedge there were so many clotheslines strung up on poles, bowed under the weight of wet clothes and sheets. Nothing dried easily here—the air was cold and damp—and the constant heat of the forge had a very useful side-benefit of drying laundry.

"There you are," Quardi hailed her. The forge was one of the few solid buildings in the camp, made entirely from wood. It had three sides and a roof, and the heat coming from within delighted her. Since yesterday she had been cold to the bone, and not even her soft, warm bedding could chase away the shivers that wracked her.

She dodged dripping washing, and ignored the sky raider guard standing to one side, but she knew he was watching her.

"Here I am," she said, and pulled on the thick leather apron Quardi handed her. He was sitting in the wheelchair he'd cobbled together from things the sky raiders had taken from Barit, and he gave her thick leather gloves and a scarf for her hair.

They worked in a steady rhythm, falling back into a pattern repeated many times in the last two years when Taya had helped him in his forge back in Pan Nuk.

She'd enjoyed the work, even though she was busy enough dying the levik wool that came from the village co-operative.

Everyone had a herd of leviks in Pan Nuk, although Eli, Kas, and Harvi had the three biggest herds.

Had. They were all gone now.

She'd started dying the wool when Kas went to Gara and found a bale of colored wool fetched double the price of an undyed bale.

Her dark crimson-maroon was the most highly sought after, with the pale creamy yellow a close second.

She'd tried for months to replicate the blue of the scarf Kas had lied about buying for her. She wondered now if any of the presents she'd given him for Garek had ever been delivered.

He'd made three trips to Gara since Garek left, to negotiate the deals that kept Pan Nuk a prosperous little town. She'd given him a maroon tunic to protect Garek from the cold of winter, and a dark brown cloak of levik wool to match Garek's eyes. She'd imagined him wearing them, thinking of her, and the sudden realization that he may never have received them brought stinging tears to her eyes.

Working in the forge brought her too close to him. To the old days. Despite its relative comfort, she almost preferred the mine. At least there, she wasn't constantly reminded of what she'd lost.

A wind came up, snapping the sheets and clothes around them, and playing havoc with the fire of the forge.

"Come hold this up for me," Quardi said, a thin, bendable sheet of wood in his hand. "I need the flame steady for what I'm doing."

This was it. She could hear a tremor of excitement in Quardi's voice.

She took the shield from him, and he made her stand with her back to the guard, the wooden shield just below her chin, blocking Quardi completely from the guard's sight.

The heat of the fire wafted over her face and stung her cheeks.

Quardi drew the shadow ore from his sleeve and set it in a clean, small pot. "Let's hope its melting temperature is lower than my pot's," he muttered, and left it, moving on to other work; tapping out a mold he'd made earlier. The guard shifted, but Taya couldn't concentrate on him any more.

So near to the ore, her heart was beating like it wanted to burst from her chest. Nausea burned her throat and she wondered if she could stand much longer on legs gone weak and soft.

Quardi had warned her that raw ore was different to the iron he was smelting from the items the sky raiders brought him. They were already tempered, their impurities stripped out from when they were smelted the first time on Barit.

He didn't know what would strip the impurities from shadow ore, what the process was to get to the elemental metal.

This was an experiment in every sense.

Quardi came back and lifted the tiny pot with a long-handled clamp, swirled it a bit and tilted it to the light to get a better look. "Beautiful," he breathed. He tilted it in her direction, keeping it low so that the guard could not see over the shield.

The melted ore glowed red hot. Taya could feel the pull of it, and when the shuffle of the robotic legs of the guard behind her shot a spike of fear through her, she used the emotion to fling the tiny liquid mass into the air.

She felt something, like water sifting through her fingers, and realized she'd left whatever impurities there had been at the bottom on the pot.

The purity of the molten ore sang to her.

Now she had to decide what would be useful to her.

Something sharp.

The guard shuffled again, and panic joined fear in her chest. A knife? She suddenly couldn't think of what kind would be best, and it didn't look as if there was enough ore for that, anyway.

The ore floated, startlingly cohesive. So full of possibilities. Too full. And yet, there was so little of it. She was paralyzed by indecision.

The slender shards of ore that had lain at her feet yesterday gave her an idea, and on a spurt of nervous energy she split the small ball up into ten thin, sharp needles. When the guard shuffled behind her again, she dumped them in the bucket of water beside the fire in a rush of panic.

Steam hissed up, and too scared to turn around, she fixed her gaze on Quardi. He'd put the small smelting pot behind him and was calmly filling a new, larger one with scrap—the iron tips of arrows, bucket handles, and a kettle he had smashed to bits.

The guard stepped even closer, close enough to look over the shield at what Quardi was doing, the corroded metal of his armor bumping her elbow.

A minute ticked by, and eventually Taya turned, lifting the shield to the guard. Her arms were shaking from holding it so long, and she couldn't stand him behind her any longer. He took it automatically, and she got to work fetching more of the scrap the sky raiders had stolen, piling it up near the fire.

She looked over at Quardi, and their eyes met.

He looked far too cheerful.

"WHAT DO you plan to do with my ship?" Falk stared dully at Garek from the floor.

He'd spent the night in Garek and Opik's room, loosely tied and lying on a thin pallet, but Garek had removed the bonds so he could eat. Garek didn't want him too cramped and stiff. An appearance of normality was everything.

"I'm going to steal it, and fly until I find another sky raider craft, and then I'll follow them. Find where they are taking their prisoners." Garek broke off a piece of the surprisingly fresh, fragrant bread made in Haak's kitchen, added some butter and honey, and handed it to Falk. The serving boy from the kitchens had also brought up a jug of hot, spicy galal and Garek poured both of them a cup.

Falk sat up and took the cup with both hands, gave a sigh of pleasure as the first sip went down his throat. He took a bite of the bread, and then looked at it in surprise.

Garek took a bite himself and chewed slowly. It was early still, but they had to get a cart and enough wood and tools to look as if they were carpenters. Opik was out looking right now, promising Garek he had friends who could supply what they needed.

"Not that I'm not curious about where they go and why, I truly am, but why are *you* so interested? Interested enough to try to fly something completely beyond anything Barit has ever seen, and then to make contact with our most dangerous enemies."

"I'm not planning to make contact with them if I can help it. At least, not friendly contact." Garek drained the last of his galal. "What is your deal with Aidan Hansard?"

Falk went still, then continued eating his bread, taking his time.

Furiously thinking how to answer, Garek had no doubt.

"Why do you ask?" Falk said eventually.

"Because he seemed upset that we'd made off with you last night. I recognized him right away."

"Maybe he's the guard the town master appointed to keep an eye on my safety." Falk held out his cup for a refill of galal. Garek poured for him, and then for himself, as well.

"Aidan didn't much like the town master, the way I remember it," Garek eased back in his chair. "And his conscription year ended the same time as mine did, just over a week ago." He took another bite of bread. "My guess would have been that he got out of here as quickly as he could, but, as he's still here, he's working some plan of his own. He certainly would never sign up for a permanent position."

Falk said nothing to that, and an idea wormed its way into Garek's head.

"You're selling secrets to him, aren't you? The secrets of the sky raider craft." He'd always had the impression that Aidan came from a lot of money. His clothes and his spending were just a little too extravagant. He could have simply been someone who played fast and loose with his earnings, but something in his manner told Garek he was used to being obeyed and having servants pick up after him.

He knew Aidan hadn't enjoyed the Guard. He'd wondered occasionally why he'd stayed.

Conscription was a full year, with no early release, but if his family were as wealthy as Garek guessed, he could have found a way out. But Aidan had stuck to it, although not in a 'make the best of it' way.

He didn't take the service seriously, and was continually insubordinate. He didn't follow orders without question, and while he wasn't completely disruptive, he riled the guard master as much as possible.

For that, Garek had liked him.

Falk was staring at him. "That's quite a leap you're making."

Garek shrugged. "I'm right, though."

Falk looked away, and when he turned back it was with eyes that glittered with frustration and annoyance.

Garek gave him a lopsided smile. "I don't care what your deal with Aidan is. I don't care about anything but getting into that craft and making it fly. The sooner you help me with that, the sooner I'll be gone."

"That craft is everything to me. Months of research. But I haven't managed to work out how to fly it, so for you to think you can just get in and make it go is . . ." He ran a hand through his hair, blew out a breath. "And even if you *could* do that, which I very much doubt, if you think the town master isn't going to look at me very closely when the thing disappears, you're wrong. I'm the first person he'll suspect."

Garek set down his plate and his cup. "You wouldn't even have that craft if it wasn't for me. Now tell me, what have you learned about it?"

Opik knocked softly at the door, and stepped inside, carrying the fresh scent of crushed leaves and coming rain with him. "Found someone who can lend us their cart and gear, but it'll only be ready by eight."

Garek gave a nod, and Opik slid onto the other chair at the table, helped himself to some food.

They both looked at Falk.

"All right. I'll tell you what I know, but at least tell me why. Why are you doing this? It's an incredible risk."

Opik opened his mouth, but Garek shot him a look. The old man closed it again.

Garek gathered the plates and cups onto their tray. "All you need to know is it's a risk I'm willing to take."

TWELVE

"HERE." Quardi held out the ten thin needles of shadow ore she'd made that morning, and the firelight glinted off them as they lay in his palm.

Kas leaned across Taya and lifted one, touched the tip and let out a startled cry of pain. "Sharp." He sucked the tip of his finger, and held the needle to the light. "Why did you make this, particularly?"

Quardi made a face. "My question, as well."

Taya shrugged. "I was too afraid of the guard to think of anything else. It wasn't enough to make anything significant, anyway."

Pilar took the needle from Kas and leaned in even closer to the fire to see it better. "It's well made, for all that, Taya. They aren't identical, but they are smoothly formed. It would take a mold to get them like this in the usual way. And even then, they'd need to be sanded down." Although he'd seen what had happened to Kas, he touched his finger to the tip as well, and winced.

Taya took the needles from Quardi gingerly, and Pilar dropped the one he'd taken into her hand.

She didn't feel as sick as she had this morning, but the ore affected her still, made her lightheaded.

She tried to lift the needles into the air simply by thinking about it, like she'd done down the mine, and she could feel them stir on her palm, like something alive, waiting to break free.

Eventually she looked up, caught Kas staring at her. "I can't lift them."

"You'll still need a strong emotion for that. At least at first."

She sighed. "I think I should keep these on me. To practice when I have a chance." She frowned. "They're terrified of the ore coming close to them, though, and they've made us build the stockpile far from the landing area at the mine. I think the shadow ore makes their equipment break down, like the diggers down the mine. But Min, you brought the piece we just smelted with you, and they didn't notice and the transporter didn't break. I can only assume it's because it was such a small piece."

Noor moved across and looked at the needles without touching. "I'm pretty good at hook weaving." She tugged at an intricately woven hair band that pulled her dark, tight curls back from her face. "I found some interesting yarn in the Stolen Store. It has a stretch to it. I could make you a headband like this, weave the needles into it like decoration." She bent her head, so Taya could examine the head band, and when she straightened, Taya gave a nod.

"Could we make stripes across the band, and hide the needles inside them?" She touched the ore. "The sky raiders will recognize this if they see it, and they do not want any of it near them or their ships."

"Makes you wonder why they've gone to so much trouble for it." Pilar stretched his back and lifted his arms, wincing. "I didn't realize how good I had things, helping Quardi in the forge. Today was hard work." He looked across at Quardi. "For mining the seam, our picks work well enough, but we need to build a hand-cranked crusher to separate the ore from the rock once it's taken above ground."

"Why would you help them like that?" Min had been unusually quiet, sitting with her dinner near the fire.

"It's not them I'm thinking of." Pilar shrugged. "We have to do the work. Might as well make it safer and quicker."

She conceded the point with a nod of her head. "Our turn to do the dishes?" she asked Taya.

Taya gave a groan and nodded. She stood and carefully slipped the shadow ore needles into her pocket. Min was gathering everyone's bowls, and when they had everything, they walked together to the river.

They were in the rhythm of cleaning and rinsing at one of the four wooden washing basins on the river bank when Taya noticed something odd about the water. It rose in little spikes, before collapsing on itself. She stopped stacking bowls and stared.

"You draw the water Change, don't you?"

Min looked up, stricken, and all the little water spikes in the basin collapsed. She rubbed a hand over her forehead. "I do it without thinking. It's an exercise, and when I'm distracted or tired, I forget to make sure I only do it where no one can see."

Taya touched her arm. "You're with the Illy now. We consider that normal." She paused. "Well, not normal, but special."

Min looked at the dirty dish water, and made a hundred spikes of water rise up for a moment, then let them collapse. "I can't work it right here. It isn't the same as in Kardai. I could make much bigger spikes, and whirlpools. Even small waves."

Taya nodded. "Kas and the other Changed in camp have also found that. There is too much difference in the earth and the air on Shadow for them. Or the mix of elements isn't the same. You're the only one in camp who can call the water Change, but it isn't surprising that you're having the same problems as the others. This isn't Barit."

Min stood, and instead of tipping the basin on its side to drain the water, she funneled it back into the river in a wide, shallow arc.

"Next time, I'll get you to fill the basin like that, too." Taya grinned at her and nudged the bucket she'd used earlier to fill the big tub.

Min blushed. "Keeping quiet about it is so ingrained." She looked across to the Kardanx side of the camp. "Not that it helped. Too much happened when I first called the Change. Too many people saw too much."

"I heard the Kardanx kill their Changed. You're lucky to be alive." Taya followed her gaze. The Kardanx sat around their fires, eating and talking, just like the Illy, but the laughter was louder, the talking easily edging into shouting. Too many men, too close together. With too much blood on their hands, and the time to think about it.

"They were working their way up to killing me." Min turned her back on the Kardanx camp. "The law makes it impossible to kill someone who calls the Change without the permission of the *haidai*. A *haidai* is like the Illian lieges, I think."

"And they didn't get permission?"

"The *haidai* is my grandfather." Min crouched down to pick up an armful of bowls. "He disowned my mother when she moved in with my father. They didn't even have a Kardanx marriage ceremony. My mother had received an excellent education, far better than most women get in Kardai. It made her angry that the very oaths the men swore to protect and honor women were used against them, as a way to keep women from equal power.

"She came to realize that over time, whatever could be twisted to give women less agency was twisted. So that the life of women in Kardai now bears almost no relation to the original way of things when the Mother oaths were first sworn."

Taya took her share of the clean bowls and stood. "What happened?"

"She tried to make changes, to recall the old ways and the women who had ruled with men, studied with men, and fought with men for the honor of Kardai. She was banished to the mountains where my grandfather had a small house. My father was living in the village near the house and they fell in love. Maybe it was the final rebellion my mother could think of." Min drew in a deep breath. "Whatever their reasons, I think they were happy."

"They're dead?"

Min nodded. "Killed by bandits when I was seventeen. The mountains are full of them."

There was something in her voice, though.

"You don't think it was bandits, do you?" They had reached the area where the bowls and cutlery were stored, but they were the only ones there for the moment.

"No." Min set her bowls down carefully. "I think they were murdered. I think it was pure luck I was in the woods that day, and wasn't killed with them, and I think ever since, my grandfather has been working on killing whatever conscience he has left so that he can order his granddaughter murdered, too."

"Why would he kill them at all? Surely he could have ignored them? Let them be?"

Min fussed with the spoons. Then braced her hands on the rough counter and bowed her head. "In Kardanx inheritance law, there is a strict hierarchy. The children born of a man and his first wife get almost everything. If the wife dies and a man takes a second wife, the children from the second marriage get only a fraction of the father's wealth. If there is any to get. The same goes for a woman who is widowed and remarries. Her children from her first marriage inherit her and her first husband's wealth, not her children from her second marriage."

"And your grandfather remarried."

"Yes. He has a son with his new wife. And only if my mother were dead could her half-brother inherit my grandfather's lands and wealth. For years some of the *haidai* have been trying to change the law to exclude daughters, to protect them, naturally, from greedy men who would only marry them for their money." Min made a face. "But there are enough *haidai* who only have daughters who don't like that idea, and have fought any change. The women who inherit still have to put the land and wealth in the hands of their husbands anyway. So they aren't burdened with the terrible, terrible weight of controlling their own finances, of course."

Taya thought of something. "The fact that you call the Change surely made it easier for your grandfather to kill you? If it's within the law."

"The *haidai* can only order the death of a witch if he's personally seen him or her call the Change with his own eyes. And my grandfather has steadfastly refused to see me since I was born." Min pushed away from the counter, and stood tall.

Taya could find nothing to say to that. She reached out a hand, and touched Min's shoulder.

"It's funny. In the days before the sky raiders came and took everyone in the village, I had a strong feeling of being watched. I think my grandfather was about to make his move." Min laughed, and there was a genuine, wry humor in it. "The sky raiders probably saved my life."

"Unless . . ." Taya looked over at the Kardanx camp one last time. "Unless they scooped up your grandfather's assassins with everyone else."

THIRTEEN

THE GUARDS SEEMED MORE PERPLEXED than suspicious. Garek could tell they weren't used to Falk bringing workmen with him.

"For the frame over the craft," Falk muttered to one of the two guards at the gate, running a hand through his hair. Garek had given him hot water and a comb after breakfast, but he still looked as if he'd just rolled out of bed. "Let them in, will you?"

After a moment of hesitation the guard cheerfully opened the side gate so they could bring the carpenter's cart and horse around the outside of the tower. Opik's cheeks were flushed with exertion and his white hair stuck out from under his hat—he looked like a pix from the tales Garek used to hear around the fire as a child, completely harmless and friendly.

Someone had to balance out Garek's dark broodiness, Opik had told him, when he'd mentioned it as they were setting out. Otherwise they'd be arrested by the guards for sure.

Garek left him to lead the cart around and entered the main tower entrance right behind Falk, a scarf wound about most of his face, and a hat pulled low. The sudden cold snap of a false autumn was a boon, allowing him to cover up. He knew two of the guards by sight, and had the feeling he'd seen the other two at some time or another.

Once through the door, Falk disappeared off into the gloom, but Garek stumbled to a halt, gaping. Opposite the door, a large section of the tower's stone wall had been removed, opening the space out into the inner courtyard. A wooden structure had been built up against the tower, making the area the size of the circular tower and the inner courtyard combined.

He forced himself to focus back on Falk, his eyes a little better adjusted to the darkness, and saw he'd walked to a massive cogwheel. Falk turned a handle and as he cranked, the circular roof of the wooden structure lifted up and back on itself in sections, flooding the area with light.

There, in the inner courtyard, was the sky raider craft—a sleek silver disc nestled between two crescent-shaped brackets. He'd had a good look at it when he'd brought it down, but Garek was still awed. Although . . .

"What have you done to it?" Panicked, he ran forward and lifted a hand to what had once been the smooth silver of the ship's side.

"I haven't done anything." Falk tugged at his already-wild hair. "I'm spending more time trying to find a way to reverse or at least stop the disintegration than I am on working out how the damn thing is built and works."

A large double door to one side of the wooden structure swung open, and Opik stepped through. He let out a low whistle. "Bigger than I thought it'd be. They look smaller up in the sky." He left the horse and cart where they were and walked across to stand next to Garek. Rubbed a finger over the bubbling metal. "Rust?" He frowned. "Is this rust?"

"Sort of." Falk joined them. "More vigorous than rusting, and given we're three hundred standards from the coast, nothing to do with salt. I think it's the make-up of our air. Wherever the sky raiders come from, their climate is very different. Their metal breaks down on contact with our atmosphere."

Breaks down was right. Garek looked at the ship with a sinking heart. Would this rotting hulk even fly any more? He'd risked time and energy to come to Gara to steal this ship because it was already down and someone had been studying it, but looking at the large blisters of disintegrating metal, he wondered whether to abandon his plan of stealing this one and instead take down a new one.

"If our air is so poisonous, why are they so keen to be here?" Opik walked under the disc and looked up at the ladder Falk had placed there, leading into a neat circular entrance to the ship.

Falk patted the side gently. "I don't know. When Garek brought the ship down, that opening was like that. I think that's what the pilot used to escape, and fortunately it didn't close again. But even though it was open, most of the air inside the ship was unbreathable when I first got in there. More of the bad air was being pumped in all the time. That was the first thing I did—work out where the pump was and change it to pump our air, in case I ever triggered that door closed while I was inside it."

"How'd you change the type of air it was pumping?" Opik asked.

"I had to wear a mask with a tube going out of the craft so I could breathe, and then I found and took off the vent cover. There was a dial of some kind, a glowing light under glass, and I turned it, and checked the air, turned it and checked, until I got the right mix of gases. I ended up sick in bed for a week, after breathing in all that poison."

"You think the solution is permanent?" Garek hadn't thought of the air he would breathe in the craft. "I hope it keeps pumping Barit air when I take it up into the sky."

Falk shrugged. "It's worked so far, but I haven't had a chance to focus on it. I've just been trying to preserve the ship. Almost everything I do is focused on finding a way to stop the disintegration."

"And? Have you found a solution?" Garek joined Opik at the bottom of the ladder, and started to climb.

"Nothing." Falk paused. "Please don't touch anything in there."

Garek turned back to look at him from halfway up the ladder. "If I'm going to fly it, I have to touch."

"What happened to the sky raider flying this thing?" Opik started up the ladder as well.

"I hit the craft with a strong blast of air, and flipped it. The loud noise they make cut out and I saw something drop out of the craft. If it was the pilot, he was in a type of padded suit with something on the back that let out a little spurt of flame. He got clear of the falling ship and went straight up." Garek shrugged. "Didn't see him come down, so he probably got away. I was too busy controlling the ship's fall to the ground to pay attention."

He pulled himself up the final rung and stepped onto the smooth floor of the ship, and as his foot touched it, an amber light flickered to life, lighting the pitch darkness of the interior. A small whirling sound started up. Most likely Falk's air pump.

Opik whistled again as he joined him, and then Falk pulled himself in, as well. "That's why I don't like unnecessary visits inside. I don't know how long the lights and pump are going to last. Every time someone steps in here, it must be using up whatever is fueling them."

Garek ignored him and moved across to the sculpted seat set on a slender column that rose from the floor. He lowered himself into it and stared at the solid wall in front of him. "How do they see out?"

Falk walked forward, and despite his irritation at their intrusion, there was an edge of excitement in his movements. He tapped something above his head. "There's a thin line here, you can barely see it. It goes along the entire circumference of the disc, and there's another one here." He pointed to a parallel line at knee level. "I think it's a window. My guess is when the ship is operating, this lightens and becomes transparent."

"And how do they power and fly the craft?" Garek leaned back in the chair and suddenly realized how comfortable it was. As if it had been made for him. Or someone just like him.

Interesting that the sky raiders were the same general size and shape as they were. Well, a bit bigger, because Garek was head and shoulders above most people.

Since their ships had first appeared in the sky, the sky raiders had become the bogey men of Barit. Monsters from everyone's darkest nightmares.

"I don't know how they pilot it. I've searched every inch of this craft for a lever or button or opening that would turn it on."

"On your own?" Opik walked around the perimeter, tapping the walls.

"I'm the only person the town master has allowed to study the craft." Falk didn't say more than that, but Garek could read between the lines. The town master was keeping any discoveries made as secret as possible. With just Falk to watch, he could have more control, although even that hadn't worked that well, if Aidan had found a way to bribe Falk already.

"Where's the privy? Where's the food?" Opik arrived back at the ladder. "Just looks like one big round room."

"I can only imagine this is a small craft, like a raft on a boat. The people-stealers, like the one that flew over the city yesterday, are about ten times this size, and there will be a larger vessel somewhere up in the sky, too high to see. Perhaps not even in the atmosphere, where it will surely be subject to the same deterioration as the small ships." Falk traced the thin line of the dark window with a fingernail.

Garek examined the armrests of the chair, smooth extensions of the curve of the seat. He ran his fingers over the metal, but even here there were irregularities, small bubbles of deterioration. There was a hole at the end of the left armrest that didn't look like a reaction to the Barit atmosphere, though. Garek peered closer, and then pulled the sewing kit each guard in the Garamundo barracks was issued to mend minor rips in their uniform from the bag over his shoulder, and pulled out a needle.

"What is that?" Falk frowned. "What are you doing?"

Garek pushed the needle into the hole. The hole curved slightly, and he had to alter his angle before he reached the end. He heard the faintest snick, and then pale golden lights flashed to life on the arm rests, as if the metal was just a thin transparent skin with the lights below it.

Behind Falk, the wall went from black to gray to transparent, and they were suddenly blinking as Star light shone in.

Falk turned to look out into the enclosed area, and then slowly turned back.

"Three months," he said, and there was almost nothing in his voice, his dark eyes narrow and snapping. "Three months I've been working on this, and you just sit down—"

"You weren't curious about that hole?" Garek looked down at the lights that seemed to form the shape of dials.

"I didn't notice it! I've only sat in that chair twice, and both times, I was looking for something more obvious than a tiny hole at the one end!" Falk's voice was fraying at the edges. "I've been trying to save this ship so I could have a proper look at my leisure."

"Well, maybe they have very long, thin fingers," Opik said, peering down to look at the little hole. "Or long, sharp claws, eh?"

Garek lifted his gaze to the old man. "Hmm."

He stretched out his arms, bent his fingers, and yes, if he had long, sharp claws, that hole would be very nicely placed. "I think you have it."

It was good to know in advance he'd be facing claws.

One thing was clear, Falk couldn't help him fly this. He knew nothing.

No time like the present, then, to try and get this into the air.

"Maybe you should get my supplies." He looked up at Opik again and jerked his head to the ladder.

"What? Now?" Opik's eyes widened.

Garek nodded. "Time is wasting and I might not have another chance. If it will even lift off, in its current state."

"And the book-boy?" Opik slid his gaze to Falk.

"Get him off, too." Garek studied the lights on the arm rest again.

"I'll get your stuff out the cart. Let's go." Opik waved to Falk, then started down the ladder. "Garek wants to get this thing up."

Falk stalked forward, and crouched beside the armrest to look at the lights himself. "You're not going to try and fly this now. I need to study it."

"Sorry." Garek grabbed Falk's wrist, and Falk jerked his gaze up. "I mean to get this working before it falls into a thousand pieces of rusted metal and I have to waste even more time trying to bring down another ship. Get off with Opik, and if you want to make yourself useful, help him bring up my supplies for the journey. You can take notes as you watch me fight this thing into the air if you like. As soon as I've got my equipment, I'm going to start pressing on these light buttons and you aren't going to be in the ship when I do."

Falk stared straight into his eyes for a long beat. "You're serious." His words were hushed.

"At last you seem to understand."

"You're insane."

"That may be." Garek gave a twisted smile. "Now get off the ship, Falk."

Falk backed away, walking slowly, and then looked down when the ladder rattled. Opik came up the ladder with the food, water, and the few bags with tools and clothes Garek had brought along hovering in the air in front of him. Garek kept forgetting the old man could draw the air Change.

Falk raised his arms in a gesture of surrender at the sight. "Just tell me what's the rush?"

Opik piled everything in a corner and gave Falk a grin. "He won't tell you." He walked back to the ladder casually. "See you back at home, then."

"With luck. Thank you for your help." He gave the old man a nod. "Time's up, Falk." Garek touched the pad of his forefinger to the light-dial at the end of the armrest.

Nothing.

He pushed harder. Still nothing.

Then he remembered what Falk had said about the light dial behind the air vent. He moved his finger in a circular motion, following the outside of the glowing dial, and the sound he'd come to dread over the last year rumbled from beneath his feet, louder and louder as he moved his finger further and further around the disc of amber light.

"Star take it, Garek!" Falk ran for the ladder, temper and jealousy burned into his features. As he swung down, he gave a cry, and disappeared abruptly as if he'd lost his footing.

The rumble of the engines had certainly destabilized the ladder, and Garek hoped Opik had the sense to move it. It would block the opening if he ever found the correct button to seal himself in.

He studied the panels again, and thought the straight line of lights under his righthand fingers might be up and down. He'd have to work out how to turn when he was in the air.

He ran the tip of his forefinger gently up the line, and felt the craft strain beneath him, wanting to lift up. He went higher, and the scream of the engine drowned out everything. He traced his finger on the dial under his left hand even further along the circle, giving it even more power, then tried again.

The ladder clattered, and he looked across just in time to see someone tumble into the craft. The ship lurched once, and then lifted, hovering, and as it did, a metal sheet slid across the opening to close them in.

He wavered a moment, not knowing whether to try and get rid of his unwanted passenger, or whether any delay would give the guards the chance to bring him down.

Then the man who must have pulled Falk off the ladder and scrambled inside rolled to his feet and Garek saw his face.

Garek set his finger on the up-down line and pushed hard upward.

As the craft shot straight into the air, shuddering as it clipped the retracted wooden roof of the building, he watched Aidan Hansard lose his footing again.

FOURTEEN

"I'M NOT sure having assassins after Min will make much difference." Pilar put an arm around Noor and drew her close to make room for Min and Taya when they returned to the fire. "Most of the Kardanx are after both your blood anyway."

Min shook her head. "Wishing me ill and killing me are two different things. I've lived with the threat of death over me for a long time and I've come to understand that even if someone wishes you dead, taking a life is never easy."

"You think the Kardanx will threaten you but not actually hurt you, but these assassins will?" Kas leaned closer to the fire, just like he used to at home, and Taya felt a deep sense of loss that Luca and Garek weren't here.

"Won't actually hurt her? You're forgetting one thing. Most of the Kardanx men killed someone just before the sky raiders took them." Taya still couldn't fully stretch her mind around it.

Min looked up, and the firelight glinted off her eyes. "I won't defend them, but I will say it would have been hard for them. They would have been ordered to do it by the village heads, and it's a deeply ingrained part of the Mother religion. But it wasn't easy.

Reading a few lines every Thanks Day from the Guardian and putting into practice what those lines say—they are very different things. I was with them all the way from Barit to Shadow, straight after they'd done it, and most of the men were in shock. Some were crying, and it takes a lot to make a Kardanx man cry."

"You were lucky they didn't try to kill you and the other women with you in the ship." Noor spoke softly, and Taya had been thinking the same.

"Some did try." Min rewound a piece of thread around the bottom of her plait. There was a shake to her voice. "One was screaming over and over, 'Why should you be alive, and her not, why should you be alive?'"

"What happened?" Quardi spoke for the first time.

Min shrugged. "They didn't have weapons, obviously, and so the sky raiders had time to stop them while they were beating and strangling us. After that, they put bars between the women and the men. They used that white flash on them, to stop them. Like when they caught us."

The fire popped and crackled in the silence.

"That explains why they didn't try to kill you when we got to camp and there were no more bars separating you." Pilar's voice was quiet. "To have that a second time . . ." His voice faded away.

"There are other things the men can do, though, that won't leave us dead." Min hunched her shoulders. "I feel bad for the women still there, although two have family members among the men. One wife who was on the other side of the village, whose husband didn't get to her before the sky raiders, and one whose son prevented his father from killing her."

There was silence again.

"That wife . . ." Noor's voice trembled. "How can things ever be the same between her and her husband?"

Min nodded. "And the woman whose son protected her . . . she won't speak to her husband, and he slinks around, ashamed and confused, and the son is ostracized by most of the other men, although there are some who think he was right. Other men whose sisters were killed or whose mothers were, who think it was wrong."

"I've been watching the Kardanx women when I can, after what happened to Jerilia." Kas rocked a little on his seat. "I think Ketl chose to grab an Illian because the Kardanx women who are left are seen as untouchable. It's not just that they're afraid of the lightning again. They're thinking more clearly now."

"I hope so. If they harm them . . ." Taya had always thought her gift was reading the subtle changes in body language everyone gave off, understanding people better because of it. Before she knew she could call a Change. So she would start watching, too.

"We'll do something if they change their behavior." Kas rubbed her shoulder.

"And what can we do?" Pilar asked.

Taya looked over at him across the cheerful dance of the flames. "I'll go to the sky raiders again."

Kas squeezed her shoulder. "I agree. I'll go with you."

No one else spoke, but around the fire, Taya thought the mood swung away from gloom and helplessness, and into determination.

"GAREK. I thought it was you last night." Aidan spoke from his position on his back, head canted awkwardly against the curve of the wall.

Garek didn't answer, his focus on the sky as he shot the craft upward.

The ship shuddered, and he turned and saw he'd hit the roof of the tower, causing a shower of clay tiles. The side of the ship dipped and then he gave it even more power and shoved his finger up with force, and suddenly they were above Gara.

Now to figure out how to turn.

He studied the lights as they rose ever higher.

It made sense that it would be easy and at last he noticed the horizontal line just at the curve of the arm rest.

He moved his finger left and one side of the craft dipped and they turned toward the east, the direction the sky raiders usually went after an attack.

Aidan grunted as he slid along the floor again and then pulled himself to standing. He gave a cry and jerked back from the window when he realized how high they were.

Garek didn't know if it was because he called the air Change, but he felt no fear at all. Just a deep sense of satisfaction that he had managed to complete the first step in his plan.

He knew he should feel awe at the technology he was controlling, but he'd had over a year of watching the sky raiders and their strange, amazing ships. He no longer saw them as wondrous. They were deadly. They were weapons used against his people. And if he could turn that around and use them right back, he'd shelve any wonder and awe for later.

"So which liege has put you up to this?" Aidan spoke again, leaning against the wall with his eyes determinedly not on what was happening outside. "I'll match what they're paying you, and double it."

"Will you?" Garek started ascending at a steep angle. He hadn't caught sight of a single sky craft to follow. Finding one would have been great luck, but he hadn't expected it. The sky craft numbers were less now, and it had always been unlikely. He would go up as high as he could and look for the bigger ships. The people-stealers. "How do you know I'm not working for the liege of West Lathor?"

"If you were, you wouldn't be stealing this. You'd have permission."

"True." Garek moved his finger up again.

"What are you doing?" Aidan was nervous now, leaning close to the massive window and angling his head so he could look out. "You're going higher."

"Yes." Garek looked at him directly for the first time.

"What's going on, Garek? Who are you working for?"

Garek shook his head, looked at the dials under his fingers again. "No one."

For the first time, his former colleague straightened away from the wall. "You're doing this on your own? I know the powers that be in Gara poisoned any goodwill you might have had when they forced you into another year, but stealing their sky craft seems an odd revenge."

Garek glanced up at him again. "Who are *you* working for? Or is the bribe you're offering me out of your father's purse?" Just behind Aidan, through the window, he could see the sky darkening as they flew upward, and he felt the first uncomfortable lurch of fear. Because beyond it, all he could see was darkness.

Aidan jerked at the comment on his father, and then, sensing Garek's change in mood, turned and looked out of the window. Went very still as they angled up through the deepest indigo blue. "What do you know about my father?"

"He's rich."

Aidan gave a low laugh. "Out of everything you choose to say about him, you pick the one thing he most dislikes about his position."

Garek didn't respond, he could feel the craft shuddering a little under him, and he focused all his concentration on keeping his finger steady on the acceleration lights.

"I've watched you from the moment I arrived in Gara." Aidan turned back for a moment then faced the window again. "I kept my eye on you, and paid others to do it when I couldn't."

Garek raised his brows in surprise at that.

Aidan pressed a hand against the clear window. "In the year I've known you, you haven't once given a hint that you're mad. And I tend to believe you're working alone. No liege could have found you and recruited you to do this in the six days since you left Gara. So what are you up to?"

Garek found he didn't want to tell him. He had never trusted Aidan before, because he had the cocky sense of entitlement of a rich

boy who would always escape the consequences of his misde-
meanors. His offer of a bribe and his deal with Falk had deepened
Garek's mistrust, because it told him Aidan was in someone's camp.
And his attitude and confidence indicated he was high up in the
hierarchy.

Given he was the same age as Garek, that was unlikely unless he
was family to whoever he was working for.

Much though Garek hated Garamundo, he would not support
someone trying to bring down West Lathor's liege. There would only
be suffering for everyone if that happened.

If Aidan was working for another liege, then he was a spy who'd
spent a year studying the way Gara's Guard worked and exploring
the city. It was clever, and it was a betrayal of every guard who'd
walked the walls with him.

"At least tell me where we're going." Aidan only spoke again
when they broke free of the air that wrapped around Barit like a
comforting blanket, the air that Garek understood, and controlled. It
was disorienting to leave it behind, and still, nothing would change
his plan.

"We're going to find the people the sky raiders have taken."
Garek kept his gaze on where Barit curved away on the horizon. He'd
keep them within sight of Barit until he had no other choice but to
strike out in another direction.

He needed to find a people-stealer or the big ship Falk had
hypothesized was up here.

Aidan didn't respond, and eventually Garek flicked his gaze
his way.

"Why?" Aidan slid down to sit against the wall, and for the first
time since Garek had met him he looked truly serious. The slightly
amused, condescending attitude was gone.

"One of the people they took is very important to me."

"You thrust us off Barit in a rusted hunk of metal to rescue one
person?"

Garek lifted a brow. "Firstly, I didn't invite you along. I'd planned to do this alone, but you forced yourself onboard. And secondly, no, not just one person. Since I'm going to the effort, I'll try to rescue everyone if I can."

Aidan covered his eyes with his hands. "How could I have missed the fact that you are mad?"

Garek's lips quirked. "I'm not the person who forced his way onto a sky craft as it was being piloted for the first time by someone who didn't know what they were doing."

Aidan let out a bark of laughter. "I thought you were stealing it for another liege. I couldn't let it get away."

"You were willing to risk your life to stop another liege getting some small advantage?" Garek moved his gaze away from Aidan, his eyes back on the horizon as he looked for a big ship. "I don't care who has control of what."

"What do you care about?" Aidan's question was soft.

Garek shook his head. "None of your business."

"It is my business now. Whether you like it or not, I'm in it with you."

There was a thin edge of temper in Aidan's voice.

"I'll tell you what I'm doing," Garek said. Aidan was right that he had little choice. "But if you cause trouble, or endanger my plans in any way, I will kill you."

Aidan gave a quick laugh at that, and then stared at him through narrowed eyes. "You mean that."

Garek caught the flash of Star light off something in the distance and turned the sky craft in its direction. "Oh, yes. I mean it."

FIFTEEN

AS TAYA APPROACHED the pile of newly hacked ore, she hunched against the underground chill. It cut through the thin fabric of her tunic, and she decided from tomorrow she was bringing a coat. Now she was back in the dark, cold tunnels, she missed the warmth of the forge fire.

Pilar had offered to go in her place again, give her another day with Quardi, but she'd refused. There was no reason why she and Pilar couldn't swop permanently; in fact, they got another strong back with Pilar in her place, but she had brought herself to their attention too many times already to make a fuss.

She squared her shoulders as she approached the growing pile of rock the men had hacked off the main seam. The feeling of disorientation was getting less, but she avoided the pieces that had too much shadow ore on the surface. She was less able to handle the skin contact than she was the pieces where it was buried deeper in the rock.

Noor had made good on her promise to weave a headband, and the shadow ore needles nestled out of sight in its thickly embroidered bands. When she'd put it on, the skin on her scalp had prickled with awareness and she'd wanted to rip the headband off, but she'd grown more used to it as the day wore on.

And she'd prevaricated long enough.

She hitched up the shoulder of her tunic, a soft tassel weave from the east, ran hands grubby with sweat and dust down her sides, and then hefted a rock from the pile.

"All right?" Min lifted her own rock.

She gave a nod. "Better."

Min had been withdrawn since they'd discussed the assassins, and as they made their way up the long passage Taya walked as close behind her as she could. "I shouldn't have said what I did last night. I didn't mean to worry you."

"No. It's good you did." Min was breathless as she carried the heavy rock up the sloping tunnel. "I hadn't thought the assassins might also be taken by the sky raiders, but why not? I wouldn't be able to tell. When the sky raiders hit me with that lightning and I dropped to the ground . . . " She stopped talking for a moment, and Taya shivered with her. She would never forget the agony, the white-hot, terrible pain of that moment.

Min shook herself free of the memory. "When they grabbed me and put me in the ship, there were already fifty or more Kardanx in the holding room. I recognized some people from the village, but there were so many strangers, the men who'd been watching me could have been standing right in front of me and I wouldn't have known. It can't hurt to be wary."

"More wary than we are already?" Taya shifted the rock in her arms to get a better grip. But Min was right. They had adjusted to the dangers here. They knew the threats, and this was a new one.

One more thing to add to the list.

The tunnel curved sharply ahead, caused by the broken-down mechanical diggers' strange and erratic digging patterns. A side shaft, one of many, branched off from the main route up ahead—evidence of the sky raiders' failed attempt to get at the shadow ore without the forced labor of the people of Barit. This shaft always made her shiver though, as it blew cool, damp air out into the main thoroughfare.

As she and Min passed it, she steeled herself against the chilly fingers that seemed to reach out from the darkened entrance, and then screamed as real hands shot out of the shadows and grabbed both Min and her around their waists.

She was thrown with great force down the passage and landed hard on the rough, rocky floor.

She hit her head on something—probably the rock she'd been carrying. She got her elbow beneath her and, in a daze, tried to lift herself up. She couldn't work out where she was in the darkness.

A groan came from main tunnel, a mournful moan, and for a confused moment she thought it was someone else who'd been hurt.

"Get back, Taya." Min smacked her with wildly waving hands in the dark, and then got a grip under Taya's arms and pulled her deeper into the tunnel as the groan became a shriek and then a rumble as rocks and soil collapsed in front of them.

The weak light coming from the side shaft's entrance winked out.

A few small stones landed on Taya's feet, and she shook them off. Her head pounded as she struggled to sit up straight.

"What happened?"

"Ketl, and one other, at least, attacked us. I only saw the two of them, but there could have been others." Min pulled her back a little more as what sounded like two or three small rocks crumbled from the ceiling and fell with sharp cracks onto the floor. She couldn't see anything in here. It was utterly dark.

"But what did they do?"

"They destroyed the props that were holding the entrance to this tunnel up. The poles were probably already close to collapsing anyway. I caught a glimpse of them and they were almost rusted through, but just before it all came down, I saw Ketl swing something at one of them."

Taya shuffled on her behind until she hit the wall, then leaned back against it. "If no one saw them, they'll pretend to know nothing about it. No one will wonder why the props gave way, the only mystery will be why we were down here in the first place."

"Even if some people did see Ketl, do you think he'll care?" Min's voice was bitter.

"He'll care." She reached out and patted Min's leg, which was pressed against her side. "You think Kas won't make a fuss about this?"

"Maybe." Min's voice was grudging. "But if Ketl managed to make sure no one was around, your brother may not realize we're gone until it's time to go home. And then they'll have to look for us. Dig us out. Do we even have that long?"

Taya took a deep breath and sneezed as the dust got up her nose. "I think there's air coming from somewhere. I can feel it blowing on my skin." She licked her forefinger and lifted it up, felt the chill of a breeze coming from the end of the tunnel.

"I can, too." Min's tone had calmed from panicked to thoughtful. "You think there's a way out?"

"We've got nothing to lose. I just wish we had a light."

"Me, too." Min reached down and helped her to stand. Taya's head was still thumping and her left side started to burn now she was upright. She ran a hand down her tunic. The fabric had been ripped and torn and she sucked in a quick breath as her fingers brushed over weeping grazes along her side.

"Do you think the sky raiders can see us, with that machine they have?" Min had started moving, and Taya limped after her.

"Maybe. That's a good point. They certainly knew who sat in protest the day they shot Quardi. They must have some way of distinguishing which blob of light is which."

"So they'll know Ketl and his friends were here, and that they threw us in."

"I would guess, yes. They may know already, or maybe they only look at the screen when they realize something's wrong. We mostly behave now, so they haven't had to keep such a close watch in a while. But they should be able to see where we are. Unless . . ."

"Unless?"

"Unless there is a lot of shadow ore in the rock that came down, in which case, their equipment might be useless. Have you noticed that the big outside screen doesn't show much detail where the men are mining. Not like in the passageways."

Min sighed. Then cried out in pain.

"What is it?" Taya stopped and carefully extended her hand. She eventually touched a rough, rusted surface.

"I hit my shin against something. I think it's a digger."

Taya could hear Min hitting the digger with her palms, feeling her way, and she trailed her hand more gently in Min's wake.

"Dead end." Min's voice caught.

"Not completely dead. Can't you feel the air flowing in from somewhere?" Taya refused to accept they were trapped here.

If only there was some tiny glimmer of light so she could see.

She brushed up against Min and moved past her, then came up against the cold hard stone wall that was the end of the tunnel. It was rough and jagged from the work of the digger, and she was careful as she ran her hands down it, slowly getting lower until she was crouched in front of the digger's spiky tracks. She extended her arm out slowly and then shuffled left until she was at the tunnel's midpoint, wincing as the movement tugged on her scraped and bleeding side.

"Here. The air is coming from here." She leaned forward, and where she expected to find the tunnel wall, she found nothing but air. Hopeful, she inched forward, and eventually found the edges of a fissure in the rock face.

"There's a crack. I don't know if it's wide enough for us to fit through." She rose carefully, aware the digger's scoop might be directly above her, and pressed herself against the opening.

She had to turn sideways, and the sharp, rough texture of the rock snagged and pulled at her tunic, scraping the skin that wasn't covered as she forced herself through.

It hurt, and panic gripped her for a moment when she thought she was stuck and wouldn't be able to go either forward or back.

"Taya?" Min's call, frightened and uncertain, stiffened her resolve and she pulled hard, felt the skin at the back of her shoulders give as she stumbled out into a wider section.

It still wasn't spacious, but at least she'd keep from being scraped and battered if it stayed this wide.

"Taya?" Min's voice rose.

"Here. It's a tight squeeze and you may bleed a bit, but it gets wider."

"All right." Min's words exhaled in relief.

Taya could hear her pushing her way through the narrow space.

"There's a bit where I thought I was stuck, but I managed to get through," Taya said into the dark when she thought the sounds were more panicky than they had been. "I just lost some skin, that's all."

With a grunt of effort, Min collapsed into the wider pocket of space with Taya, and Taya helped her up, holding her close in a hug.

"We made it."

They stood quietly for a moment, and Taya turned her head left.

"Do you hear water?" It explained the cold, damp air that was blowing down the tunnel at them.

"Yes." Min shivered, and Taya didn't blame her.

The water in this place was dark and strange.

"Hold onto me," she told Min, and started walking toward the sound, running her hands along the passage on both sides so she could feel if there were tunnels branching off it and testing the ground in front of her cautiously with each step.

The tunnel kinked left then right, staying more or less the same width, like a jagged fissure in the rock.

Min had grabbed hold of the fabric of her tunic near her waist, and Taya could hear the quick in-and-out of her breathing.

She was glad she wasn't in here alone.

Time seemed to be elastic in the dark, and she didn't know how long they'd walked when Min finally started talking.

"What was your life like in West Lathor?" Min's fist had loosened a little, so she was no longer holding onto Taya's tunic with a death grip.

"The work I did, the friends and family I had around me, were good." That was what Taya'd held on to for two whole years.

"I hear a but . . ."

"Someone important to me had to leave to complete his year in Garamundo." She shrugged, and then was angry at herself for making the gesture. It wasn't okay.

"You sound angry." Min hesitated.

"I am angry." She shook her head. "The sky raiders appeared for the first time near the end of his year, and Gara made him stay."

"He was serving his conscription? My father mentioned this. I have a feeling it's why he moved to Kardai. To escape this service."

That made sense to Taya. If Min's father hadn't wanted to serve his time with his liege, he would have had to run. She'd wondered why he'd moved to a place which reviled anyone who could call a Change. "Did he not want to do it at all, or did they try to extend his time?"

"I don't know. I do know he was very angry about it, the few times it was mentioned. It upset him so much, my mother and I avoided it."

"I understand that anger." She could say no more about it. She knew well enough anger would solve nothing. But until the sky raiders had grabbed her, she'd clung to the belief that patience would be her salvation. She could out-wait Garamundo.

Now that had been taken, too.

"When is he due to be released?" Min asked softly.

"Around about now. Any day now, he'll return to Pan Nuk, and find us all gone." He'd look for answers. Hopefully find Luca and take care of him. It was the best she could hope for.

Given the sky raiders' focus on efficiency and speed, she had long ago worked out they would not take the time to return them to Barit when they had enough shadow ore.

They'd leave them here on Shadow to starve.

"What about you?" She forced her mind away from the darkness of her thoughts. "Do you have someone in Kardai?"

"No." Min laughed, but there was no humor in the sound. "Yusemi was a small town. Like your Pan Nuk. All the men there knew who I was, what I was. None were ever interested in a relationship with me. Having sex with me, yes. Some were very interested in that. Some didn't care much whether I was interested back or not, despite all having sworn loyalty to the Mother. I'm sure they all read the Guardian every Thanks day, too."

"They tried to rape you?" It wasn't unheard of among the Illy, but women had as much legal and social standing as men, and very few got away with it. The punishment was extremely harsh. At least ten years in the labor camp, and no right, ever, to marry.

"The price if they were found guilty is steep in Kardai. It's death. But they didn't think the *haidai* would take an interest if I was the victim, and they may have been right. As it was, they kept forgetting one of the reasons I was alone was that I could call the Change."

"You called the Change to protect yourself." Taya found satisfaction in that. The thing that made Min different was the same thing that protected her.

"Yes," Min said. "I will never be sorry I can call the Change."

They both fell silent again, and the only sounds were the rush of water, getting louder all the time, and the rustle of their clothes and the tap of their feet as they walked.

Taya slowed, taking tiny steps, as the sound rose to a roar. A fine mist settled on her face, coating her cheeks and forehead in dew.

It took her several minutes to realize that she could now make out the rock around her, her hand against the wall, the ground she was walking on.

She stopped dead. "There's light up ahead." She barely breathed the words.

"Sky raiders?" Min's breath was hot in her ear.

Taya raised her shoulders in a shrug and started forward again, even slower than before.

The light was strange, like everything else here, a murky color rather than a pure white.

It was a relief to see the way, though.

Perhaps she would have struggled to see clearly if she'd come directly from above ground, but being in the dark so long, even the dimmest light helped illuminate everything around her.

She could finally see the long crack they were walking in rose up so high above their heads there was no indication where it ended. The walls were rough, looking like they'd been violently ripped apart, and now she could see what she'd only felt before, the sparkle and glint of shadow ore.

The light grew brighter, in tandem with the thunder of the water, and Taya took one last, cautious step around a sharp turn in the tunnel and stopped.

She was standing on the edge of a narrow ledge about four feet above the floor of a massive cave.

At the far end, to her right, water geysered out of a hole in the wall at least twenty feet above the cave floor, landing on a jumble of boulders. Over time it had hammered a deep pool out of the rock at its base, and then worn a groove across the gently sloping cave floor. The channel running the length of the cave and then disappearing to her left was smooth, looking almost hand-carved, like the stone gutters on the houses in Pan Nuk.

But as amazing as that was, what made her catch her breath and gape were the lights.

Min stood right behind her, her hands gripping Taya's shoulders. "Is that . . . moss?"

Taya nodded. "It looks like it."

The ceiling was so high above them the light didn't reach it, but moss clung to the walls, to jutting rocky overhangs, to the floor, and it glowed, not just one color, but many, which explain why the light spilling down the narrow crack had been so murky.

There were subtle pinks, blues, greens and yellows.

Insects with wide, fluttering wings darted from patch to patch. One flew erratically past her and she saw its body was tiny, its wings white with a subtle black pattern.

She moved aside to make room for Min, and then peered over the side of the ledge they were standing on. There were rocks and rubble below, and she crouched and then climbed down cautiously.

Everything was slick with water, and tiny droplets clung to her hair and beaded at her temples, sliding down the sides of her face.

Nausea rose as soon as she stood on the uneven cave floor and she had to bend and put her hands on her knees and breathe.

"The shadow ore?" Min asked, clambering down beside her and putting a hand between her shoulder blades.

She nodded, her eyes fixed on the moss she was standing on. Its leaves were intricate and succulent, the light it emitted coming from them as well as the tiny, delicate flowers. And the parts of the floor not covered in moss, she noticed, were dark with ore.

She fell to her knees, unable to tell whether the roaring her ears was from the waterfall or her reaction to the ore. Her hands burned as they landed on the ore-rich rock, the searing heat traveling up through her arms, embedding itself in her skin.

She'd wondered, in the last few days, how Garek and Kas, who could call the Change for something really abundant, like air and earth, had coped with the disorientation. They had both been thirteen when they'd called the Change. And had literally been surrounded by their element.

If they could handle it, she could, too.

"My father threw me in the river when I started to call the Change." Min said quietly, crouching beside her.

"Was it bad?" Taya could barely speak, her breath short, her body switching from being hot to suddenly wracked with chills.

Min nodded. "But once immersed, I never felt sick again. It was good for me."

"Maybe this will be good for me, then." Where on Barit could she ever have been immersed in shadow ore? Perhaps this was the only way to truly claim her Change.

She shuddered in a breath, and then fell to the ground, the pain from her earlier injuries flaring as she landed on her scraped side.

The last thing she saw was the flutter of white and black wings.

SIXTEEN

"WHAT'S YOUR PLAN?" Aidan stood to the side, staring at the massive ship in front of them.

The reflected light Garek had turned toward earlier had become this behemoth and he wondered just how happy Falk would be to have been proved so right.

"We find a way in." There wasn't much else he could do, although he was very aware that Falk had altered the air inside this sky craft. They wouldn't be able to breathe if they left its safety.

"You think they'll let us enter?"

Aidan was regaining Garek's respect a little at a time. He wasn't dwelling on his helplessness, or his deep dislike for what Garek was doing. He'd decided to deal with reality.

"This is one of their ships, why wouldn't they?"

"Yes, but it's been missing for months."

Garek hesitated, then decided he might as well start sharing a little with his unwilling passenger. "I don't think they'll be keeping track. Unless there's another group out here with sky craft of their own, I'm guessing they assume all ships that are theirs are piloted by their people."

Aidan gave a grunt. "I see your reasoning, but it's a big risk to take when you can't be sure."

"We aren't going back, so we have little choice but to hope my guess is accurate. And I'll say again, this was supposed to be a solo run."

Aidan sighed. "So who's this person you're rescuing? Family?"

"You could say that." Garek intended to make Taya his family. And there was the small matter of his own father and Taya's brother, as well. However much the old man and him grated against each other, however much Kas may wish him dead or on the other side of the world to his sister, Garek couldn't, wouldn't, leave them behind.

"How do you even know they're alive?"

"Because until two months ago, the sky raiders were taking people. Now, they're taking food, clothes—whatever supplies they can. I don't think the people who designed this," he waved at the craft's interior, "are desperate for our food and clothes, do you?"

"They're stealing food to feed their prisoners." Aidan gave a slow nod. "You'd be a good general." He said it grudgingly. "You think the right way."

Garek didn't answer, because something bulky shot out from under the big ship, and he saw it was a people-stealer. He slowed the sky craft's approach a little to watch it.

It turned away from them, aiming for Shadow.

"You going to follow it?" Aidan asked.

Garek was tempted. But he didn't know where he'd be going, and he didn't want to waste his only chance.

"No. We go in, see what we can find out in the big ship."

"How are we going to do that? We don't know much about the sky raiders, but we know we don't look like them."

"No. They have claws, and we can't breathe their air, anyway."

Aidan sucked in a breath, and Garek guessed he'd just remembered that Falk had had to recalibrate the air in the ship. "So we're confined to this ship?"

"That's right." Garek hoped they could slip the sky craft into what was surely a loading and maintenance area and observe for a bit. There was a lot a busy transport hub could tell the patient watcher, and he could be patient when it was important enough.

"You know, I said I didn't know you were crazy before, but there was something that always bothered me about you. I should have trusted my gut." Aidan's face was calm as he spoke, his tone neutral.

Garek didn't much care what spoiled rich boys thought of him, so he simply shrugged.

Aidan's face lost its calm, and his lips tightened. "You genuinely don't care what I think, do you?"

"No. But my guess is you're going to tell me anyway." Garek kept their speed steady as they closed in on their destination.

"Maybe that's why I like you despite your charming personality. You don't care where a person comes from."

Garek laughed at that. "You've got that right."

Aidan crossed his arms over his chest. "You answer to a higher power, is that it? Some kind of strange abstinence thing? Because the behavior that got my nerves jumping about you back in Gara was that you never once took up an offer of sex. Not this last year when I served with you, and the other guards told me not the year before, either. And you weren't short on invitations, my watchers and I both saw that."

Garek stared him down blandly and eventually Aidan looked away with a jerk of temper.

A higher power?

Garek couldn't help the chuckle that burst out of him. Maybe he'd share that with Taya one day. Because he *was* getting her back. "When you say you like me because I don't care who you are, remember, that comes with a distinct downside. Just because you want to know why I've done something doesn't mean I'm going to answer. It's none of your business. You're obviously used to snapping your fingers and being obeyed. I don't jump for you, or anyone."

"That's an arrogance all its own, isn't it?" Aidan turned back to face him, lips in a tight line. "You carry that mantle about you, knowing there's no one who can physically take you down. But that's not because you've earned it. You were born with the power of your Change."

Garek shrugged. "I've worked to get to my peak. I've supplemented the strength of my Change with physical strength. What have you done? Sulked at being in the Guard? Splashed money around? Deliberately been a thorn in the administrator's side? And now I discover, also spying on the security set-up at Gara. Betraying every guard you had anything to do with."

Aidan froze, eyes wide. "That's what you think I've been doing?"

Garek sneered at him. "You bribed Falk, and you risked your neck because you thought I was making off with the sky craft for another liege, which tells me that's exactly what *you* were planning to do with it when Falk worked out how to fly it."

Aidan shook his head. "I hadn't thought of it like that. But you're wrong."

Garek ignored him. They were getting closer to the mothership, and he needed every ounce of concentration.

"Garek, listen to me. You don't trust me, which means you won't let me have your back, and we're going to need that going in to that thing." Aidan looked over at the ship that was now looming over them, monstrous and overwhelming.

Garek flicked a glance at him. "What can you possibly say to change my mind?"

"You don't care who I am? Fine. That *is* something I appreciate, no matter what you might think of me. And I admit that I behaved like a petulant child when I got to Gara. I can see you think very little of me for it, and I deserve it. But I'm not betraying the Gara Guard, because they may report to the town master, but the town master reports to the liege of West Lathor. And the liege is my father."

Garek managed to keep his attention fixed on what looked from this distance like a narrow opening in the ship's underbelly. He hoped it didn't look like such a tight squeeze when they got closer.

"Nothing to say?" Aidan asked him.

He shook his head. "I guessed you were some high-end rich boy. You threw your weight around in Gara too much to be anything else."

He noticed Aidan winced a bit at that.

"But you understand now, I wasn't a spy for the enemy? My father wanted me to understand Gara from the inside out. We knew no one in the Guard would likely recognize me, I haven't made any official visits from Juli to Gara since I was a teenager. And my father wanted someone he trusted to check out the intelligence he'd received, word that things weren't as they should be. That the Gara town master was actively working against his own liege."

"Only because he's let too much slide for too long." Garek had thought that for a long time.

Aidan winced again. "My father hasn't been himself since my mother died, but that's no comfort to anyone who's had to deal with Gara for the last two years. I accept that."

"Do you?" How nice for him.

"You're truly angry, aren't you? You like me even less now you know who I am." Aidan's shock made Garek want to laugh again.

"As you've already pointed out, princeling, I don't care who you are. You say you weren't betraying the Guard, I believe you. But I'll still kill you if you do anything to mess up my plans."

"You're a bastard, you know that?" Aidan turned back to the window.

Garek shrugged. He got that a lot.

SEVENTEEN

"WAKE UP, TAYA. WAKE UP!"

The last words were hissed with such terror, Taya forced her eyes open.

She was lying close to where she'd fallen, pulled up under the slight overhang of the ledge they'd climbed down from.

Min held her around the shoulders and she gave Taya a little shake. Pain shot through Taya's side and she groaned.

"What's wrong?"

Min slumped in relief. "There are things up there." She pointed to the ceiling.

Taya blinked and shuffled her legs a bit so she was more or less upright. The light was diffuse, with no single source, and each one so weak, it was impossible to see the vast ceiling above.

"How long have I been out?" She rubbed at the bump on her head from when Ketl threw her down the shaft, and gingerly pulled her tunic from her body where it was stuck against the open scrapes, hissing at the pain.

"Ten minutes or so." Min shivered. "Soon after you collapsed, something came diving down from above. It nearly clipped my head."

As she spoke, a dark shadow swooped silently over them, at the last second angling its body with its wide wings to rake the ledge above them and bringing soil and tiny pebbles down on their heads.

Min made a low sound in the back of her throat and put a hand over her mouth.

"What is it?" Taya brushed dirt off the top of her head, her hair so damp from the spray of the waterfall, it was more like rubbing mud.

"Not it, them. More than one." Min pointed again and Taya saw more shadowy shapes swooping above.

"They weren't doing that when we got here."

"No." Min shifted, pulling up her knees and hugging them tight. "I think we disturbed them."

Whatever they were, Taya knew she hadn't seen anything like them above ground in the camp. The animals they'd encountered on Shadow so far had been strange creatures, furtive and mostly small. These were the biggest she'd seen, and they were bold by comparison, attacking rather than running away.

She closed her eyes and tipped back her head to rest against the stone wall behind her.

"How are you feeling?" Min's voice was soft, almost contrite. "I'm sorry I shook you awake."

"Besides the headache and scrapes from when Ketl grabbed us, I'm all right."

"I feel like an idiot for panicking like that." Min rocked a little, back and forth. "Do you have garls in West Lathor?"

Taya looked over at her and gave a nod.

Min shuddered. "There's a cave of them up above my village, and they come down in the summer when the lake fills up with croakers to feed." She shuddered again. "Slithers with wings, my mother used to call them. Once, when I was about twelve, one got into my hair. I've never been able to be reasonable about things landing in my hair ever since."

"It's okay. I'd panic if something strange grabbed at my hair, too."

"You didn't look good when you collapsed, are you sure you're all right?" Min searched her face.

"Yes." The nausea was gone, along with the strange feeling of disorientation. She didn't feel her normal self, though. She felt excited, little fizzes of anticipation rising up inside her and bursting, so she could hardly stop herself shaking.

She reached for what she was looking for, unsure herself what it was, and a piece of rock the size of a fist lifted up beside her.

"I hope that's you doing that," Min whispered.

Taya blinked. "It is me. Although I didn't . . ." She was going to say she hadn't meant to, but she realized she had. Before, when she'd confronted Ketl in the tunnels, and when she'd manipulated the ore with Quardi, it had felt like she was slightly apart from herself, like someone else was making the ore do what it was doing. But now, the feeling was a tug inside her, as integral as breathing. She lifted the rock higher and one of the creatures from above had to dodge around it as it came in for another dive.

"We need to find the way out. And it's most likely that way." Taya pointed left, to where the river disappeared into the gloom.

The other entrance, where the water poured into the cave, looked impassable. It was a wide crack in a sheer wall of stone, broadened and rounded over time, the water spewing from it under enormous pressure. Even if they could climb up to it, they wouldn't have the strength to fight the current. Unless . . .

"Can you manipulate the water? If we had to go that way?" Taya studied the waterfall for any sign it was possible.

"If there's no other choice, we can find out. But let's try the other way first." Min looked up at the swooping forms. "If we can get there."

"I have an idea." Taya stood cautiously, then ducked as another winged shadow dived at her. It didn't make a sound. Not even its wings gave it away.

The rock she'd reached for was still floating beside her, and she lifted it up higher, above her head, and concentrated on reaching for another one. A piece dark with shadow ore rose and she set the two spinning around her head.

She found another rock, and then another.

The four were all roughly the size of her fist and they deflected the attackers, forcing them to pull up before they got in too low.

"Let's go."

Min crawled to were Taya stood and rose up inside the little safety zone Taya had constructed, her hand grabbing Taya's tunic like she had in the tunnel.

Another creature swooped in, but instead of flying away, it landed on a large patch of moss growing on the wall near where they'd entered the cave.

For the first time, they got a good look at what it was.

Ugly.

Very ugly.

It was black all over. Its eyes were black and gleaming, and the only part of it that reflected the light. The skin covering it was hard to make out. She didn't know if it was fur or feathers, but whatever it was it lay sleek and close to its body. Its wings were tucked in, but they hung down on either side, longer that its torso.

It clutched the wall with its feet and the claw of one hand, and extended the other towards them in what was an unmistakably aggressive move. But it was the flat, almost squashed, face that radiated the most menace. Its mouth was open, and against the faint blue of its tongue, she could see teeth that seemed to be as black as the rest of it.

"It looks as dark as the shadow ore," Min said and swallowed. "Like it's absorbed it."

"I'm already starting to feel tired, so let's go before I can't move the rocks any more." Taya had forgotten that part of the Change in the excitement and joy of her power. That calling it took effort.

Kas called his carefully, because as village head, he always felt the need to keep some power in store for an emergency. So he called the Change for useful things, repairing or building earth walls, keeping the paths and roads in good condition, by doing a little each day.

Garek—well, he sometimes used his up in one big gulp of power, but he suffered for it afterward. And when he'd been younger, before he'd courted her, when she'd watched him come into his Change as a tall, lanky teenager, she'd once seen him collapse in the street.

Quardi had left him there as a lesson.

No one ever found out who had put the pillow under his head, or the blanket over him after darkness had fallen.

Taya swallowed her smile. If they didn't start moving, she'd be the one lying passed out on the floor. And Min would be left alone to deal with the cave flyers.

She grabbed Min's hand and they headed left, angling to where the fast-flowing stream disappeared into the darkness. Neither of them was particularly fast. Taya was stiff from lying on the stone floor, and from her cuts and scrapes, and Min hadn't fared much better.

She tried to speed up, using the moss light to negotiate the best path.

It was interesting that the moss didn't grow in the part of the cave they were aiming for, didn't grow above a certain height, either.

Taya was fascinated by plants. They provided the color for the dyes she created for her wool.

She wondered what this moss might do in a dye. If she could transfer the luminescence to levik wool, she could name her price per bale.

She pushed the thought aside and concentrated.

The rocks she had lifted weighed on her, heavier and heavier with each passing moment. She and Min had made it halfway across when she realized she was at her limit. The rocks had already dropped to just above her head, and were sinking with every step she took.

"I can't hold them much longer." She had to force her lips to move through the stabbing pain growing behind her forehead.

Another cave flyer swooped, this time close enough for Taya's hair to flutter in the wind it caused.

They were closer to the stream than to the back of the cave.

Min must have been thinking along the same lines as her, because she gave a grim nod as they both altered course for the water.

"Keep hold of me," Min said. "I don't have as much control over this water as the water on Barit, but what I do have is better than nothing."

Taya forced the rocks up a little as another flyer swooped, and the moment it passed, dropped them with an involuntary cry of relief.

"Go."

They ran, both ducking as a flyer dived at them again. Taya felt the scrape of claws on her upper back, the tug of her tunic as it was caught and then ripped.

They reached the edge of the stream and jumped in.

She didn't know what Min had expected, but she'd had the impression the stream was relatively shallow. She'd actually been worried it wouldn't be deep enough to shield them from attack.

She needn't have been.

The water closed over their heads, and they sank like stones.

On Barit, the water always seemed to cradle her, to allow her to float with ease, but Shadow water had no buoyancy.

It was also absolutely dark. She couldn't see Min, and was grateful that their hands were still clasped together as the strong current dragged them along.

Min tugged her closer, and then clamped both arms around her, pulling her flush with her body and resting her chin on Taya's shoulder.

A strange feeling of lightness grew around Taya's head, and suddenly, there was no water touching her from the neck up.

She couldn't see what Min had done, but she drew in a tentative breath.

"No talking, save the air," Min whispered in her ear and Taya swallowed her questions, careful to take as little air as she could.

A few drops of water fell on her head, but, although her heart sped up in panic, the bubble around them held, and she tried to see where they were.

It was impossible.

The moss glow did not penetrate below the stream's surface.

They were moving swiftly, and every now and then she bumped into the smooth, slick walls of the channel.

"I can't hold the water back for more than another few seconds," Min warned, and Taya took a last breath, as deep as she dared.

The water collapsed inward, making her ears pop with the change in pressure.

Her shoes had touched the bottom many times, and now she waited for them to make contact again and then pushed upward as hard as she could, pulling Min up with her.

They broke the surface for a fleeting moment, Taya looking backward first, to see how far they'd come.

The river had swept them to the back of the cave, the area in deep shadow, and relieved, she turned to face the other way before the water sucked them down again.

It was impossible to see where they were going, but there was a new roughness to the water, a choppiness that hadn't been there when they'd jumped in.

She sucked in a huge breath just before the water closed over her head, and heard Min do the same.

Once under again, the strength of the current was more noticeable, and she tightened her grip on Min.

It felt as if the water was trying to pry them apart.

Since they'd jumped into the water she'd forced her headache to the background, but now, holding her breath in the cold, dark waters, it muscled its way forward and began to stab at her brain. She kicked out with both feet to get to the surface again, needing another gulp of air with a frightening desperation.

Min's arms seemed to tighten, to keep her down, and Taya struggled against them, and broke free.

She swallowed water and air when she came up, choking and gagging, and reached out with both arms to find Min again.

She caught hold of Min's shoulder with one hand, and flailed with the other to keep her head above water, crying out as she hit her hand against a rock ceiling.

She coughed and sucked in more air, panicked at the thought of being in some kind of tunnel. What if the water level rose and there was no air gap?

She put her legs down, found she could reach the floor, and using her arms to brace herself, fought the power of the stream and came to a stop.

Min slammed against her and she stumbled back a few steps and then managed to hold fast again.

"You all right?" Min gasped for breath.

Taya gave a jerky nod. "Headache. Had to get some air."

"I'm getting it too. Calling the Change too much does that. I usually don't because calling the Change too much in Kardai is dangerous. I haven't had a headache since I was a teenager." She was quiet for a moment and both of them slowly got their breath back. "I'm not an expert, because no one talked to me about the Change in Kardai except my father. But I think what you did back there is hard. You're strong, Taya. Very strong."

Taya was glad to hear that. Her whole life she'd wondered why Kas had been born with the earth Change and she hadn't.

But she had.

And she wondered how many were like her. Had the power to Change, but the element that resonated with them was buried too deep beneath the ground, or too high up, for them to ever come in contact with it.

Min's teeth started chattering. "It's cold."

"We have to go on, agreed?" There was little chance of making it back, as far as she could see.

"Agreed."

"There's no point taking risks we don't need to take, though. Let's go slow. I'm afraid of reaching a part where there's no air gap."

Taya started moving again. It was hard to walk, but she was too scared to let the water carry her along in case she couldn't stop again. She moved forward slowly, taking deep breaths and trying to ignore the cold that seemed to seep into her very bones.

She lost track of time in the darkness, the only anchor Min's occasional touch, confirming they had each other and were not alone.

When the current strengthened, she was grateful the floor and walls of the tunnel were not as slippery and slick as the channel in the cave had been. She moved even slower, inching her way along, fighting against the tug of a current that wanted to grab her and run.

When she took a step and found no tunnel floor beneath her, she went under with a cry of surprise, and Min dragged her back.

She coughed the water out of her lungs, trying to move back against the flow. It was impossible.

"There's a deep hole?" Min asked, her voice strangely disembodied in the pitch dark.

"I think so. The ground falls away." Another fit of coughing wracked her body.

"What do we do?"

Taya closed her eyes, took a deep, deep breath.

"What can we do? We have to go on." The thought filled her with terror. "Once we commit and let the current take us, we won't be able to go back."

"I don't want to do it."

They were silent for a beat after Min's words, and then they both burst into laughter.

"No." Taya's arms shook under the strain of holding herself in place against the pull of the current. "I don't want to, either."

"Hang on tight to me. If I have to, I'll find some power from somewhere, and either make another bubble or do something else."

"All right." Taya took a last breath. "Get ready. Go!" They both dropped their hands from the tunnel walls and hugged each other close, lifted their feet, and let the water sweep them away.

EIGHTEEN

THE ENTRANCE beneath the sky raider's ship was lit with a faint green glow. It had an extended lower lip and was far wider than it was high. They were in a small sky craft, though, and there was more than enough room.

As they came closer, Garek saw the green glow was more like a solid wall of light, and he slowed the craft down so much they were almost drifting as they hit it. They passed through, and found another green wall blocking their way.

Aidan made a sound of panic, and Garek's finger hovered over the acceleration lights, but before he could make a decision, they hit the second wall.

"A wall that isn't a wall." Aidan's face was tense, awash in the green light. Unlike the first barrier, this one seemed much thicker.

"They've worked out how to harness light." It was an idea that had been brewing in Garek's head since the light-dial had lit up under his fingers. "They use it to power their flying ships, and I think they're using these walls of light to keep the air they breathe inside the big ship from escaping out."

At last they broke free of the wall and he gently brushed downward on the up and down lights.

They dropped, not hard, but with a definite jolt, and Aidan grabbed at the wall for balance.

"It's busy out there." He crouched down, out of sight.

"I don't know that anyone can see into this window." Garek hoped they couldn't. "I've seen a lot of sky craft, and they all look solid silver from the outside, and I can't imagine they were all flying blind."

"You mean, you think they bend light, so we can look out, but no one can see in?" Aidan swiveled to look at him. "That old man who was with you, just before I climbed the ladder I heard him exclaiming that the windows looked solid, even though you'd opened them."

Garek nodded his head. He stood and walked carefully to the window, bending low, just in case, and joining Aidan in a crouch. It was the first time he'd moved since they'd taken off, and he was stiff from sitting for so long.

Aidan was right. They had come through into a hive of activity.

Sky raiders strode about, calling to each other as riderless carts carried boxes and pallets toward a massive open set of double doors or toward one of the two people-stealers parked beside them. The carts moved seemingly under their own power; nothing pulled them, no one drove them.

He stared in wonder, and was aware that Aidan was doing the same.

Just as he'd guessed, the sky raiders had claws. Their hands were massive and broad, much bigger, proportionally, than any other appendage. They either had pale yellow skin, or a smooth fur covering their limbs. All wore long, dark pants, but some were shirtless, and others had vests on. Men and women alike.

West Lathor was known to be a slightly prudish place, but Garek didn't find the scene shocking so much as interesting. The sky raiders operated with efficiency and focus. There was no joking or teasing, as he imagined would be the case if the same situation was played out in West Lathor, or in Illy in general.

"They're big," Aidan said.

They were. The average height looked around the same as Garek, and he was used to being head and shoulders taller than most. Their hair contributed to the impression. There was a lot of it, and it was bushy, in various colors from light brown to almost white.

"Something's happening." Aidan crouched suddenly, and Garek angled his body to see.

Another of the riderless carts had moved forward, this time with no cargo, and then disappeared around the side of their sky craft.

There was a faint thump and a tiny shudder went through the craft, and then they started moving forward, deeper into the huge space.

"Getting us out of the way," Garek guessed. He saw where they were headed, toward a short line of sky craft, set to one side.

"Do you see what they're doing with the people-stealers?" Aidan asked him. He'd turned and walked to the other side of the sky craft, so he could keep watching the loading.

Garek gave a grunt of acknowledgment. Most of the pallets and boxes were being transferred from one people-stealer to another.

"They're a bit different. Do you see it?"

Aidan frowned and then nodded. "The one they're loading up is bigger. It's more like a cargo vessel."

"Hmm." Garek tried to remember what the people-stealer they'd seen leaving the big ship earlier looked like. Had it been one of these bigger ones?

He hadn't been paying enough attention.

Their sky craft jerked to a stop, and now that they were next to a few others, Garek saw theirs was in the worst shape. That made him nervous. Someone might feel the need to fix it.

Would the sky raiders be waiting for someone to disembark? And what would they do if no one did?

He shook the feeling of worry off and concentrated on watching the scene in front of him. If they needed to get out of here quickly, their craft had a clear run across the loading area to the light wall.

"Those are the silk bales that were taken coming into Gara a week ago." Aidan spoke almost under his breath as he watched someone take the bales out of a riderless cart and stack them to one side of the people-stealer's hold. "What could they possibly want with them?"

"I see tools, pots and pans, and crates of fruit going in with those bales. My guess is they're just taking whatever they can steal and passing it on. Because they don't need any of it for themselves."

"Passing it on to the prisoners?" Aidan leaned a shoulder against the window.

"People need clothes, food, and equipment to survive. The sky raiders want them for something, so they're trying to keep them alive." Garek hadn't wanted to think about what that something could be, but seeing the sky raiders working so well together, the calm, methodical way they loaded the people-stealers, the fear he was carrying eased a little.

They seemed logical. Focused. Not the crazed, evil devils they'd become in the minds of the people of Barit. Whatever they wanted of those they'd stolen, it was likely not depraved, but practical.

You didn't give someone you were torturing silk and the finest Illian grapes. Unless, he conceded, you didn't know the value of the items you were taking, which could well be true.

"Why do you think they took our people?" Aidan asked.

"They need them to do something they can't do themselves."

"But look at them." Aidan's hands clenched into fists as they watched the sky raiders wheel three big metallic structures to the people-stealer's loading ramp. The structures looked strangely humanoid, with a bulbous glass head and strange mechanical legs and arms. One of the sky raiders touched the chest part of one of them, and the glass opened, one half lifting up. The sky raider swung up, putting his foot on what must be a built-in step, and Garek saw there was a seat inside the glass dome. The dome closed, and the strange mechanical thing stepped off the pallet that had been wheeled in, and walked into the people-stealer's hold. It moved to one side, up against the wall, and stopped, and then the glass dome opened and the sky raider got out and walked to the next one on the pallet.

"Look at that!" Aidan was as riveted as Garek as the sky raider moved the second mechanical person into place and went back for the third one. "What can we possibly do that they can't?"

The one reason Garek had come up with had placed Taya and the others from Pan Nuk on Barit. But if that was so, why bother bringing their stolen supplies all the way up here only to take them down again? Why not simply take them directly to where they were holding their prisoners?

"Garek?" Aidan was watching him.

"I thought it was because they needed something from Barit, and they couldn't breathe the air. That's the one thing we can do that they can't."

Aidan's eyes widened. "That makes sense, but . . ."

"But where on Barit are they keeping them?" Garek nodded. "And they'd take what they steal directly there, not back up here."

"So you think that's wrong? They aren't keeping them on Barit?"

Garek nodded. "It's definitely wrong. But they're alive somewhere. Why steal them, just to kill them? And why spend time stealing supplies, if you don't need to keep them alive?"

Something banged against the side of the sky craft, and Garek spun, saw a sky raider was pushing a metal ladder on wheels beneath them.

It was far more sophisticated than the wooden ladder Falk had been using.

"They're coming in," he murmured to Aidan and moved toward the circular depression in the floor that could slide open.

"Hold you breath when it opens," Garek warned as Aidan came up beside him. "The air out there is poison."

Aidan nodded. "Do you know how to close it up?"

Garek shook his head. The door had closed automatically before, as he was lifting off. When it opened, the outside air would rush in. He needed a plan.

He drew the air in the sky craft to him, making it denser, giving it substance.

A circle of light suddenly blossomed right next to his foot, and he crouched beside it, noticed that the part of the floor that had lit up was slightly raised, easy to miss if you weren't looking for it. The door opened suddenly and he shuffled back a little, still crouched low. The air around him wanted to rush out into the hangar, and the air in the hangar wanted to flow into the sky craft. He could feel it nibbling at the edges of the tight ball of air he was holding.

A head popped up through the hole and he reached down and grabbed the sky raider by his throat and hauled him up.

As soon as he was inside, the man started to gasp and choke.

Aidan was on him before Garek could move, which was a good thing, because he needed more and more strength to hold the air inside. He could feel the pressure building at his feet as the outside air pushed, and held the air inside closer still.

He pressed the circle of light, hoping it would close the door, but nothing happened.

With a grunt, the sky raider rolled away from Aidan, his hands clawing at his throat.

Garek pressed the light button again, his eyes on the sky raider as he writhed on the ground, eyes wide as he took in Aidan and Garek. He tried to say something, to shout out, and Garek stabbed at the button again.

The door closed.

With an exhale of relief, he let go of the air and then watched as the sky raider arched up, eyes too wide and protruding in his face and then went still.

He walked over, and he and Aidan looked down at the man.

"They look more like us than I thought they would," Aidan said.

Garek knelt beside him. This was the first sky raider he'd killed.

Usually, it was the other way around. Sky raiders killing guards.

"You held the air inside?" Aidan asked, kneeling beside him. "I could breathe the whole time."

"It was the only way. The air in here wanted to mingle with the air outside, and vice versa."

Aidan was silent for a beat. "You're a freak of nature, you know that? Gara didn't say a word about you to my father. When I joined and discovered what you could do, how they'd forced you to do an extra year, and sent word about it back to him, my father had someone steal the guard master's books for a night to see if there had been others like you they'd kept quiet about."

"And?" It wouldn't have surprised Garek if they had.

"They were doing it as a matter of course. But you, by far, were the strongest they'd ever had the privilege to have walk their walls. And they couldn't even do that right."

Garek flicked the black vest the sky raider was wearing open, and found small devices and tools tucked into interior pockets. He lifted the man's torso up by gripping his neck, and pulled the vest off him.

The fabric felt strange; smooth as silk but tough, too. He rubbed it between his fingers thoughtfully.

"It's like he's covered in velvet," Aidan commented, and Garek gave a nod in agreement. The sky raider's skin wasn't fur, precisely, but it was very dense hair that was very short and incredibly soft.

His incisors were long and pointed, and the pupils in his staring, golden eyes were not round but oval.

The man they'd killed was about the same height as Garek, and Garek eyed his pants and boots.

"It's a pity they're such a different color to me." His own skin was a deep bronze, too brown to fool anyone outside, even at a distance.

"You couldn't breathe, anyway," Aidan pointed out.

"Holding the air inside here gave me an idea. I might be able to hold some around myself, like a bubble." He looked out the window at the cargo bay. "Maybe when they finish, I can wander around, see what clues I can find." And he wanted to look at those mechanical people again. An idea was forming in his head and he needed to see if it would work, because without question, the loaded people-stealer was going to the prisoners, and he needed a way to get himself and Aidan onboard.

"We need to hide the body, too," Aidan said, pulling himself to his feet.

"Yes." Garek walked closer to the window, watching as the sky raiders moved with purpose about their business.

"I thought I'd feel happy to kill one of them," Aidan said into the silence. "But I don't."

Garek glanced at him. "It's never easy to take a life, but they created this whole situation. And they've managed to have it their way for a long time."

And if he had anything to do with it, that was about to change.

NINETEEN

TAYA LOST her grip on Min almost immediately.

The current ripped them apart and swallowed her under with a great, icy gulp.

She fought against it, fought upward, with everything she had. Dark spots edged with orange flickered at the corners of her vision as she was tumbled end over end, until she was so confused, she didn't know which way *was* up.

Something yanked her, got a hard, strong grip around her neck, and then her head was above rough water, Min holding her up as they barreled along.

She couldn't speak, she had to use all her energy to gulp air down, and with a sudden, sharp turn and a moment of free fall, they were spat out into what was a large, calm lake.

She blinked a few times, but she wasn't imagining it. Moss grew on the rocks all around them, glowing faintly and illuminating the vast space.

She tried to feel for the bottom, but the water was too deep, and Min towed her to the side, away from the rougher water below the waterfall.

Min must be calling her Change, because it seemed to Taya she moved too fast and too smoothly for it to be plain swimming.

They both grabbed hold of the slick, wet rocks.

Taya forced herself to find hand and foot holds and pull herself up.

She put a hand down to Min, saw the exhaustion on her face, and hauled her up beside her.

They sat side by side, feet just above the water, shivering in the cold.

Taya put her arm around Min and pulled her close. "Thank you."

"Call it even, now." Min managed a small smile.

"There was never a tally."

"I know." Min squeezed her back and then crossed her arms over her chest and hunched over, rubbing her arms to try and warm up.

Taya rose to her feet, her gaze going upward to check for the presence of shadow flyers, but this cave had a lower ceiling than the first one they'd stumbled into, and moss blanketed it, lighting the whole space better and leaving little hidden.

The rocks they were sitting on were almost up against the cave wall, but Taya saw the rocky shore widened considerably the further from the waterfall it got.

"What now?" Min asked, and her voice was faint.

"Let's move a little, warm up. And find the way out." Taya was just relieved for the moment they were alive. Anything else would be a gift on top of being able to breathe.

She offered her hand to Min again, and they stood side by side for a moment, looking around them.

"There's a lot of shadow ore here."

Taya looked to where Min was pointing, and her mouth fell open. A seam of dark purple glinted in the diffuse light, clear against the light brown stone of the cave wall. The seam was as high as she was in places, as narrow as her wrist in others, an undulating mother lode.

"If we told the sky raiders about this, they may get what they need quicker," Min said.

Taya nodded. "And be done with us faster."

Min put both arms out for balance as she negotiated the rocks along the shore. "Is that a good or a bad thing?"

"Bad." Taya leapt lightly after her. "When they have what they need, do you think they'll take the time to drop us back on Barit?"

Min thought about it for a long time as they picked their way around the lake. "They'll leave us here to die, won't they?"

"Not if we escape first." There had never been a lot to lose. They either risked a quick death trying to escape, or a long, slow one, trapped on Shadow.

Neither of them spoke again as they concentrated on keeping their footing, until at last they reached a smooth slab of rock on the far side of the lake.

It was still cold, but the exercise had warmed Taya. Orange light, bolder than the pale pastels of the moss, stabbed through the dim interior and Taya frowned at the sight.

"What do you think . . ?" She stumbled to a stop, looking up through a wide crack in the wall, to the sight of the Star low in a spectacular sky.

"What is it? Oh!" Min stopped beside her, and they stood for a moment, letting the warmth of the Star touch them with long, comforting fingers.

"We did it," Taya whispered. She grabbed Min's hand and scrambled up the incline until it got too steep and she had to use both hands to pull herself up.

She was breathing hard by the time she stepped out into the open. She glanced back, waiting for Min to join her before she looked around.

They'd emerged at the foot of a stark cliff face, smooth, solid rock soaring straight up. There was nothing in front of them but the barren flats that seemed to define Shadow.

Something skittered away through the scrubby, woody bush that covered the plain in front of them, rustling branches and clicking pebbles together.

Taya looked in the direction of the sound but there was nothing to see. It was probably one of the small creatures that looked like slithers with short, stubby legs that were common around the camp.

Taya lowered herself down on a rock and closed her eyes, letting the last of Star's rays warm her eyelids.

With a sigh, Min sat beside her, bumping her with her hip to get a little extra room.

"You want to stay here for the night?" Min's voice was thick with exhaustion.

"No. But I don't want to wander around in the dark, either. We've got shelter and water here. I think we'll have to stay."

"Good. Even this rock looks comfortable enough to sleep on."

Taya chuckled. "Say that in the morning." Her stomach rumbled and she rubbed it. Ketl had attacked them around mid-morning, so they'd missed lunch and dinner.

"What will we do if the sky raiders ask us to show them where we came out?" Min lay down on a flat, warm surface, eyes closed.

"I don't know." She'd have to fake confusion and stupidity. It wouldn't be that difficult, because the sky raiders saw them as a lesser form of life. "We pretend we don't know. That we just wandered around, lost."

Min snorted. "That's just about true, anyway."

Taya grinned, and lay down beside her. The heat of the rock was delicious through her tunic, warming her for the first time since they'd been trapped in the mine shaft.

The Star was low on the horizon, taking the vibrant oranges and reds with it like an actor exiting with a flamboyant swirl of a cloak. High in the indigo sky left in its wake, Barit was clear, a crescent of white and blue.

She couldn't look away, her longing for home sharper than her hunger, and a tear tracked down her cheek.

"What's wrong?"

She turned her head, found Min watching her.

"I miss Garek."

Min was quiet as they both looked up at Barit again. "Tell me about him."

Taya shifted a little, moving to a new spot, chasing the heat. "He was the town guard before Garamundo called him up. He walked the walls of Pan Nuk. Not that we actually had walls to walk." She smiled at the thought of her sleepy village having a guard walk like Gara. "He kept us safe, and broke up any disputes in town. Kas and him never saw eye to eye over me, but they were a good team. Pan Nuk was a happy, peaceful place with the two of them running things." Although it wasn't enough for Garek. She'd started to understand that toward the end. He only stayed because she was there.

"And then he was called up? To Garamundo?"

"Yes. Our district has to provide one guard a year between five towns. It was Pan Nuk's turn when Garek had been town guard for a few years." And Haret's turn the year after, but they'd had no one to send who was stronger than Garek, and Gara wanted the strongest they could find when the sky raiders started patrolling the skies.

Couldn't blame them, not really. She understood West Lathor needed the best protectors they could get when they were facing a war with an enemy they'd never seen before. But she *could* blame them for never allowing a single visit.

She'd wanted to see him so badly.

She'd had one long trip since he'd left, to Juli, the capital of West Lathor, where the liege lived, to bring a beautiful golden throw as a gift to the liege's daughter on her marriage. Kas would've tried to send someone else, but Taya had made the throw, and her gift had been chosen to represent the whole district.

Even though Juli was famous, built at the top of a waterfall, one of the most beautiful cities in all of Illy, she'd wished the wedding ceremony was being held in Gara with every step she'd taken on her journey. She wanted to go past Gara on her way back, but Kas had blocked her every move. No family was the rule while you walked the walls, he'd told her, time and again. Family distracted you.

Garek would get into trouble, and so would she.

She wondered what the town master and guard master in Gara had ever sacrificed? Whether *they'd* ever had to give someone up for two years with unreasonable rules attached.

What could it honestly have hurt to let her and Garek be together, even for a day?

Her body had absorbed all the heat it could from where she was lying, and she moved again, searching for more, and winced when her injured side pressed against a sharp ridge of rock. She'd been too cold to feel her scrapes until now.

She looked up, and found the sky was almost black, dark enough for the light generated by the moss in the cave behind them to be visible, spilling out through the crack. Barit glowed, too, as the Star's light struck it from below.

Kas would be raising the alarm back at camp. Maybe demanding they dig into the tunnel. She just hoped he'd listened to her and hidden his knife.

"What do you think's happening back in camp?" Min's thoughts must have been following the same trail as hers.

"Trouble, I'm guessing."

"Yes."

They lay quietly, and as Taya drifted off to sleep, she hoped that the trouble was all on Ketl's side.

TWENTY

THE SKY RAIDERS drifted out of the cargo bay in small groups or individually. No one watched a clock or was ordered out that Garek could see.

They worked hard and stayed until the work was done.

A few minutes after the last one left, the lights dimmed, causing both him and Aidan to tense.

"The lights knew when they'd gone and weren't needed anymore," Aidan murmured. "I didn't think it was possible when you said it before, but you're right. The sky raiders have learned how to control light."

It was just one more amazing thing in a string of them. If, when the sky raiders had arrived, they'd come and asked the people of Barit for what they wanted, they could have exchanged some of their knowledge for whatever it was. And none of this would have been necessary.

Garek leaned against the window and looked out for another five minutes, just in case someone had forgotten something, or another shift was scheduled to arrive, but the place remained quiet and still.

He walked to the panel Falk had shown him in Gara where he'd changed the mix of air in the sky craft. He studied the light gauges, trying to commit where the lights stopped on each of the three light circles to memory.

Then he turned and gestured to the door in the sky craft's floor. "When I'm ready to come back in, you'll need to press down on the button when I knock from below." His gaze lifted to Aidan while he spoke. There was probably a button on the outside, too, otherwise how had the sky raider come in? But just in case he couldn't find it, Aidan needed to be ready.

Aidan nodded, crouching beside the slightly raised circle to study it.

Garek kept his gaze on Aidan's face. If the princeling wanted to kill him, now would be the best opportunity for him.

"Don't." Aidan looked up, holding his gaze.

"Don't what?"

"Don't start wondering if I'm going to lock you out." He balanced back on his heels.

"Are you?" Garek kept his face calm.

"No." The answer was short, exasperated, and Garek believed him. Nodded.

"Good." He jerked his head to the wall of the craft. "Stand back 'til I'm out, and then take a breath and hold it before you run over and press the button to close this up."

Aidan stood and walked to the wall, leaning back against it like he was simply passing the time of day.

Garek couldn't help the upward quirk of his lips at his cockiness.

He glanced at the body of the sky raider, but he wouldn't take it with him until he'd found a good place to hide it. And if the idea forming in his head worked out, he wouldn't have to move it at all.

He drew the air to him, surrounding himself with a dense bubble of it from his feet all the way up to his head, ballooning it up above him. He crouched and pressed the button, dropping down onto the ladder as quickly as he could as soon as the door slid open.

He saw a corresponding light under the belly of the ship, directly below the one inside, and dropped a few more steps to jab at it with his finger.

Like the first time when the sky raider had entered the craft, it took three tries before the button worked.

A delay of some sort, perhaps? To stop it closing on someone by mistake?

He caught a final glimpse of Aidan, leaning down to look at him as the door closed, and then he concentrated on keeping the air around him together.

He moved quickly across the floor, grateful that the sky raiders had left the massive door of the people-stealer they were loading open. The lights flickered back on as he moved, and he stilled, turned slowly, but there was no one there. The lights had seen him in some way, and switched back on to help him see.

The idea was as intriguing as it was frightening, and when nothing else happened, he forced himself to focus on the people-stealer again.

Its design reminded him of a cart with a levered back that acted as a ramp when lowered.

The sky raiders weren't that different from the people of Barit, they just used things in ways his people hadn't thought of yet.

He walked cautiously up into the ship, aware that every breath he took shortened the time he had to explore.

He ignored the stolen items stacked on the right and went to the three strange humanoid vehicles on the left.

They were closed up, but Garek had watched the sky raider closely as he'd moved them one by one. He focused on the chest of the first one in the row.

He pressed his hand to the raised circle he found in the center, and with a hiss, the bubble head opened up.

He swung up, using the foothold built into the side of the mechanical torso, and sat down in the comfortable chair built inside.

The moment he did, lights came on and he felt the gentle flow of air from vents on either side of the chair.

It swirled around the air from the sky craft he was holding around him, eating away at the edges. He focused on the panel before him, looking for dials like the ones in the sky craft.

They were hidden from sight in the sky craft, and he guessed the same would be true here. It would be dangerous if someone could alter them by mistake.

He looked lower, crouching in front of the seat awkwardly, poison air blowing directly into his face. He found two panels and ripped the covers off both with no compunction. He could feel each breath was getting harder.

And there they were. Three dials of golden light in a row, all lit up. He needed to close the lid before he changed the air mix, or he might still suffocate.

He reached up and pressed the central button on the main panel at his eye-level, hoping it was the right one, and when nothing happened, he used his fist from right to left, smacking them all, hard.

The vehicle lurched, took a half step forward and toppled, but as it did, the bubble top closed quickly and smoothly.

Garek flung out his hands to brace himself as the vehicle hit the floor, his forehead hitting the panel in front of him hard. He ignored the pain, moving his fingers over the gauges. The bang the vehicle made as it landed had sounded massive, seemed to reverberate, and Garek forced himself to concentrate on the dials in front of him and not check to see if the noise had attracted any attention.

Bad air still blew at him. That he could taste it, feel it, meant his own bubble was almost gone, but as he moved his finger around the dials, it changed, getting better and better until he drew in a deep, shuddering breath.

He was folded into a strange position on the floor of the vehicle, and he let his head drop back against the seat of the chair in relief.

He'd done it.

He lifted himself slowly, angling himself so he could study the panel.

He started on the far right, lightly moving his finger over the smooth resin-like surface, and lights lit up under his touch, the right arm of the machine shuddering, trying to move while trapped under the bulk of its own weight. He moved on, using an down-up motion, and the bubble started opening again, and he pulled down with his finger to close it.

He worked out most of the functions, but he couldn't find a way to get the vehicle back on its feet.

He took another deep breath, pulled the air to him, changed the dials that controlled the air mix back to what it had been and opened the bubble again, slid out, and touched the chest of the next vehicle in the line.

He had the bubble open and was inside, with the lid closed and the panel removed in a quarter of the time it had taken him before. He got the air working, and then carefully moved the legs, shuffling the vehicle past the one he'd tipped over and very slowly moving it down the ramp.

There were ways of moving it that he hadn't worked out yet, because the sky raider who'd parked them had gotten the legs to bend, whereas he was only able to get a straight-legged shuffle and he was too afraid of tipping this one over to experiment.

He wobbled all the way to the sky craft, getting it as close to the ladder as he could, and then pulled the air to him again. He had the glass dome open and was on the ladder as fast as he could go. The door of the sky craft slid open before he could knock or press the button and he scrambled inside.

Aidan said nothing for a moment, his gaze on Garek's face. Then he blew out a breath.

"You're bleeding," he said at last.

Garek frowned and put his hand up to his forehead, and his fingers came away dark with blood. "Must have happened when the thing fell over."

Aidan gave a curt nod. "Lucky no one came to investigate."

"Yes. I can't say I wasn't worried about that."

"Why did you bring one of the other ones over here?" Aidan's gaze was fixed on the fallen machine.

"I've got it to blow Barit air. I brought it to get you over to the people-stealer. You can stay inside it and I'll climb into the other one."

"We're going in the people-stealer?"

Garek nodded. "You can stay here if you like, but I thought you'd prefer to come with me. They have to be loading that people-stealer with things meant for the prisoners, which means I need to be on it. If we're in the mechanical vehicles, then we'll be hidden and we can breathe our own air."

Aidan looked out at where the one metal marionette lay on its side. "What about that?"

"I'll see if I can lift it up." He started gathering up his supplies, putting the food into two piles.

Aidan worked out what he was doing and helped, stuffing things into one of the bags Garek had brought and slinging it over his shoulder. "What about him?" His gaze went to the dead sky raider.

"We leave him where he is."

Aidan opened his mouth to object, and then closed it again. "That will probably work," he murmured.

Garek moved to the door, all his gear dangling from his shoulders. "You'll have to hold your breath, but I've parked quite close to the ladder. Ready?"

Aidan narrowed his eyes. "No. But let's do it anyway."

TWENTY-ONE

IT HAD BEEN A HARD NIGHT.

In the early hours of the morning a wind had come up, forcing Taya and Min back inside the cave to escape the chill and the sting of the grit.

Taya had just dozed after that, lying on a bed of moss close to Min to share body heat. They had both been awake before the Star broke over the cliff, casting long shadows in front of them.

They drank what they could, and then Taya picked her way through the rocks and pebbles on the underground shore, piling the stones with the most shadow ore in them to one side.

When she had enough, she got Min to lift the sides of her tunic up to form a basket, and did the same, dividing the rocks between them.

"Why are we doing this again?" Min tested the weight of them.

"Shadow ore makes the sky raiders' systems malfunction." Taya shrugged. "It might be worth having a stash nearby for any escape plan we come up with."

She and Min would have to hide the stones when they got close to the mine, but it would save having to try and sneak shadow ore out of the mine itself.

They were ready to go before the Star's light had even crested the top of the cliff.

They headed around the side of the hill, edging around soaring slabs of rock. They wanted to walk directly into the dawn's light. They both glowed a little in the shadows of the cliffs while they made their way to where they could see the Star, their arms and legs slightly luminescent in the darkness, which made Taya smile. The moss they slept on had rubbed off on them, and they lit their own way on the path they forged through the dense, low brush.

As they made their way around, the hill revealed itself to be a massive plug of hard rock, sticking up like a finger into the sky. Taya would have liked to climb it, to see if she could see the mine or the camp from the top, but there were no footholds and she was too afraid of getting stuck or falling.

Instead, they'd agreed their underground journey had taken them roughly west and so they would need to travel due east, directly toward the rising Star.

"We probably didn't even go that far," Min said.

"It felt far to me." Taya knew her sense of time and distance had been compromised, though. The darkness, the pain, the panic. She wasn't even sure they were headed in the right direction, but they could see for a long distance westward from the mouth of the cave, and there was nothing but bush that way. If the mine did lie west, then last night they would surely have seen the lights around its entrance on the wide, flat plain, lit up for the night shift, but there had been nothing.

East was as good an option as any.

She reveled in the heat as the Star rose higher and warmed the air, lifting her face upward and closing her eyes to receive a Star's kiss. After hours in the pitch dark, she would never take the Star's light for granted again.

They stopped to rest around midday, and Taya scrambled up on top of the rock they'd chosen to lean against, looking in all directions for any sign of the mine.

"Anything?" Min looked up from her spot below.

Taya shook her head. "I'm getting worried. It feels like we should have found it by now."

She did another slow, full turn, listening as well as looking. To the northeast, the land rose up to form a small hill. Something glinted in the sunlight right at the top, and she focused on it, but it was impossible to make out.

"You find something?"

Taya jumped down. "Something shining. Metal, maybe? It's on that hill. It might be a good idea to head toward it, anyway. Maybe we can see a bit better up there?"

Min shaded her eyes, looked over at the hill. "I'd rather not wander around completely lost, so yes. Let's climb the hill."

Taya nodded. She forced herself to sit still and tried to ignore the nerves and fear she felt for Kas's safety. He might do something truly rash if he thought she was dead or buried alive. He'd lost Sara, his wife, along with their parents, when Luca had been only four. Now Luca was down on Barit, alone, and Taya was all Kas had left.

She prayed Quardi had the sense to take his knife away. Hoped the others could reason with him.

She stood, agitated, even though she knew Min was still tired. But Min said nothing, she just nodded and got to her feet.

Her calm acceptance helped settle Taya as she led the way. They would find their way back, and Kas would be all right. Anything else was unacceptable.

———

IT TOOK them two more hours to reach the hilltop.

They left their shadow ore at the bottom when they saw how steep the climb would be, and Taya was gasping for breath, had sweat dripping between her shoulder blades and stinging her eyes when she pulled herself up the last steep slope and found herself at the top.

She stood quietly until Min joined her, and they both took in the tall, rusting pole with a shallow bowl attached to it. The bowl faced upward, but while they watched, it moved a little to the left.

"Sky raider equipment," Min breathed.

The structure had obviously been built with the metal from the sky raiders planet—it was badly degraded. Only the dish on the top, coated with some type of gray paint or coating, looked like it wasn't about to fall to pieces.

Taya nodded. "We could break it. That would bring them running." And breaking it wouldn't take much.

"We won't have to." Min's voice was fill of suppressed excitement.

Taya turned to her, frowning, and then followed the line of the finger she was pointing.

The mine.

It felt as if a ton of shadow ore flew up off her shoulders at the sight of it.

It was far in the distance, but Taya could just make out the flash of white as the two guards patrolled in their two-legged walking machines, could see the top of the large screen where they kept track of everyone down in the shafts.

She turned blindly and hugged Min. "We did it."

"Yes." Min squeezed her back. "Let's go. It'll be dark too soon."

Taya nodded. But she didn't start down the hill immediately. She walked right up to the strange pole and dish, saw there was a little box attached near the bottom. She crouched down next to it, and peered at the lights blinking and flashing under a glass casing. "I still think if we broke this, they'd come," she said.

"Don't." Min sounded panicked. "They won't be happy with us if we deliberately destroy something. We know the way without them."

Taya nodded. "I'm not talking about now." She took a last look at the box and then straightened back up. "I'm talking about when we want to escape."

"Why would you want them to come get you if you wanted to escape?"

"Because there's usually only two guards at the mine, two at the camp, except for when the people-stealers come. If we wanted to split them up, we could take them one at a time."

Min stared at her. "How would we even do that? They shoot out rays of light, and we can't get to them in their machines."

Taya tapped at the glass, to see how thick it was. "Maybe Quardi can make more of those shadow spikes for me. I could shoot right back. It might make the vehicles they hide in stop or go crazy, like the diggers in the mine did."

"*Maybe. Might.*" Min held her gaze and then looked down at the ground. "Sorry, I sound like a coward, don't I?"

"No. You sound like someone who doesn't want to foolishly throw her life away. I don't want that either. I'm just thinking things through, Min. We'll put our heads together with the others, and we'll come up with a plan that works. But I don't think anything we do will be without a lot of risk."

And it was worth it, especially for her. If Garek was here instead of her, she'd trust that he'd do whatever it took to escape and get back to her.

"When we get back, Kas and I need to find out who's prepared to take the risks. Those who don't want to, we can plan without them. I don't want to bring anyone down with me if I fail."

"No one knows better than I do that everything's a risk. I wasn't exactly safe back in Kardai." Min turned and started down the hill. "Even though I'm afraid, I'm in."

TWENTY-TWO

THE RING of metal on metal woke Garek with a jerk.

He lay on the floor in the bubble 'head' of the metal machine, curled around the seat, and he lifted himself up carefully, keeping low and moving to a crouch, so he was just able to look out of the window.

At least, like in the sky craft, it was easy to see out of, but impossible to see in. He and Aidan couldn't have hidden here otherwise.

The lights were on in the cargo bay, and Garek noticed loading crew were carrying large boxes up the ramp. There was smoke or mist billowing off them and the sky raiders hauling them were wearing gloves.

Almost out of sight, to the far left of what he could see out of the hold, a section of another craft was visible. It hadn't been there last night, so Garek guessed a new ship had just arrived. Perhaps they'd been waiting for it, to load the final supplies before leaving.

His heart lurched in his chest. He was closer to his goal than ever. If they weren't discovered.

His gaze went to the fallen vehicle beside him.

He and Aidan had tried to lift it, but neither had enough control over the vehicles to do it, and they'd eventually decided it was better to leave it than risk one of theirs falling, too.

There was another clatter as the sky raiders walking up the ramp dropped their cargo and stared at the fallen machine in surprise.

Someone, a supervisor, walked up behind them, shouting and gesticulating, and they picked up their burdens again and disappeared beyond Garek's view, deeper into the back of the cargo hold, their smoking boxes leaving a trail of white cloud behind them.

The supervisor stared at the fallen machine and then waved someone over. Garek slipped into the chair of his vehicle. He didn't know what he'd do if they decided to check his and Aidan's, but he couldn't fail now. He wouldn't.

The sky raider who'd been summoned opened the bubble, got inside, then skillfully maneuvered the vehicle back in place.

Garek was very glad he'd remembered to put the air back to sky raider air. A machine could fall by accident, but he didn't think the same would be believed of the settings on the air filter.

When the sky raider swung back down, she looked over at Garek's machine, staring right at him, although he knew she couldn't see inside.

She stood for a long moment, and Garek lifted his hand toward the controls, his gaze never leaving her face.

She turned suddenly, and Garek saw the supervisor was calling again. With a last, suspicious, look over her shoulder, she strode away down the ramp, weaving through the steady stream of loading crew with their smoky boxes. It was frost, Garek realized, at last noticing the glitter of tiny ice crystals on the rims. Cold storage, so possibly they contained perishable food.

He'd heard the produce trains into the cities were being attacked. Now he knew where it was going.

And Gara and Juli could suck up the loss, as far as he was concerned, if Taya didn't go hungry because of it.

The last of the crew left the cargo hold and disappeared off beyond the ramp.

As soon as they were gone, the ramp rose, smooth and quick, shutting them in total darkness. The floor began to vibrate, Garek could feel it coming up through his seat.

The people-stealer was fully loaded and on its way.

He should have felt fear, trepidation, and those feelings did register, but very low down the ladder.

Mostly, he just felt elated.

Taya was out there somewhere, and he was coming for her.

FOR A LONG TIME, it seemed to Taya, the lights of the mine never got any closer.

She and Min walked through the afternoon, into the dusk, and when the big lights at the mine entrance were switched on, at first they were a welcome beacon, an easy way to find the right path.

That slowly turned into an interminable slog where it seemed they were walking in place rather than moving forward.

"Do you hear that?" Min's voice rose a little, with more energy than Taya had heard for a while.

"No." She forced herself out of her head, and paid attention again, and at last, she heard it, too. The rumble of a transporter coming to fetch the day shift.

"We're close," Min said, and Taya decided maybe they were.

The lights did seem closer, now. And she could hear the transporter getting louder.

Without saying any more, they both sped up, half-jogging across the hard-packed earth.

Taya remembered the shadow rocks just as the scream of the engine announced the transporter had landed.

"Min. The rocks." She'd carried them for so long, she'd forgotten about them. At the start of the day she'd played with them, calling her Change to lift them one at a time, then all at once, both her and Min's loads. But thirst, hunger, and exhaustion had put a stop to that, and she'd simply gotten used to the weight of them.

Now she crouched down and released her tunic, tumbling the shadow ore onto the ground. She flexed her hands, wincing as they cramped up. She rubbed at her shoulders as Min turned back and dumped her rocks on top of Taya's.

"We're just going to leave them here?" Min looked around and Taya did the same. There were no landmarks they could use to find them again.

"We'll have to." Taya rose up and lifted her arm out straight toward the camp, found she was pointing directly between the two light arrays. She noticed her skin was still glowing from the moss, something she'd forgotten about in the bright light of the day. "I'll count how many steps we take from here to the camp." She shrugged. "It's the best we can do."

"Okay, but we have to hurry." Min started her loping stride again, and Taya ran after her, counting her steps in her head with an internal voice that got louder and louder the closer they got to the camp.

She was up to eighty-six and mentally shouting when they reached the edge of the cleared area and stumbled into the light.

The transporter's ramp was lifting, and she waved her arms to attract the attention of the guard standing beside it.

He turned and went still, then strode toward them, and she and Min slowed their pace.

Taya had to close her eyes and lift her arm to shield herself from the dust as the transporter settled down again.

When she dropped her arm, the guard was right in front of her.

The night shift stood to the side, and Taya caught a glimpse of the surprise and shock on their faces.

"You all right, Taya?"

She focused on the crowd at the call, and saw it was Eli, one of the farmers from Pan Nuk. One of many friends who'd been dragged to Shadow with her. "I'm fine, thank you."

"You need help?"

A slam drowned out whatever he had to say next, as the ramp hit the ground, and then someone began shouting. Not words, but a long, drawn out battle cry.

Taya looked past the guard, saw Kas running toward her, his face battered and bruised, the hands he stretched out to her raw and bloody.

She moved around the guard toward him, but before she'd taken a few steps he reached her, drawing her up in a hug that somehow also included Min, so they were both enveloped in such a tight embrace, Taya found it hard to breathe.

"You're alive," he was saying, over and over. "You're alive."

"We're alive," she whispered into Kas's ear. "We're fine."

At last he loosened his hold, although his arms were firmly around her and Min's shoulders.

"Where were you?" The hiss of the guard's speech still frightened her, even though she knew what it was now, and she took comfort in Kas's tight hold.

"We were out there." She gestured back into what was now a solid wall of night.

"How did you get there?"

"Ask Ketl and his friends." Min spoke for the first time, and her words put a hush on the murmurs of the night crew.

"I knew it." Kas lifted his face to the guard, his eyes accusing. "I *told* you."

"What did Ketl do?" The guard's hiss was the only sound now that the transporter had landed and was silent. No one spoke.

"He threw us down a shaft and then collapsed the supports. We found a way out through a narrow crack at the back and walked for a long time through a dark tunnel."

"A narrow crack in the rock behind the mine?"

She nodded. "Well, there was no light, but it felt like a crack. There was just room enough for us to make our way through."

"And why do you glow?"

Taya looked down, saw the guard was blocking the light and she and Min stood in his shadow, and they were still shining a little.

"We slept on some moss last night that had a luminescence. It rubbed off on us." Taya shrugged. "It'll come off when we wash."

"Where were you all of today?"

Taya dropped her head onto Kas's shoulder. "We were walking back here. We didn't know the way, so we've been wandering around, lost."

"How did you find us?" There was suspicion in the guard's voice, and Taya decided not to mention the hill with its strange beacon.

"We saw the dust rising up, and then we saw the lights."

A beam shot out from the guard's mechanical arm, enveloping all three of them, and Taya had to close her eyes against the brightness of it.

The guard did not explain what he was doing and she felt a sense of violation, forced to submit to something against her will.

Kas's hold tightened. She knew he understood, felt the same, and the anger inside her that had been eroded away by hunger and exhaustion came roaring back. They *would* get out of here.

"Drink, then get in the transporter. You are malnourished and dehydrated." The guard turned and walked to the food table, scooping up two cups filled with water. Then he waited for them beside the ramp, cups outstretched.

Everything about the way he spoke and moved was imperious, assuming complete obedience. But aside from that water, all Taya wanted was the tiny shack she shared with Kas and the sweet, soft relief of her bed. She didn't mind dancing to the sky raiders' tune tonight.

As they walked, she let herself lean on Kas, lifting a hand to touch his swollen cheek.

"Ketl?" she asked.

Min made a sound, and Taya looked over at her, saw that she was staring at Kas's injuries, too.

He shook his head. "I'll tell you later."

They reached the ramp, took the water, and Taya saw everyone from Pan Nuk on the day shift had lined up at the top.

She felt the warmth of their concern, the strength of their support.

The Kardanx, though . . . they studied her and Min with worried eyes, keeping well back.

Everyone was injured, Taya suddenly noticed.

Everyone had bruises. Illy and Kardanx both.

"What happened?" she whispered.

Kas rubbed her upper arm. "Open revolt."

TWENTY-THREE

THE TRIP from mine to camp in the transporter took less than fifteen minutes.

Taya passed the time leaning against Kas, into his warmth and strength, and sipped her water. She said nothing, carefully taking in everyone's appearance.

They watched her just as carefully back.

The rule they'd established when they first got to Shadow was that there was no talking on the transporter. Even though there were almost never guards with them, and even when there was, they had to stay inside their machines to breathe.

Some things had been said in defiance, right at the start, that had led to unpleasant consequences. Kas thought it likely the sky raiders had some way of listening to them in here. Watching them, too, perhaps, although how they would do that, no one could guess.

But they could fly machines, not just in the skies of Barit, but between Barit and Shadow, between Barit and whichever place they came from, so listening and watching without being there hardly seemed a stretch.

The scream of the engines and the shudder of the ramp lowering should have had her leaping to her feet but Taya found it difficult to stand, every muscle stiff and sore.

Noor had sat on her other side for the journey, and now she slipped an arm around Taya and helped her up, while Kas helped Min. They hobbled down the ramp like two old ladies.

The Star had disappeared over the horizon, but there were the lights of the landing area, and the lights and fires of the camp. Barit shone too, as well as Lanora, Barit's moon. More than enough light to see that the jousting tent was half-collapsed and that some of the shacks were damaged.

"Most of it's been put back together again," Noor murmured, following her gaze. "I guess the night shift put in some work before they slept. They wouldn't have had a place to rest otherwise."

"It was worse than this?" Taya looked around, saw debris on the ground, doors propped up against walls.

"Much worse." Kas's voice was deep, rough; as if he'd been shouting a lot.

"Come, you look like you need to eat," Noor said, "and I know someone who will be very happy you're safe." She lifted Taya's hand, and rubbed a finger over her skin and then studied the transferred light on her own fingertip. "You look like a fairy." She flashed a quick grin. "I always thought you did, anyway, but now you've got the glow to go with it."

Taya scoffed out a laugh. "That's not true—"

"Taya!"

Pilar was pushing Quardi toward them, but he struggled in his wheelchair as if to get out and walk, and somehow Taya found the energy to run to him, crouching down and throwing her arms around his shoulders.

"We're both safe and well." She struggled to hold back her tears as she felt hot tears on Quardi's cheeks. "You can't get rid of me that easily."

He didn't chuckle at her joke. He hugged her as fiercely as Kas had done.

"Taya and Min need to eat, Quardi, and drink more water. They've had nothing since they disappeared." Kas put a hand on her shoulder, although Taya noticed he still had his other arm around Min.

"We had more water than we wanted sometime in the middle of it," Min said quietly, "but not since we started walking back this morning."

Quardi gave Taya a last squeeze and let her up. "You've had some adventures, then?" Like Noor he touched her hand and then stared at the transfer of luminescence to his own fingertips.

"So have you, by the looks of things," Taya said. "We hoped the only trouble would be to Ketl. But it looks like everyone suffered."

"Oh, some of it fell on Ketl's side." Kas said, and there was grim satisfaction in his voice. "Ketl's been tied up."

EVERYONE INSISTED she and Min tell their story first, so they took turns describing the cave, the underground river, and the thick seam of shadow ore.

Almost everyone from Pan Nuk who worked the day shift sat around them by the fire as they ate bread and plump roasted bobber.

"You think the pole and dish on the hill is a beacon?" Pilar asked.

"It seemed to be facing upward, and moving slowly, as if keeping track of something in the sky. The only thing I can think it could be for is keeping in touch with the big ship where the sky raiders go at night." Taya shrugged. "It's just a guess, but it reminded me of the West Lathor towers in the mountains and through the foothills, to communicate with Juli and Gara."

"And you left a pile of shadow ore near the mine site?" Quardi still kept reaching out to touch her, but he was calmer now.

"As much as we could easily carry. But it'll be hard to get, because they know where everyone is supposed to be when we're at the mine."

"We'll think of something. It's more than we had before." Kas offered her a plate of sliced apples, and she took a few to nibble on, even though she was full.

"What about you, now?" Min asked softly. "What happened here?"

"When Kas realized you were gone, which was when we were gathered after the shift, waiting for the transporter, he went straight to the guard." Noor was sitting between Pilar's legs, and she leaned back against him. "They hadn't realized anyone was missing, and I think that was because they weren't paying attention. They couldn't find you, and Kas started pointing at Ketl, blaming him."

"I saw the side tunnel had collapsed," Kas said, and Taya could hear the residual fear in his voice, "and I suddenly wondered if that's where you were. I tried to go back into the mine to look, but they wouldn't let me. They couldn't go with me, and they didn't want me going off on my own, looking for you."

"What happened?"

"They forced us onto the transporter, holding their weapons on us. And all that time, Ketl was smirking." Noor's voice shook a little, as if still angry at the thought.

"As soon as the door closed, and we took off, I asked the Kardanx if they were going to stand by him and protect him, or not." Kas sounded calm enough now, but Taya guessed it hadn't been like that at all.

"They didn't want to," Harvi murmured. He was one of the many levik farmers from Pan Nuk. "I could see they were tired of him and the trouble he keeps causing. But they also felt they had to support their fellow Kardanx."

"So what happened?" Min asked.

"We fought." Both Harvi's adult sons spoke together. One had a swollen lip, the other a swollen cheek. They grinned at each other.

"They fought," Noor confirmed, raised an arm and rubbed it with a wince. "*We* fought. Although at first, I tried to keep out of the way, but when we saw our chance, a few of the women and I banded together and dragged one of the men off Kas. They were just piled on top of him." She said it with contempt.

"When we landed, the guards were waiting, expecting trouble, so I think I'm right about them being able to see what's happening inside the transporter." Kas put a piece of apple absentmindedly in his mouth. "But we didn't even acknowledge them, let alone listen to them. The fight just rolled down the ramp. It was mayhem."

He looked grim, but there was something in his expression that Taya caught.

"You enjoyed it, didn't you?" she accused.

"Can't blame a man for having a bit of fun while swinging his fists," Quardi said, with a low chuckle. "We've had to play nice under very hard circumstances for a long time. This was the pressure valve release."

Taya realized Quardi had some bumps and bruises, too. She shook her head.

"Then what happened?"

"They didn't let it go on too long. That's why most of the camp's still standing." Noor shuffled until she was more comfortable against Pilar. "They shot Ketl."

"What?" Min leaned forward, mouth open in shock.

"They knew we were right. He's the only one who had anything against the two of you. When he went down, the fight went out of all of us."

"He's not dead, though? You said he was locked up?"

"No, they didn't kill him. They need him to work, don't they?" Harvi's laugh was bitter.

Kas nodded in Harvi's direction in agreement. "He was unconscious, then they dragged him to that short tree, the one on the Kardanx side of the camp, tied him with rope and left him there."

"They've let the Kardanx feed him, but they haven't said how long he's going to be there," Pilar said. "Probably not long. As Harvi says, they'll want him back at work."

"And the others?" Min asked.

"Others?" Kas asked.

"The ones who helped him." Taya said it hesitantly, because she didn't think they needed a new fight. "One, maybe two others."

Kas stood.

"Where are you going?" She grabbed his legs, she had no energy left in her to stand.

"To speak to Fayda. He's the elder they all seem to look to. Either he finds the men who helped Ketl, or we do."

He bent and pried her hands off his legs and was gone.

She started to rise, but Quardi lay a heavy hand on her shoulder. "Let him, love. He needs to do something. He didn't like feeling helpless. It's how we've been feeling since we were taken, but you going missing brought it home like nothing else."

"He'll get hurt."

"No. I think Fayda is tired of this mess. He'll find the men. He'll hand them over. They want to keep the peace as much as we do. There's enough to worry about without in-fighting."

"All right." She sighed. Used Quardi's wheelchair to pull herself to her feet.

"Where are you going?" Min asked.

"To wash the glow off, and then go to bed."

"Are you sure?" Noor tugged playfully at the hem of Taya's ruined tunic. "You're a handy lamp."

She smiled, then swiped her finger down her arm, reached down and drew the tip along Noor's forehead, leaving a streak of luminescence behind.

Noor's squawk of protest and the laughter of the group as Taya pulled Min to her feet and then staggered off toward the river, arm in arm, warmed her more than the fire and the food in her belly.

There could be no more biding time. The moment had come for escape.

TWENTY-FOUR

TIME WAS difficult to measure in the dim glow of the floor lights that had flickered to life after the big ship's door had closed.

He and Aidan had enough provisions each for at least a day, which took one worry away, and there was nothing Garek could do to speed things up, so he forced himself to relax.

He reached into his sack for the three letters from Taya he'd taken in Haret, the light coming from the cargo hold just enough to read by. He'd been strangely reluctant to read them before, and hadn't had the time, anyway, but now, with the chances of finding her much better, he pulled them out, and opened the first one.

He held it for a bit, rubbing it between his fingers, and eventually unfolded it.

Kas says even though it's your second year, the same rules apply as if it's your first. So letters aren't allowed. I simply can't accept that. It's a stupid rule to begin with, and even more stupid and cruel to be extended into the second year. I miss you. I want you here, or at least to be where you are, wherever that is. Your absence is an ache I cannot ease. I find myself wandering up to the meadow above the village and lying there, remembering.

Garek could hear her voice in his head, the low, husky sound of it. He closed his eyes, tipped his head back, and hated Gara just a little bit more.

When he opened his eyes again, he saw he'd scrunched the letter into a ball in his fist, and he carefully smoothed it out on his thigh and folded it again.

He opened the one he'd taken from the middle of the pile. The tone was cheerful and quiet, with a dry humor that was just exactly Taya, filling him in on everything that was happening in Pan Nuk in a way that made him long to be there, even though while he *had* been there, his only reason for it was Taya herself. Or so he'd always thought.

He'd always known she worked hard, but reading between the lines of the letter, she'd used his absence to throw herself into the small business she'd begun to build up just before he'd left. At the time of writing, she had discovered a way to make a new shade of green, and she was excited about it, talking about the technicalities with him as if they were sitting together at the end of a long day, discussing their work.

He hesitated before he unfolded the third one.

It was the last letter she'd written before she'd been taken by the sky raiders.

He turned the letter over in his hands, and then went very still when he saw the crinkles where splashes of water had fallen on the paper.

Taya had cried writing this letter.

He unfolded it slowly, and braced himself. Despite what Luca had told him, Taya could easily have decided it was time to move on. That she couldn't live with the heartache any more.

I'll tell you a secret. I don't think you're getting these letters. If you were, you'd find a way to reply. I know you well enough to know that, although I have a terrible feeling, as the months slip by and it's been close to two years since you kissed me goodbye, that I don't know you as well as I used to.

Change is inevitable.

I've changed, too. But however much Kas might wish it were otherwise, your place in my heart seems to grow bigger, not smaller.

I think of you, and my heart pounds just as hard as it did when we used to sneak up to the meadow above Pan Nuk.

I believe that even if you aren't getting my letters, you would find a way to let me know if I'm no longer the one for you. You told me I'm your world the day you left for Garamundo, and I believed you. I'll keep believing until I hear otherwise.

I love you, Garek, and there are less than three months until your second year is up.

If you don't come home then, I am coming to you.

Garek slumped back. His hands were shaking, and he was glad he was alone in the capsule, that Aidan wasn't a witness to this moment.

It shook him and soothed him all at once.

He folded the letter and put it with the others back in the satchel as carefully as if it were a precious jewel. The need to hide it, to keep it safe, was instinctive. It felt like he was safeguarding his heart.

He'd always thought he was lucky to have Taya. Now he knew he was the luckiest bastard alive.

She wouldn't have had to come to him, the idea was almost ludicrous, but that she had any doubt about it was something he wanted to wipe away completely.

Not even sky raiders could stop him.

Which brought him back to the present.

No sky raider had come into the cargo hold since they'd taken off.

Garek debated with himself about getting out and exploring.

He had gotten this far, he didn't want to do anything to jeopardize finding Taya, but he was also uneasy that they had no idea where they were going and what was in the cargo hold with them.

Eventually he decided it was worth the risk and drew all the air to him, creating another bubble before he opened the lid on the strange walking machine he was in and dropped to the ground.

He looked toward Aidan's machine, gave the guard signal for all was well, forefinger and thumb forming a V, the other three fingers bent.

He walked down the line of crates, interested to see nothing was in any sort of order. Crates of silk were on top of crates containing kettles, irons and spades, which were next to shoes.

As if the sky raiders had not bothered to work out what was what, and didn't care, either way.

Further down the line he found food; root vegetables, flour, and spices.

At the very back there was a large container, as big as some of the shepherd huts on the levik farms around Pan Nuk, and Garek decided to risk another minute of his diminishing air and open the door.

He pulled down on a large handle and it swung open.

Garek was enveloped in a cloud of cold air, the swirl of cloud obscuring his vision momentarily, and when it cleared, he saw fruit, meat, and bread, even pastries, stacked in the cool space.

It was like a cold store, dug beneath a house, only the cold didn't come from being below-ground or because of ice blocks, but from some mechanical method.

He was so amazed, it took him a moment to realize something was making a noise; a loud, repetitive beeping.

He heard the sound of voices coming from behind the container, and closed the door, running to his machine.

He had just gotten the lid closed when two sky raiders walked into view, talking to each other, neither looking particularly worried.

They checked the ice box door, found it closed, and looked around for a few minutes, chatting as they did so.

Neither looked armed and neither looked particularly alert.

They couldn't conceive of any real threat, he realized.

They had written off the people of Barit as no danger to them, and they must have control of these skies, or be the only race with access to their technology.

They were smug in their own superiority.

He sat quietly, watching them as they completed their inspection, walking past him and Aidan without a second look, and then eventually returning to the front of the ship.

Garek was close to hitting the button to raise the lid and climb out for a second time when he felt the vibration of the deck below his feet, a rumble that was more sensation than sound.

He felt the surge of adrenalin, the pure excitement of something about to happen, just as he always had when he'd been on patrol, walking the walls of Gara, and had spotted a sky craft.

Every sense sharpened, every muscle tensed.

The rumbling shook the crates, made the machine he was in shudder, and for a moment, he was worried he would tip over.

He had the sensation of dropping suddenly, his stomach left behind for a moment before it caught up again, and then the ship seemed to settle on the ground, almost like a bobber, settling into its nest.

The ramp dropped, and light flooded into the bay.

Garek craned his neck to see out.

There were some structures, a tent of some kind and what looked like a jousting flag flapping in a brisk wind.

Nothing happened for a good five minutes, and then men and women started walking up the ramp.

He stared.

Eli walked past him, picked up a crate, hefted it in his arms and then walked away.

Eli. Breathing the air normally. Walking free.

The five minute wait must have been to let the sky raider air out, and the Barit air in.

Garek allowed himself a moment to close his eyes and simply let the relief envelope him.

He had found them.

He waited, hand near the button to open the dome, gaze fixed outside to make sure there were no sky raiders to be seen, until Eli returned for another crate.

There were others, two women he didn't recognize, and four or five other men, but he let them come and go.

As soon as Eli walked past him again Garek opened up, dropped softly to the ground, hit the close button and then ran to Aidan's machine.

Eli's head had come up the moment the dome opened, eyes wide, but Garek put a finger to his lips.

Eli was a farmer, one of the many in Pan Nuk, and he'd always been big and strong, but now Garek saw his muscles were defined, his shoulders broader and bulkier than they'd ever been.

He had a sharper, harder look.

Eli slowed his step, looking over his shoulder and taking his time to get to the crates, but not stopping, which told Garek there was someone supervising the unloading.

He hit the button at the center of Aidan's machine and it opened, and Aidan jumped down.

Garek could tell he was holding his breath, just in case, and grinned.

"Breathe, princeling."

Aidan shot him a filthy look, and then caught Eli watching them.

"I don't know why I'm surprised to see you, Garek." Eli shot a quick look out the back of the bay, stepped forward and thumped Garek on the back and then pulled him into a bone-crushing hug.

He was far happier to see Garek than he'd ever been before.

"You always were a crazy bastard. Should have known you'd come for her."

"How do we get off unnoticed?" Garek asked, heart lifting at the mention of Taya, and Eli looked out again.

"I'll go first, trip and drop my crate." He picked up a crate, handed it to Aidan, then took another and shoved it at Garek. "Take these and wait for the guard's attention to swing to me. Deliver your load to the store, you'll see the others coming and going from it. Then hide behind it 'til I'm finished and can come for you."

He set aside a couple of other crates.

"What are you doing?"

"Finding something that won't be damaged if I drop it." Eli lifted the crate of shoes and turned, ready to walk back down again.

"Where is . . . ?" Garek found his throat was tight and speaking almost impossible.

"On day shift. She'll be back tonight."

She was alive. He would see her soon.

As if he could read Garek's face, Eli nudged his arm with an elbow before turning and walking away.

"She'll be just as happy to see you." He looked over his shoulder, giving Aidan a curious but friendly look, and then stepped aside for two of the men coming back up the ramp.

Garek watched him go.

"Come on, get moving." Aidan bumped him, and he forced himself to focus. The two men Eli had maneuvered around gave them both a startled look, and he simply nodded in greeting, then looked down at the crate in his arms.

He had the one with the kettles, irons and spades, he noticed, which surely also wouldn't have broken if dropped, but which was a lot heavier than shoes.

Aidan had already started walking and Garek picked up the pace to catch up. The air was strange here, different, and he realized he hadn't even asked Eli where they were.

Not that it mattered. It could be the shadow pits of Dethbarelle for all he cared. As long as Taya was here.

TWENTY-FIVE

THE STORE WAS a sturdy canvas tent, large and full, set up with a wooden platform made of old crates inside so nothing rested directly on the ground.

The two women who'd been ahead of Eli stepped out and then stopped at the sight of them. Their eyes were as wide as the men's had been, but they said nothing either, their gaze flicking to the guard who stood, grim and massive in his mechanical machine, above Eli on his knees, throwing shoes back into his crate.

Aidan nodded politely and stepped out of their way, and Garek belatedly did the same, allowing the women to edge past them and head back toward the transporter.

He ducked into the gloom of the tent, found a place for his crate and waited for Aidan to do the same. Then he walked to the back and rolled under the canvas, coming up in a crouch amongst a small village of tents and shanty houses, built out of anything the prisoners could use for cover and protection from the elements.

The jaunty flag he'd seen earlier snapped and flapped in the cold wind above a white and red tent that dominated the other structures, sitting in the middle like some kind of temporary town hall.

Aidan joined him, but when Garek looked over at him, he wasn't taking in the small, makeshift town. His gaze was fixed upward.

"Look," he said, pointing, and Garek tipped back his head.

Froze.

A planet hung above them, white and blue, with a tiny white crescent beside it. The crescent had a strange shadow on it, one that Garek recognized. It was what distinguished Lanora, Barit's moon. Which meant he was looking at Barit. And that meant . . .

"We're on Shadow?" He breathed it out, in wonder and in disbelief.

"You certainly take me to exciting places," Aidan choked out. "When you're my head general, I hope this travel bug will have worked its way out of your system. Or you'll have West Lathor conquering the whole of Barit."

Garek shook his head, so stunned at the idea of where they were, it was easier to focus on Aidan's words instead. "Why would I want to be your head general?"

"Because you'd be very good at it, and West Lathor would be untouchable. No one would attack us if they knew they'd be facing you, and the other Illian states would finally stop looking at my father's domain as a good place to expand."

Garek considered it. "That logic has something to recommend it." He'd been prepared to run with Taya, but his instinct had always been to stay and fight. And Juli, the West Lathor capital, wasn't Gara. Was most likely better.

"But you're not the liege yet, princeling, and between the Gara town master and the guard master, I'm either marked for assassination or more forced conscription."

"You suspect this, or you know?" Aidan cocked his head to the side.

"When I got home and found out the sky raiders had taken my whole village—"

Aidan sucked in a breath at that, and Garek sneered at him. "You didn't know a whole village under your father's protection had been taken?"

Aidan shook his head, and Garek shrugged it off, there was no point in being angry about it now.

"When I found my village was gone, and I headed back to Gara to use the sky craft I'd brought down to look for them, I passed a whole party of guards headed in the direction I'd just come from."

"You think they were coming for you?"

"I know it. Utrel hates me, but the town master thinks he needs me. He tried to get me to sign up as a permanent guard before I left for home, but I told him I'd think about it. I hadn't seen my family for two years, and I just wanted to get back."

"Would you have gone back to Gara?"

Garek shook his head. "I'm no lapdog. I'd have refused to follow Utrel's orders sooner or later. He was already scared I'd take his job. I wasn't prepared to spend my time waiting for someone to try and push me off the wall. And besides . . ."

He didn't finish. He was going to say he would never bring Taya to Gara. And that he would never again be where she wasn't, but the thought of her was too big at the moment. It swallowed him up and made him completely mute.

For the last two months, as he'd walked the walls of Gara and looked up at Shadow, lit up like a second, enormous moon by the Star, Taya had been there, trapped. He'd been looking right at her, and hadn't even known she was gone.

"Ready?" Eli was suddenly beside them. "Follow me."

Garek rose smoothly, moving behind him in single file, and sensed when Aidan did the same.

Garek let himself slip into guard mode, looking around him as he walked, taking in the neat, innovative homes that had been constructed from whatever people could lay their hands on. There were no guards in mechanical suits to be seen. Just the one overseeing the unloading.

As he thought that, he heard the roar of the transporter take off behind them, and felt the brief sting of grit against the back of his neck as it blasted away.

"You came at a good time," Eli said.

"What do you mean?"

"Well," Eli rubbed the back of his neck, seemingly reluctant to clarify, and all of Garek's instincts went on alert.

"What, Eli?"

"Because yesterday, we thought we'd lost her. She was missing until last night. Gone over a day and a half. Kas was beside himself. I thought he was going to get himself killed. If you'd landed in the middle of that, things would have gone completely out of control."

Garek didn't contradict him. "But she's not missing anymore?"

"No, she and her friend found their way back safe and sound. Against the odds, by the sound of it."

"What happened?" He realized his hands were shaking, even though the danger had passed and he didn't even know the details. What would he have done if he'd gotten here and found he'd just missed her. That she was gone?

He shut down the direction of his thoughts.

"He happened." Eli stopped at a gap in the tents, and jerked his head in the direction of a man tied with rope to a tree.

There was deep anger in Eli's voice, and Garek stopped. Turned to stare. He could feel a Change building but it was off-center, wrong.

"No, no, no. None of that. No calling the Change. Come on now." Eli was standing in front of him, gripping his arm. "Hear the whole story, and hear it from Kas and Taya, before you throw your weight around here and disturb the hard-fought balance. All right?"

"There's a balance?" His voice was almost guttural, but he let go of the Change. Eli was right, he couldn't throw himself into a situation he didn't understand.

"Now there is. Since Kas spoke to the Kardanx elder last night. Sounds like they've got a couple of factions at play there, and I'm not sure the elder is even the one we should be dealing with, but it's a start. We've got enough on our hands without in-fighting."

"He's Kardanx?" Aidan spoke for the first time. His gaze was on the bound man, too.

"Yes. Half of the prisoners are Kardanx, half Illian. Only those from Pan Nuk are from West Lathor, though. The rest are from a village in Harven, except for five from Dartalia, caught on a journey through the mountains." Eli looked away from Garek at last and studied Aidan. "Who are you? One of Garek's friends in the Guard?"

"We walked the walls together," Aidan agreed with a nod. "I'm Aidan."

"Eli of Pan Nuk. Former levik farmer, turned slave to the sky raiders." Eli's face didn't show anything but guileless humor, but Garek saw his fists were clenched. He turned and started walking again, and with one last look at the Kardanx, Garek followed him again.

They worked their way along a narrow path cut between the dwellings, heading toward what sounded like a river.

Garek could hear it flowing, but then another sound caught his attention. Coming from the same direction as the rushing water was the ring of metal on metal. He stumbled on a tent peg and just managed not to grab Eli's shoulder to steady himself.

Eli moved to a wooden hut and crouched behind it, turned back and motioned them to do the same.

"Thought I'd bring you here so you know you can't approach him 'til the day shift returns." He pointed, and Garek saw a three-sided building tucked up against the curve of the river. It was surrounded by washing, snapping in the breeze, so the two men within the building appeared and disappeared from view as the sheets and clothing whipped about.

But there was no mistaking who they were.

His father sat in a strange chair with wheels attached, hefting his hammer as if he were back in the grange at Pan Nuk. Pilar stood beside him, the thin, lanky frame Garek recalled of the younger man gone. Now he had muscles. Like Eli's they were hard and sharp, and his shoulders had broadened.

Garek started to rise, and Eli put a hand on his shoulder. "Look."

Garek followed his finger, saw the guard standing so still, he'd almost disappeared into the background, blending in with the flapping white sheets.

"They always watch him. In case he makes a weapon."

Garek frowned. "Why's he sitting down while he works?"

"They broke his legs, the first day we went down the shafts. Quardi refused to work, and they made an example of him."

Beside him, Aidan sucked in a breath.

It was the first sign of violence they'd seen, and Garek had to admit even he'd felt more relaxed since they'd come to this open place. He'd expected a jail of some kind. Cages or locked doors. The small village, Eli's free run of the place, had made him forget this was a prison. It was just a very big one.

"Will he be all right?" Aidan was the one who asked the question, Garek was too busy studying the old man, looking for clues as to how he was holding up.

"He'll be all right. They fixed him up as soon as they realized how valuable he was to them. But it will be a few weeks yet before he's out of the chair."

"So what should we do?" Garek asked. His father lifted his head, looking around as if he could feel eyes on him, and then Pilar distracted him and he turned back to his work.

"I need to sleep. I'm on the night shift. I'll take you to Taya and Kas's shack, and you can wait for them there," Eli said.

Garek nodded, and Eli carefully backed away from the forge and led the way deeper into the left side of the camp.

Every step he took was one step closer to Taya.

Garek breathed in the strange air, and forced himself not to whoop with joy.

TWENTY-SIX

TAYA WALKED past the collapsed tunnel over and over through the day, and every time she did, she found herself trying to call a Change. Especially if she was on her way out, carrying a large rock rich in ore.

The feeling shuddered through her and she fought to keep it contained.

Someone had moved the rubble to one side, clearing the way to make it easier to navigate the passage to and from the ore face, but smears of blood were still visible on some of the rocks.

She knew they hadn't allowed Kas back in to look for her, so they didn't come from his hands. Ketl and his friends, perhaps?

She hadn't had a good look at Ketl when she'd left this morning, didn't know if he'd been injured while bringing the tunnel down. She'd looked across at where he was tied up, but he'd been too far away for her to notice details.

"We aren't all like Ketl, you know."

She turned her head.

A young man walked up the tunnel from the direction of the seam where the men were working. He was in the awkward stage between his teen years and adulthood, face streaked with dirt. He spoke with a thick Kardanx accent, but she could still understand him.

"No group is all the same," she conceded. "But it's hard to see that when you don't speak against him."

He looked back down the passage, where the sound of picks on rock echoed, and blew out a frustrated breath. "They're fools. They're so scared of the Illy, they acted without thinking, aligning themselves with someone who pushes the very edges of the Mother religion."

He said the words with contempt.

"Why are they scared of the Illy?" She hadn't known the Kardanx feared them. Couldn't think why they would.

"Because if it wasn't for the buffer of West Lathor, some of the other Illian states would already be testing our borders. As it is, we hear the other Illian lieges are looking to take West Lathor from your liege, given his weakened state, and then they will sweep into Kardai."

"The Illian Council has to agree to any change of borders within Illy. I haven't heard of any moves in that direction."

The youngster shrugged. "Perhaps because you are from West Lathor. Wouldn't you be the last to know if your state was going to be carved up?"

"Perhaps." She hoped he was wrong, but she knew the liege was failing in his duties to West Lathor. He had barely left Juli since his wife died. It was hoped his eldest, his daughter, Kalia, would take the throne, and step up as liege in her father's place. But instead, she'd chosen to leave for the south east with her handsome new husband, with his high cheek bones, tall, lanky frame, and skin so black, it shone with a blue sheen.

The sight of them coming down the palace steps on their wedding day had struck the crowd mute, so striking and beautiful were they, even though Kalia's mother's death still hung like a pall over the whole city.

When Taya had presented her wedding gift to the princess, she'd thought Kalia was barely living in the present. She wanted to be gone so badly, Taya guessed she would hardly remember any of the details of her own wedding.

"I can perhaps understand the people of Kardai's fear if they think an invasion is likely, but why would the Kardanx here on Shadow be afraid of us? We're in the same position as you are."

"Because of your witches." The boy looked at her in a way that told her he had seen what she'd done to Ketl the first time she'd called her Change. "There are recriminations back in Kardai these days over whose idea it was to kill off those who call the Change. No matter that the decision was made two hundred years ago, and those who made it are long dead. Questions are being asked about why we still stamp them out when we find them."

The rumble of rocks falling filtered up the tunnel and Taya turned, saw the boy did the same. They both held still until the shouts and calls of the men told Taya that everything was all right.

She blew out a breath, and forced her shoulders to relax.

"I've always wondered why the Kardai hate the Changed." She couldn't see how the Changed would be at odds with the Mother religion.

"You're not alone." His lips twisted in a wry smile. "It hasn't gone unnoticed that there are really only people from two villages on the Illian side of this camp, because the Illian Changed protected you from the sky raiders. The Kardanx here . . ." His shoulders hunched. "We are from everywhere. Major cities, small villages. The sky raiders took us with impunity. Some of the men spoke to those on your side before Ketl caused all this trouble, and they reported back that you were all from very remote villages. That your Changed patrolled the cities and the countryside, and forced the sky raiders away to easier pastures." He gave a bitter laugh. "We could do nothing but duck our heads and hope they didn't take us."

"Taya?" Min walked toward them from the outside. Taya knew she'd been here too long, if Min had already deposited her load and returned for more.

"Dom." Min inclined her head in greeting to the young man, and

Taya remembered the story Min had told her of the son who'd saved his mother from murder by his father's hands. She didn't think Min would show any other Kardanx man the same respect.

She looked at him again, with different eyes. "Are things beginning to get difficult on your side?" she asked him.

"Since Ketl tried to kill you . . ." There was the sound of footsteps from the end of the tunnel, and he turned away, the reaction nervous and afraid. He started walking toward the entrance but only took three steps before he stopped and looked over his shoulder. "Yes," he said. "Things are getting difficult."

Then he was gone, striding away to get water or whatever it was he'd originally left to do.

Taya realized she was still holding a rock thick with veins of shadow ore, and she hefted it up onto her hip. "There's a change in the air. Can you feel it?"

Min nodded. "But don't get your hopes up. Dom has his supporters, and he lives with his mother and the other women—he's seen as their protector. But he's too young to be a leader and too many of the men look at him and see their own shame and failure. They can't bear to even speak to him."

"If his fellow Kardanx won't listen to him, that's fine with me." Taya knew she sounded cold; she felt cold. "When we have a workable plan of escape, I'll go to him rather than deal with anyone else from that side."

Min gave a slow nod. "He'd at least be interested in cooperating with us."

Taya hefted her rock again and then headed for the entrance, all too aware she'd been down here too long.

She passed Dom coming back the other way as she stepped outside, but neither caught the other's eye.

There would be a time and place for that, and it wasn't under the watchful eye of the guard.

For now, she just needed to get through her shift. Tonight, they would plot and plan.

"TAYA." Eli walked down the ramp ahead of the rest of the night shift, his lips quirked in a grin.

"You look as happy as a tirn in a clear summer sky," she told him, smiling back, even though every muscle in her body seemed to ache.

"No, that will be you, in about fifteen minutes." He leaned in, hugging her close with one arm, his lips stopping just near her ear. "You will never believe—"

"You're holding up the change-over." The guard loomed over them both.

Eli's grip on her arm tightened for just a moment, although his face gave nothing of his fury away.

"Tell me later," Taya said, stepping out the way. She didn't want to cause trouble and have the guards watch her more carefully than usual.

"I will." He shook off the anger and as he walked toward the mine entrance, she saw laughter and a happiness in his eyes she hadn't seen since before they were taken. "Enjoy your evening, Taya."

She looked over at Kas, saw he was frowning at Eli's back.

"What was that about?" Kas waited until the last of the night shift had disembarked and they were walking up the ramp together.

"I don't know, but he's excited about something. There's something back at camp he thinks I'll be happy about." She could only guess a transporter had come in with supplies, and Eli had found something he knew she'd like.

They were silent as usual on the way home, but when she stepped out of the transporter into the camp ten minutes later, she found herself strangely reluctant to move.

Eli had seemed like his old self, bursting with mischief, and it made her long for the long summer days before Garek had left for Garamundo, when everything was full of possibility, and she was the happiest she had ever been.

She turned her head, looked over to where Ketl had been tied up, and found he was gone.

A chill ran through her, fear and anger woven together in a hard knot.

"You knew they'd let him go sooner or later." Kas stood beside the Stolen Store, face visibly hard even in the gloom as he also looked over at the empty tree. "I didn't see him come off the transporter at night shift, but he must have been given night shift duties, so he kept himself hidden in the crowd. Which suits us." He turned away and lifted the Store's flap. "It's full. The transporter did come today."

Taya forced herself to move, forced herself to shake off the strange sense of foreboding she had.

She followed Kas to their little hut. It was her habit to set out her towel, soap, and clothes on the crate outside the door before she left in the morning so she didn't track dust from the mine into their small space, and she scooped them up and headed off to the women's partition on the river bank.

Min was already there, and Noor, and they washed quickly in the chill wind.

"What did Eli have to say?" Noor asked, pulling a sunny yellow robe over her head. It had deep pleats, which showed a burnt umber when they parted, and she looked regal and beautiful. She could be a lady at the Juli court, rather than a farmer who made levik cheese for her living.

"He said there was something at camp that would make me very happy, and I think he must have had to unload the transporter when it came in after we left this morning because Kas said the Stolen Store is full. We can go look after dinner, see what he was talking about."

"We can go shopping." Min smiled as she wriggled into her green gown and then she and Noor waited for Taya to finish drying off and pull on her own clothes.

They walked to the line strung up near the forge, hanging the clothes they'd washed in the river, and then made their way to the fire, talking softly.

Taya tipped her head to one side, caught her hair and twisted it in her hands to squeeze more water out of it.

Usually, there was a low murmur of voices around the fire when everyone gathered for their meal. It was Quardi and Pilar's turn today, and because they worked in the camp, it was usually a more elaborate supper than anything the miners could rustle up.

With new provisions having come in, Taya would have expected even more noise as everyone tucked into whatever fresh produce had been delivered, but it was quiet.

She frowned, slowing her steps.

Noor and Min picked it up too, their feet slowing along with Taya's as they approached.

Twelve faces turned their way as they stepped into the fire's glow, and then it was as if the world fell away.

There was a face looking over at her; older, two years older, but still the same. Sharp cheekbones, dark eyes, dark hair cut short so when he called the air Change none of it would blow in his eyes. Stubble shadowed his jaw, stark against the bronze of his skin.

He stood, even broader in the shoulders than she remembered, his muscles heavier, the power of his frame evident.

And then she called out his name and ran, found herself swept up in air and flying, her feet off the ground as he opened his arms, and at last she was home.

She closed her arms around his neck, felt the scratch of his beard against her cheek as he buried his nose in the place where her neck met her shoulder and inhaled her scent.

She reared back, grabbing his face between her hands, and looked into his eyes.

"They took you too?" she breathed.

His eyes widened and he shook his head. "No," he whispered back. "They don't know I'm here. I've come to rescue you."

And then he moved his head forward the fraction he needed to for their lips to meet, and once again, the world fell away, and she was right where she was meant to be.

TWENTY-SEVEN

GAREK SWUNG Taya in his arms so that his back was to the avid, curious stares of the group, his body blocking her from view. Most were familiar, but some were new, and even those he knew had never truly approved of his pursuit of Taya.

She pressed her forehead to his and he felt the hot wash of her tears as they dripped down. For that alone he wanted to level this camp and slam every sky raider ship into the ground.

Her arms tightened around him, and careful not to crush her, he lifted her even higher so her feet were dangling off the ground.

She was thinner than she had been, more delicate, it seemed to him, but also stronger.

She laughed suddenly, leaning back a little to wipe away her tears and then stroked his cheek with her hand. "I am so happy."

He smiled back at her, his arm supporting her back, his fingers tangled in the hair at her nape, lost in looking at her, breathing her in.

Kas coughed discreetly behind them, and he decided that was progress, too. Kas had been anything but discreet at trying to keep them apart before.

Taya sighed but didn't try to get out of his arms, so he turned back with her still held tight and faced the crowd.

Aidan's face was almost comical in his astonishment.

Garek grinned at him. "You wanted to know why I behaved as I did in Gara? This is my higher power." He put Taya down gently.

For a moment, Aidan didn't get it, and then their conversation about Garek turning down offers of companionship from his fellow guards or the women of Gara came back to him and his eyes widened. Then he laughed ruefully, shaking his head.

Garek hesitated. He wanted to take Taya somewhere private, but he didn't know where was safe, and he knew he needed more information before he did anything.

Kas was looking at him with questions in his eyes, and pointed out a spare crate beside the fire.

Reluctantly, Garek clasped Taya's hand and walked to it. When he sat beside her, she snuggled up to him, leaning in so her head was on his shoulder, their arms looped around each other.

He didn't think he'd ever felt happier.

He was sorry Luca wasn't here with them. It would make the moment perfect.

He suddenly realized Kas would be worried about his son. "Luca is well."

"You've seen him?" Kas moved so fast, Garek was reminded that Kas could call the Change very well, too. He crouched in front of Garek, and Taya put her hand out, resting it on Kas's shoulder in support and sympathy. "Where is he?"

"In Haret. They've taken in everyone from Pan Nuk who wasn't stolen."

"The town master of Haret did that?" Taya sounded uncertain. "That's generous of him."

"No, it's what he owes Pan Nuk." Kas spoke almost viciously. "You spoke to him?" His eyes were wary now, as he held Garek's gaze.

"He told me Haret's lack of a strong Change guard was why I had to do two years. But he's right that Gara would have found some way to keep me, no matter what. Better Haret owed us the debt, and took everyone in."

Kas leaned back, gave a nod. "Quardi says you weren't captured." "That you found a way onto one of their ships and stowed away."

"He stole a sky craft which he'd previously brought down over Gara," Aidan said. "Then he flew us off Barit to the sky raiders' mothership and from there, found a way for us to get onboard the transporter coming here."

"That's truly amazing." Kas rubbed his face and Garek noticed his knuckles were swollen and abraded, like he'd been in a fight.

"I was motivated." Garek pressed his lips to the top of Taya's head.

Quardi laughed at that. "You make me proud, boy."

"And who are you?" Kas rose up and turned to look at Aidan as he walked back to his seat. "What was your role in this?"

"He's the liege's son. Aidan of Juli." Garek spoke before Aidan could pretend to be a simple guard again.

There was the sound of a few indrawn breaths, but Garek's attention was no longer on those around the fire, but on the small group of men who had come quietly through the camp from the Kardanx side and now stood just outside the fire's light.

Kas stood again. "Fayda?"

"Yes, it's me." A man stepped forward, flanked by two men on his right, one on his left. He looked like a Kardanx prayer man, and probably was. Not as old as Opik, more Quardi's age, in his late fifties. Young enough to still be considered useful to the sky raiders.

"We've found the two who helped . . ." Fayda's eyes flickered to Taya and then went back to Kas. "Helped Ketl. We let the sky raiders know."

"What's happened to them?" Kas asked.

"The sky raiders need them to mine, so my guess is they'll move them to night shift." Taya tilted her head to look up at Fayda.

He conceded her words with a nod. "The punishment for the two we brought to them is that they'll work straight through for a full day, today's day shift and now night shift, and then they'll be on night shift permanently. Ketl is also on night shift. They untied him and took him this evening. Those three won't cause more trouble with you."

"What trouble did they cause?" Garek asked.

"I'll tell you later." Taya caressed his hand where it was resting on her thigh.

"I was coming anyway, to tell you about the two who confessed to helping Ketl, but I would have come to find out about the two Illians who sneaked into camp today." Fayda nodded to Garek and to Aidan. "Two from our side saw them climb out of the sky raider guard machines in the transporter and then one from your camp created a distraction so they could disappear among the tents and shacks. Did I hear correctly that one of them is the son of an Illian liege?"

"You did," Aidan said.

One of the men to Fayda's right made a sound in his throat, as if he were going to spit phlegm. He angled his head to Fayda. "You tell us that Kardai is better, but here we are, taken whenever the sky raiders wanted more workers, forced to do unthinkable things, while the Illians have such good protection the sky raiders have to take them from remote villages. And when they are taken, the Illians don't just sit back and thank the Mother that at least *they* are safe, they send a warrior and the liege's own son after them." The man pointed up, jabbing his finger to where Barit hung in the sky. "They sent people from Barit all the way to Shadow. The people we live next to as neighbors. They managed something none of us could ever have dreamed of before the sky raiders came."

"Are you a warrior? One of the Changed the Illy use to protect themselves?" Fayda watched Garek, his face tired, his words heavy.

"We are called guards, but yes, I call the Change, and I walked the walls of Garamundo."

"And how did you do it? How did you get here?" The man on the left's voice was low and very intense.

"I brought down a sky craft when I was protecting the city. When

I learned that my home village had been taken, I worked out how to fly it and came looking."

"And why did the liege's son come with you?" Fayda turned to Aidan again.

"We take the loss of any West Lathorian seriously," Aidan said. "But a whole village? That was unacceptable to us."

There was silence, nothing but the crackle of the flames.

Garek resisted giving Aidan an incredulous look. He knew what the princeling was up to. Stirring the discontent that everyone around this fire would be deaf and blind not to realize was fomenting on the Kardai side, holding up West Lathor and the Illy as the model of good government.

"You have a plan to rescue your people?" The second man on Fayda's right spoke for the first time.

"We have some ideas. Right now, we're just greeting Garek, because he's been fighting the sky raiders for two years. Quardi is his father, and Taya is his intended, and none of us have seen him for a long time." Kas shifted, and Garek could see he was unwilling to promise the Kardanx anything yet.

"Will you factor the Kardanx into your plan?" Fayda asked. "Will you involve us?"

"We'll speak to Dom," Taya said.

There was another silence at that. Garek could see her words were not welcome, to Fayda at least.

Kas said nothing. He didn't contradict her, he simply watched her, letting her take the floor.

"Why him?"

"I think you know." Taya's eyes glittered in the light, and there was that angle to her jaw, that tilt to her head, that told Garek nothing would move her on this. She would dig in as deep as she had to, she would not change course.

Fayda stared at her, and something in her face must have made him realize arguing would be futile. He nodded.

"We'll come to you when we're ready," Kas said, and his words were not what the Kardanx wanted to hear. Garek could see them shift nervously.

They understood that they were being brushed off for the moment, and might never be included.

"We could make things difficult," the one on the left said.

"You could," Garek agreed reasonably, memorizing the man's face.

He seemed to understand the scrutiny was not a good thing and shuffled so that Fayda mostly blocked him from view.

Fayda gave him a furious look over his shoulder. "We will do nothing of the sort."

Kas nodded at him, Garek simply stared, blank-faced, and then the Kardanx turned and left.

There was silence as they waited for them to get out of hearing distance.

"Is what he said true?" Taya asked, looking over at Aidan. "About the liege caring we were taken?"

Garek barked out a laugh. "He didn't even know the whole of Pan Nuk had been taken until I told him this morning."

Everyone stared at Aidan.

The princeling looked ashamed for the first time since Garek had known him. "I don't think anyone but Garek could have conceived a plan as audacious as this one, but we should have known about Pan Nuk. Word was sent to Gara?"

Garek nodded. "The town master of Haret sent word. Not that Utrel passed it on to me. I had to find out when I came home to a deserted village."

"Well, that lie you told certainly stirred up trouble for Fayda." Kas said it in a way that told Garek he wasn't sure yet if that was to their benefit or not. "Why did you come, princeling, if you didn't even know what Garek was up to?"

"He jumped into the sky craft at the last minute, trying to stop me from taking it." Garek hugged Taya closer. "And even I didn't know how far this journey would take me. I simply followed the clues to Taya."

Taya turned her head to look at him, her eyes so full of warmth and delight he wanted to drown in them.

"Eat." Quardi rolled up to them, interrupting, holding out two plates piled with delicate fruits, warm bread and skewers of bobber roasted over the fire.

Taya took the plates, smiling at his father. "You must be as happy as I am, Quardi."

His father laughed. "Perhaps not quite as happy, but happy enough."

She passed a plate to Garek, kissing the side of his neck as she did so, and then settled back against him to eat.

"What was that for?" He realized his voice had gone guttural again.

"Because I can." She paused with one of the delicate green grapes from West Lathor held just in front of her lips. "We should eat." Her eyes conveyed mischief. "Then I'll show you the lay of the land."

The smile he sent back to her was hot and slow. He didn't think he could speak anymore, so he concentrated on eating.

Out of the corner of his eye he noticed Aidan watching him.

There was astonishment again on his face, as if he still couldn't get his mind around this new Garek he was seeing. But there was something else there, too.

If Garek were to guess, he'd have said it was envy.

TWENTY-EIGHT

ANTICIPATION MADE the reality all the sweeter.

Since Garek's arms had closed around her at the fireplace, Taya had imagined how it would be when they were alone.

Now they lay side by side on a piece of canvas spread over the patchy grass between the back wall of Quardi's forge and the river.

It was the most secluded place in camp.

She'd imagined a hot, passionate coming together as soon as they had some privacy, but instead they both lay still, arms and legs entwined. Her hand gently smoothed over his chest, and his tangled in her hair.

She looked upward, at where Barit hung above them in the sky, a shining reminder of how far he'd come for her.

"I didn't get any of your letters." Garek's voice was a low rumble against her palm.

"I guessed that." She felt a brief, hot fury at Kas, but that faded as soon as it rose up. "I didn't get the scarf you sent. Well, I did, but Kas didn't tell me it was from you."

"Who did he say it was from?" She felt the tension in him under her palm.

"He said he bought it from a trader coming over the pass."

Garek relaxed again. "I got the clothes you made me. Whoever delivered them told me my father had sent them, but I knew better."

There was a smile in his voice.

She smiled, too.

A thought occurred to her. "If you didn't get the letters, how did you know about them?"

"Luca told me when I got home. I took three. One of the first, one from the middle, and the last one. I read them on the way here."

She turned, found him watching her with an intensity that sent a shiver through her.

"I missed you more than I ever thought possible."

His words cut straight to her heart and she wriggled, going up on her elbow to lean forward and brush her lips against his. Her hair fell in a curtain around them. "To me, it felt like a wound I couldn't heal from."

He slid his palms up to cup her face and angled his lips over hers.

Heat washed over her, making her limbs tremble and her heart stutter, and then they were pushing at each other's clothes, desperate for each other. As she raised her hands to help him pull her dress over her head, Taya didn't feel the chill of the night air, she was surrounded by Garek, his skin hot and smooth under her fingertips.

He caught her sighs in drugging kisses and she caught his groans the same way.

They had been too long without each other and every touch, every caress made them burn faster, like a pyre doused with oil.

His hands and tongue, the thrust of his body, brought her to a shuddering, gasping release faster than she wanted, and his came right on the heels of her own. But afterward, as she lay against him, soaking in the heat of him and letting herself float on the happiness having him back brought her, just the smoothing of Garek's hand up her side was enough to stir her desire again.

He rose up over her, calmer now, his lips following the line of her neck. He nipped at her collarbone with his teeth and she arched into him. Her hands traced the smooth skin over hard muscle on his back and they were both lost again, holding each other close, rocking a slow, tender rhythm to a deep, soul-clenching climax.

When they lay still again, sated and happy, Garek pulled her half onto him, so her thigh lay across both of his, her head on his chest. "I'll never let anyone separate me from you again."

He stroked down her back; long, languid caresses from her shoulder to the curve of her buttocks and she kissed his chest, listening to the steady thump of his heart.

"I'll never allow it, either."

They lay quietly, but she could tell he was as awake as she was. She was just happy to be holding him again, but she knew the moment his mind turned from the beauty of the moment to other things.

"Was this what the Kardanx did to you?" Garek's voice was calm, but when she lifted her head, she saw the steady burn of rage in his eyes as he noticed the healing scrapes on her side.

"In a way." She kissed the tip of his chin. "But I managed to do my own rescuing. Well, Kas got him tied up, but between Min and I, we saved ourselves."

He held her gaze for a moment, and then relaxed again. Nodded. "I still want to know."

"Do you know much about the Mother religion?"

Garek shifted beneath her carefully. "A little. There's a small community of Kardanx living in Gara."

"Well, one of the passages in the Guardian is about protecting women at all costs. Even if you have to kill them to save them from torture or dishonor."

Garek's eyebrows rose. "He tried to kill you? To save you?"

"No. Well, yes, he tried to kill me, but not because of that. What I'm trying to say is that you'll notice tomorrow that the Kardanx here are mostly men. Only six women were spared, one because her son saved her from his father."

"Dom?" Garek guessed.

She smiled at him, because despite two years apart, he still knew her so well. "Yes. Dom. But the point is there aren't many women on the Kardanx side, so Ketl tried to grab Jerilia one evening. Kas and some of the others tried to get her back, and I persuaded the sky raiders to intervene."

"They stopped him?" He sounded surprised.

"I told them it would slow down production, so yes, they stopped him. He didn't like it. Then later the same day, the sky raiders insisted that the Kardanx and the Illy keep to their sides of the camp, and Min chose to join the Illy. Her father was Illian and she calls the water Change, so she was in constant danger on the Kardanx side. Ketl didn't like that, either, and again, I managed to get the sky raiders to stop him."

"Taya." Garek lifted her chin and she realized his fingers were shaking.

"I know, I'll drive you to an early grave. Kas already gave me the lecture, but I wouldn't let Min go back against her will."

"So then Ketl came after you."

"Yes." She could feel his distress and she ran her fingers through his close-cropped hair. "Except, I had a surprise in store for him. Ever since we've been working the mines I've felt sick, and Kas said he was sure I was calling the Change."

Garek went still under her.

"I know." She gave him a small smile. "A little late in life to discover it, but it's the shadow ore. The thing the sky raiders need us to get for them. It must be buried too deep on Barit for me to ever have sensed it. Here, I'm covered in its dust, having to haul rocks rich with it. I was feeling so sick, so disoriented, and then Ketl attacked me and Min, and I dropped the rock I was carrying, and suddenly, I had control of the ore. I used it to hurt him."

"How badly?"

The eager way he said it, she understood he hoped it was very badly.

"I pinned his body to the rock with the ore."

He made a hum of appreciation, and she couldn't help the low laugh that escaped.

"Your father smelted some for me the next day, and so now I have some needles of it." Her hair band was outside the door of her room, but she could show him later.

"But even though Kas warned the Kardanx to keep Ketl in check, he was too humiliated by our confrontation to leave it alone. Two days ago, he and two others grabbed Min and me and threw us down a side shaft and then collapsed the tunnel entrance on us."

"They had to dig you out?" Garek's hand was on her upper arm now, holding her like someone was about to rip her away.

"There are so many collapsed tunnels, no one noticed. Kas realized we were gone when it was time to go home. By then, Min and I had found another way out, but it took us a long way underground and we had to sleep in a cave full of shadow ore, and then spend almost a full day after that walking back."

He was quiet for a while, his arm tightening around her, pulling her even closer. "I'm not Kas," he said at last.

She nuzzled him. "I know."

"Don't try to downplay things, then."

Surprise kept her silent for a beat. "You have changed."

He would never have called her on that before.

"Taya." He sounded implacable.

She sighed. "It was dark and dangerous, we were attacked by strange creatures, and if Min hadn't been able to call the water Change, we'd have drowned."

He kept his strokes light, but she lifted her head again, saw the way his jaw was clenched.

"And he'll be free to wander around from tomorrow?"

"I think so. Now we've broken through to the ore, they're pushing as hard as they can to get as much as possible. They need strong backs like his and the two who helped him."

He thought about it. "They're on some kind of schedule, do you think? They've got some kind of time limit?"

"It could be. But if they do, I don't know why. It could be anything." She'd wondered before if they had a deadline of some kind, or whether the sky raiders were simply worried about the atmospheric damage being done to their equipment and wanted to get what they needed and get out as quickly as possible. "I don't even know how they plan to transport the ore, it messes up their systems so badly."

Garek lifted up on an elbow, looked down at her. "You've worked that into your escape plan?"

"Quardi told you about it?"

He shook his head. "I know you and Kas. You've got a plan."

She nodded. "We have. You don't think I wasn't trying to get back to you just as much as you wanted to get back to me?"

He smiled. "I know you were."

She felt the tears suddenly flood her eyes, and couldn't do anything about them. "I can't tell you how many times I wished you were here. Not to save me, just to be with me. Because it hurts to not have you in my life."

He lifted a fingertip, brushed a tear away. The look on his face made her go still.

"You look like you want to commit murder." She tried a wobbly smile.

He kissed her cheek where the tear had been. "That is because I do."

TWENTY-NINE

GAREK DIDN'T KNOW where Kas and Aidan ended up spending the night, and he didn't care. He was just happy they'd left Kas and Taya's hut to Taya and himself.

It wasn't something Kas would ever have permitted when he and Taya had been together before he went to Gara, but there had been a shift of power between the siblings.

Taya was an equal partner to Kas now, and he'd obviously decided he no longer had the right to act as if he were her father, although he'd taken that role since their parents and Kas's wife had been killed in a rockfall walking over the pass when Taya was fourteen and Luca had been four.

Garek had slept lightly, holding her close on her soft bed, and was awake to hear the camp stir to life, as the occupants got ready for another day down the sky raider's mine.

He swallowed his anger at the thought of Taya being used as a slave, knowing the best revenge would be the destruction of the sky raider base, and the rescue of all the workers.

She stirred, and he rose up on his elbow to look down at her.

"Now this is the way I like waking up."

He grinned at her, but the sound of someone outside had him rolling to his feet.

"Taya?"

It was Kas, and Garek stepped outside to greet him, closing the makeshift door behind him so Taya could change.

Kas was watching him steadily.

"Thank you." Garek knew last night could have been made much more difficult if Kas hadn't decided to play nice.

"She deserves to be happy. You make her happy." Kas shrugged.

"You didn't always feel that way." Garek kept his voice low.

"No." Kas shook his head, looked down. "I knew you were always the one as far as she was concerned, I just hoped she'd find someone else. Because everything about you screams trouble."

"I don't go looking for it." Garek was tired of hearing how he was trouble, when he made every effort to stay away from it.

"No." Kas gave a surprisingly friendly chuckle. "I don't suppose you do. You didn't choose to look like you do. And you didn't choose to be as talented about calling the Change. Still doesn't mean I'm thrilled about having you in the family."

"What does that even mean? What do I look like?"

"Like a warrior from the old tales." Taya stepped out, dressed in a plain shift that was clean, but had deeply ingrained stains that told him this was what she wore down the mines. She grinned as she shrugged into a coat that was a little too big, but that seemed warm enough to settle the worry and anger that rose up in him. "Kas wants my intended to be someone he can easily cower. Someone he can boss around. And he's always known that wasn't going to be you."

Kas gave her a sour look and stepped into the hut, closing the door behind him with a little more force than necessary.

Taya winked at Garek, and he felt the strange sensation of falling for her all over again, his heart stuttering in his chest at the way she pulled on boots in preparation to work as slave labor for an alien force with humor and mischief.

When she leaned forward and kissed him, he struggled to keep his touch light.

"So what are you going to do today?" She sat down on a log propped up against the shaky wall of the shack.

"I'll watch the sky raiders. See where their weaknesses are." That was one thing he was good at.

"Try to get some rest as well." Kas emerged, his clothes as rough and stained as Taya's. He'd always been strong, but now Garek could see almost every muscle defined in his arms. "It would be good if you and Aidan could sneak out of camp tonight, check out the signal tower Taya found when she was walking back from the cave."

Garek lifted a brow at Taya and she shrugged.

"We were so busy, I didn't have time to tell you about that." She suppressed a smile at Kas's scowl.

"We'll talk about it tonight, give you some provisions. I was wondering how one of us was going to go out and find it and still function on their shift, but you don't have that problem."

Garek nodded. "I'll make sure we rest this afternoon."

"Well, let's have breakfast," Taya looked upward. "The transporter will be here soon."

She slipped her hand into his and squeezed, and that's why he was smiling like a fool as she led him to the fire.

"IT MAKES ME A LITTLE SCARED, you know." Aidan crouched beside him behind one of the huts as the transporter landed with the returning night shift, the blast of grit spitting against the wood like rain against a tin roof.

"What does?"

"You, behaving like a real person."

Garek frowned at him and he grinned.

"I shared a room with your intended's brother last night. They obviously grow them taciturn and monosyllabic out Pan Nuk way."

Garek didn't understand his spike of anger at Aidan's words, nor his compulsion to react. "They also make them loyal to their own out there. If I'd been taken, Kas and Taya would have tried to get me back, too. If only the rulers of West Lathor could learn from their own citizens."

Aidan went quiet.

The sound of the transporter's engines faded into the distance, and Garek straightened, waiting for Eli.

If he knew the farmer, Eli would already have made it his business to watch the sky raiders while he could during his rest time.

"You have an uncanny knack of knowing exactly where to stick the knife in." Aidan's voice was low and angry. "I admit, my father has let West Lathor down, but he's not disloyal. Pan Nuk should not have slipped through the cracks, my father should have known about it, and you're right, having the Gara town master against us is no excuse, because we do have a spy in his office. Now, can we move on?"

Garek turned his head, gave a nod. "I won't bring up your tenuous hold of West Lathor again. Just be warned that you don't get automatic respect where we're concerned. Your father failing to be a good leader has endangered us all. I've seen what's going on in Gara over the last two years, and I know things are at a tipping point. Before, your father's Iron Guard made every other provincial leader think twice about making moves on West Lathor, but there are rumors that that's changing."

"That's because the Iron Guard has disbanded." The words were quiet.

Garek hid his shock and held Aidan's gaze. "We'll talk about that later." He heard footsteps heading their way and now wasn't the time to talk about the loss of a major strategic strength back home.

He needed to keep his concentration on getting them all out of this mess. The good thing was now he wasn't alone. He had Taya, Kas, his father, and people like Eli to help him. And they knew a lot more about this place than he did.

Eli walked past the shack, saw them and gave a quick nod. "It's my turn to make breakfast, we can talk while you help me."

Garek stepped in along side him, and Aidan took his other side, and they walked back to the cooking area that seemed to be the Pan Nuk meeting place.

He asked Eli about it.

"There's about thirty Pan Nukkers on the day shift, about ten on night shift. You'll recognize most of them when they finish washing up and come to eat."

"Where do the ones taken from Harven and Dartalia gather?" Aidan asked him.

Eli pointed to the right, but whatever place he was talking about was obscured by the shacks and huts. "It was unwieldy for us all to eat in one place, and hard for one or two to make food for so many, so we split up into two. We get along well enough, but ended up staying close to those we know."

"And on the Kardanx side?" Garek asked.

Eli shrugged. "They seem to have smaller groups, because they're not from just two places like we are, but all over. The women stick together, though. They only allow a few men into their circle from what I've seen. Dom, the one who saved his mother, and a few of his friends who support what he did."

"Some don't?" Aidan's voice was soft with surprise.

Eli shrugged. "If they do, then they're admitting they were wrong. That they shouldn't have murdered their wives and daughters."

There was silence as Eli crouched in front of a low cupboard set under a canopy to one side of the fireplace and pulled out the golden flat grains common to the north of West Lathor for making porridge, and handed the sack to Aidan. "Four cups of this into six cups of water into that pot should be enough."

Garek watched as Aidan took the sack as if he'd been asked to make porridge every day of his life, accepted the cup Eli handed him and went to grab the pot standing near the fire. As he walked off toward the river to get the water, Garek caught Eli's quick grin.

Grinned himself.

"Here, you can chop the fruit." Eli lifted out a large flat bowl of mixed fruit, and a wooden board, and Garek began peeling and chopping with the bluntest knife he'd ever used. He guessed that was deliberate on the sky raiders' part. Eli bent over a bowl where he mixed flour, oil and water into a thick paste for flat breads.

He sprinkled some strange seeds into the mixture and Garek took a few and sniffed them. The spicy, musky scent was good.

"Falimar. From down south. I'd heard about it, but never tasted it until I came to this Star forsaken place." Eli gave a flat laugh. "Ironic, really."

"You'll get back home," Garek told him. "We all will."

Eli sent him a sideways look. "I believe you, only because I know you'd cut out your own heart rather than fail Taya. I saw it from the start, which is why I've always thought Kas was wasting his time trying to get her to look elsewhere."

He used an empty bottle to roll the flat bread out, and then used the trivet which held a grate over the flames and slapped the dough down on it.

The smell that wafted up was so good, even though he'd already eaten, Garek realized he was hungry again. He tipped the fruit into the bowl Eli had slid his way.

When he turned toward Eli, he saw Hap and Lynal, frozen in their tracks, staring at him.

"Garek?" Hap stepped forward, uncertain and off-balance.

"Hap." He flicked his gaze to Lynal, gave a nod. He recalled Luca telling him both had tried to come calling for Taya during the second year he was away, thinking he'd given up on her.

He told himself he couldn't blame them for trying. If he'd been them, he'd have tried, too.

"How? Did they take you?" Hap stopped in front of him, bent his arm at the elbow, and Garek hooked his thumb around Hap's and clasped his hand.

"Eli didn't tell you?"

"Can't be sure they're not listening in at the mine, especially since Ketl threw Taya and Min down that shaft." Eli shrugged.

Hap took a step back. "You got here on your own?" He chanced a quick glance at Aidan, walking back from the river with the pot cradled in his arms.

"Brought down a sky craft, flew it up to the sky raider's main ship and then stowed away on a transporter to get here." Garek shrugged.

Lynal whistled. "I like Taya, but not that much."

Garek raised a brow. "And that's the difference between you and me, Lynal."

Eli gave him a sharp look, but relaxed when Garek didn't say anything more. "Play nice, boys. We all know Taya made her decision a long time ago, and even if Garek hadn't managed to defy all the rules and get up here, she'd still choose him over anyone else."

"True." Hap grinned, and clapped Garek on the arm. "Who's your friend?"

"Aidan of Juli." Aidan set the pot down by the fire.

"The liege's son?" Lynal frowned.

"We walked the walls together at Gara," Aidan said. "And now we're here to get you out."

Garek stared at him.

"Well," Aidan conceded, "Garek's here to get you out. I'm just along to help."

"No." Garek would have to put a muzzle on Aidan's mouth. "I'll admit I came to save Taya, but it looks like you've already got the workings of a plan to escape. I can help, because I don't work shifts and they don't know I'm here. So tell me where you think their daytime vulnerabilities are, and I'll spend the morning watching them to see what I can contribute."

Eli gave a slow nod. "That'll work."

It would have to, because Garek was getting Taya off this planet, no matter what.

THIRTY

NO ONE SPOKE much while they finished breakfast, and then Eli and the others went to wash and sleep.

Garek waited until the camp settled down into silence, the hammering and murmured conversation from his father's forge the only sound.

Aidan shadowed him, a quiet and easy companion.

They watched the guard standing over his father for a while, then angled their way through the shacks so they were looking at him face on.

"It's hard to say because of the tint in the glass, but he could be asleep in there for all he's doing." Aidan spoke for the first time.

Garek nodded. "Given they've only got two guards on the ground at the camp, you'd think he'd be moving around more, checking on my father but also doing a general sweep."

Eventually they slipped away, working their way to the Stolen Store and the open area where the transporters landed.

The lone guard stood absolutely still, his mechanical outer shell pointed in the direction the transporter went that morning.

As if he stood watching it go, and had forgotten to turn back to the camp.

"It's almost too tempting to think they're this lax, but they've been here for two months, and they think they have all the advantages."

"We're thinking like guards from the wall with sky raiders attacking daily. We're always on alert. They haven't had a serious threat in a long time, and the closest they've come to danger is when you slammed that sky craft down. And you're the only one to have ever done that, as far as I know."

Garek nodded, conceding the point. He and Aidan were both battle-ready and honed from months of attacks. These guards thought they were unassailable, with prisoners who had nowhere to run and no option but to toe the line.

They sat and watched the guard for another half an hour, and eventually he turned and moved closer to the Stolen Store, but seemed to hunker down as if he'd switched most of the machine off.

"Like we were in the back of the transporter," Garek decided. "Saving power."

He moved back from their position, slowly enough for Aidan to keep up with him, and then quietly made his way to the border between the Illy and the Kardanx camp.

Unlike the Illian side of camp, where everyone slept, men still walked around, talking loudly, or simply sat in front of their makeshift houses to soak up the light of the Star.

"It's like they don't want to sleep," Aidan said.

Garek shrugged. "Perhaps what they did to their women weighs on them in their dreams."

Aidan looked at him. "Do you really think they did that?"

"Didn't you understand that from last night? That's the reason there are only six women on the Kardanx side."

Aidan said nothing, and they settled in, watching a man walk listlessly between the shacks, with no clear destination.

"How can a society come back from that?" When Aidan eventually spoke, his throat sounded raw.

"Especially when they have the alternative, the Illian side, staring them in the face every day." Garek wondered how much that had affected them. Seeing the Illian women, if not happy with their situation, coping just like the men, strong and determined. And the six women from their own side doing the same.

"Are you going to include them in the escape?" Aidan shifted, turning with the man they were watching as he stumbled and then reached out a hand for balance against a wall, and simply stood with his head hanging.

"That's not my choice to make. Kas, Taya, and the others will need to decide. I don't think they're a stable, united group. When you told that whopping lie about caring what happened to Pan Nuk to stir them up, you were much more successful than I thought you'd be. They were very quick to criticize their prayer man. Something tells me that's not usual practice."

"Garek." Aidan drew in a deep breath, and then blew it out. "All right, you've every right to feel aggrieved by my father's poor grasp of the problems in West Lathor, and yes, I was lying to stir things up, but what I said *would* have been true if I'd known about it. My father would also have been appalled if he knew about Pan Nuk, I promise you."

Garek didn't respond. He watched the man eventually push away from the wall and disappear deeper into the Kardanx camp.

"I knew my parents loved each other, but I could never have believed my father would take my mother's death so hard. And my sister was the one who was supposed to be the next liege. She tried to take over when things started slipping, but it wasn't as if my father was dead. He kept insisting he was fine, that he could do it, so she was stuck, with no real power to act, but with the knowledge that things were getting worse. He started accusing her of trying to usurp him, when all she wanted was to keep things going, to make sure things didn't slide."

Garek turned and looked at him, saw he was leaning back in a crouch against a wall, looking above the roofs of the Kardanx camp to where Barit hung, white and gray, on the far horizon.

"When she met Prince Hasi at a diplomatic event a year ago, it was as if she fell in love at first sight. He seemed to feel the same. They were almost never apart from that moment, and my father made life so hard for her, the idea of returning to the south east with him, to work with him in ruling Baltar, was a good use of her education and training, and it put her with the man she loved, and away from the heartache of watching my father fall apart. From the unfairness of him blaming her for becoming what he had trained and encouraged her to be."

"But that left you alone to deal with the mess." Garek didn't blame the princess. It sounded as though she'd made the best choice she could.

"Yes." Aidan gave a half-laugh. "She felt a heavy weight of guilt for leaving me, but it is what it is. She stayed and tried to make it work for a year after she met Hasi, but eventually she conceded defeat. And in a way, she's carrying on the tradition of my mother. My mother was born a Nordren, she followed my father to West Lathor after he met her up north. She was the one who started the Iron Guard."

Garek leaned back with Aidan, enjoying the heat of the Star light on his face. "That reminds me. You say the Iron Guard has deserted your father?"

"They were never my father's men and women. They were my mother's. When she died, they continued on for a while, but my father's orders were either erratic or non-existent. Rose Hanson, the general in charge, brought my father an ultimatum while I was with him. She said they were not players for his amusement, they were a weapon to be used wisely and strategically. That they couldn't justify the recruitment process, bringing new babies in, was how she put it, under the current terms. That if he couldn't behave like the ruler my mother had been, the Guard were falling back on the signed agreement with my mother and leaving for the homes some of them hadn't seen in ten years."

"And your father's response didn't reassure them?"

Aidan shook his head.

"What does the Iron Guard do that's so special, though. Why wouldn't they have been home in so long?"

"I don't know. My father wouldn't discuss it." Aidan rubbed at his forehead. "I just know that the Iron Guard's reputation has made West Lathor safe for a long time. And now the whispers have started that it's disbanded, greedy eyes are looking our way."

Garek contemplated it for a while, letting the sounds of the camp settle around him, slowly getting quieter and quieter.

He wasn't sure when he sensed eyes on him, but he turned his head slightly, and saw a man in the shadows a few shacks away.

He rose to his feet in a fluid motion, and the man stepped out into the light.

Ketl. He recognized him as being the man tied to the tree yesterday.

Anticipation sang in his blood.

Aidan coughed quietly. "You're blurring, Garek. Stop calling the Change."

He tried to settle, but not that hard. He didn't want to settle. He wanted to feel the surge of anticipation and adrenalin he usually got before battle.

"You weren't on night shift, and you aren't on day shift," the Kardanx said. "How is that?"

"They don't know we're here. Didn't the prayer man tell you after they visited us last night?"

"I worked the night shift." Ketl scowled, and Garek felt the first touch of hope that there could be a compromise with the Kardanx. If they weren't even exchanging gossip with Ketl, then perhaps they had truly cast him out of their circle.

"How did you get here, then?"

Garek shrugged. "I brought down one of their sky craft and flew here."

"Why?"

"To rescue the woman you tried to kill."

Ketl stiffened, and Garek took a step forward.

"Just remember, we don't want to attract attention." Aidan spoke softly.

"Your woman needs to learn to keep her mouth shut."

Garek drew in a steady, even breath. "My woman is a person who's allowed to speak as much as anyone else."

"So, you're here to rescue her. Why wouldn't I run to the sky raiders about this?"

"Why would you cooperate with the enemy?" Garek slid another few steps closer.

"She did," Ketl spat. "She went straight to them."

Garek simply shrugged.

"You planning to rescue the rest of us, too, or is it just her?" Ketl's eyes narrowed.

"More than just her." Garek didn't know if they were taking the Kardanx, but he knew he didn't want to take this piece of garbage.

Something of his contempt must have shown on his face, because Ketl took a step forward into the open space between shacks, put his hands on either side of his mouth, and gave a shout.

"Guard!"

"Shit," Aidan swore behind him, but Garek ignored him.

He called the Change, ripping the air out of Ketl's lungs and forming a bubble around his head with air as thin as he could possibly make it.

Ketl's shout cut off, and his hands went to his throat.

"I hear the guard coming," Aidan whispered. "From behind us."

Ketl dropped to his knees, his face going red, his lips blue.

"You shouldn't have shouted." Garek crouched in from of him. "I didn't make it all the way from Barit to have my plans destroyed by you. I risked my life to save Taya, do you honestly think I wouldn't sacrifice yours?"

"Garek." Aidan had grabbed his arm, and was trying to drag him away.

He kept the air around Ketl's head thin as he let himself be pulled away. Aidan got him behind a shack just as the guard lumbered into the clearing.

Ketl was gasping and Garek gave another hard yank of air.

Aidan didn't speak, but he kept tugging and Garek allowed himself to be led away.

"Are you crazy?" Aidan pulled him to the hut closest to the river, so the sound of the running water drown out their conversation. "Why would you bring attention to us like that?"

"He threatened our escape plans." Garek raised his brows. "You saying I should have let him get us and probably everyone else killed?"

Aidan took a deep breath. "You're right." He loosened his shoulders. "But seeing him die like that, like that guard on the big ship . . ."

Garek put a hand on his arm. "He might not be dead. I'll need to go back to check."

"What are you going to do if he's alive?" Aidan asked.

"What do you think I *can* do?" Garek asked. "Do you think he'll suddenly decide to keep quiet?"

Aidan shook his head.

"That's what I think, too. So I'll finish the job."

THIRTY-ONE

TAYA DIDN'T KNOW HOW, but she knew Garek was watching her as she walked down the transporter's ramp. She forced herself not to look for him, just as she'd forced herself all day to present a calm, neutral facade, all the while hugging her joy close.

She bent her head and closed her eyes against the stinging, swirling dust as the ship took off behind her.

Kas and Min were walking, heads together, in front of her, and she slowed down even more, wondering where her lover could be hiding.

When an arm reached out from behind a wooden hut, she gripped the outstretched hand with a smile and swallowed the laugh of joy she felt as she was lifted up and swung around, set gently against a wall.

Kisses rained down on her eyes, her cheeks, and then stopped, so her eyes fluttered open and she saw Garek's lips hovering just over hers. He had shaved, and smelled of the spicy soap made from dala bark that Kas and Quardi used.

"My heart is too big for my body," she whispered to him, rubbing her lips against his smooth skin, and he made a sound like the groan of a steel girder before it collapses, and slanted his mouth over hers.

She tightened her hold around his waist, kissing him back.

When he drew back, she saw black smudges on his cheeks, rubbed off from her face to his, and she stopped him leaning in again with a hand against his chest.

"I'm making you dirty. And I really need to go clean up."

He eased back reluctantly and lifted up a small bag. "I've got the things you left outside the shack this morning. Let's go."

He took her hand and tugged her along, and she followed him, bemused. "This isn't the way to the women's wash area—"

"That's because you're not washing there tonight."

She let him lead her, happy to trust he knew what he was doing, and when he took her behind Quardi's forge, where she'd brought him the night before, her breathing sped up a little.

He moved a screen aside for her and then put it back in place when she'd stepped through.

He'd obviously already been here. Had set things up.

There were two screens, making the area completely private, and in the small area between the back wall of the forge and the river was one of the large basins Quardi used to cool the tools he created.

Steam rose up from it.

"A hot bath?" Her fingers tightened around his.

He smiled, pleased with her reaction. "I asked my father to heat some water for you, then I carried it back here when he finished for the day and the guard left."

This was beyond thoughtful.

She kicked off her boots and pulled off the filthy shift she was wearing. When she stepped knee deep into the hot water, she let out a gasp at the feel of the soaking heat on her poor feet.

She let her head drop back as she wiggled her toes, and then raised it again when she realized Garek had gone quiet.

He was staring at her.

"You are beautiful."

She saw the heat in his eyes, and felt a responding blossom of heat in her belly.

Suddenly shy, although she didn't know why, she crouched down and then sat, reacting to the sudden heat of the water with a shiver.

"You have soap?" she asked, her voice husky and low.

He lifted it out the bag he had set on the ground.

He walked toward her, and she realized they'd never been this intimate before.

They'd made love in the meadows above the village, they'd walked hand in hand down the street, had stolen kisses in doorways and in her garden, but last night was the first time they'd ever slept the night in each other's arms, and he had never been inside her bathroom while she bathed.

He moved around the basin and crouched behind her and she immersed herself completely in the water, coming up with her hair wet and sleek against her skull.

He seemed to hesitate a moment, as if he, too, suddenly realized how intimate this was, and so she reached back and drew his hands down to her head, and he began working the soap into her hair.

"That you did this, created this little piece of luxury for me, makes me love you even more, when I didn't think that was possible."

"It was my pleasure." He leaned forward, cheek pressed against hers, and she felt him smile. "Seeing you standing naked in the tub . . . That turned out to be just as much a gift for me as for you." She laughed softly as his hands worked the lather through her hair, firm and gentle, and then strayed down to her breasts.

And then, suddenly, she wanted out of the tub now, and into his arms. She rinsed her hair out and then took the soap from him so she could quickly finish.

When she stood and turned, water cascading off her, she saw he'd stepped back and taken off his clothes.

He was magnificent.

Strong—he'd always been strong—but in the last light of the day she could see the sleek muscles, the way he'd grown even more into his powerful frame in the two years he'd spent in the Guard.

Steam wafted off her skin, and everything felt hot, inside and out.

His hands shook as he stepped closer and lifted her out of the tub, let her body slide down his.

She reached down, gently closed her hand around his erection as he bent his head to her breast.

"I can't wait," she whispered, and she thought he might have muttered "Thank the Star" as he lifted her up against the wall of the forge.

Then neither of them spoke again, for a long time.

HIS FATHER HAD MADE excuses for them, something Garek never thought he'd see in his lifetime.

Certainly not when what he was excusing them for was the most incredible sex of Garek's life. Watching Taya as she'd stood, naked and uninhibited in that tub . . .

He had to concentrate on moving the food from his plate to his mouth, because that image kept wiping his thoughts clean of anything but the warm, sweet-smelling woman tucked up against his side.

He looked up and found Kas staring at him, hard-eyed. He stared back, and eventually Kas concentrated on his food.

After the small talk, everyone ate the meal in relative silence, anyway. They were tired and hungry, but there was a tension among them, too.

"You watched us land this evening?" Kas scraped the last scraps from his plate and set it down on the ground.

"Aidan and I wanted to see what the security protocols were so we know what we need to overcome if we're going to take the transporter for ourselves."

Taya lifted her head from his shoulder. "And?"

"And if they had protocols at the start, they're not bothering with them anymore."

"They think we've got nowhere to run. They seem to be unable to consider that we would take to the skies," Taya said.

"That's exactly it." He wound his hand in her wet hair and lifted it off her shoulders. "They don't understand their own impact on us. They've expanded our horizons with their existence and their technology, but it's like they're incapable of realizing that's given us new options."

"What else did you do?" Noor asked.

"We spent the morning checking the weaknesses Eli has already noticed, then ..." He rubbed a hand on his thigh, "then we had a run-in with Ketl."

There was a general intake of breath.

"He sought us out, and he threatened to tell the sky raiders I was here, that I planned to help you escape."

Kas's eyes glittered fury in the firelight, and beside him, Taya seemed to vibrate.

"He started shouting for the guard—"

Quardi sucked in a breath. "That's what that shout was?"

Garek nodded.

"We wondered." Pilar looked between him and Aidan. "Do you think he told the guard anything?"

"I think he would have. I killed him before he could."

There was silence.

"How?" Kas asked. "The day shift is off the hook, but if the sky raiders look for the perpetrator, some of the night shift might be under suspicion. If they decided to search—"

"I didn't lay a hand on him," Garek said.

"Then how?" Kas frowned.

"He sucked the air right out of his lungs." Aidan spoke with a calm he hadn't had earlier. "Garek did the right thing. That bastard was going to throw us all over the cliff, just to get petty revenge."

"I didn't realize you could suck the air out of someone's lungs," his father murmured.

Garek said nothing to that.

"So it'll look like a natural death?" Kas asked. "The fact that we haven't heard anything means that might be their conclusion."

"I hope so. The guard arrived while he was still alive, and I managed to draw more air from him while the guard was standing over him. It may have appeared to be a fit or seizure."

"That's good," Kas murmured. "That's actually very good. It was one of the reservations I had about sharing information with the Kardanx. Ketl was always going to be a problem."

There were nods around the circle, and Taya hugged him a little closer to her.

He looked down at her. "I went back to check if he was dead, and saw the guard carrying him away like a thing, not a person. I'd rather not have had to kill him."

"He was his own worst enemy," she said quietly. "There were so many times he could have chosen a different way, and yet he always took the most destructive path."

"Some people can't help themselves," Min said into the silence, and they watched the fire leap and dance for a while.

"So what now?" Quardi asked at last.

"Aidan and I will go check out the tower, as discussed."

"When are you leaving?" Taya's question was soft.

"As soon as everyone is asleep." He wanted more time with her, but he'd have all the time he wanted when they were safely back on Barit. He refused to even contemplate failure.

"You got supplies?" Kas asked and Garek nodded.

Quardi had closed the forge early today, telling the guard the tools he'd made needed to cool overnight before he could work them again, and he and Pilar had put together food and water for two days, just in case he and Aidan got lost or were delayed.

He'd also given them canvas to sleep on, and warm blankets to wrap themselves in at night.

"What are you going to do if it *is* a communications tower?" Kas asked. "Are we ready to make our move now?"

Garek had thought about it all day. "Taya says it took her and Min about four hours to walk from the tower to the mine. That's not insignificant, but it isn't that far, either. Unless an opportunity arises that we just can't turn down, I think we should simply find out as much about it as we can, come back and discuss it, and formulate our plan."

There were nods of agreement all around.

"Don't forget to bring back the shadow ore Min and I brought from the cave. It's near the mine site, and I'll tell you exactly where." Taya looked over at his father. "We'll need to find a way to transport it back home without sending the transporter's systems crazy. Maybe an iron box, or something? Because now that I've called the Change, I think I need it."

"We also need to talk about the Harven and Dartalians." Aidan leaned back on his elbows, his plate on his knees. "The way you speak, you're including them with you in a rescue."

Kas nodded. "They're our friends. We don't eat together, but that's more a logistical issue than anything else. We are friends in the mines, and that goes for the day and night shifts."

"Do they know what you're planning?" Garek asked.

Kas nodded. "I've discussed it with Luci, the town master of the Harven village that was taken. She also speaks for the Dartalians, because they were on their way to her village for trade when they were taken in the mountains. They know her and respect her."

"Does she know that the liege of Harven has plans to invade West Lathor?" Aidan asked.

His words were met with blank incomprehension.

"Invade?" Taya asked, and there was something in her voice that told Garek this wasn't the first time she'd heard this.

"What do you know?" Kas asked her, and Garek realized he'd also heard the change in tone.

Taya shrugged. "Dom told me, when I spoke to him in the mine. The rumor in Kardai is that West Lathor is no longer the buffer to invasion it used to be. That the liege," she shot a quick look at Aidan, "the liege's grief has caused the other Illian lieges to consider trying to expand into West Lathor, and when they do, the way to Kardai is open to them."

"That's . . . not good," Noor murmured.

"No." Kas eyed Aidan. "Are you saying we shouldn't help them because their liege wants to take advantage of your father's situation?"

Aidan shrugged. "No. They most likely have nothing to do with it, and may not even know what's being planned. However . . ."

He looked upward at Barit, and Garek could see the way his mind was working, as clear as if it were written on his forehead.

"You want to make sure the liege of Harven knows who rescued his people and how," he guessed.

Aidan looked at him, surprised. "Well, yes. And I was thinking along the lines of having as many people as possible in Harven witness their return. It would make it very difficult for their liege to advocate attacking us after we managed such an amazing rescue."

Taya laughed. "A neat solution, and one with no blood shed on either side. I like it."

"Me, too." Kas seemed thoughtful. "But that means we'll have to deliver them to the Harven capital, not their village."

"They may not be averse to that. They'll need help from the liege anyway, to get their village back on its feet again. All their leviks were taken, same as ours. Their homes will need repair." Pilar shrugged. "It's better for them to go straight to their liege."

"I'll sell it to Luci that way." Kas nodded. "And the Dartalians?"

"Same thing." Aidan smiled. "They're further from West Lathor, their liege is less likely to be involved, but at least she'll think twice about lending her support to another liege who wants to invade."

"What about the Kardanx?" Min asked. "We know we'll be taking our allies, but what about our enemies?"

"That depends." Garek didn't know if it was his place to say this, but everyone looked at him expectantly. "From a pure strategy point of view, you'd have to decide if they can listen to orders, if you trust them. And if we decided to do this quietly, with as few people as possible to maximize success, then I would say we leave them out of it."

"That's the thing," Min spoke, her voice quiet. "I don't trust them in general, but to get off this planet, to get back home, I think they'd do whatever they had to."

"Will they?" Taya was the one who spoke now. "Some of them are very conflicted about what they did to their women. And there are factions and power struggles within their camp that aren't in ours."

There was silence as they thought it through.

"What it comes down to," Noor said, "is could we look up into the sky at Shadow every day when we're safely back home, and be comfortable with having left them here."

"No," Taya whispered. She swallowed. "No."

"Perhaps what we need," Aidan said, "is two transporters. One for them, one for us, so we don't have to deal with them."

There was more silence. "We'd have to have two anyway, if we're taking them," Kas said at last. "One wouldn't be big enough for all of us. We'd need to steal one of the big provision ships Garek and Aidan arrived on for us all to go together."

"If we take two transporters," Garek looked over at the Kardanx side of the camp, "they can be responsible for themselves. I got the feeling last night they want to be more involved than simply being rescued."

"It's their pride," Min said. "But I would make it clear they need to follow our lead, or we'll leave them out."

"They came to us, asking in, so yes, they'll have to follow our lead, but I don't know if we can trust them to do that." Kas rubbed stiff fingers along his temples.

"Well, why don't we ask?" Garek wanted to go into the camp anyway, get a sense of what was happening, what the guards had told them about Ketl. "Nothing like the direct approach."

"Now?" Quardi seemed surprised.

"Best Garek and Aidan know now what type of plan we're considering before they head out to find that tower," Kas said.

Kas agreeing with him was so strange, Garek didn't say anything straight away.

"And if we can't trust them to help?" Quardi asked.

"Then we get both transporters by ourselves, and hand one over." Garek looked around the fire. "We have decided we have to help them leave, yes?"

Everyone nodded.

Garek stood. "Who's coming with me?"

Aidan stood, as Garek knew he would, and so did Kas. But when Taya did, Garek shook his head.

"Taya, no."

She angled her head up to look at him, and he saw shock, and hurt, in her eyes. "Yes."

"Why?" He couldn't see any benefit to it, and she would be putting herself in possible danger. "Aidan, Kas, and I all trained as guards. If things get ugly, we can fight our way out of there."

She was silent for a moment, looking down at the ground, and he thought he'd won the argument. Then she looked up, eyes narrowed, and he realized his mistake.

"I want to come because I have strong feelings about them. Because I've agreed to help save them when everything in me wants to leave them behind to rot, beside the women and Dom, and perhaps a few of his friends who've stood by him. I've already made some progress talking to Dom, the only man over that side worthy of the name. If he thinks the others won't cooperate, I'd rather he came over to our side with his mother and her friends, and we can save just them rather than risk us all dying here because of those bastards."

"That's true," Min said, standing and walking over to Taya's side. "She and Dom talked about it the day Garek arrived. I don't think he'd easily trust anyone else."

Garek looked over at Kas. He stood, arms crossed, face hard to read. "The Kardanx don't listen to women, usually. No matter what we all might think of that, it's their way."

"I don't care about their way," Taya said, her voice quiet. "I'm not trying to soothe their cultural feelings. We're saving them despite what they've done. They can accept it, or be left out, but they are the ones who will need to adjust, not us. Why should *I* pretend to be less to make *them* more compliant?"

Why indeed? Anyone who needed Taya to be less was a fool. "I just know you've never had to fight, Taya, and I want to keep you safe."

She looked at him, and he thought he was forgiven. "If they can't deal with me now, in this camp, how are they going to deal with me when we escape? If I'm not safe with them now, when will I be?" Taya tilted her head in query.

Kas blew out his breath. "Good point."

Garek reached over for her hand, brought it to his mouth. "Promise me you'll get behind me if things go wrong."

She had put on the headband he'd included in the things he'd taken from outside her door for her bath, and now she fiddled with it, pulling out a sharp-looking needle.

She threw it upward, but instead of falling it hovered in the air and then floated over to him, spinning lazily as it did.

He heard Aidan gasp and he jerked in surprise.

He'd forgotten.

In his defense, he'd only had one day to get used to the idea that she could call the Change.

He'd even nodded when she asked him to remember to bring the ore she'd found, but still hadn't thought about it in real terms, especially as his own Change was dampened here, not nearly as strong.

He lifted a finger in awe and touched the tip of the metal shard. Blood welled.

"Maybe," she said, "you should stay behind me."

THIRTY-TWO

KAS AND GAREK STRODE AHEAD, leaving Taya to walk behind them with Aidan of Juli.

Taya didn't recall him from his sister's wedding, but if he'd been walking the walls of Gara with Garek, that would explain it.

She used the time to take off her headband and pull out the shadow ore needles. She didn't think the Kardanx would be foolish enough to cause trouble, but then she couldn't believe most of what they'd done so far.

"You call an interesting Change," the princeling said, his eyes on the shadow ore in her hand.

She shrugged. "I would never have known it if I hadn't come here. If there is shadow ore on Barit, it's nowhere near Pan Nuk, or buried too deep below the ground."

"It makes you wonder, doesn't it? If we can all call a Change of some kind, and those of us who can't, simply haven't found our calling yet."

She nodded. "Finding myself able to do it this late in my life has made me think the same." She looked over at him. "But you must call

a Change already, surely? You wouldn't have walked the walls
without it."

He grimaced. "The water Change. But not as strong as Garek."

"Who is?" she asked softly.

"No one that I've met or heard of," he conceded.

"You should try to call the water Change here. The water is
different. Min calls it, too, and she can't do it as well here. It may be
the opposite for you."

He gave a nod and then she noticed his demeanor change as they
walked past the jousting tent and into the Kardanx camp. He went
from casual, almost laconic, to watchful and dangerous.

A man who hid behind a mask of irreverence and studied indif-
ference.

The Kardanx must have some system of keeping watch, because
she could hear the change in tone of the murmured conversations
around them.

They had been spotted.

Garek slowed, looked back at her, a quick glance to make sure she
was all right. He stopped and so did Kas, waiting until she and Aidan
were right beside them.

They were in an open space, a misshapen area onto which six or
seven doors opened, with a narrow walkway leading out to the main
cooking and washing area on the Kardanx side of the river's loop.

"Why are you here?" someone asked from the darkness.

Kas spoke for them. "We were invited."

There were murmurs, and then Fayda appeared.

"I'm pleased to see you. Come, let's talk by the fire."

Garek put a hand on Taya's shoulder, holding her back when she
was about to step forward. He studied the crowd.

"Please walk behind me." His face gave nothing away.

She hesitated, then nodded, moving behind him and letting him
lead the way.

Kas was ahead with Fayda, and Aidan brought up the rear.

Their positions spoke of distrust and suspicion, which she

supposed was fair enough. That was how things stood between the Illy and the Kardanx.

When they were free of the crowded huts and shacks, Taya saw the open area was similar to their own, except there were more fire pits, and each one was smaller.

Fayda led them to the biggest one in the center of the space, and indicated the low logs and crates they were using as seating.

No one, it turned out, wanted to sit.

"I don't see Dom," Taya said after a long moment of silence.

There was a mutter at her words, a low rumble, and Fayda turned to Kas.

"She speaks for you?" His voice held a challenge, as if Kas's masculinity was somehow on the line if he answered yes.

She laughed at the same time as Kas did. Fayda's eyes widened.

"You find it incomprehensible that an intelligent, brave, and loyal Illian would be tasked with speaking for us?" Aidan asked into the silence.

"They can't see past the fact that she is a woman to any of her attributes," a voice said from the darkness of the river bank, and then Dom stepped forward, dripping wet, as if he'd been in the river. "I hear you're looking for me?"

He looked like he'd been beaten. His cheek was swollen and his lip was split. But they hadn't had it all their way. His knuckles were bleeding, so he'd gotten some punches in.

Fayda blanched visibly at the sight of him. "Who beat him?" he asked, looking at the crowd that had formed around them.

No one said anything.

"This is a problem," Taya murmured.

"We thought you didn't want them talking to him," someone called to Fayda from the back of the crowd.

"I beat him." A man stepped forward, looking as rough as Dom, with a swollen cheek and a hand against his ribs.

"Dar-nagel . . ." Fayda shook his head, and there was a slump to his shoulders. "He is your *son*."

Taya watched the prayer man, sceptical about his every move, but she thought he might actually be genuinely saddened by this.

"What's your plan?" Dom ignored his father, looking at Taya instead.

"We are going to investigate something we think can help us escape. If it's what we think it is, we'll put a plan in place to steal two transporters, and leave."

"How will we fly the transporters?" someone called from the crowd.

"I'll show Dom how to do it," Garek spoke up. "So it would be to all your benefit if he is fit and able to be your pilot, because he's the only one I'm prepared to share the secret with."

"You're the one who flew here to rescue your village?" another man called.

"I am."

"And your companion is West Lathor's liege?"

"The liege's son," Aidan said.

There was the buzz of voices.

"What is it you are going to investigate?" The man who asked the question had been one of three who'd come with Fayda last night.

Taya shook her head. "That's not something we're prepared to share with you."

A number of men blinked at her, too astonished at her refusal to even respond.

"You don't trust us," Fayda said.

"No. Why should we?" Kas asked, looking from face to face in the crowd. "You have not been our friend, even far from home, with a common enemy."

"I'm surprised you're helping us at all. Why not just leave us behind?" one of the men asked, sarcasm heavy in his voice.

"We discussed that." Kas's words caused absolute silence. "You killed your women, which we find abhorrent. You tried to assault and then kill the women in our camp, which we find unforgivable. To all of us, they seem the acts of men who are morally bankrupt, who need to hurt or denigrate to make themselves feel strong. That an entire culture can accept this as perfectly reasonable is anathema to us. And yet, we've decided our consciences will not be easy if we leave you here. We've decided we will help you. But for our plan to work, we need people we can trust on our side, and we had doubts before coming here about your trustworthiness. With this recent attack on Dom, the one person you knew we were prepared to deal with, that has turned out to be a valid doubt. I'm not sure where we go from here."

"I don't know, either." Fayda sat down, crumpling like a limp rag.

"We don't have the same ideas on public and private life, but we are facing an enemy that cares nothing for either of us. Can't we put our differences aside for the time it takes to get free?" The man who spoke was another of the three who'd come last night.

"That's well said." Taya spoke up. She smiled at the speaker. "As long as you realize that it is *you* who will have to put your differences aside. Not us."

GAREK UNDERSTOOD why Taya was provoking them. She wanted to test how firm their commitment to cooperation would be.

But while he didn't think what she'd said was all that inflammatory—Kas had said much worse—the words were no sooner out of her mouth than the man lunged at her, hands out.

Garek reacted without thought, even though he wasn't as strong here as he was on Barit, he was still strong enough. He lifted the attacker up at least two feet, out of reach of Taya.

It was only after he'd lifted the man that he saw the shadow ore needles, hovering in what looked like a swarm at Taya's attacker's throat.

There was a moment of almost incomprehension as everyone processed what happened.

"She shouldn't have spoken like that," Fayda said, jumping to his feet, and Garek was so angry at his deflection of responsibility, implying the attack on Taya was her own fault instead of making his man take responsibility for his own actions, that he slammed Fayda back down.

The prayer man hit the log he'd been sitting on and then sprawled onto the ground as the momentum toppled him over.

"Where we come from, men take responsibility for their lack of control. We don't shift the blame to our victims."

There was a sharp intake of breath from some in the crowd, and Garek wondered how many had enough intelligence and insight to have understood this a long time ago, and had simply never spoken up.

Silence stretched out, and then, surprisingly, a stream of water, a single arc, as if from a spout, came from the direction of the river and hit Fayda in the face.

Garek noticed Taya looked sidelong at Aidan and then tried to suppress a smile.

Fayda coughed, struggling upright, and then dragged himself back on the log.

His eyes were fury itself.

Perhaps not the peace they had hoped to foster when they'd come over here. He also found it strange that no one had mentioned Ketl.

He'd thought about not bringing it up, but perhaps it was better to put it in the open as a lesson of how far he was prepared to go.

"Let him down," Fayda said at last.

"I'm waiting for something first." Garek looked at Taya, and she met his gaze and gave him a smile so true and pure, he lost his hold on her attacker for a moment, then grabbed him again.

From the looks around him, the Kardanx took that as an intimidation tactic, not the loss of concentration of a man in love.

He didn't set them straight.

"What is it you're waiting for?" one of the other men who'd come with Fayda last night asked. The one who'd verbally attacked his own prayer man.

"An apology, you idiot." Dom laughed. "Do you still not understand she is a valued member of their group, and neither she nor they will tolerate an attack on her?"

"I . . . apologize." Taya's attacker spoke to Garek, not Taya, so Garek turned him in the air, the shadow ore needles following the movement in a show of precision from Taya he was astonished and proud of, so that her attacker was facing her directly.

"Try that again," he suggested softly.

"I apologize." His voice was monotone, and most definitely not sincere.

The needles moved forward slowly and touched the man's skin without breaking it.

"I don't believe you," Taya said.

"You'll never get a genuine apology from him. He killed his own mother, his wife, and his three daughters in the name of the Mother religion. Saying sorry for a mere attempted assault is not something he's capable of." Dom's words fell like blows on the man. He flinched and closed his eyes.

Tired of it all, Garek dropped him without warning, and watched, entranced, as Taya's needles flew up and landed in her open palm.

"It seems you insist on making it easier and easier for us to leave you behind," he said. "It will be safer to leave you—the less people we have to move, the better."

"We will abide by your plans and rules. And Dom will not be touched again." The man who had argued with Fayda last night looked around at each face in the crowd, and Garek had the sense control had just been wrestled away from the prayer man. "You have my word. My name is Jona."

"Good." Garek caught his gaze. "You should know, I had a run-in with Ketl this morning."

A murmur swirled around the gathering like a breeze stirring leaves.

"Did you, now?" Jona's gaze didn't waver from his.

"He threatened to tell the sky raiders I was here and to reveal my rescue plans. And it wasn't just a threat. He actually called out to them." Garek broke eye contact with Jona and looked around. There wasn't a person who wasn't staring at him. "When he called them, I killed him."

Another murmur.

"I have traveled a long way, and put myself in danger every step of the way to get here and save my people. I would like you to realize that if anyone thinks to jeopardize that in any way, it will be the last thing they ever do."

"Ketl died of a seizure, he wasn't killed by you." The man who'd tried to hurt Taya had pulled himself to a sitting position, a sneer on his face.

"A seizure like this?" Garek asked. As he pulled the air from the man's lungs, as he watched him scrabble at his throat and then writhe on the floor, he wondered if he was going to stop.

Taya touched his arm, and to his surprise, he did let up.

The man choked and sobbed as he hauled in breath after breath.

"Warning received?" Garek's voice was quiet.

"Warning received." Jona's face was pale. "Who *are* you?"

"The future general of West Lathor, and the most powerful Changed in the history of the Illy," Aidan said, and Garek sent him a quick, frowning look.

"We'll let you know our plans in a few days, when we've found out what we need to know." Kas's voice seemed to cut through the tension, bringing everyone back to a semblance of calm. "Until then, carry on as usual."

Jona shook his head. "You have a warrior who can literally steal our breath. Nothing will ever be usual again."

THIRTY-THREE

GAREK HAD DRAWN Taya into a dark corner and kissed her goodbye until they were both breathless before he forced himself back to the fire place to gather up the provisions and equipment his father had assembled for them.

Leaving her when he'd only just found her again was a physical pain in his chest, making it hard to breathe.

He used leather straps to fashion rough backpacks for both himself and Aidan and then Aidan stood beside the river and compacted the water on the choppy surface into stepping circles so they could cross it without getting wet.

Everyone agreed that moving toward the mine and from there to the tower on the opposite side of the river was the safest way for them.

The sky raiders only ever patrolled the camp side.

Taya took his hand, eyes glittering with tears he could see she was determined would not fall, and squeezed. "Be careful."

He squeezed back. "You, too." He leant in for one last kiss and then glanced over her shoulder at Kas.

They exchanged a look.

It was the first time they had both been in accord when it came to Taya, and Garek couldn't help the quick grin that escaped. Kas would watch over her, with his life.

Kas raised his eyebrows in return, but Garek thought there might have been a hint of a smile on his lips, too.

Garek straightened and Aidan gestured with his hand to the water. Garek could just see the large circles of calm the princeling created, and he used them to run across the water.

Aidan did the same, and then, with a wave to everyone on the other side, they plunged into the darkness.

Garek had only gone a few steps when he realized he needed to have one last look over his shoulder.

Taya stood on the bank, silhouetted against the camp fire, as if standing watch.

She lifted up her hand, brought it to her lips, and, although she must think he was long gone, most certainly couldn't see him, she blew a kiss after him anyway before Kas drew her away.

Garek caught it in the air and pressed it to his heart before he turned back. And didn't care that Aidan had seen that.

"Was she your childhood sweetheart?" Aidan's voice sounded wistful.

Garek kept his attention on the ground in front of him.

Although it was flat, small, sturdy tufts of vegetation grew haphazardly across the landscape, tripping them up in the darkness. Their long, thin leaves were also sharp enough to cut skin.

"I've known her my whole life, but I wouldn't call her my childhood sweetheart." Garek remembered her as an adorable child, but he'd had little to do with her, considering her far too young to be interesting to play with. "She's two years younger than I am, and I was always big. Big enough to play with the older children."

"And her brother most likely steered her away from you." Now there was a teasing edge to Aidan's voice.

Garek snorted out a laugh. "Kas was town guard when I first called the Change. He moved on to town master later, and I took over town guard duty, but as part of my training, when I was eighteen, he sent me to work in all five of the towns in our region. He was right, I did learn a lot on how to be a good town guard by observing all the different methods of doing it, but I'm pretty sure he also did it because he thought Taya already had a soft spot for me."

"Did she?"

He had never told her, he wasn't sure why, that he'd always known who had put that pillow and blanket over him when he'd shown off as a cocky sixteen year old and collapsed in the street.

The sweet smell on the pillow beneath his cheek, the gentle touch of hands that tucked the blanket around him.

Oh, yes. He'd always known who it was.

"I'm not sure. She was always happy to see me, sweet and generous, but I think she was like that with everyone."

He thought of his two years in the various small towns near Pan Nuk.

He'd bedded his first women in those towns, relieved to experiment with people who hadn't toddled around with him since they could both walk.

And then he'd come home for good, as Kas's duties as town master made him too busy for him to be both guard master and town master. He'd called Garek back, and on that very first day, when he'd knocked on Kas's door and Taya had opened it, calling to Kas behind her, he had fallen irrevocably in love.

Thank the Stars, thank every single one of them, that she had fallen in love right back.

"I know now why you turned down any relationship with the women in Gara's guard, but how did you keep them so friendly with you after saying no?"

"Because, interestingly enough, they respect a man who's committed and faithful to his lover." He knew there was an edge of sarcasm in his voice, and he fought to rein it back. It wasn't for him to judge Aidan and his dizzying array of bed partners. "Also because when they were with me, they weren't subject to the harassment they received from Utrel and his chosen few. Another issue your father should know about and sort out."

The law of the Illy was clear. Since the Day of the Women almost one hundred and fifty years earlier, when every woman had put down her work, no matter what it was, and gathered silently for a full day in town squares across the country, refusing to do anything, grinding the entire country to a halt, the law had been unequivocal. Everyone was treated the same.

"I know it. I heard you threatening a few of the guards who took Utrel's harassment as an excuse to follow his lead. I sent a dispatch about it to Juli."

"And?"

Aidan shook his head. "Nothing." They walked for a good five minutes before he spoke again. "I'm going to have to overthrow my own father when we get back, aren't I?"

Garek thought he already should have done it, but then, he knew how complicated families could be.

"Yes."

THEY FOUND the tower just after the sun rose, almost walking straight past the steep hill in the half-light as they powered over the rough ground as fast as they could.

They'd skirted the mine site after midnight, moving beyond it quickly even though Garek would have liked to have gotten closer and seen more of it, how it all worked.

But it would not do to be seen by the transporter in the morning light, and so they used the darkness while they could.

It was the sound of the far-off roar of the transporter bringing the day shift that had pulled them from their focus on the ground. Garek had paused a moment and turned back to look, even though there was no way he could see it, and had spotted the hill to their right.

"You think that's it?" Aidan asked him.

"If it isn't, it's elevated so we can see what the alternatives are," Garek said.

They drank some water and shared some of the fruit Quardi had packed, and then set off, walking for another half hour before they reached it.

There were a few smooth rocks lying at the foot of the hill. They looked out of place, mottled thickly with veins of dark purple ore.

Shadow ore, Garek thought as he picked one up and smoothed his thumb over it.

He guessed they had been dropped by Min or Taya.

He put them carefully into his pack and then left it in the shade of a rock. Aidan did the same.

The climb was steep. They had to pull themselves up rocks by finding hand and footholds, but the morning air was still cool, and they reached the top in less than fifteen minutes.

And there was the tower.

It was made of metal similar to the stuff the sky craft he'd stolen from Gara was made of.

It had been here for a while by the look of it. Parts of it were rusted away almost completely, just as Taya had said.

To bring this down would be risk free.

No sky raider would think sabotage was at work for even a moment when they saw it.

The little gray dish at the top of the tower made a whirring sound and moved a little to one side, and Garek wondered what it was tracking, or doing.

He crouched to look at the little glass fronted box at the bottom, and saw the lights flickering behind it.

"When the dish moves, the lights dance around more energetically. When it's still, this one," he tapped the corner of the glass cover, "blinks at a steady rate, but as soon as it moves, look—"

He moved back so Aidan could see.

They stared at the lights, looking up and back down at the box a few times to confirm.

"What does that mean?" Aidan sat back on his heels, his gaze going upward.

"I think information is being sent when it moves." Garek felt like he was feeling his way. "I don't know what information, but they wouldn't have built this if they didn't need it, so when we're ready, we can bring it down, smash the box."

"And then?" Aidan leveled his gaze at him.

"Then they send someone to find out what's happened. My guess is a transporter with one of the guards in those suits."

Aidan tipped his head to one side. "And when we jump them?"

Garek smiled. "Well, we know how to open those suits, and the sky raiders can't breathe the air." He shrugged. "It will rid us of some of them, probably gain us a transporter."

"So, what now? We just leave things the way they are?"

"It didn't take us that long to get here. If we go back to the mine now, find those rocks for Taya, we could be back in camp before the day shift even finishes."

"We're eating something first," Aidan said.

"Sure." Garek rose up, led the way back down the hill.

"And don't think I don't know why you're in such a hurry to get back to camp by tonight." Aidan sounded distinctly grumpy.

"Wouldn't you rather be back at camp by nightfall? It'll be more comfortable."

"That's not why you're in such a rush," Aidan said.

Garek grinned. "When you worship a higher power, princeling, you worship a higher power."

"You're never going to let me forget that, are you?" Aidan muttered, but Garek could hear him chuckling all the way to the bottom.

THIRTY-FOUR

TAYA HAD HOPED Garek would be back by the end of day shift, but had forced herself not to expect it.

It made sitting in front of the fire now, with his arm pulling her close, all the more wonderful.

"That little box at the bottom lights up when the dish moves," Garek was saying. "We watched it for a while. I think when it does that, it's sending information somewhere. How, I don't know."

"So if you destroy it, they'll come looking. How quickly, I wonder?" Kas asked.

"If they don't come immediately, what will you do?" Luci, the town master of Cassinya, the Harven village that had been taken like Pan Nuk, sat with them. A short, dark man sat beside her, one of the Dartalian traders who had also been scooped up in the sky raiders' abduction.

"We wait until they do." Garek shrugged. "The plan is to kill whoever comes and take their sky craft, whatever that is. The rest of you will need to be ready when we return with it, to help us take the other one."

"And if the sky craft comes back, and you aren't in control of it?" The trader leaned forward, skepticism in every line.

"Then we're dead or couldn't risk jumping them, and you have to either wait for us to come back, or make a new plan." Garek was blunt.

The trader blinked. "You think they aren't going to ask some hard questions of us if they have to kill you out there?"

Garek said nothing for a beat. "Most likely they will. If you think there is such a thing as a risk free escape plan, you're living in a different world to me."

"Particularly," Taya kept her voice low, "as the ones taking the most risk in this plan are Garek and Aidan. Or would you like to wait at the tower and try to take the sky raiders instead?"

Luci shook her head, looked sidelong at her companion. "It's just the first time we've heard the details. We're trying to come to grips, that's all." She put a hand on the trader's shoulder. "Zek lost two friends in the raid, they jumped off the pass rather than be taken, and none of us want to see more deaths."

"What do you think is going to happen when they've got enough shadow ore?" Quardi asked. "You think they're going to bother taking us back home?"

Zek looked at his feet. "No. Forgive me. I didn't mean to suggest that some of us should carry no risk. We're all at risk, just being here. And what frightens me more than the sky raiders realizing we're trying to escape and harming us is the thought of what will happen when they leave us here. Because then, my prediction is that we'll be killing each other, near the end. Just to survive."

It was something that had crossed Taya's mind, too. In her imagination, the end was as ugly as could be.

"What happens if they send one of the small sky craft?" Pilar asked. "There won't be room for enough people on that."

"If that happens, we'll have to take it down and wait for them to wonder why it hasn't come back up, or isn't answering, or whatever the protocol is, and send another one down, until we get a transporter." Kas looked around the assembled group, and Taya decided he looked better than he had since he'd arrived.

It was as if a firm plan had brought the old Kas back.

"What if all this works?" Luci asked. "What if we do get two transporters. What then?"

"We head straight for Barit." Garek's hand curled a little tighter around her shoulder. "Either they have some way of knowing where their transporters are, or not, but we should assume they can track them in some way, like they track you down the mines."

"So, they'll come after us." Quardi nodded.

"And?" Zek leaned forward, elbows on knees.

"And, they don't have any transporters to spare. And they need you to work the mine. They won't risk damaging their equipment or their workforce. If they do, they'll have to start over, and my guess is they are far enough away from their home world, they can't afford to do that."

"That makes sense." Kas nodded. "So what do you think they'll do?"

"I don't know." Garek shrugged. "I just don't know."

"It doesn't matter. How can we know everything, plan for everything?" Taya asked. "The alternative is certain death. We have to take the chance."

Luci nodded, and after a moment, so did Zek. The rest were already in agreement on this, and she felt her heart give a little skip.

This was happening.

They were going to get out of here.

LATER THAT NIGHT, naked and lying draped over Garek, Taya stroked a hand down his chest.

"You didn't say it at the meeting, but you do have an idea of what they'll do when they realize we're gone, don't you?"

She lifted her face up as he looked down, and their gazes locked.

He gave a nod.

"They'll come after us, won't they? They'll follow us down to Barit and they'll try to take us back."

His arms closed tight around her. "I will never let that happen."

"I have a way that might stop them." She'd been thinking about it ever since she'd seen how far they'd put the shadow ore from the transporters. "For it to work, we'll have to be on the ground already so it doesn't affect the transporters."

"You're talking about the shadow ore?"

"Yes." She rested her head more comfortably against his chest. "If your father can smelt more ore into long, spear shapes, that would be good. I could aim them better, that way."

"You think you could pierce the shell of their craft?" His fingers tangled in her hair.

She shrugged. "From what I've seen it do so far, yes. What do we have to lose, anyway?"

He gave a hum of agreement. "We'll need more ore, then. What you and Min brought back from the caves won't be enough for an offensive. And you need some for yourself, for later."

She hugged him closer. "There's a lot piled outside the mine entrance. We need to see if anything masks its effect, otherwise we can't risk putting it in the transporters."

"It'll be risky to test," Garek said.

He was right. If they did it before the escape attempt, and it didn't work, they would be found out. And if they tested it after they got the transporter for themselves, and it didn't work, they could destroy the transporter, their only way off Shadow.

"Don't worry about it now." Garek smoothed a hand down her back. "We'll find a way."

And they would, she thought as she drifted off to sleep. They really had nothing to lose.

THIRTY-FIVE

TAYA CHOSE a piece of shadow ore from the pile by the rock face deep in the mine that was small enough to hold in her fist and fit in her pocket, but at least five times bigger than the small piece Min had brought in the transporter and which she'd worn to and from the mine in her headband ever since.

There was a growing pile of pieces too small to be worth carrying out set to one side, and she was spoilt for choice.

More than one of the men working the seam knew what she was planning and gave her a nod.

Kas simply put down his pick, wiped his face with the shirt he'd tucked into the waistband of his pants, and touched her cheek with calloused fingers. "Be careful."

She nodded, found a bigger piece that was worth carrying out and made her way through the twists and turns of the tunnel.

When they'd first been sent to the mine, they'd avoided the screen that showed them as nothing more than blobs of colorful light, but they'd gotten used to it, and their path from the deposit site where they dropped the ore to the entrance of the mine had gotten closer and closer to the gently humming black box with the massive screen perched on top. It was the quicker route.

When Taya had outlined her idea at breakfast, asking for suggestions on what to test the ore with, Noor had pointed out that the screen went fuzzy when they walked past with the shadow ore, but didn't when they were coming back from the deposit site empty-handed to get the next load.

No one else had noticed this, and Noor had looked both surprised and pleased at the praise as everyone realized the importance of it.

They'd drawn more people into the scheme, some from Pan Nuk, some from the Harven village, all to keep watch at the right time to see if the screen was affected when Taya walked past it with the ore or not.

To test if the small piece even had the power to affect the screen, Taya deposited the big rock, and then walked past the screen with the rock in her hand.

She didn't dare look up to see the effect. She'd simply kept her head down and walked back into the mine.

When she got deep enough down the passage, she slowed so Noor could catch up with her. Noor gave her a nod.

"Not as much as the rocks we bring up, but a definite wobble," she said.

The next time, she put it in the pocket of her jacket. Because, wouldn't it be handy if the soft fibers of the dar bush, from which most of the clothes on Barit were made, worked?

But Noor gave a quick shake of her head. "It wobbled again."

The next time she stood by the rock face to fetch another rock, she wrapped the small rock in silk.

She'd gone through all the different fabrics they had access to by the afternoon, with no success. Every time she caught Min and Luci's eye as they passed one another, it felt depressing to see them shake their head.

"It would have been more surprising if one of them had worked,"

Noor consoled her as they stood outside beside the long trestle table with its jugs of water and assortment of mugs.

Taya had a roughly crafted wooden mug in her hand, and she held it up, thoughtfully.

Noor narrowed her eyes. "I see where your mind's going, but how are you going to carry a cup past the screen without attracting attention?"

"I don't know." Taya swallowed the last of the water, looked at what she had available on the long, rough wooden plank. There were numerous wooden cups, some very basic, like the one in her hand, others ornately carved. Some were worn and cracked with age, others looked as if the sky raiders had stolen them straight out of the carpenter's shop.

There were silver cups, too, most of them tarnished by use and lack of polish. There was also cosil, the bronze colored alloy used for most tavern tankards.

She didn't want to try the silver and cosil, because even if they did work, there was hardly an abundance of either in the camp.

She thought through her options.

The guard stood between the table and the mine entrance, the swiveling head of the machine he was in turning at regular intervals. When it swung toward the mine entrance, Taya dropped the rock into her empty mug. She poured water into it, then poured water into two more empty mugs and balanced them awkwardly in her hands.

"Watch the screen," she said to Noor. She heard her friend hiss with frustration behind her, but she'd already turned away and started walking.

She angled toward three of the men who'd come out from working the seam for a short break. They stood in the sun and breathed the clear air.

She didn't know any of them well, they were from the Harven village, but Luci would have told them what Taya was doing today, most likely, and even if she hadn't, they knew there were plans in play for escape. They'd cooperate. She hoped.

She walked deliberately past the screen, forcing herself to keep her gaze on the men, and then hailed them with a smile.

"You look thirsty."

She could sense the guard's interest, saw his head swing in her direction. He couldn't see her face, only those of the men, all three of whom were blinking at her in surprise.

"Play along." She mouthed the words, hoping they were quick enough to catch on.

"Thank you, Taya. Most welcome." A man who Taya thought might be named Pete, held out a hand to accept the cup.

"There's a piece of shadow ore in there," she murmured to him as she handed it over. "Drink up and pretend there isn't."

She handed the other cups over to the remaining two. "You're the lucky ones. Water only." She sent them a tiny smile.

They seemed a little stiff at first, not as natural as she'd have liked, but they did well enough.

Pete drained the cup and then coughed a little.

"Went down the wrong way," he gasped.

"Bit of grit on the ore?" she asked so quietly she didn't think even he could hear her, but his gaze caught hers and she could see he was laughing.

"Felt bigger than a piece of grit, but never mind. I'm happy to sacrifice for the cause." The murmur was low and then he went absolutely silent.

Taya turned, found the guard had walked right up behind them.

"Break is over." He spoke in a monotone, but Taya thought she could sense suspicion.

Hopefully it was all in her head.

She gave a meek nod, took the cups and walked back to the table as the men turned back to the mine.

Just in case Noor hadn't gotten it the first time, she made sure she walked directly under the screen.

"Stop."

The guard's order made her freeze.

Her back was still to him, and she tipped the cup with the ore in it, so the pebble fell to the ground.

It glinted, clean from the water. Far too clean.

"Yes?" She turned back to face him, scuffing her feet to make as much dust as she could.

He leaned over her, looking at the cups, then looked up at the screen.

"Do you have shadow ore on you?"

The words made her heart sink, because it meant the screen was fuzzy.

She held out her hands, smudged with dirt from carrying the rocks. "Just the dust."

"No, something more." The machine he sat inside made a few strange sounds, and he pointed to the ground. "That. There."

She looked down, but she already knew he was pointing to the piece of ore she'd tipped out.

Thank goodness it looked dusty again.

She picked it up, held it out to him. "This?"

The guard made the machine take a step back.

"What's it doing there?"

Taya shrugged. "Perhaps it got caught in someone's clothing and fell out?" She took another step forward, as if trying to give it to him.

"Take it to the pile and get back to work," he said.

She slipped it into her pocket and nodded. She put the mugs back and then walked casually past the ore pile, tossed the rock into the heap.

When she got back into the tunnels, Noor was waiting for her at the seam where the men were working.

Kas dropped his pick, and Pete and his two friends moved closer to her so they could overhear.

"What happened?" Her brother looked a little sick.

"I tried to see if wood would mask the ore, took a cup of water to Pete with the ore inside." She smiled over at him as he was making no effort to hide he was listening in anyway. "But it didn't work."

"That's where you're wrong," Noor said. "I don't understand it, but when you walked toward them, the screen stayed the same. It was only when you returned that it went fuzzy."

"What was the difference?" Kas asked, and Taya leaned forward grabbed his face and gave him a smacking kiss on the cheek.

"The difference," she said, "was that Pete drank the water."

THIRTY-SIX

"WATER?" Quardi said as they discussed Taya's findings over dinner, and Garek could see his father was already thinking about what containers he could make.

Night had swept over the sky, and a wind cut through the camp like a honed blade, making everyone slow and jerky as they stumbled to the fire and huddled around its heat.

Anger and frustration that Taya, that all of them, had to work until they were exhausted hummed just under his skin. They were tired and had gone to clean themselves with slow, hunched steps, despite their excitement at their discovery.

As they discussed possible containers for the water, though, there was a new sense of urgency. After the talk last night, it was as if most of the camp had woken to the fact that escape was a tangible possibility.

"Wood isn't a long term solution, but it's the most abundant material," Pilar said.

"It doesn't need to be long term. It shouldn't take more than two days to get to Barit. At the longest." Garek shrugged.

There was silence.

"Why do you say that?" Kas asked.

"It took us half a day to get to the mothership, and no more than half a day to get from the mothership to Shadow." Garek looked at Aidan for confirmation, and he nodded. "Most of our time was wasted. Looking for the mothership, learning to fly the craft, and we spent a night in the mothership before we left it. It could easily take us less than a day."

"It took us . . . a week?" Garek didn't like the uncertainty in Taya's voice. "I thought it was a week."

"I thought it was longer," Noor said.

"Why would they have delayed?" Aidan asked, and Garek could see that was what was disturbing everyone.

"Maybe they were seeing if we survived the white lightning." It was Quardi who spoke. "There are only a hundred and fifty, maybe a hundred and sixty of us here, but there was talk long before we were taken of people being stolen by the sky raiders. I think they were calibrating their white lightning canons to debilitate but not kill."

"You think those others were killed? That they were waiting to see if we didn't die before they bothered taking us to Shadow?" Noor's eyes were wide.

Quardi nodded. "Where are the other people, otherwise?"

Garek's arm tightened around Taya. Because his father was right. As a guard, he knew far more people than just those who were here had been taken. He'd been so happy to find Taya, he hadn't thought about it, but what else could have happened to them? It was just pure luck Taya had been in the group where they'd gotten the strength of their weapon right.

"Then we were the lucky ones." Kas focused on the positive, shaking everyone out of their shock.

"Yes." Quardi looked at Taya, and Garek knew his father was thinking the same thing he was. "And if it's just a day or two that we have to worry about, that means wood will work. Metal will, too."

"We'll never get away with using the metal they give us for tools," Pilar said, and Garek could hear the alarm in his voice. His father was sometimes reckless enough to try things like that.

"We don't want to tip our hand," Kas cautioned, and Garek was grateful. Sometimes his father dug in, just because it was Garek who was doing the criticizing.

"Whatever we make, it has to be done carefully, so no water escapes." Taya spoke quietly, but everyone listened. "They are . . ." she seemed to think about the word she wanted to use. "They are *frightened* by it, even though they seem desperate for as much of it as they can get. Which means if water leaks out, and exposes some of the ore while we're flying away, it could be catastrophic."

"So no short cuts," Min murmured, and everyone nodded.

"No short cuts." Quardi shifted in his wheeled chair.

"I'll let the Kardanx know what we need, and Luci's group. They can start finding wooden planks." Kas stood.

"Without making it obvious to the guards," Garek warned, and Kas nodded.

"Unobtrusively and quietly."

"You think the Kardanx will be careful?" Taya asked.

"I hope so." Kas looked over at him. "And I'll remind them that Garek won't be happy if the guards get suspicious."

That was fine with Garek.

He didn't mind being the monster they feared. When it came to getting Taya free, he'd be their worst nightmare if he had to.

He stood as well. "Let's spread the word through camp. We need to get things moving."

"What about shaping the ore?" Quardi asked. "Taya says she needs it in long spears."

"We'll have to do that after we've taken the camp. I'm not sure how long we'll have between taking one of the transporters and having the second come to investigate, but that's the window you'll have to work on them."

"We can stoke the fires when Garek leaves to bring down the tower," Pilar said. "Make everything ready, and then use Taya to shape it."

Taya nodded. "You can't do it with the guard watching. He'll know it's shadow ore if he gets too close."

"What's the timeline?" Kas asked. "What deadline should I give Luci and the Kardanx?"

"Two days," Garek said. "That's long enough for them to find enough wood, to get their heads in the right place for the escape, but not too long to live under the fear and adrenalin of knowing we're about to put ourselves in danger."

Aidan nodded in agreement, and so did Kas.

"Two days it is." Kas disappeared into the dark and Taya rose up beside Garek, slipped her hand into his.

"Let's go scavenging."

Everyone else stood except his father, who shifted again in his chair, looking frustrated.

"Bring whatever you find back here. I'll sort it," he said.

Garek hesitated. "Do they check here?" It was such a communal space, they would be stupid not to check it regularly.

Taya shook her head. "In the beginning they did. Not any more." His father tried to move the chair a little way away from the fire, and Taya must have seen more in the move than he did, because she crouched in front of him, rubbed a hand over his knee. "I know you get angry about these legs," she said, and he could hear the depth of love and warmth in her voice. "You think they hold you back, but without you, we couldn't smelt the ore at all."

He was used to his father blustering and being difficult and annoying, but instead of brushing Taya off as he expected, Quardi leaned in and kissed her cheek.

"Luckiest day of my life, when my boy fell for you," he said, and she laughed softly. Garek could see from their body language this was a well-worn ritual between them.

"No," she answered, and Garek could tell from his expression of delight his father knew what was coming. "I'm the lucky one."

She looked over her shoulder at Garek, her eyes still alight with laughter at their private joke, and in that moment, as their gazes held, there was nothing he wouldn't have done for her.

THIRTY-SEVEN

TWO DAYS FELT TOO LONG, and not long enough.

Now that he stood back on the hill, crouched down beside the tower with Aidan, Garek went through a checklist of their preparations.

They were solid.

Containers had been made, mostly by Aidan and himself, supplies had been quietly gathered and stored.

Everyone had put together a small bag each of belongings to take with them.

His father had concocted some elaborate story to cover why he needed to keep the furnaces burning through the night tonight, and that had the additional benefit of keeping one of the two guards focused on what he was doing, rather than watching everyone else.

He and Aidan set out before the transporter had picked up the night shift, taking advantage of the early darkness to get a head start.

While they'd been walking, they'd watched the transporter return to camp with the day shift and then angle up into space, silhouetted against Barit.

Garek had stopped to track it, and had only continued on when the bright blue flame from its thrusters winked out as it left Shadow's atmosphere.

Now, although at least two hours had gone by since then, he checked the night sky one last time before he stood with a piece of Taya's shadow ore in his hand.

It had been Taya's idea to use it against the little box of lights at the bottom of the tower.

"The ore might interfere with the way it works, but it's also really hard, so you win both ways," she'd told him as she put it in his bag that morning.

He'd nodded, then tried to smooth away the worry on her face as she'd buckled his knapsack again, gently cupping her cheeks and kissing her goodbye.

She hadn't said anything more; she hadn't needed to.

He could see her fear for him and her excitement at the thought of escape in the way she hugged him close one last time.

He didn't know why, but now he kissed the smooth, thickly-veined stone for luck, raised his arm and hammered it into the glass-fronted box.

A buzzing sound came from the now broken box, and he pressed the rock against it and the lights fizzled again, then spluttered out.

"Target struck." Aidan used the guard terminology for a direct hit, and Garek approved. They had taken the war to a strange place, but this was an extension of what they'd both been doing in Gara.

With the box destroyed, they found a flat piece of ground to stand on and grabbed hold of one of the horizontal metal bars which made up the tower, pulling downward.

They'd chosen the place with care while they'd waited for the cover of night the last time they were here, finding the most rusted part of the metal structure.

It groaned in agony, and they let go and moved out of the way, but though it had definitely tilted, it wasn't quite bent enough to fall.

"Again." Garek grabbed hold, waited for Aidan, and then grunted with effort as they took the strain.

On the third attempt, they only just got out of the way as the whole structure toppled, the metal screeching like an injured snuffler as it went down.

Garek dusted the rust and grit from his hands. "Let's get into place."

They'd both agreed the sky raiders would not land on top of the hill. There was no room, no flat surface big enough. So they climbed down, taking up hiding places among the rocks at the bottom.

Garek made sure he could still see a lot of sky from his position.

"What if they send a guard from the mine?" Aidan asked.

"Then they'll only have one guard at the mine." It would be crazy for them to do that. Two guards was ludicrously few as it was, but Garek admitted that they may feel secure enough to do that.

He thought it through. "Then we take the guard. Carry on waiting." If the sky raiders were stupid enough to send the second guard when the first didn't come back, that would actually be a windfall.

They waited in silence, and Garek was grateful for the thick jacket Taya had taken from the store for him. It was levik leather, the dark gray of it making him almost invisible in the darkness, with a lining of soft levik fur.

The wind whistled and moaned, cutting an icy path across the flat plain. It was probably colder because the sky was so clear, but that was to their advantage, and sure enough, the flare of bright blue flashed high in the night sky after just over an hour of waiting.

"Here we go," he murmured, and Aidan grunted in response.

The craft that came down was the same as the one that took everyone to and from the mine, a normal transporter with no weapons on it that Garek could see.

It circled the hill, taking in the fallen tower.

That's right, he thought, just a simple failure of your metal, something you already knew. There is no danger here.

Taya had raised the possibility that they would be able to see Garek and Aidan using the same technology they used to keep watch over them in the mine.

Kas had argued that was a very specific set-up, a complex one, and he didn't think it likely to be a feature of the transporters.

It didn't matter to Garek. They would know he was here soon enough—having a little warning wouldn't save them.

The transporter landed and the doors slid back. Two figures emerged from the blunt, rounded front of the craft without any caution at all. They swung down using footholds built into the side, both in some kind of thick suit of dark blue with a full helmet.

Garek had wondered if they'd bring guards in their metal machines like the ones at camp and the mine, but these two seemed to be it.

He waited for them to walk past him, rose up and struck the one at the back on the helmet with the shadow ore rock.

He heard the fizzle of something from the hard shell, and the pilot lifted both hands to the helmet as if he couldn't work out what had happened.

Garek struck him again, and this time, the pilot turned.

Garek couldn't see his expression, but he guessed it was surprised.

The man grabbed him, trying to head butt him with the helmet, and Garek slid to the side, hooking an arm around the pilot's throat so he could hit the helmet again.

Something snagged at the sleeve of his jacket, and he pulled at it, realized as the helmet suddenly came loose that it was the catch where the helmet attached to the neck of the suit.

He pulled again, getting it up past the pilot's chin before taking an elbow in the ribs. He heard the sweet hiss of escaping air.

"I've got him." Aidan said and Garek shoved the pilot at him, turned to the second pilot, who was only just turning back, only just realizing they were under attack.

She struck out with a wild punch that hit Garek on the shoulder and he was knocked back by the blow. The sky raiders were big, but so was he, and he was grateful that the suits they were wearing included gloves, so their claws were sheathed.

He threw the shadow ore at her head, where it hit her helmet between the eyes.

This time, he saw a spark of dark purple that seemed to leap from inside the helmet to arc against the ore before it fell to the ground.

The pilot lifted her hands to her helmet, scrabbling at some lights flickering on the side, but Garek called the Change and knocked her down with a gust of air. He was on her in a moment, wrenching the clasp at her neck and hauling the helmet all the way off her head.

They stared at each other.

She bared long, sharp teeth at him, snapping at him, then panicked when she realized she couldn't breathe.

Garek leaned forward and snapped her neck, unwilling to watch her suffocate for however long it took.

He looked over and saw Aidan had done the same.

"This wasn't easy, but it didn't feel wrong. They stole our people." Aidan moved over to look down at the pilot Garek had killed.

"Yes." Garek picked up her body, straining under the weight, and dragged it behind one of the thick bushes that grew on the hill.

Aidan lifted his one, eyebrows raised, and Garek nodded, made room for the second body beside the first.

"Let's go change the air settings in the front area where the pilots sit, then wait to see what they do if the transporter doesn't report in."

"You think they might send a guard from the mine?"

Garek shrugged. "If they don't, we'll fly to the mine as decided. We've got a few hours to play with." He regretfully set the shadow ore down on the ground. It wouldn't be safe to take it.

"Do you think either of them had time to get off a distress signal?" Aidan took a last look at the bush and started toward the transporter.

Garek followed, his gaze going to the sky, watching for another flare of blue light. "I don't know. They're so complacent, I hope even if they did, it won't be seen as urgent."

When they reached the transporter, Garek was pleased to see the doors had been left open. For a quick get away, probably.

All to the good, because he had no idea how he would have opened them otherwise.

He left Aidan on the ground, keeping watch for any sign of the sky raiders, and climbed into the front compartment.

The whole craft was powered off, and he pulled out his needle and poked it into the tiny hole built into the arm rest of one of the pilot's chairs to start it up, just as he'd done with the sky craft in Barit. The doors slid shut with a snap but he ignored that, and knelt down to find the air mix gauge as the vents began to pump their poison. He set it to replicate Barit air in less than a minute and found how to open the doors a moment later.

Aidan climbed up the side.

"Anything?"

The princeling shook his head. "Where do we wait? In here?"

Garek considered it. "One in, one out."

Garek dropped to the ground and moved away from the transporter to find cover. With a shrug, Aidan pulled himself in and closed the doors.

Garek settled in to wait.

The plan they'd hatched had been built on guesses, but the guess was the sky raiders would send a transporter, and they had. The next step was for him to fly the transporter to the mine a few hours before shift change, hoping to force the guards to investigate, and when they did, ambush them and open up their suits.

It was the most unpredictable and dangerous part of the plan, but everyone on night shift had been told to head into the shaft when they landed.

The guards couldn't get them there, and wouldn't try anyway.

They needed their workforce alive.

An hour passed, and then two.

Aidan opened the door and stuck his head out. "They aren't coming."

"No. We don't have time to wait any longer, anyway." Garek swung back up into the pilot's chair and powered up. As they rose, and banked off toward the mine, a voice came through from somewhere, a low growl of a voice.

He exchanged a look with Aidan, lifted his finger to his lips.

Kas said he thought the sky raiders could see them in the back of the transporter, that they listened to them, too. If that was the case for the pilot's part of the transporter as well, they were in more trouble than he'd like. But there was nothing he could do about it now.

They were at the mine about five minutes later, and he knew he used too much power when he set the transporter down, he could hear the engines whining louder than they did when it landed in camp to fetch Taya.

Aidan winced and he waved an apologetic hand in acknowledgment.

He landed well enough, though, gentle and feather-light.

Aidan turned and clasped his forearm in the traditional guard handshake. "May you walk the walls tomorrow," he said.

"May we both walk the walls for many years to come," Garek responded in kind, and he realized the familiar pre-battle ritual settled him.

They both slipped out of their chairs and hunched low, crouching just out of sight beneath the window. Garek lifted slightly to look out, saw the guard was approaching.

"I don't know how he's going to look in here. That machine won't be able to climb up."

It didn't need to, he discovered. Its legs extended, and as soon as it rose high enough, Garek hit the button to open the door, lunged out, and pressed the release button in the center chest of the machine, opening the glass dome.

The guard inside looked up at him, dumbfounded, and Garek leaped in with him, grabbed him and threw him out onto the ground.

He bent for the moment he needed to change the air gauge settings, and then jumped to the ground after the sky raider.

The guard was scrabbling at the leg of his machine, trying to climb back up it, but he'd already breathed in the air, and he was choking and gagging at the same time.

Garek looked up, saw Aidan had climbed into the machine and closed the lid again, turning it to face the mine.

Even if it wasn't dangerous to both the transporter and the night shift, they had decided not to even try to shoot the other guard with the weapons included in the arms, because they didn't have any idea which button it was.

Garek grabbed the guard and started dragging him to the back of the transporter, fighting him the whole way.

The other guard, who'd been facing away, toward the mine's entrance, turned to see what was going on and Aidan moved toward him, lumbering forward clumsily.

Garek had to trust him to be the distraction he needed while he got the other guard out of sight.

The sky raider refused to go easily. There was keen intelligence in his eyes; fury, too. He fought as if he still had a chance to live, never letting Garek get a good enough grip on his neck.

When he realized there was going to be no air he could breathe, a sense of resignation came over him, but still he refused to give in. He swiped at Garek, trying to rake him with his claws, but he was weak enough by then that Garek was able to hold his arms down. He died breathing the poisonous air of Shadow instead of fast and clean.

"You should have left us alone," Garek told him, letting him go and stepping back as he wheezed in his last breath. "Why couldn't you leave us alone?"

A grating, shrieking crash came from the other side of the transporter, and Garek turned away from the sky raider, ran to the front to find the guard machines locked in a strange embrace.

The one closer to the mine was the one containing the sky raider, Garek guessed. It looked as though Aidan had tripped his machine up and was leaning on the other guard.

Aidan must be trying to extricate himself, because the arms and legs of his machine were doing strange things, and the other guard was trying to push Aidan off him.

Garek ran. As he reached them, he saw Eli step out of the mine entrance, but he had to ignore him, ignore everything as he called the Change for a little boost up to slam his hand onto the button that opened the glass dome.

The sky raider flinched back as he was exposed, and then scrambled for the button within to close it up again.

Aidan managed to get one of his machine arms in the way, and it only closed partway.

"Get some shadow ore," Garek shouted to Eli, saw him run to a pile of rock to one side.

He came running back with a piece the size of his head and threw it at Garek.

He caught it, boosted himself again, and managed to shove the shadow ore through the opening before he dropped to the ground.

He danced backward, watched Aidan open his own dome, get free, and scramble out of the way.

The guard's machine made a strange sound and then went quiet, and the two intertwined mechanical giants went down, toppling slowly to the sound of grating metal.

The guard wriggled through the gap in his dome, eyes bulging, one hand clawing at his throat.

Eli came to stand beside Garek and watched the guard crawl toward them. They both took a step back when he tried to grab them with a sharp-clawed hand. Then he shuddered and lay still.

"They killed every single one of my leviks," Eli said, looking down. "They ruined me, and stole away my life. They stole my whole world."

Garek glanced over at him. "We'll make sure they're sorry for it, although when we get to the camp, it probably won't be as easy as this was."

Eli frowned. "We've been thinking of ways to kill them since we got here. There isn't one of us who thought what you just did was easy."

Aidan joined them as the rest of the shift started emerging from the mine.

Several looked over at the transporter, then at the guards, and whistled in quiet appreciation.

"You're a fearless bastard, Garek." Lynal murmured as he took in the mangled heap of machinery and the dead sky raider in front of them.

"Yes," Eli said, and Garek was surprised at the warmth in his voice. "But he's our fearless bastard."

THIRTY-EIGHT

TAYA KNEW Garek would be gone when she got back to camp after her shift, but knowing it didn't help ease her fear. He was in danger, and all she could do was be ready to move when he returned.

She washed quickly and dressed in guard clothes; pants that were bias-cut and stretchy, a soft long sleeved shirt she had to pull over her head and a leather vest with lacing that she could tighten for a perfect fit. She hadn't had to ask for these or barter for them like the more popular finds from the Stolen Store, they had languished in there for a long time, obviously made for a woman guard. There was . . . not exactly a taboo on it, but not many were willing to don the clothing of a guard if they weren't one. It was disrespectful to those who called the Change, because it was a symbol of the year they'd given up.

Taya had no such reservations. She had given up less than a year's worth of time here on Shadow, but she didn't think any guard would have preferred to take her place.

She'd remembered the clothes when Kas had first confirmed she was calling the Change, and had gone to find them. They would be perfect for what lay ahead, but she didn't forget the soft silk dresses.

They were both a symbol of her captivity and a reminder that not everything about this strange abduction had been negative. There had been things to learn, and joy to experience.

She packed her favorite two gowns in the bag Garek had found for her yesterday, rolling them up tight and pushing them down to the bottom.

Then she went to get some dinner, laughing at the comments at the sight of her in her guard gear. Kas looked pensive as he handed her a plate, but neither of them spoke.

She knew she needed to eat, that it was wise, but she found it almost impossible to swallow the fragrant flatbread past the icy knot of fear in her throat.

She looked toward the mine, and Kas slid a warm, strong hand along her shoulder.

"You know him. He got all the way here. He isn't going to fail now."

She drew in a deep, shuddering breath. Nodded. And managed to force half the food on her plate down.

Then she put together two plates and walked to the forge, where Quardi and Pilar were stoking fires.

The guard watched her carefully.

She ignored him, handing the plates over and fussing around Quardi as she usually did.

"How's it going?"

"The fires are hot." Quardi smiled an almost demented grin of victory. "We're going to have to start smelting something soon, or he might get suspicious."

"He already is." Pilar leaned forward, pushing his hair back from a sweaty forehead with the back of his hand.

"Do you have something to smelt?" Taya asked and they nodded.

"I was hoping Garek would be back before it came to that, but it doesn't matter. We've got enough we can do."

"Did you notice a transporter come down after the night shift left?" She hadn't, but she couldn't watch the sky every second.

They shook their heads.

"Doesn't mean anything. We're under a roof here, and busy most of the time." Pilar patted her knee.

She nodded, stood from her crouch, and looked over at the guard.

Saw he had turned toward the landing area, and then she heard it, too.

She walked out of the forge, keeping her stride steady, but fast.

A transporter was coming in.

She walked past the guard, ignoring him, and glanced back at Quardi and Pilar.

Pilar was standing, face tense, but Quardi was smiling that same demented smile.

She slipped into the narrow path between the shacks and huts, making her way to the camp fire.

Kas was waiting for her, his whole body tense.

She'd removed her headband, had her pieces of shadow ore in her hand.

"Let's go." Kas started walking as the transporter came to a rest, disappearing from sight behind the big jousting tent.

As she followed, she sensed others coming with them. Men and women walking quietly in the dark, making their way through the narrow alleys and spaces between the houses.

She caught sight of Jerilia, and exchanged a nod as she noticed the woman was clutching a piece of wood in her hands.

Everyone was carrying something, she realized. Using parts of their huts or shacks as weapons.

They stopped at the last line of huts, and she and Kas crouched low, leaning against a rickety wall and peering around.

The guard was moving toward the transporter. It was quiet now that the engines had powered down, no sound but the wind blowing.

The doors didn't open, and the guard seemed to hesitate. He'd been moving toward the back of the transporter, probably out of habit, but he changed course, walking toward the front, to the pilots Taya had never given much thought to, because she'd never seen them, not even once.

He tapped on a panel, and a door slid open.

What happened next was so fast, she struggled to make out what was going on in the strange orange illumination of the landing area lights.

It looked like the dome top of the guard's machine lifted up, and someone—Garek—grabbed the guard from his seat and threw him onto the ground.

He dropped down after him, and perhaps called his Change a little to heave the guard further from his machine.

She could hear the sounds of choking, of coughing, and then nothing.

Kas seem to take that as his signal, because he ran out into the open toward the transporter, and Taya followed close behind, shadow ore at the ready.

Garek met them halfway, and she had to force herself not to touch him, because this wasn't the time.

But she was so very happy he was alive and well. She forced her hands into fists to stop herself reaching out to him.

With a gentle whine, the back of the transporter opened and then Aidan climbed out of the pilot's door and dropped softly to the ground beside them.

Eli and a group of other night shift workers ran down the ramp.

"Where're the others?" Kas asked and Taya realized only about half of the shift had come back from the mine.

"They're sorting through the pile of shadow ore so when we go back and get it, we have the best pieces," Aidan said.

Garek stepped closer to her, and she couldn't help reaching out to touch his arm.

"Is the guard still watching my father?"

She nodded.

He grabbed her hand and pulled her out of the landing area, running for the forge. Kas was at her heels, Aidan just behind him.

They passed a few people who melted out of their way and then followed them, too.

Garek slowed as they got close and pulled her down into a crouch a little distance away.

"The guard will definitely be on alert. He's suspicious," Taya whispered. "He stopped watching your father right away when the transporter came in, turned to look at the landing area. But I'm sure he couldn't see what just happened. There're too many buildings and tents in the way."

Garek nodded and slid a hand along her nape, gave her shoulder a gentle squeeze.

She turned her head, kissed his cheek, and then lifted the hand holding her shadow ore shards. "Just as we discussed?"

Garek nodded.

She stood, straightened her shoulders, and took a step forward. Found herself pulled back against a big, hard body.

"Be careful." The whisper was a low murmur in her ear, rumbling through her.

She didn't want to show her nerves but there was no hiding them from Garek, he must feel her heart pounding beneath his hand.

He let her go, and she sucked in a deep breath, shoring up her courage. He would be right behind her. So would Kas, and plenty of others. And she could help them all by disabling the guard as quickly as possible.

She took the turns, left, right, and then she was at the forge.

The guard turned in her direction, and she forced herself not to falter, to keep walking as if she were merely returning for the plates she'd brought earlier.

She looked over at the guard, making it casual, noting the areas on the machine that protected him that would be good to target. She raised her hand as if to wave to Quardi, and let the needles of shadow ore go, sending the slivers of metal into every joint on his machine she could see.

The dark tint of the glass dome flickered and then went clear, and she saw the guard's face. Even though it was alien, she could read the astonishment.

Then he snarled, his upper lip lifting to show long incisors. The machine lurched, as if he was trying to take a step toward her, but the knees had locked up, and the whole thing toppled over.

She ran backward, just as Garek and Kas ran forward, past her.

Garek hit a circle of light that had lit up in the center of the body of the machine, but aside from a strange grinding sound, nothing happened.

"It's the shadow ore. It's affecting the operation of the buttons." He looked over his shoulder at her. "Can you get them out?"

She ran over to him, called the shadow ore back from the places closest to the lights, leaving the shards in the legs and arms.

Garek hit the button again, but nothing happened.

"I'm taking them out of its arms now," she warned him, and pulled them out, but the damage must have been permanent, because the arms remained stiffly outstretched and unmoving.

The guard pressed his face up against the glass dome, staring at them with teeth bared.

Taya couldn't help but smile at him, and it wasn't a nice smile at all. He drew back, startled, as if it suddenly occurred to him that he was no longer in control.

Pilar emerged from the forge as she pulled out the shards from the legs, and he was carrying a hammer. The huge one Quardi had made to shape the picks and shovels they used at the mine.

"If you don't mind," he said politely to Garek, and when Garek stepped back, Pilar raised the hammer over his head, muscles bulging and straining in his arms, and brought it down on the glass.

There was an ominous crack, and Taya saw a hairline fracture on the dome, but it held.

"My turn." Eli was there suddenly, still dusty and sweaty from the night shift.

Pilar handed him the hammer, and he lifted it with the ease of enormous strength. When he hit the glass, Taya could see the vibration run along his arms.

Another crack appeared.

Jerilia stood behind him, and even though she visibly struggled to lift the hammer high enough, she still managed it. And perhaps because of the angle she struck it at, the crack she made seemed deeper than the other two.

"Anyone else?" Kas asked as he took the hammer from her. "Because we have a time issue."

One man stepped forward as a few others hesitated, and then shook their heads with regret.

It was a Kardanx, although not one Taya recognized. Maybe he was from the night shift. He took his turn, crying out a strange call as he brought the hammer down. Again, cracks spread like winter frost, but the glass held.

He handed the hammer reluctantly to Kas and her brother lifted it, vengeance personified as he drew it up over his head; neck and arm muscles bunched and flexing, leg stepping back, and then driving forward as he brought it down with a crack that echoed louder than a thunderclap. The dome shattered, collapsing in on itself, the glass seeming to disappear, although she realized it had merely disintegrated into minute pieces.

The sky raider launched himself out and stood, staring at them all.

He took a breath, and there was surprise and panic on his face.

"Hard to breathe?" Jerilia asked.

Taya had never heard her so cold.

The guard turned to her, but when Kas moved a little, the guard's head swung back, took in the hammer.

He took a second breath, one that seemed to rasp and tear at his throat, and then he looked back at the ruined capsule that had been his lifeline.

"Not so powerful now." Eli took a step closer.

Taya glanced at him, and there must have been something on her face to cool his bloodlust, because he caught her eye and stopped.

It took so little time, after that.

They all stood and watched as the guard fell to his knees and then face first into the ground. He went into a spasm, like a fit, convulsing until he lay still.

They were all silent for a moment after he gasped his last breath, and then Garek pulled her to him, pressing her cheek against his chest, holding her close.

She held on until she felt him shift back.

"We need to get moving," he said. It seemed to rouse everyone from wherever they'd all gone in their heads.

"Let's go," Kas called. "Everyone knows what they have to do."

And just like that, they were moving. Taya grasped Garek's outstretched hand, and they left the guard lying face down in the gritty black dust as they headed back to the landing area and the transporter.

But she couldn't seem to walk away without looking back one last time.

"He would have left you to die on Shadow without a second thought." Garek stopped tugging her along.

"I'm better than he is," she replied. "It seems . . . wrong to be so callous."

"It's not callous. We didn't kill him for fun. He would have stopped us. Prevented us leaving if he could."

She sighed. Gave a nod.

"And for taking you, forcing you to work here, I would kill him again." He looked upward. "I'd kill them all."

She slid a hand up his cheek. "Ruining their plans is enough for me."

He seemed to come back to himself, leaned forward and nuzzled a spot just above her ear. "We need to hurry."

She nodded against his cheek, and then let him take the lead back to the transporter.

The clock was ticking, and they had a planet to escape from.

THIRTY-NINE

"NEARLY YOUR TURN TO run the show," Quardi told her, as Taya stepped back a little from the intense heat of the fire he had going.

She'd gone with Garek back to the mine, and Dom had come along, to watch Garek pilot the transporter, and then learn to work the controls. They'd loaded the ore into their boxes of water, and brought them back to camp, with Garek making Dom land and take off three times on the way.

Quardi had assembled a small group to help him at the forge, and everyone else had been given a shift watching the skies for anything coming in.

Those not on watch slept. It was understood everyone needed to be up and as fresh as possible tomorrow morning, when the day shift transporter came in.

If it didn't, Taya didn't know what they would do. It would mean the sky raiders knew something was wrong.

But until that happened, they were operating on the belief that their captors were too arrogant to think anything could hurt them or disrupt their plans.

"Ore's liquid," Pilar called from under the heavy canvas hood he had on to protect his face from the intense heat. He stepped back and waved to the team standing beside one of the long wooden boxes full of water.

They each took a corner and lifted it, bringing it closer to the flames, setting it down and then backing away, shielding their faces.

"Ready?" Quardi asked her.

She nodded. She'd spent the time as they were waiting for the ore to smelt thinking of what would be a good shape.

She reached out to call the Change, jerked as her senses locked on to the ore. She pulled it up, feeling the elemental metal separate from its impurities, letting it stretch in a long, thin cylinder, and when she had something about half her body length, she cut it off from the molten liquid and concentrated on the tip, making it as sharp as she could.

When she was done, she moved it above the box, and dropped it into the water.

There was a bang, and steam shot up in a hiss.

Everyone ducked instinctively but nothing else happened.

"Whew." Pilar wiped his brow, edged closer to the box to look in. "That was a surprise."

Garek exploded from between two tents on the opposite side to where she stood, his face wild.

"Just the water reacting to the heat of the ore," she told him when his stricken gaze fixed on her. "We're all fine."

His eyes snapped to his father.

"It happens. You know that." Quardi had hardly reacted, Taya noted.

Garek looked at her again, and then blew out a shaky breath, gave a sharp nod. "You going to do that again?" he asked.

"I want to see if this one's any good, first."

Pilar already had the clamp in his hand, and was lifting the spear out of the water and moving it to a second box of water to let it cool even more.

"It feels light," he said. "Lighter than iron, anyway."

It barely sizzled as it went into its second cold water bath and after a moment, Pilar used the clamp to pull it out, brought it over to her and Quardi.

They bent over it and then she felt Garek behind her, his arm tugging her back against his chest as they all peered over the spear.

Steam wafted off it, so it was still hot, but it had an almost pearlescent sheen to it. She took the clamp from Pilar, and gave a nod. "It does feel light."

She passed it to Garek and he agreed.

"This won't be cool enough to test for a while, and we don't have the luxury of time," Quardi reminded her.

She nodded. "It looks all right. I'll have to trust it'll be strong enough."

She turned back to the pot, and Garek gave her a last squeeze and disappeared back into the darkness, to oversee the watch.

There was enough ore for Taya to pull four more spears from the pot, and when she'd used up as much as she could, Pilar tipped out the slag and impurities that were left, and added the next lot of ore to smelt.

She moved on to the second fire.

She'd seen a picture once, when she'd been in Juli for the princess's wedding, a wall mural depicting the Iron Guard going into battle.

It wasn't a true depiction, as far as she knew. The Iron Guard patrolled the West Lathor border, and they were fearsome, but West Lathor hadn't been to war for a long time, and the Iron Guard had only been formed twenty years ago.

Nevertheless, something in the picture had spoken to her. There was a truth to it, and Taya had thought perhaps the artist had watched the Iron Guard do their patrols, or train in their barracks. They had looked real.

In the painting, the guards had been wearing armor that looked like the scales of a slither, overlapping iron hexagons that hung from leather breastplates and arm guards, and from leather helmets that protected the ears, nape and throat as well as the head.

Clothing had become her business, as the dyed levik wool she sent to Gara and Juli became more and more popular. She thought more about the end product than she ever had before, about how the colors would influence what the wool was used to make, and she'd stared at that picture for a long time, thinking of ways the strange decoration could be used for the general population.

Of course, that was back when she thought the iron hexagons were only for protection. Before she understood what calling a specific element could mean.

Even now, she didn't know how they would release the hexagons and use them in a fight, but back then, when she'd gotten home to Pan Nuk, she'd had Quardi make her thin circles instead of hexagons, and she'd sewn them in a way that they overlapped on woven fabric.

The iron had turned out to be too heavy for the cloth, and she'd given it up. It seemed leather was the only thing that could hold the iron without tearing and she wasn't in the leather decoration business.

But if shadow ore was that much lighter than iron, and it had felt like it, she would try again. Make something both light and protective, and lethal, for herself.

She lifted a small amount of ore out of the second pot, and formed the most perfect circle she could. It seemed to want to form a circle, she realized. It was almost no work to pull the ore up and let it spread until it was about the size of her palm.

She would have chosen to make them smaller if she'd had time, but that would have taken much longer.

As it was, the only hard part was the tiny hole she made at the top.

She drew up more and more ore, until she had over twenty circles, and then dumped them in the box. She was only able to make another forty before the ore ran out, and she went back to the first pot again.

"The ore's nearly ready," Quardi told her, and she realized she was thirsty, and there was the hint of a headache, slinking like a thief toward her. She walked to the small jug someone had set on a table, poured some water and realized the team Quardi had gathered to help him were all staring at her.

Most of them sat on the ground, looking exhausted but bemused.

"What?" She tipped back her head and swallowed half the water in one long gulp. "Shouldn't you try and get some rest?"

They'd finished moving all the boxes of water close to the forge fires, she saw, and there was nothing else for them to do.

"Watching you is too interesting." Noor pulled herself up. "But yes, I need some sleep."

It broke the thrall everyone seemed to be under, and soon it was just Pilar, Quardi and herself.

"How much ore is left?" She had the sense she couldn't waste a drop. She would need it—need it like she needed to breathe or eat— when she got back to Barit.

"We filled the first pot again, and I'll put these last few pieces in the second pot." Pilar had tipped the second pot out, so the slag lay, glowing, on the ground. He set the pot down on the fire and threw three pieces about the size of her fist into it. "That's all of it."

She had to make sure they could fight when they got to Barit, but if the spears lodged in the sky craft and they managed to fly away, she would lose them. She would have the shards in her headband, she would have the circles, but she wanted a knife, too, or a short sword. Something that was a true weapon.

The pieces smelting in the second pot would have to be enough, she decided. Because none of it would matter if she was dead, or Garek or Kas were dead. She needed to protect them when the sky raiders tried to take them back, so she needed the full pot in front of her to go toward more spears.

She managed to get six spears out of the pot, and she could feel the act of doing this over and over was making her better at it, making her more accurate.

When she got to the second pot, got the nod from Pilar that it was ready, she pulled everything out at once, shaping it into a long straight blade with a pommel below. Too long, she realized, and cut a piece off the top, made a small knife with a handle using the excess.

She stood for a while, until she was happy with the length and width of the blades.

She was about to toss them into the water, when Quardi lifted his hand.

"Wait. Your blades are too thick at the edges. Give them to me to shape."

She laid both on the anvil and then stood swaying for a moment to the sound of Quardi pounding with his hammer.

If felt as if each strike was drilling into her head, her headache darkening her vision at the edges.

"Time to crash?" Pilar asked her.

She nodded, unable to answer, and then Garek was there, helping her to bed.

"Will you stay?" she managed to mumble as he lay her down on the soft, wonderful mattress, but she didn't know if he answered her before the headache pulled her under.

FORTY

THE SOUND of running jerked Garek awake. He was standing, opening the door of the hut, before Eli even reached it.

The sky was still dark, although with a hint of gray on the horizon that told Garek dawn could not be far away.

That meant he'd managed to get five hours of sleep, and he felt the better for it.

"They're coming?" he asked, looking upward.

Eli nodded. He stepped away from the door and pointed above the roof.

Garek joined him, watched the flare of blue fire making its way toward them.

When he'd joined Taya an hour after he'd put her to bed, they'd been ready in every way. Everyone from the Illy and the Kardai side had their orders.

"They're coming in too early for day shift, so they know something's wrong," Eli said.

"Aidan awake?" Garek asked.

Eli nodded. "He was bunking with me, anyway. He's already waiting by the guard's machine for you."

Garek looked back into the hut, saw Taya was still asleep.

"Called the Change too much," Eli said, with a sympathetic nod. "Do we need her for this fight?"

"It wouldn't hurt." But he wasn't sorry there was a good excuse to keep her out of it, either. "She's no good to us at half-strength."

Eli nodded. "Half-strength may be better than nothing, though."

Their voices must have roused her, because she blinked and sat up. Regret rode him, and he wished he'd left with Eli right away.

"They're coming?" Her voice was husky.

"Yes. I'm getting in position." He hesitated. "Are you able to help?"

She gave a nod, scrambled to her feet. "Go. I'll see you there."

He turned to do just that, realized he didn't want to without a kiss, and went back for it.

She smiled against his lips as he bent down, holding him close, and then he forced himself back from the warm, sweet smell of her and ran to the transporter.

Eli kept up with him. "Why do you think they've decided to come now?"

"They may have only just realized they have a craft missing."

Eli's eyebrows rose in disbelief.

"They don't think they have anything to fear from us, and they seem confident they're the biggest, baddest things out here."

"So what do they think happened?"

"Maybe that something broke?" Garek guessed that's exactly what they thought. He hoped so, anyway. This would go much more easily if it was the case.

He arrived in the landing area, and Aidan waved. There were people standing just out of cover all along the edges of the landing area. Everyone was looking up.

Garek could sense the tension, and the excitement.

"Want me to get in now?" Aidan pointed to the guard machine.

Garek nodded. He'd managed to land the transporter close to it when they'd come back from the mine with the shadow ore. It looked as if the guard was talking to the pilots.

Aidan could move around in it, if necessary, make it look like there was a guard inside there.

"Let's hope they don't go to the mine first," he said, as he watched the craft with its blue trail swoop lower.

Nothing would tell them things weren't as they seemed louder than the abandoned mine.

"If they do?" Kas was standing beside him now, stepping out of the darkness silently.

"I'm hoping they'll come straight to the transporter. If they go to the mine, they may still think something simply went wrong. I don't think they'll jump to the right conclusion until we actually attack."

Kas gave a hum of agreement. "Taya?" he asked.

"Just woke up. Says she's all right." He looked down the narrow pathway between the shacks to their hut, and saw her coming, still in her guard uniform, although for some reason she wasn't wearing her coat, despite the chill. Her hands were in her hair as she braided it off her face.

She looked tired, pale beneath the dusky gold of her skin, and the need to get her away from this place became a deafening drumbeat in his blood.

"How many do you think will be in there?" Kas tensed beside him as the craft banked right, angling toward them. It was five minutes away at most.

"If we're lucky, two. If not . . ." He shrugged. "We deal with it."

"We're ready to deal with whatever comes." It was Jona, stepping out from the Kardai side, flanked by Dom and another man.

"Dom needs to stay back," Garek said. He looked directly at him. "Only engage if we clearly need help."

The boy hesitated.

"You aren't a trained guard," Kas told him. "And there's no time to teach anyone else how to fly the transporter if you're hurt too badly to do it. So you need to be safe until we have the situation under control."

Jona touched Dom's shoulder. "We can't leave without you." There seemed to be respect there, which was different from a few nights ago.

Dom gave a nod, shared a quick look with Taya and then walked back into the camp, disappearing among the tents.

"If he does get hurt?" Jona asked.

"Then we teach his mother," Taya said. "Or you stay behind."

Both Kardai men drew in a sharp breath.

"Are you ready?" Garek asked her.

She nodded, held up the shadow ore shards, and Jona took a step back.

"Don't let them get near the transporter," he said, panic in his tone. "I saw what they did to that guard machine by the forge."

"I've taken them on the transporters before, so it isn't enough to affect them while it's on me. But I know the stakes," Taya told him. "I'll be careful. Garek and I have talked about when and where I'll use them."

The sound of the transporter's engines were audible now, and Garek gave the guard signal for everyone to take cover. Then smiled at himself when only the few from Pan Nuk and Harven who had done guard duty complied.

"Go hide," he said.

"What about you?" Jona asked.

"Don't worry about me." He turned, following Taya to the Stolen Store, the closest structure to the landing area, and waved her deeper into the shadows. He crouched in front of her, his body shielding her completely.

"You don't fool me," she whispered, shuffling so close to him she was right up against his back, her lips almost touching his ear. "I know you wish I was still sleeping in the hut."

He grunted, his eyes on the transporter as it came in to land.

She kissed the side of his neck, a quick, hard press of lips and then she burrowed her face in his shirt as the grit swirled around them.

He put his hand on her knee, squeezed, his gaze never leaving the transporter.

It settled, and once the dust had stopped flying, Aidan turned the guard machine to face it.

That was good, Garek thought. It would have been odd if a guard hadn't turned to see the new transporter.

They waited, seconds ticking by so slowly, they felt like minutes.

Eventually, Aidan started walking toward the ship.

Risky, but Garek agreed they needed to do something to get things moving.

Aidan's walk was more a lumber, stiff-legged and jerky. When he got to the doors, Garek moved forward, ready and focused.

The pilot doors stayed closed, but he heard the unmistakeable sound of the back ramp lowering.

Aidan didn't move, and Garek realized he probably couldn't hear it, encased in glass and metal as he was.

Garek held still, the warmth of Taya still pressed against his back, and watched to see who came out of the back.

Four sky raiders, all in the same dark blue suits as the ones he'd killed at the tower.

Now he had to decide whether the pilots were among them, or whether they were still inside.

"What now?" Kas came up behind them, crouching low.

"I have to get into the pilots' area and kill the pilots if they're there, then fly the transporter a short distance away, so they can't fly off with it. We won't get another chance at one." The sky raiders may think they were untouchable, but Garek would bet losing two trans-porters would make them sit up and take notice. There would be no more opportunities after this.

"I agree. We'll deal with the four in the blue suits that have stepped outside. You take the transporter. I'll let everyone know." Kas slipped away.

"You want a diversion?" Taya whispered. "To get to the pilots' door?"

"No." The word came out more harshly than he intended. He swallowed. "Taya, please don't risk yourself."

Then before she could argue, he ran, bending low, and keeping to the shadows.

The four sky raiders who'd stepped out were walking toward Aidan in his guard machine, and Garek felt a leap of relief as Aidan moved away from the front of the transporter, heading for the open area in front of the jousting tent.

The sky raiders attention moved with him and just as Garek moved to the other side of the transporter, out of sight, Aidan seemed to stumble, and the machine fell over.

Garek guessed he hadn't meant that to happen, but it shocked the sky raiders into action. They ran forward, and Garek slipped around the back, swung up the small ladder on the side, and hit the button to open the pilot's door.

The door opened with the familiar whoosh of air as the outside atmosphere mingled with the strange sky raider air in the cabin.

A sky raider turned to him, helmet in hand as if about to put it on. He stared for a moment, shocked, and then lunged for a button on the side.

Garek dived in, drawing as much air as he could with him and hit the helmet out of the pilot's hand as he straightened from closing the door. The pilot panicked as he tried to breathe air that was a mix between Shadow and sky raider and Garek took advantage, moving in and striking him hard on the side of the head with his elbow. The pilot grunted and stumbled back, but the system was pumping more sky raider air in, and Garek could see him getting stronger.

His window of opportunity was closing.

The pilot lunged, claws out, catching the leather of Garek's coat, and Garek threw himself forward, bringing them both down hard on the floor.

Sharp claws dug into his chest, he could feel them sinking into his skin, tightening their hold.

He ignored the pain, enveloping the pilot in the air he'd brought in with him and got his hands around his throat. He tried to draw what air he could from the sky raider's lungs, but there was so little to get hold of that he had to accept the sky raiders' air was just too different from Barit and Shadow for him to work with it.

The pilot bared his incisors, tried to bite, but Garek slammed his head back against the floor, tightening his grip around his throat as the sky raider sunk his claws deeper.

The door suddenly opened on the camp side of the transporter, and Garek lifted his head in surprise.

A sky raider in full suit and helmet stood on the rung, and the pilot beneath him twisted to look, shouted something in the sky raider language.

Garek used the chance to pull in armfuls and armfuls of air, flooding the chamber.

He felt the claws loosen, then retract, and he levered himself up, shoved the sky raider trying to climb in off the side of the transporter.

When he turned back, he saw the pilot was scrabbling to get his helmet.

Garek went on his knees, found the dial beneath the console and moved it to the Barit setting, keeping his attention split between getting the correct mix and watching the pilot.

The pilot had just managed to fasten his helmet when Garek got it right. The door was still open, and Garek levered up, grabbing the pilot and throwing him out.

The sky raider managed to grab hold of the side, and Garek leant over him, unclasped the helmet and pulled it off.

Shock flashed across the pilot's face, and then Garek swung the helmet and struck him with it.

Blood flew, a strange, dark brown blood, and then the pilot fell.

Garek looked out over the landing area, saw the other four sky raiders were surrounded by Illy and Kardanx. The one he'd thrown earlier seemed to be favoring his leg.

He couldn't see Taya at all, and hoped that Kas had managed to keep her back.

Then he closed the door, used his pin to start the engine, and lifted the transporter out of the sky raiders' reach.

As he banked over the river, he saw a flash of white lightning, saw it again. It seemed to be originating from one of the sky raiders, and as he turned the transporter to keep the window of the pilot's cabin facing the landing area, he saw Eli fall.

He looked desperately below for a flat place to land, and then, just when he found something, he saw the sky raiders were edging away from the attack team from the camp, moving toward the other transporter.

He'd known that was a possibility, had discussed it with Aidan, Kas, and Luci, so there were people under the transporter, ready to step forward and cut off the sky raiders' route, but as he landed, before the swirling dust obscured his vision, he saw the flash of white lightning again, and wondered if they had a chance.

He was only four hundred meters from the landing area at most, but it would have to be enough, as he compromised between getting back quickly to protect the other transporter, and making it difficult for the sky raiders to take this one.

He leaped out of the craft, running as fast as he could toward the camp.

He had wondered if the sky raiders would bring any weapons to investigate what was happening at the camp.

Now he had his answer.

FORTY-ONE

TAYA WATCHED KAS, Luci, Eli, and six others from both villages who'd once been guards move forward after Garek had run behind the newly landed transporter. There were at least ten Kardanx as well, all big.

Aidan toppled over in the mechanical guard and then opened the dome and crawled out.

She saw the sky raiders react to that. Their faces were hard to see through the helmets, but they all stiffened, their focus on Aidan as he climbed to his feet.

She gripped the shadow ore shards a little tighter, started moving forward, feeling the cold slow her down a little.

She hadn't been able to find her coat when she'd woken, remembered she'd taken it off last night when she'd been so close to the forge fires.

There hadn't been time to go looking for it.

She was still crouched down, and she moved closer, keeping low as their team spread out, wooden planks and shovels gripped two-handed in front of them.

"What is happening here?" The hiss of the translation was clear in the silence. "You." The sky raider pointed to Kas. "Tell me. The rest, return to your sleeping quarters."

Kas pointed to himself, as if confused who they meant, and stepped in closer.

Then he must have called the Change because dirt puffed up at the feet of the sky raider who'd spoken to him, and he ran forward, shovel raised, and swung it in an arc. It connected with the sky raider's shoulder, and he stumbled back, hands up in surprise.

One of them turned and ran back to the transporter, and Taya stood, stepping forward to stop them, but a Kardanx was already after them.

She'd been told to stay back, to only use the shards if and when they were really needed, and so she hesitated.

"Taya."

The soft call came from behind her, and she looked over her shoulder, saw Noor, standing with Taya's coat held in one hand.

She reached for it, grateful, and then frowned as it seemed to tinkle.

"I sewed the circles on it for you," Noor said, dark circles under her eyes. She looked pale with fatigue. "We'll have to take them off before you can get in the transporter, but I woke early, and Quardi told me what you intended to do with them."

Quardi probably talked Noor into this, thinking it would protect her, Taya decided, but she slipped it on and sighed as warmth enveloped her. "Thanks."

Noor nodded, and it was only then that Taya saw she was holding one of the picks Quardi had been working on in her other hand.

Taya turned back to the fight, saw Garek push the sky raider off the side of the transporter, and saw the Kardanx who stood below slam a piece of wood into him as he lay on the ground.

Kas swung his shovel again, drawing her eye, but the sky raider he was aiming at moved out of the way and then the one who Garek had pushed off the side of the transporter rolled to his feet, moving a little slower after his fall and the hit the Kardanx had gotten in, but without panic or obvious distress.

They were behaving strangely, and she leaned forward, dread curling in the pit of her stomach.

They didn't look worried enough by this attack.

"Is Min in place by the river?" Taya hadn't seen Min this morning, but that had been the plan. For her to call the water Change and use it against the sky raiders anyway she could, if they made it that far.

Noor nodded. "Everyone's in place. This is what we've been waiting for for so long. Pilar wanted me to stay back, he's there just near Eli, but it's everyone's duty to fight now. Everyone's."

More of the camp came out of the shadows into the light cast by the high, angled lights around the landing area, all of them with crude weapons raised, and still the sky raiders looked more curious than afraid.

"Something's wrong," Taya said, and stood. As she did, the limp body of a sky raider without his helmet fell from the pilot's door and then it closed. A moment later dust blasted out from under the transporter, and it lifted off.

The sky raiders looked back and up briefly, and for the first time, they seemed to be paying attention.

Eli advanced on one, and suddenly white lightning lit up the night, enveloping him, and everyone froze as he toppled to the ground.

Not one of them had forgotten the white lightning. The terrible pain of it.

Taya saw everyone go still, and some take a step back.

She couldn't blame them.

The sky raiders started moving toward the other transporter, and dread grabbed her in its cold, hoary claws.

"No."

They needed both transporters. The sky raiders could not get the second one.

She saw Kas dodge a blast of white lightning, then Luci went down as she was caught in a stream of it.

And the four sky raiders moved closer and closer to the transporter.

Taya ran, ignoring the cry from Noor behind her, ignoring everything. She ran in an arc that would get her to the transporter before the sky raiders, to block them off, although she reminded herself she couldn't get too close, covered in shadow ore as she was.

They noticed her, and one of them swung her way as she sprinted the last few meters to get herself in front of the ship.

He shot her before she could let her shards loose, and as the lightning hit, she felt the burn of nausea at the back of her throat at the memory of the pain.

But there was no pain. Not this time.

The lightning hit her coat and seemed to leap back toward the small black device held in the sky raider's hand.

The sky raider gave a cry, high-pitched and terrible, and went down.

For a long moment, the other sky raiders were absolutely still.

Taya looked down at herself, saw the shadow ore circles sway with her movement, and looked up again, eyes fierce.

She took a step toward them. Let go of three of her shards. She embedded them in the closest sky raider's suit, two in the center of his body, one just under his helmet.

He staggered back, trying to pull them out.

She let go of the other seven shards and as they found their mark, Garek leaped out of the darkness, screaming a wordless battle cry like a garpal from the shadow pits of Dethbarelle.

He was on the sky raider closest to her before she could take another step, ripping off his helmet.

Kas grabbed another, now also immobilized by the shards, and she saw the new Kardanx leader, Jona, fiddle at the neck of the third, work it out, and rip it off with a triumphant cry.

Garek let his sky raider fall, choking and gasping, and made his way to her without looking back.

She put her hands on his arms, saw blood smeared on his chest and looked up at him, eyes wide.

"Just a few scratches," he said, his expression so blank it was frightening. "You?"

"Nothing at all. Thanks to Noor's sewing. And your father." She lifted an arm, let the circles jingle, hoping to snap him out of the terrible cold in his eyes.

He traced a finger over one of them and forced a smile. "The old man just keeps redeeming himself over and over, doesn't he? Soon, I won't be able to hold a single grudge against him."

She laughed, low and huskier than she'd meant to. Let him dip his head and kiss her lightly on the lips, although she could feel him holding back, reining himself in with massive control.

He drew back and looked to the side, at the sky raider who had tried to hit her with white lightning, his face a mask of such pitiless loathing, she swallowed.

"They used that same light to capture us," Taya said, and bent down, picked up the black device carefully. "I suppose it works as well on them as it does on us." She handed it to Garek. "And now I know one reason why they want the shadow ore so badly."

Garek lifted his gaze from the device resting on his palm to her face. "The shadow ore deflects the lightning?"

"It bounces it straight back."

"Which means they want to use it against people shooting it at them."

"They're in a war?" Taya frowned. "A war with themselves?"

Garek shrugged. "Same as we often are."

Oh. That made so much sense.

Garek slipped the device into the pocket of his coat, crouched beside the sky raider and took his helmet off. "He's dead, but it could be because the suit stopped creating the right kind of air for him, not the lightning."

"Eli." Taya suddenly remembered. She looked around desperately, saw Jerilia was kneeling beside him and ran over.

"He's alive." Jerilia looked up. "It's just like when they took us."

Taya nodded, felt the relief drain her of all energy.

"What now?" Jerilia angled her head up as Garek joined Taya, pulled her close to him with an arm around her shoulders.

"Now we put the shadow ore in their water boxes, and we go. As fast as we can."

FORTY-TWO

THEY SLIPPED off Shadow like thieves in the night, with Garek flying them over the horizon and then up, up, up, and right, toward Barit.

Kas, Taya and Aidan stood watch at the window that encircled the pilot's cabin, searching for any sign they were being pursued.

Garek had found a way to open the pilot's area to the rear, so they could switch out the watch with others when they got tired. Dom kept the second transporter slightly to the right and back a little, allowing Garek to take the lead.

Taya felt her heart flutter in her chest as Barit got closer. She had planned and plotted for this, but hadn't truly believed she would achieve it.

She thought she would die trying, and that had been enough.

She turned to look over at Garek, sitting at the controls, and their gazes clashed.

She shivered.

She'd loved him for a long time, but the Garek she'd fallen for was gone. The new Garek was harder, more focused, and fortunately loved her just as fiercely.

"Come here," he said, and she walked over to him.

He put an arm around her waist and lifted her onto his lap, and she curled into him, breathing in the scent of him, letting it fill her lungs and settle on her skin, letting the heat of him seep into her bones.

"I was too far away, when the sky raider shot you," he murmured into her ear, his hand smoothing her hair over and over. "I was running flat out, but I was still too far. And I saw them bring Eli down earlier. I thought he was dead, and that I was watching them kill you in front of my eyes." His hold on her tightened.

"I couldn't let them get the transporter," she whispered back.

"I know." He buried his nose in her hair. "But I never want to be in that place again. Too far away, and helpless. Like when they took you the first time."

They sat that way for a long time, until Taya slid off his lap and went to find Noor and check on Min, who was watching the containers to make sure the water didn't leak out.

Jerilia was keeping watch over Eli, and one of Luci's family sat beside her, but neither had moved since they'd been shot, although both had a steady pulse.

She, Pilar, and Noor put together a meal, and persuaded Kas and Aidan to let others take the watch. They sat on the floor at Garek's feet and ate quietly, no one in the mood for laughter or the light banter they'd used at the camp.

Hour after hour slid by, and she knew it wasn't her imagination that everyone grew more and more tense as they got closer to Barit.

No one slept. No one felt safe enough, relaxed enough, to close their eyes.

They had been flying for half a day at least when Aidan, who was back on watch, straightened.

"They're coming." His voice was steady.

She moved to the window, saw the lights of three sky craft to the left.

The word spread through to the back, and Taya could hear the murmurs of worry.

"Do you think they'll be able to catch up with us?" she asked.

Garek shrugged. He hadn't moved from the pilot's seat since they'd taken off, and his face looked drawn. Tired.

"They have a dilemma," Kas said, and there was satisfaction in his voice. "They can't afford to lose either us or the transporters."

"But they won't do *nothing*," Min argued from the connecting door.

"No. They won't do nothing." Taya agreed. "But let's hope they wait until we land before they act. So that we don't crash."

"And they may not understand how I brought down that sky craft I used to reach you, but as soon as we land, they'll find out soon enough." Garek smiled. "I'll be back on Barit, and I'll be able to call the Change better."

"So will I," Kas agreed. "So will the other Changed with us."

The words seemed to bolster everyone, but as Taya looked back out at the lights converging on them, she wondered if it would be enough.

They had her spears. They had their Changed. They had the brave men and women who'd fought for their freedom at the camp, but there was no question who had the upper hand.

She shivered at the thought of the white lightning. The sky craft following them seemed to get closer, but so did Barit.

The ships following them were the small ones, the ones that shot the white lightning when they'd been taken back in Pan Nuk.

So they'd be facing that again when they landed.

"We can't bring what's following us to the Harven capital," Kas said, as if his mind was working along the same lines as her own. "We know they'll use their white lightning. It won't be safe."

Taya looked over at Garek, saw him nod.

"We'll have to pick a place that's far from anywhere. Fight them off, and then carry on with the victory lap Aidan wants us to make in the name of West Lathor."

Aidan grunted from the window, still keeping track of the sky craft. "Something tells me it won't be that simple."

"No. It never is." Garek laughed, but there was no bitterness in it. Despite the shadows under his eyes, he looked like he was genuinely looking forward to the confrontation.

It scared her more than anything else could.

THEY'D MADE BETTER time than Garek thought they would. He knew which way he was going this time, of course. Barit was hard to miss.

And the sky craft were still behind them, not quite caught up yet, which was another thing he'd never dared hope for.

He angled the transporter in a shallow trajectory as they came into Barit's atmosphere, and had Kas check that Dom was doing the same on his right wing.

Not that he could do anything about it if Dom tried to come in too hard. There might be a way to communicate with him, transporter to transporter, but Garek hadn't found it.

Oceans flashed far below them as they hit a layer of cloud and then broke through into clear sky.

He had no idea where they could be, no landmarks to use to orientate himself, and most of the landmarks would have been meaningless to him, anyway.

When it came to Barit, he had never left West Lathor.

Someone came through, Zek, the merchant who'd accompanied Luci to their planning sessions, and Kas made room for him at the very center of the window.

"Looks like Baltar," he said, pointing to the jagged coast line below them, and Aidan drew in a sharp breath.

"My sister's in Baltar," he said, looking down as well. "West Lathor is northwest of here."

Zek gave a nod. "We could come down on the Endless Escarp-ment, if you're looking for someplace uninhabited."

He stood beside Garek, showed him which direction he needed to head, and Garek adjusted, banking them left and going even lower.

"What a way to travel, eh?" Zek looked around the pilot's cabin. "Imagine the possibilities if we all had access to something like this. The Endless Escarpment wouldn't feel endless any more."

Garek grinned. "No. I would agree this is better than walking or going by cart."

It was a pity that in time, the transporter would fall to pieces in the Barit air.

He swooped even lower, and now he could see the wide road that wound through the natural undulations of the escarpment.

Far in the distance he could see dust rising from a caravan of trav-elers, but a few kilometers ahead there was a flat, straight stretch of road and no one to be seen.

"Everyone not carrying the wooden boxes of ore, get ready to get out and scatter. The more spread out we are, the harder it'll be to get us. Those carrying the ore, get a good distance from the transporters, then run yourselves." Kas had moved to the doorway at the back, and got quiet murmurs of confirmation in response.

"They're still following us." Aidan angled his head as Garek came down to land.

But Garek had taken that as a given, and piloted them in, heard the scream of engines behind him when Dom overcompensated on power as they landed, both craft kicking up a massive swirl of golden dust.

"That's good," he said.

"The dust?" Kas asked.

He nodded, caught Kas's eye and remembered he was talking to someone who called the earth Change.

"We could use this." Garek couldn't help the surge of anticipa-tion that rose up in him.

He shifted his gaze, saw Taya watching him, a look in her eyes that told him she'd seen his eagerness and was afraid for him.

"We obscure their view, you throw your spears," he told her, and she gave a tight nod and moved out of his sight, into the back to help carry the ore out.

He powered down, opening the back door as he did so, and judging from the clatter of feet, there was a rush for the outside.

He opened both pilot doors as well, left them for Aidan and Kas and ran to the back, grabbed the side of one of the long boxes and heaved it up with a mix of men and women from Harven and West Lathor.

They jogged down the ramp and followed those carrying the other boxes in front of them.

Garek twisted his head around and up, looking for the sky craft, but saw nothing until they set the boxes down.

He ripped the lid off his one, saw Lynal, his old competitor for Taya's affections, pull off another, and someone from Harven levered off the third.

"Those not running, look for the sky craft," he ordered, because no one seemed to be heading off as Kas had ordered.

These were all former guards, he realized, or potential guards, men and women with strength and training they wanted to put to use as much as he did.

The dust was still swirling as Dom revved the engines, and the door hadn't opened yet.

Dom was too rattled maybe, or having some kind of trouble.

As he thought it, the back ramp dropped down, and the Kardanx streamed out in a tight group.

Some headed for him, others saw the Illy were scattering and did the same.

Two knelt on the ground, dust almost obscuring them, and touched their lips to the soil of Barit in thanks.

He used the swirling air, lifting the dust higher, and blanketed those running for cover with a dust cloud just above their heads.

Aidan and Kas had been looking up, standing beside the transporter, but then the dust got thicker, and he realized Kas was funneling more of it into the air. Both men moved closer to him, where there was still some visibility.

And then the sky raiders came.

He was an expert at spotting them in the sky, had spent more than a year of his life doing just that.

The glint of silver, the far off whine of sound.

Aidan heard it, too, cocked his head to one side, and Garek pointed.

Everyone looked up. Everyone except Taya. She bent down and took a spear from its water bath.

"If some of you are staying and can't call a Change, then your job is to hold spears for Taya, and hand her one when she needs it."

Zek and Lynal nodded, scooped up a few spears each, and others did the same.

"You'll need to stay with me so I have access to the spears." Taya spoke for the first time since they'd landed, and he was suddenly swamped by an emotion he couldn't describe, seeing her with a spear over her shoulder, in the tight-fitting clothes of a guard. "If you need to run for any reason—if they start using white lightning or if they're going to capture you—drop the spears so I have a chance of getting to them. The sky raiders won't go near them."

Garek could see none wanted to admit to the idea of running away, but everyone nodded reluctantly.

"Did you tell Dom to keep the engines running?" Kas asked, as the transporter kept kicking up dust.

Garek shook his head. "I didn't tell him how to turn it off. But it's working for us."

Kas gave a grin in response and even more dust rose up, which Garek flicked upward so it looked like a miniaturized sand storm.

"Don't waste too much energy," Taya warned them, stepping close to him, close enough that he could reach out and run a hand down her back.

"It takes almost nothing at all, with us working together," Kas told her, and Garek wondered if he'd understood that before. He usually worked alone, but Kas was right—with a combination of the two of them, he could do this all day without burning out. Either of them could have created the same effect by themselves, but with a considerably bigger drain on their reserves.

"They're coming in for a low swoop." Aidan had kept his gaze skyward.

It was an intimidation tactic. The sight of the gleaming silver craft, so alien to everything on Barit, the roar of sound, the low pass.

It snapped Garek back to himself, and he called the Change fully, settled in to a place where the air was thick and syrupy and reached for the air around the sky craft diving toward them.

Usually he couldn't do this, because the sky raiders were after either people or goods, and that meant built-up areas. The time he'd brought the sky craft down, it had been just outside the walls of Gara, into a farmer's field.

He had the same freedom here. Actually, more.

Last time, he'd tried—and succeeded—in bringing the ship down in one piece for them to study. He had no such requirement now.

He felt the pilot try to pull up from his swoop, sensed the wobble as the sky raider fought his controls, could almost, almost taste the panic as the engines couldn't find enough power, and then hammered the air above the craft down like a fist, slamming it into the ground.

It crumpled in a scraping, shrieking cartwheel, getting smaller and more misshapen until it came to a steaming, groaning stop at least five hundred meters from them.

"One down," he said with satisfaction as he drew back from the Change.

Kas was staring at him with his mouth open. "You've come a long way from when I trained you," he said. "And I thought you were too strong for your own good then."

Aidan was also watching him with a face that said a lot was going on under the surface. Only Taya looked at him with appreciation and wonder and a fierce satisfaction. She slid her arm around his waist and pulled him close.

It frustrated him, always had, that he had to hold back, not use his full ability, to make others more comfortable.

But Taya didn't want him to, and he reveled in the freedom that gave him.

"Headache?" she asked him, as he looked up once more, searching for the other two craft.

They'd be more cautious now.

He was almost certain they wouldn't understand how the craft had been brought down.

"No headache." He kept his gaze up as he answered her. "I probably should have one, but not yet."

She nodded. Hefted the spear on her shoulder and stepped a little away from him. "That them?" She pointed and he saw the telltale glint high in the sky.

"We need more dust cloud," he said to Kas, and they both got to work again, billowing it up from where it had subsided when his attention had been elsewhere.

Clearly, Kas had been too focused on what he'd been doing to concentrate on it as well.

"I don't know my range," Taya said, eyeing the second craft as it came in, higher than the first, more wary, but low enough to reach. The third stayed even higher, almost impossible to see.

Garek knew his range, though. He called his Change and reached again.

The pilot must have felt something, because the craft rolled away just as Garek hammered down. He caught one side of the wing, though, flipping the craft on its side, then flipped it again, so it was upside down, and then slammed again.

But this sky raider was more intuitive than the other one. He or she flipped back upright just before the craft hit the ground, and the pilot was able to skip it across the ground like a flat stone across water.

The crunch and screech of metal against the rocks and stones of the escarpment were clear, even over the engines of Dom's transporter. It hit something, probably a boulder, and began to spin.

When it came to a stop, its engines were still running.

"We need to shut it down." Garek thought it was possible it could still fly.

He looked up again, caught a glimpse of the third craft hovering high above. Waiting.

"Let's go." Taya's voice snapped his attention back to the ground. Her call hadn't been for him, it was for her spear carriers. They all started running toward the downed craft.

Garek hesitated. The first sky craft was a smoking, crumpled mess, and no matter what, it wasn't going anywhere. The second one still looked dangerous, but the third worried him.

The pilot must be watching, trying to work out what had gone wrong. And he or she wasn't going to make the same mistakes as the others.

Suddenly, the second craft lifted up.

The sounds coming from it told him it was in some trouble, there was a grating sound, but it got some height, hovered.

A flash of white blinded him. When he could see again, he blinked.

The spears were out of Lynal and Zek's hands, out of everyone's hands, floating in the air in a criss-cross pattern, and white lightning was dancing over them.

No one was down. No one.

The spears fell, except one, which flew into Taya's hand, and then she heaved it at the sky craft.

Garek reached for his Change, caught the spear, gave it extra power, and felt his Change mesh with Taya's for a moment, like he'd done with Kas. Complimenting her strength, as she complimented his.

The spear struck the front of the craft, piercing the window, and the whole craft dropped to the ground.

Taya did, too.

She'd burnt herself out.

But anyone could throw the spears physically. He realized now that's why Taya'd heaved it herself, she'd been trying to save her strength, but she'd been too late. It had run out.

He heard her call something to one of her helpers, saw Lynal run past her and leap up to the window, pull the spear out, and run back.

That was good.

He didn't think the sky craft was going anywhere, but it was better to have as much ammunition as they could get.

There was a sound above him, and with cold certainty, he knew he'd kept his attention off the third craft for too long.

He looked up, just as it came flying down toward him.

FORTY-THREE

SHE'D REACHED HER LIMIT.

Taya forced herself to her knees, took the spear Lynal had retrieved, and used it to help herself to her feet.

"I'm close to empty," she told him. "But we can still use the spears, we just have to throw them."

"That was quite a throw," Lynal said.

She laughed. "That wasn't me. That was Garek."

Lynal looked in Garek's direction, and his face went pale.

She turned, saw the third craft coming down, so fast . . .

Hefting the spear on her shoulder, she ran toward it. Garek was looking up, and she saw him blur a little, knew it was a level of Change she had yet to reach.

The sky craft flipped, but it righted itself and banked away, then came down with a scream of engines, the dust it blew up mingling with the dust Kas was still pumping into the air.

"Call your people, get them back in the transporters, and we will let you live." The hissing voice of the pilot was everywhere, amplified in a way Taya didn't understand.

It felt like magic. She knew it wasn't, but it was frightening, all the same.

She reached Garek's side and wasn't surprised when he held out his hand for her spear.

She gave it to him, looked behind her, and waited until Zek reached her, took one of the three he was holding.

Garek didn't give any response to the pilot, didn't say anything. He simply threw the spear, making it spin as it arced up and angled down to the roof.

The sky craft reversed back, and the spear landed just in front of it, almost obscured by the sandstorm.

She handed Garek her new spear, grabbed another from Zek but before Garek could throw again, white lightning shot out of two small tubes at the front, the first time she'd seen where it came from.

The shots were aimed like a warning, flaring from right to left in front of them, but the screams were all too real as clusters of searing white crawled over four Kardanx who were crouched down between Dom's transporter and the one the Illy had used.

Before the screams had died away, Taya turned to Garek, sucked in a breath when she realized he wasn't there.

She searched, frantic, through the swirling dust, blinking against the grit in her eyes.

There.

He must have run, because he had almost reached the sky craft, and Aidan was ahead of him.

The princeling turned and crouched a little.

Garek ran full tilt at him, got a boost up, and she saw the spear leave his hand. Penetrate the front section of the craft.

He jumped down, ran back and grabbed the spear that had missed, and then rammed it into one of the white lightning tubes.

There was a horrible smell of burning, and then relative silence, as the engines stopped.

The only noise now was the sound of Dom's transporter, and Taya realized it was getting on her nerves.

The sound of metal clattering on rock came from behind her and she whirled to see what it was.

Zek had dropped his last spear. He stood staring at the downed craft. "He got them all."

She thought that's what he said, because the headache that hit her like a vicious, vindictive strike forced her to her knees, and then over to her side.

She was a baby when it came to calling the Change, and she'd overextended.

Through the dark buzz, as purple and orange lights flashed behind her eyes, she remembered that time, long ago, when Garek had fallen in the main street of Pan Nuk.

Guess it was her turn.

SHE WOKE SLOWLY, aware of a vibration beneath her, and what felt like her coat under her head, the warmth of something covering her, as well.

Murmurs and quiet conversation floated in the air around her, along with the sounds of feet shuffling and clothes rustling.

She opened her eyes to the familiar dimensions of the transporter, and slowly lifted herself up on her elbows. The warm covering was Garek's coat, tucked around her, and she smoothed a hand down it.

Min crouched down beside her, smiling, and handed her a wooden cup of water.

She sipped it gratefully, her throat feeling like it was coated with dust, which it probably was, given how much of the stuff Garek and Kas had thrown into the air.

"Where—?" She coughed, and had to drink some more.

"On the way to Harven. We're nearly there, I think. Zek is acting as navigator."

So they had gotten away.

"The Kardanx? The ones who were hit?" She closed her eyes at the memory and shivered. That is what had once happened to *her*. To all of them. Somehow, seeing it done to someone, seeing those sparking white lights crawl like bloodsuckers over the Kardanx was horrifying. It was like the lightning was alive. A creature that enveloped its prey.

She felt nausea rise in her throat, and slowly sipped a little more water, breathed deeply.

"They're unconscious. Garek let the Kardanx kill all three pilots. The one in the first craft was nearly dead anyway, but the other two were very much alive." Min looked off to the side, as if remembering it.

Taya struggled to sit, leaned against the cool metal wall. "It disturbed you?"

"I wanted them to do it, and then I felt sorry for the sky raiders." Min shrugged.

"They wanted blood, then?" she asked, understanding the need. "They would have died eventually if we'd left them there."

"Garek said they needed to die. Just in case the sky raiders rescued them and they told their commanders what happened. What we can do. What defenses we've worked out. Maybe they can send messages up to the sky above, maybe not, but it was better to make sure they couldn't share our secrets."

It was harsh, but Taya knew the element of surprise was also the only edge they had, when everything else was stacked against them.

"Taya." Quardi rolled up to her, and the delight on his face warmed her, dispelling some of the chill Min's words had settled on her shoulders. Before this was over, there would be many more times they all had to make hard decisions.

"You didn't leave me lying on the Endless Escarpment to learn my lesson, I see," she teased him, forcing the darkness back a little.

He frowned, then she saw the moment he recalled the Garek-in-the-street incident, because he threw back his head and laughed. "That was you, with the pillow and the blanket, wasn't it?"

"I have no idea what you're talking about," she said to him, and used the wall behind her to pull herself to her feet, hooking her finger in the collar of Garek's coat. "You were all right? In the transporter?"

Quardi had stayed inside, watching over Eli and Luci. His chair would have been useless on the rutted, uneven road, and even worse off it, and it had made sense for someone to stand guard, just in case a sky raider had gotten inside.

Quardi patted the mallet still lying across his lap. "I was the safest one of all of you."

Taya kissed him on the cheek, and then walked unsteadily forward, one hand on the wall, until she reached the pilot's chamber.

Garek turned his head, his eyes hot, and she stumbled over to him, draped his coat over his shoulders and let him pull her onto his lap.

"When I heard my father laugh, I knew you'd woken." He smiled against her forehead.

"I told him I was grateful he didn't leave me lying there to learn my lesson."

Garek's smile broadened. "It wasn't quite a pillow and a blanket, but I did carry you into the transporter and pillow your coat under your head."

"Like I said to your father, I have no idea what you're talking about." She pressed her lips to the side of his neck, then at the sound of Kas clearing his throat behind her, stood up and went into her brother's arms.

When he'd squeezed her hard and let her go, she went to the window to look out. "The Dartalian Range?"

She had never seen mountains from above, and pressed her face against the window to drink it in.

"That's The Finger," Zek said, pointing out the peak.

"Oh. I've heard of it, but I never thought I'd see it. It does look like a finger."

She caught a glimpse of silver out of the corner of her eye, felt the prickle of fear run down her arms as she turned, and then blew out a breath when she saw it was Dom's transporter, once again a little behind and to the right.

"Dom all right?" she asked, looking back at Garek.

"He's tense, but yes, he'll last until we get to Harven's capital." Garek looked less strained than he had before they landed on the Endless Escarpment, even though he hadn't slept for nearly a day, and had called the Change at least three times.

"What?" He frowned, catching her staring at him, and she shook her head, blew him a kiss.

"How long until we're there?"

"Luf is a week on foot from where we are now," Zek said. "I have no experience on how long it will take to fly. But it took me two months to reach the Endless Escarpment, and we've done it in a few hours, so soon, I expect. Very soon." He looked around the transporter with a gaze that said he was thinking just how much money and time he would save if only he had one of his own.

She could see the last row of mountains, like sentinels standing watch over Harven, slightly lower than those deeper in the range, but sheer, the gray, jagged cliffs an almost impenetrable wall.

"Cassinya is just down there." Luci came in, looking a little pale, but otherwise recovered. She stood beside Taya and pointed down. "There on the foothills. The gateway to Harven from Dartalia."

"You have children?" Taya asked, thinking of Luca, of her and Kas's relief when Garek had confirmed he was all right.

"Two, but my parents were also left behind. I know they'll have taken care of them."

She nodded, and stood quietly as Luci took over the directions from Zek, exclaiming with interest at the landmarks she'd only ever seen from the ground, as well as ones she'd missed before.

"I didn't know that old fort was there," she said, and Taya saw the one she meant, a ruin that looked as if it had been gnawed down by time, standing at the end of an overgrown track that was hidden from the main road by a thick wood. "I've passed that way many times, and had no idea."

"Look, it's a short cut to Luf, if you can navigate the track," Zek murmured. He pointed to where the track bypassed the fort and continued on, meeting the road at a point Taya guessed was closer to the capital city.

"You're right. But it looks impassable." Luci tapped the window thoughtfully.

Zek gave a reluctant nod, but Taya guessed he would at least try to use it, the next time he made his way from Cassinya to Luf.

"And there we are," Luci said, her voice soft in the cabin. "Luf is ahead."

Taya raised her gaze from the ground below, and saw in the distance a walled city, like Juli and Gara, crenellations clear in the afternoon light. It sat on top of a low hill, the walls sitting like a crown on a head.

There were flags flying and she caught the glint of armor on the walls.

Even though she wasn't home yet, it felt good, this first step in bringing the Illy home.

She glanced sideways at Aidan, standing with his feet apart, hands clasped behind his back, gaze fixed on the city before them.

He was most likely thinking how best he could use this situation to West Lathor's advantage, and she couldn't fault him for it.

It would be good to have a strong leader again. Someone who put West Lathor first.

And if she guessed right, this would be the first step he took on the road to becoming her liege.

FORTY-FOUR

"WHERE IS a good place to land in the city?" Garek asked, looking across at Luci. "It'll need to be big enough for both transporters."

Luci glanced over her shoulder from her position at the window. "I've been thinking about it and the park in front of the palace makes the most sense. It's a public venue on holidays, otherwise entrance is limited to those with permission from the liege. There won't be a crowd we could hurt by mistake, and there is plenty of space."

"It's at the center of the city?" Garek asked.

Luci nodded, and he banked left rather than going straight over the front gates. He kept the transporter tilted to one side, following the city walls until he'd done a full circuit.

He wanted everyone to see them. As many witnesses as possible.

Luci frowned, turning to him as if to question it, but then held her silence as he banked again and descended in a tight spiral to the park that sat atop the hill, nestled in front of a palace that was a massive rectangle with arched windows and doors.

The park was full of trees but there was an open area where people could congregate, and he landed as close to the edge of the woods as he could, giving a less steady Dom more room.

"You going to power down?" Aidan asked him.

He shook his head. "Not yet. This is your show now."

Aidan hesitated, then inclined his head. "If we need to leave quickly, it's best you're at the controls."

"You think they'll attack us?" Zek asked.

"We're the enemy, as far as they know," Kas said, and Zek gave a reluctant nod.

"Guards are running toward us, but they're being cautious." Aidan stood at the door, looking out.

"Are you going to open up?" Luci asked him, and Garek shook his head.

"We'll wait until someone senior arrives. My guess is the young hotheads will have gotten here first."

Luci gave a snort of laughter at that. "So says someone who was once a young hothead."

He was still young by most measures, but she was right. His days of stupidity had ended a long time ago.

He saw Kas grin at Luci's words, and heard Taya laugh softly.

She stood with her brother and Zek, out of the way, keeping watch out the window.

"There's the liege's general. Carey Faloni." Luci was leaning against the window.

"The look on his face is priceless."

"Don't laugh at him." Luci was dead serious now. "He's a pompous ass and he has no sense of humor, let alone the ability to laugh at himself."

"I think we can risk opening the door," Aidan said. "As soon as they see Luci, they'll be at least interested in hearing from her before they start shooting their arrows."

Garek pressed the button, and the door slid back on itself.

"General Faloni." Luci leaned out of the door, her hands cupped on either side of her mouth so her voice carried. "Can you call the liege, please?"

Even over the roar of both his and Dom's engines, Garek could hear the shouts as the Luf residents caught sight of her.

"I'm no sky raider," Luci called in response to something someone must have called to her. "But I'll explain when the liege gets here." She angled her body, facing inward for a moment. "I'd tell that fool Faloni to get his guards to lower their weapons, but that'll have the opposite effect."

Garek nodded. They could withstand any number of arrows. He knew that from his time fighting the sky raiders on the walls of Gara.

Luci stood silently, waiting, even though Garek guessed questions were being called to her. He knew when the liege arrived, because both she and Aidan straightened.

"My liege," Luci called. "I am Town Master Luci of Cassinya. About two months ago now, most of the adults in my town were taken by the sky raiders. We were taken to Shadow, and forced to work there."

She stopped, swallowing, and Garek realized she was overcome. Now that she was free, she was able to release the tight grip she'd had on her fear and rage.

"Who is that beside you?" The call must have been extremely loud for Garek to hear it over the engines, and he guessed they were using a speaking horn.

"This is the liege of West Lathor's son. He and one of his guards from West Lathor found a way to rescue us, and agreed to bring us home." Again, her voice broke.

"West Lathor?" The question sound like it had been wrenched from the liege's lips.

"The sky raiders took people from the Illy and Kardai. Half of the Illy are West Lathorians. Their liege sent his son to bring his people back."

Garek's gaze jerked to Luci's back at that. She couldn't have said it better from Aidan's point of view. Did she understand what Aidan was trying to do? The game he was playing?

Aidan looked over at him, eyebrows raised, so Garek knew he was as surprised. Perhaps the Kardanx weren't the only ones to feel the sting of being forgotten and left to rot.

There was silence, as if Luci's words were being absorbed by the crowds.

"We wish to leave the transporter, to set foot on our home soil." Luci opened her arms. "Please ask the guards to lower their weapons."

Someone called something sharply, and Luci's shoulders relaxed a fraction.

"I would speak with Valtor's son, too." The words were measured.

"I will gladly speak with you," Aidan called back, bowing his head briefly.

"And the guard that came with you."

Aidan hesitated, turned back into the cabin. "What do you think?"

"Habred, my liege, won't like being denied." Luci's voice was soft, and unspoken in what she said was that she might be blamed in some way for their lack of cooperation.

Garek nodded. "I'll power down. Kas and Eli can stand guard." He rose from his seat, picked up the bag he'd set at his feet and made his way to Kas and Taya, making sure his back was to Aidan, Luci and Zek.

Never show all your cards. That had been a lesson he'd learned from Kas when he'd trained under him.

But he didn't think that applied to family.

He dipped into the bag and took out two of the four slim, palm-sized black boxes he'd found on the sky raiders at the camp, holding them close to his body. He handed them both to Kas. "One for you, one for Eli. I think you press the button and it shoots white lightning." He kept his voice so low, only Kas and Taya could hear him. "Keep what it can do a secret between you and Eli."

Kas took them with a nod and they disappeared from sight.

"I can stand guard outside too," Taya said. "They might not see me as much of a threat."

Garek hesitated. That was true, but he didn't want Taya anywhere near guards with bows who might just let their fingers slip.

"I'll be careful." She looked sidelong at Kas. "Kas won't let me be anything else, anyway."

"It'll help that we won't look like we have any weapons." Kas said.

"I can take the shadow ore shards out. They won't understand what those are, either."

"I'd rather you don't give up your secrets too easily," Garek told her.

"Is my Change a secret?" She frowned.

He and Kas exchanged a look.

"The Iron Guard has kept the same secret for a long time. There has to be a reason for that." Garek couldn't say why he felt the flames of fear licking at him at the thought of Taya's Change being widely known, only that his instincts had never steered him wrong.

She studied his face for a beat, then gave a nod. "Aidan and Luci are waiting. You better go."

She went up on her toes, kissed him goodbye, and he let the gesture steady him.

She was here and she was relatively safe.

"We go out the back?" he asked Luci, and she nodded.

He closed the pilot door.

Kas moved out of the pilot's chamber, to the back. Garek watched him put a friendly arm around Eli, and then waited for them to reach the door before he pressed the button and lowered it to form a ramp.

Light flooded in as it came down in a smooth, silent motion.

"Wait." Luci's voice cut through the murmurs of excitement. "Let Aidan and me step out first, then the Cassinyans, you can step out, too, but don't go far from the transporter. I need to negotiate where we'll stay with the liege."

"And if he can't take us?" someone called.

"Then we'll take you home." Garek didn't think the liege would deny them, though.

There was silence, and then nods of agreement.

The ramp hit the ground, and Aidan walked down it, waited for Luci at the bottom.

Garek came up behind them, eyes taking in the way the guards had surrounded them, the crowds of people just beyond. The sheer number of townspeople would make the situation almost impossible for the Guard to control.

The people would soon start working their way through the guard ranks, he guessed. He wondered how the guards would respond, but hoped with their own people milling about, they'd be very careful.

He looked back at the transporter, saw Eli and Kas were standing at the bottom of the ramp.

There was no sign of Taya, and satisfied, he turned to face the delegation before them.

FORTY-FIVE

TAYA STOOD at the pilot's door and from its window watched Luci and Aidan bow to the liege of Harven, noticed Garek did not.

He was behind them, so it was possible to excuse the lapse, although she was sure there was no lapse at all. He simply refused to lower his guard. His gaze would be taking in everything.

She'd seen him look back, seen him relax, and knew she'd been right to stay back, although she wanted to be standing between Eli and Kas, looking at the palace gardens of Luf, and seeing what threat there was to Garek.

He could concentrate on his own safety, and that of Luci and Aidan, because she was safe.

They couldn't live their lives with her always keeping back, but she was willing to give him this for now, when he'd just found her, while everything was still raw and new.

The guards parted, and Garek disappeared from sight as they moved forward, and the guards reformed their line.

She walked into the back area, saw Quardi, Pilar, Noor and Min were sitting together, looking out into the gardens at the crowd of onlookers and guards.

Those from Cassinya were all standing near the top of the ramp, craning their necks, their gaze fixed on the crowds.

"Will Dom know what we're doing here?" She hadn't given much thought to the Kardanx, but the sound of their transporter's engines was hard to miss.

"Garek and Dom discussed it before we left the Endless Escarpment," Min told her. "He knows we're here to drop off the Cassinya, that his people have to wait inside the transporter."

"The Harven Guard might get a little twitchy at the sight of eighty Kardanx tumbling out in front of their liege's palace," Quardi confirmed with a laugh.

"They're twitchy enough as it is," Taya agreed. It felt as if things were getting more tense, not less; the guards looking behind them now and again as the crowds pushed closer.

"Stay back!" The words boomed out through a speaking horn, and everyone froze. After a moment, the crowds did seem to ease back a little, but one little boy, precocious, daring, darted past the line and ran for the ramp.

A woman screamed from behind the guards. The little boy stumbled at the sound, fell flat on his face, and started to cry.

"Someone needs to go out there and pick him up," Kas said. "They need to see we're safe."

One of the Cassinyan women, Gera, who was waiting in the group near the top of the ramp, walked down, arms loose at her sides. She was someone Taya knew and liked, a day shift worker who was as strong and brave as anyone.

"I never once thought we'd be treated like we were dangerous," one of the Cassinya villagers said. "All I could think of was that we'd be home. That everyone we'd left behind would be happy to see us. It never crossed my mind we'd be facing armed guards."

Gera crouched beside the boy and murmured to him, and it felt as if the crowd held its breath.

The boy had stopped crying and Gera extended a hand, helped him up, and then waved her hand toward the crowd.

The boy looked longly back at the transporter, but Taya agreed with Gera's handling of it. It would only induce panic if she allowed the boy inside to look.

The crowd seemed to breathe out in relief, and slowly, more and more Cassinya villagers walked down the ramp to join Gera where she stood in the sunshine.

Some of them simply stood, heads back, drinking in the Star's light. Others looked over the crowd, as if to find a familiar face.

More than one did.

There were shouts of greeting, calls of support.

Eventually, someone called for their story.

"We were taken to Shadow," Zek answered. He was one of those who'd seen a familiar face, and Taya guessed he would be known to many traders in the city. "We were taken to work in a mine, because the sky raiders can't breathe our air, and they needed us to do the work for them."

There were comments and opinions voiced around them, but mostly, Taya could see, the crowds were insatiable for more.

"We lived in a camp, made up of tents and wooden shacks, whatever the sky raiders brought us from their raids on Barit."

Again, the exclamations, as they finally began to make sense of what the sky raiders had been doing.

"So how did you get free?"

Zek pointed the way Aidan and Garek had gone. "There is a guard from West Lathor. He is very strong. The people of his village were stolen, just like we were. And he had managed to bring down one of the sky raiders' sky crafts. He and the liege of West Lathor's son made a plan to take the craft, follow the sky raiders back to their base, and rescue us."

There was silence at that.

"Did they know the base was on Shadow?" someone called.

Zek shook his head. "How could they? But that didn't stop them. They found a way to us, and then together, we made a plan to escape. We've fought off the sky raiders three times, and thanks mainly to that guard from West Lathor, we won every time."

"Who is in the other ship?" This was from one of the guards, who were as absorbed in the story as anyone else.

"Only half the prisoners were taken from the Illy. The other half are from Kardai. They're in the other ship. It was decided that the Cassinya villagers would be taken home first."

"It's almost impossible to believe," a large man who'd worked his way almost to the front called out.

"That's true. It is very hard to believe." Gera spoke, wiping her cheeks with the back of her hand, and Taya realized while Zek had told their story, many of the Cassinya villagers had started weeping, as if finally giving themselves permission to let go. "I thought I would die up on Shadow when the sky raiders no longer had a use for us and left us there to starve. But here we are. Some of us know people here in Luf. If my cousin Veri is in this crowd, then I know someone, too. This will be my fifth visit to Luf, although by far the most memorable."

There was a wave of quiet laughter at her words.

"We are standing here, alive." Gera took up her statement when the sound had died down. "We walked out of a sky raider ship, which you saw us do with your own eyes. And the liege of West Lathor's son and the guard Zek told you about are now talking to our liege, along with our town master. It may be impossible to believe, but sometimes, the impossible is true. I know I will always give the impossible a chance now. I've lived it."

There was a hum as she finished, and as she wiped away her last tear, the voices rose, and then hands rose into the air. There was a sharp clap, then two, then one again, and then a shout. "Welcome!"

"What is that?" Noor asked and Taya shook her head.

"I don't know."

"It's the Harven Welcome, used to welcome back those who've been away at war," Quardi told them.

The Cassinya villagers were crying openly now, and Taya felt tears prick her own eyes.

"That was well done, then," she said. Because they were like combatants who were coming back from the front line.

They deserved a hero's welcome.

FORTY-SIX

GAREK HEARD the sound of a thousand hands clapping as one. Once, then twice, then once again.

"Welcome!" The shout echoed off the palace walls.

Habred looked up, and the look on the liege's face told Garek he wasn't pleased to hear it.

"They're giving us the Welcome." Luci looked in the direction of the palace gardens, and from the smile on her face, Garek guessed she was as happy about it as Habred was angry.

"So they should," Aidan said, and although he wasn't looking at the Harven liege, Garek knew he'd seen Habred's scowl and was happy to poke at him. "You are heroes. Victims who fought back against a more powerful enemy force."

"How do I know any of this is true?" Habred said, and Garek looked up and met his gaze.

"Did you not see the sky raider ships we flew in on?" he asked quietly. "Are you saying Luci has lied about her entire village being taken. That we have lied about our village?"

"I know the village of Cassinya was taken, some of the elders of the village made a report, and I sent guards to check the story. We gave them assistance." Habred said the words unwillingly, but he had to say them, Garek knew, because there were enough advisors standing around them in the hall of the palace that he needed to make it clear he had cared about his people, had followed up, at least.

But he also knew he looked weak in the face of a rescue of his people by West Lathor. A rescue beyond what he and his advisors and his guards had ever contemplated.

He knew it. Aidan knew it.

So did everyone else in the room.

"Don't feel bad at being unable to do more," Aidan said. "We could not have contemplated the rescue if Garek hadn't brought down a sky raider craft."

Habred inclined his head, the movement jerky and stiff. "I hadn't realized West Lathor had made so much progress in the fight against the sky raiders."

"We put our people first, liege, as I'm sure you do, too." Aidan's words were smooth. "We've had little time to send out missives, our focus has been on keeping West Lathor safe from attack."

His words weren't in any way aggressive, and yet Habred blinked.

Oh, yes. He had definitely been party to the plan to take West Lathor. Garek was certain of it.

They were standing in a pit of vipers.

"We need to leave soon," he said to Aidan, quietly, but loud enough for Habred and some of his advisors to hear. "The second transporter still has its engines running, and we need to get the Dartalians home before we can go home ourselves."

"The Dartalians don't want to be let off here?" one of Habred's advisors asked. She had been quiet through the whole conversation, but Garek had noticed that her focus had been absolute.

"They were originally headed for Luf when they were taken," Garek told her. "But they have been away for over two months now, and word may have gotten back to their families that they were taken. They want to be returned home to reassure their loved ones that they are all right."

She nodded.

"If you ever need anything, Luci, just send word and West Lathor will help you," Aidan said.

Habred recoiled. "We know our obligations to Cassinya. We don't need help from another province."

"Forgive me." Aidan's voice was suspiciously humble. "I meant no disrespect. It is just that Luci and the people of Cassinya have become like family to the people of Pan Nuk. They worked in the sky raider mines together, they slept in the same camp, and we all fought together to get free. It is a bond that won't be forgotten."

Garek kept his face neutral, but he wanted to smile at the fury that ignited in Habred's eyes at that.

He had been outmaneuvered.

Some of the advisors, perhaps those not yet aware of the plans afoot to shuffle the Illian borders in Harven's favor, smiled at Aidan.

"You do your liege proud with such sentiments. And Harven won't forget your service in bringing back our own, and in such a way . . ." The advisor who spoke waved a hand in the air. "It will go down as legend."

That, Garek thought as they walked out of the hall, was exactly what Aidan was hoping.

———

"WHAT DID the Dartalian liege have to say?" Garek spoke to Aidan as soon as they rose above the towers and walls of the Dartalian capital, Valian, into the growing twilight.

He'd kept his thoughts about how things had gone in Harven to himself as they'd flown Zek and his colleagues to their liege, aware the trader didn't miss much with his dark, intelligent eyes.

"Susa was never a serious threat to West Lathor," Aidan admitted, "but not because she isn't strong. Dartalia is just too far north, with too many mountains in between, for an easy attack on us. But she might have been approached for support on the Council, either from Habred or others who are closer."

"You think she was?" Kas leaned against the front window, looking down at the mountains below.

"I do." Aidan's eyes gleamed. "She seemed a little guilty, a little too effusive when she thanked me for saving her people when we said goodbye."

"As long as she withdraws support, that's what matters," Taya said. She was sitting on the floor, her eyes closed.

"They owe us for helping their people." Eli was also leaning against the window, his gaze outward, on the far horizon. "But the fact that we control these transporters? That makes them afraid of us, too. Because anything the sky raiders did in these things, we can do, too."

"Except I haven't found how to shoot white lightning from this." Garek hadn't tried very hard either. He didn't like the idea of the white lightning, although if he worked out how to use it, and he had no choice, he would.

"It doesn't matter. They don't know that. And even if all we can use it for is to move people very quickly from one place to another, or bring in supplies, that is a massive advantage." Aidan knocked his knuckles against the wall. "It's a pity these things fall apart in our atmosphere."

"Not something we should make public knowledge." Kas lifted his head. "The scientist who was studying the sky craft you stole, did he have a solution for the deterioration?"

Aidan shook his head. "It was Falk's main priority, but he wasn't able to work out how to slow it. I'm surprised Garek got that craft in the air it was so close to collapse."

Taya opened her eyes, caught his gaze.

He could see the fear for him, the acknowledgment of the risks he'd taken, in her eyes.

"We're all safe," he said to her, and after a moment she nodded, closed her eyes again.

"We aren't going to let Dom take his transporter home to Kardai, are we?" Eli asked into the silence that fell over them. There was almost no noise from the back, as most people had curled up to sleep or rest.

"No. We'll take them to Juli, and we'll organize transport for those who want to go home. Those who want to stay can also do so." Aidan tipped his head to look out the window at where Dom's transporter trailed them faithfully. "We're not giving them the second transporter. It's ours."

"The women will choose to stay, I'm sure. Dom and some of his friends might stay with them." Taya's voice was husky with exhaustion.

"You need to drop us in Pan Nuk first," Eli said. "We don't all need to go to Juli."

"No." Kas's hands fisted, and Garek saw Taya lift her head, open her eyes. She reached out and grabbed her brother's hand.

"I can't wait to see Luca." Taya looked up at Kas. "In fact, Garek should land at Haret rather than Pan Nuk. That's where the heart of Pan Nuk is right now. Only Garek and I need to take Aidan home to Juli. We can talk to the liege."

Kas relaxed. Gave a sharp nod. "That works."

Kas's hands were shaking, and Garek wondered how hard it had been for him to go to Luf and then Valian while all the time, he had Luca waiting for him in Haret.

He pushed the transporter a little faster, and after a moment's hesitation, Dom matched his speed.

It was time to go home.

FORTY-SEVEN

LANORA, Barit's moon, was low on the horizon when the transporters settled outside Haret's gates.

They didn't wait for the town master, or the guards, this time. Garek lowered the ramp and Kas led the way down.

"Garek?" Opik called from just within the wooden walls.

The gate he'd destroyed was only half repaired, Garek noticed.

"It's me."

There was a cry from the shadows, and then people spilled out of the darkness as everyone in the transporter followed him and Kas down.

"Luca!" Kas shouted, his voice cutting through the noise, and then a thin, sleep-tousled boy wove his way through the crowd and threw himself into his father's arms.

Garek watched them. They stood silent, just holding each other, Luca lifted off the ground and hanging, completely enclosed in Kas's embrace.

Taya slid her arm around Garek's waist, rested her head on his shoulder. There were tears streaming down her cheeks. "Thank you."

This had been about her, and only her, but reuniting everyone with their families, he conceded, was a very satisfying consequence of his plan.

"You did it." Opik had worked his way through the crowd, hugging and shaking hands with friends, and now he stood in front of Garek, face creased in a wide smile.

"Opik." Taya reached out, pulled the old man into a tight hug and kissed his cheek. "You helped Garek in Gara."

"A little," Opik said. "Dodged guards all the way back, too."

"The ones that we passed on the way to Garamundo?" This was something Garek needed to know, not that they were going back to Gara, but it would be useful to know who'd been after him.

And he would have to help Aidan deal with the mess in Gara eventually.

Opik nodded. "We crossed paths again at an inn halfway between Pan Nuk and Garamundo. They were on their way back. I tried to eavesdrop on some of their conversation, and it seemed they didn't know Pan Nuk had been taken when they set out. They weren't happy to find it deserted.

"Then, when I left the inn the next morning, I heard travelers coming up on the road behind me, and went to ground, saw two new guards on the same path. I followed them all the way to Pan Nuk. They looked around, then went on to Haret.

"I slipped in after them, got everyone to pretend I'd been around all along."

"They ask questions about me?"

Opik gave a curt nod. "If you'd come this way. Where you'd gone." Opik shrugged. "What you'd expect."

"And the answers you gave?"

"A version of the truth."

Garek turned at the voice of Lait Pollar, Haret's town master. He waited, and Pollar shook his head.

"You did it, Garek. I thought you'd come back empty-handed, or we'd get word you were dead. But you did it." He looked at the trans-porters, face awestruck.

Taya slid her hand into Garek's, and looked over at Pollar. "Thank you for looking after our people."

The town master forced his gaze to her. Nodded. "It was our duty and our privilege. And I've just spoken to the liege's son. We thought you'd be in trouble, but instead, you got official sanction. You've proved me wrong, Garek. I thought you'd bring trouble on our heads."

"I may still." Garek looked back at Opik. "There are those in Gara who would defy the liege. Who would not like me to lend him my support."

"You've become a bone to fight over." Opik watched him with clear eyes. "It makes sense they'd want a man who can fly to Shadow and bring back two sky raider craft."

"We support the liege." The town master spoke a little louder than he needed to, so everyone would hear. "If some in Gara would play traitor, we will resist them."

"And the liege is glad of your support." Aidan came up behind the town master, clapped a hand on Pollar's shoulder.

"Opik was telling us what information was given to the two guards who came sniffing after me." Garek exchanged a look with Aidan, and he gave a faint nod. He'd keep any questions he had until later.

"We told them you'd come back to Pan Nuk. Found it deserted. That you hadn't known everyone had been taken. That you left, angry and upset, and we had no idea of your plans."

So, truly a version of the truth, but without giving anything away.

"That's good." He heard the engines from the transporter Dom was piloting rev a little higher and sighed. "The Kardanx need to get out of their transporter, too. We need to go, but we'll be back tomorrow. We need to get the liege's son home."

"So soon?" Opik looked at the transporters with a hunger to know more.

"We'll come back tomorrow afternoon or evening. But first . . ." Taya dropped Garek's hand and walked to Kas, put her arms around both him and Luca and then staggered back a little as Luca threw himself at her. She rocked with him from side to side, and Garek heard her murmuring in the little boy's ear.

When she raised her head, she was looking for someone. "Min? Will you come with us, or stay?"

Min was standing with Noor, and she hesitated. "I have never seen Juli, but . . ." She looked from Kas to Luca then shook her head. "I'll stay."

So it was only Aidan, Taya and himself who walked back up the ramp, closed it, and lifted off before most of Haret knew they were going.

Garek could see shock and disappointment on the faces below.

"They wanted to thank you. To catch up with us all." Taya stood beside him and must have seen the expressions, too.

"We'll be back soon enough."

And they would be. It was only an hour to get to Juli, and as they came in, the moon had risen in the sky, gilding the small city in silver light.

Juli had been built in the middle of the Finoval River, which flowed around it and then tumbled like two frothy white plaits on either side of the city, down the hill. Clever engineering over hundreds of years had built up walls below the city, so that instead of just perching at the top of the waterfall, the city was terraced, with towers and houses all the way to the foot of the hill, with the river in free fall on either side.

The moonlight reflected off the calm water in the small lake at the base of the city, and also off the armor of the guards on the walls.

Garek caught glimpses of movement as he came in, thought he might have heard the thud of arrows against the side of the transporter, although that may just have been because he expected to hear it.

"Over there." Aidan pointed to the wide wall at the top of the city, the thick, curving stone holding back the Finoval River where it first encountered Juli, and was forced to make its way on either side.

There were guards standing along the wall looking up, but they ran when Garek swooped along the length of the wide space and set down at the far end to give Dom more room.

An arrow hit the window as he settled down, bouncing off harmlessly.

"You'll be shot in the eye if you stick your head out the door." As he spoke to Aidan, another arrow made a tiny ping against the glass.

"I think you're right." Aidan looked out, frowning. "Can you open the door part way, so I can shout to someone?"

Garek shook his head. "If it's possible, I don't know how to do it. Both of you, take cover. I'll open it, then you can start shouting."

Taya moved to the back area, crouching to the side of the door and Aidan went on his haunches below the pilot's door.

Garek opened it and another arrow hit the window, but none came through the door.

Garek guessed no one was in the right position to manage a shot like that.

"It's Aidan," Aidan shouted. "Get me the guard master."

No more arrows struck the side.

"Aidan?"

"Vent, it's me. Tell the guards to lower their weapons, unless they want to explain to my father how they came to shoot his son."

"You're really in that thing?"

"I really am. Call Dartan up here. I won't come out until I'm sure no one has anything sharp aimed at me and my friends."

"Your friends?"

"I didn't steal two sky craft on my own, Vent. Aside from anything else, I can't fly both of them at once." There was a light-hearted note to Aidan's voice, and Garek guessed the princeling and his father's guard master were old friends.

A booming laugh reached them. "Weapons down." In contrast to the laugh, the order was sharp.

"You want to come over here, see it's me?" Aidan asked him.

"Might do."

Garek saw a shadow detach itself from one of the guard houses along the wall and walk toward them.

A big man, he carried no bow in his hand, although he had a sword strapped to his waist and he walked with confidence.

"What Change does he call?"

Aidan looked over at him. "Earth Change."

Garek nodded, keeping his eye on Vent as he walked around the side of the ship.

"Up here," Aidan called down to him, and leaned out.

"It looks like you," Vent said. "But how on the Star did you come to be in one of these abominations?"

"Long story." Aidan swung his leg out, stopped about halfway down the ladder. "You called Dartan?"

Vent nodded. "Come down, no one's going to shoot you, or they'll be thrown off the wall."

Aidan dropped out of sight, and Garek powered down the engines to an idle.

"What are we going to do with the shadow ore?" Taya had come back into the chamber, dropping to a crouch beside his chair and looking up at him.

"You want it out the transporter?"

"I don't want someone to make off with it. Wherever it is, it needs to be safe, and I'd prefer it goes with me."

"Then it goes with you. We'll get Aidan to organize people to carry it to whichever room we get to sleep in tonight."

She nodded. "You think it's safe to stand?"

He didn't know. In Gara, he'd have said no, but that's because Utrel, the guard master he'd served under, was as slippery and untrustworthy as a slither.

"You can come out," Aidan called from below.

"Let me be sure," Garek whispered to Taya. He stood, drawing air around him, ready to step into the inbetween in a moment, and moved to the door to look down.

Aidan was standing beside Vent, but as Garek began to lean out, the princeling stiffened and turned.

Garek turned with him, saw a small entourage had appeared at the head of the stairs. They stopped dead at the sight of the transporters.

"It's safe, Dartan. We stole the transporters from the sky raiders."

A man in the small crowd stepped forward. "Aidan?"

Aidan walked toward him. "Yes. I've had some adventures since I saw you last."

Garek saw Dartan flick his gaze to the transporters again, narrow his eyes at the sight of Garek, and then focus on Aidan.

"I'd be very interested to hear it. Can you shut down the noise?"

"When we're sure no one is going to shoot us by accident." Garek kept his tone cool.

"And you are?" Vent was the one who asked the question, and Garek guessed he was blurring a little at the edges, because the guard master was tense now, where before he'd been much more at ease.

"Garek. I walked the walls of Garamundo with Aidan."

Vent relaxed a little at that.

"He's saved my life more times than I can count," Aidan said, and Garek flicked him a surprised look.

He supposed that was true, but then, if it wasn't for Garek, he wouldn't have been in danger in the first place.

"Do we have the word of the liege all will be safe?" Garek asked, and Aidan winced but said nothing against the demand.

Dartan looked between the two ships. "How many are we talking?"

"Eighty Kardanx in that one, just three of us, me included, in this one," Aidan told him.

"Kardanx?" Dartan frowned.

"We let the Illy that were captured off at their own homes, but we won't let the Kardanx keep the transporter, so they had to come with us here. I promised them accommodation until we can organize them passage home. I'm sure you'll agree it's better to have both ships under our full control at all times?"

Dartan blinked at that, but then gave a slow nod. "I see the sense in that. They will be accommodated."

Garek walked back to his chair, opened the back ramp, and switched the transporter off.

Dom must have seen that as the signal all was safe, because Garek heard the ramp on the other transporter lowering, and the Kardanx began to emerge slowly from the back.

The pilot's door opened, and Dom climbed down.

When he reached the ground, his legs were unable to support him, and he collapsed.

He'd been in that chair for a long time with only a short break on the Endless Escarpment. Garek dropped to the ground himself and ran over to him, helping him to his feet.

Two of Dom's friends took over, slinging his arms over their shoulders as they half carried him to the knot of Kardanx gathered near the stairs.

"You did well," Garek called after him.

"Never want to hear an engine again," he called back, and Garek grinned.

Aidan stood with Dartan, his attention on the Kardanx as they were welcomed and invited down the stairs.

"Taya needs to keep the ore close," he murmured in Aidan's ear when at last the princeling's attention swung his way. "Can you arrange for someone to carry it to our room?"

"You can have my sister's quarters, seeing as she's no longer here." Aidan called four guards over and gave them instructions.

The palace was close to the wall, almost part of it, and there were covered walkways leading to it. It was a whimsical building, with slender towers and courtyard gardens, and it looked pretty in the moonlight.

Dartan gave one last command to a thin woman who seemed to be his assistant, and then made his way over to them.

"My father?" Aidan asked, softly enough only the three of them could hear.

Dartan glanced at Garek. "He's fine."

"Garek knows all my secrets, Councilor. How is my father really?"

Dartan sighed. "He alternates between raging at you and your sister for leaving him, and accusing you of trying to take away his power."

"So, the same as before, then."

Dartan shook his head. "He's worse now. He's been drinking more. He had long stretches of being clear-eyed, but now . . ."

He trailed off, and Garek looked in the direction of his gaze.

A man in a big coat, too heavy and thick for the weather, was being helped along by two guards on either side.

Aidan went stiff beside him. "Father."

"I heard my son was back, traveling in strange vehicles."

Aidan moved forward, bowed. "I have taken part in a daring rescue and have stolen two of the sky raiders' craft in the process."

"Stolen. Hah. You always were a thief." Spittle flew from the liege's mouth, and Aidan took a step back, his face blank.

After everything they'd done, after all they'd been through, the princeling did not deserve this public humiliation. And the liege was the thief here. He had stolen the hope of West Lathor by refusing to step down.

"Stealing from the enemy is usually considered a good thing." Garek let his voice carry a little.

Aidan shot him a look that told him he would pay for his interference later.

"From the enemy?" The liege frowned at him.

"Unless you consider the sky raiders our friends?"

There was silence as everyone waited for the liege to respond.

"You're trying to trick me? What is this?" The liege frowned at him, and Garek saw his eyes were watery and unfocused. He was deep in the drink.

"This is your son, and two sky craft from our enemy." Garek knew from experience there was no talking sense with someone this far into a bottle of firebrand.

"Ah." The liege seemed to find the answer acceptable. "Good. Carry on!" He waved a hand in the air and then pivoted on his heel, almost falling over in the process.

The guards grabbed him, and ushered him away.

"Can't you switch that cursed transporter *off*?" Aidan snapped the question at him, rubbing above his ear as he held Garek's gaze, fury and embarrassment in his expression.

They had both decided not to show the Kardanx how to start the transporter or shut it down, only how to fly it. An extra measure to ensure no one could force Dom to fly to Kardai, but that meant only Garek could turn it off.

He inclined his head, allowing the show of temper without comment. "I can." He looked for Taya, saw her standing on the ramp, speaking to the guards assigned to move the ore, and satisfied she was safe, walked toward the craft.

He had almost reached the ladder when a noise made him look upward, but before he could focus on the night sky, the most indescribable pain enveloped him in a sheet of white light.

And then nothing.

FORTY-EIGHT

TAYA WATCHED the guards take the strain as they hauled the long wooden boxes down the ramp. Her shards were in a small box of water, even though she'd carried them without protection in the transporters many times.

No one had wanted to take the chance when it wasn't necessary.

The box was no bigger than her palm, and she carried it down herself, lifting the lid and grabbing them in her fist when she stepped onto the wall.

She flicked the water off them, stuck them in the deep pocket of her coat, and as she withdrew her hand, was blinded by light.

She had to close her eyes to stop the lights dancing in front of her vision, and when she opened them, Garek was lying on the ground, and a small sky craft was hovering over Dom's transporter.

A circular door opened underneath the sky craft and a sky raider dropped out, dressed in the same thick padded suit with a helmet that they'd worn when they'd invaded the camp.

Instead of falling, he hovered, and she saw there was a pack on his back that made a humming sound.

She moved slowly to the side, to where the guards had dropped the boxes, and opened the lid of one.

She called, and the shadow ore rose up from the water, two long spears of it. It was so much easier to do than when she'd called the Change on Shadow, they rose higher than she meant them to.

"Stop." The hiss of the sky raider had her lifting her head.

"Go ahead, shoot at me." Taya adjusted the spears, so one was above each shoulder.

"I will shoot *him*." The sky raider pointed to Garek. "He's still alive now, but he won't survive a second hit at this strength level."

Taya drew in a breath. They *knew*. They must know. Somehow the sky raiders from the Endless Escarpment had managed to let them know she had shadow ore, that it would rebound on the shooter. "Then you will die."

"I think you would prefer to save him than kill me."

"What do you want?"

Behind her, she could hear shouting, could hear Aidan giving orders. She ignored it all.

"I will take back this ship. If you do not throw the *xjila*, then your friend will live."

While he'd been speaking, the sky raider had lowered himself down to the open pilot's door, and with a strangely athletic twist, landed inside the pilot's cabin.

"If you or your friend in that sky craft shoot at me, you know what will happen, but if you shoot at anyone else, I will have no hesitation at throwing these spears at you. And you know the likely outcome of that."

"We will have the *gytrin* aimed at your friend until you can no longer see us. So be warned. If you throw, he will die."

They were at a perfect impasse. Taya itched to go to Garek, but she stood, spears vibrating at the ready, as the door of Dom's transporter closed and it lifted in a hover, and then shot straight up into the sky.

The sky craft followed more slowly, rising directly above Garek until it was swallowed by the night sky.

She ran to him, forgetting the spears were still above her shoulders until she knelt at his side. She set them aside on the ground, felt his pulse.

Aidan was beside her a moment later.

"Alive?"

She nodded.

"We should have realized they'd never give up so easily." He looked upward.

They should have, but they had all thought they'd lost them. The sky raiders must have been following them, or found them again on their way back from Harven.

"Let's get him settled." Aidan called over more guards, and Taya scooped up the shadow ore spears and stood when they lifted him up.

Everyone was staring at her, either sidelong or openly, and she frowned in confusion.

"You called your Change." Aidan tapped one of the spears with a finger. "No one has seen anything like that before."

She'd forgotten to hide it, but there had been no time, anyway. And with Garek's life at stake, she didn't care. She'd do it again without a second thought.

She shrugged.

"There was no choice, I understand that." Aidan waved at the guards standing beside the boxes. "I'll make sure the ore goes to your rooms. But Taya. Don't speak about it if anyone asks."

She frowned at him, but he looked so serious, she gave a nod and then followed the guards carrying Garek.

She thought she'd be happy to be here. She'd enjoyed her visit before, enjoyed the beauty and the uniqueness that made Juli a city to be proud of, but there was something wrong.

The liege was unable to walk in a straight line. There was tension among the guards, she got that just from the few minutes of talking to them, and the administrator, Dartan, seemed to have a permanent frown on his face.

Taya realized she just wanted to take Garek and go home.

FORTY-NINE

GAREK WOKE to the sound of someone getting out of the bath.

There was a soft splash and then the rustle of drying.

He must have been hearing the sounds for a while, he realized, because he felt in no danger.

He knew it was Taya, that he was safe.

He had been hit by white lightning. That was his last memory, and he forced himself to unclench his muscles as anger at himself swept over him.

He should have known the sky raiders would never be so easily defeated.

It could have been Taya shot. Or she could have been taken again, while he lay unconscious.

But that hadn't happened.

He used that knowledge to calm down.

A fire crackled in a nearby hearth, and he felt the gentle heat of it warming the air.

He lifted his lids slowly, saw Taya, with her back to him, pull a gown on. It fell to her waist and she wriggled her hips as she smoothed it down her thighs, then her hands came up and she twisted her hair and pinned it on top of her head.

He must have made a sound because she turned, her eyes going straight to him.

She ran to him, throwing herself beside the bed he was lying on and gripping his hand.

"You're awake." Her voice was a quiet whisper.

He hauled her up, lifting her over his body and into bed with him, and she snuggled in close, her hold tight.

"How long was I out?"

"All night."

The light coming through the window was gray, and he angled his head, saw it was overcast and threatening rain. The sound of the waterfalls drifted up to the window.

"What happened?"

"They must have been following us. Waiting for us to land. They took Dom's transporter."

"Did you use the shadow ore?"

She shook her head. "I was going to, I had it ready, but they said they'd shoot you again. That you'd die if they did it a second time."

He went still, thinking it through. "They'll be back for the other transporter."

She nodded. "They will be. We need to hide it."

She was right. And they couldn't hide it just anywhere. It had to be away from any new victims the sky raiders would be tempted to scoop up.

Because there was no way they would easily abandon all the equipment and time and effort they had put into the mine and camp on Shadow.

"What else? Where are we?"

"We're in Aidan's sister's old rooms. I haven't spoken to anyone but Aidan since you were hit. But there's someone outside the door, as if they're keeping watch or guarding us. I'm not sure which. But I decided to treat them as friendly and asked for a hot bath when I woke up, and I got one, so maybe they aren't watching us."

"Or maybe they are, but they're being polite about it." Aidan would want to keep both him and Taya happy, but Aidan wasn't in charge here.

That job was held by a liege who had fallen down a deep hole.

"There are strange tensions here. Everyone is nervous and I don't believe it's our arrival. I think it's been that way for a while." Taya shifted, getting more comfortable.

"Did you see the liege when he came up?"

"Yes. He looked buzzed." She looked up at him for confirmation.

He nodded. "Buzzed, and dark with it. Some get happy when they're that drunk, he had an edge. He came across as petulant and self-absorbed."

"He wasn't like that before."

"No. Aidan looked in pain when they spoke. I think his father is not the man he was. And Aidan needs to step up before he does any more damage to West Lathor."

"So we have trouble on two fronts." She didn't sound worried, though. She sounded resolute.

He grinned, bent and kissed her forehead. "Maybe three. Don't forget the other Illian provinces looking to take West Lathor for their own."

"This isn't over by a long way, is it?" Taya nestled her head under his chin.

"No. I have the feeling this is just the beginning."

None of it mattered, though. He had her back and safe. Everything else, they could handle.

In fact, the Illy, the sky raiders . . . they could fall into the shadow pits for all he cared.

And if the sky raiders came for Taya again, he would make them wish they hadn't.

THE SKY RAIDERS SERIES

Sky Raiders is the first book in the Sky Raiders space opera trilogy. It won the RT Reviewers' Choice Award for Best Futuristic Romance in 2018.

Other books in the series are Calling the Change and Shadow Warrior.

You can visit Michelle Diener's website at www.michellediener.com and sign up to her new release notification list to never miss a new release, as well as gain exclusive access to INTENDED, the prequel novella to the Sky Raiders series, available only to members of Michelle's new release notification list.

ABOUT THE AUTHOR

Michelle Diener is an award winning author of historical fiction, science fiction and fantasy.

Michelle was born in London and currently lives in Australia with her husband and two children.

You can contact Michelle through her website or sign up to receive notification when she has a new book out on her New Release Notification page.

Connect with Michelle:
www.michellediener.com

ACKNOWLEDGMENTS

Thank you to the team of awesome readers, editors and authors who help me make my books as good as they can be. This journey would be a lot more lonely without you. The amazing cover is by Lana Pecherczyk.

Made in United States
North Haven, CT
18 December 2023

46009788R00211